CRYSTAL CADETS

Written by
**ANNE
TOOLE**

Art by
**KATIE
O'NEILL**

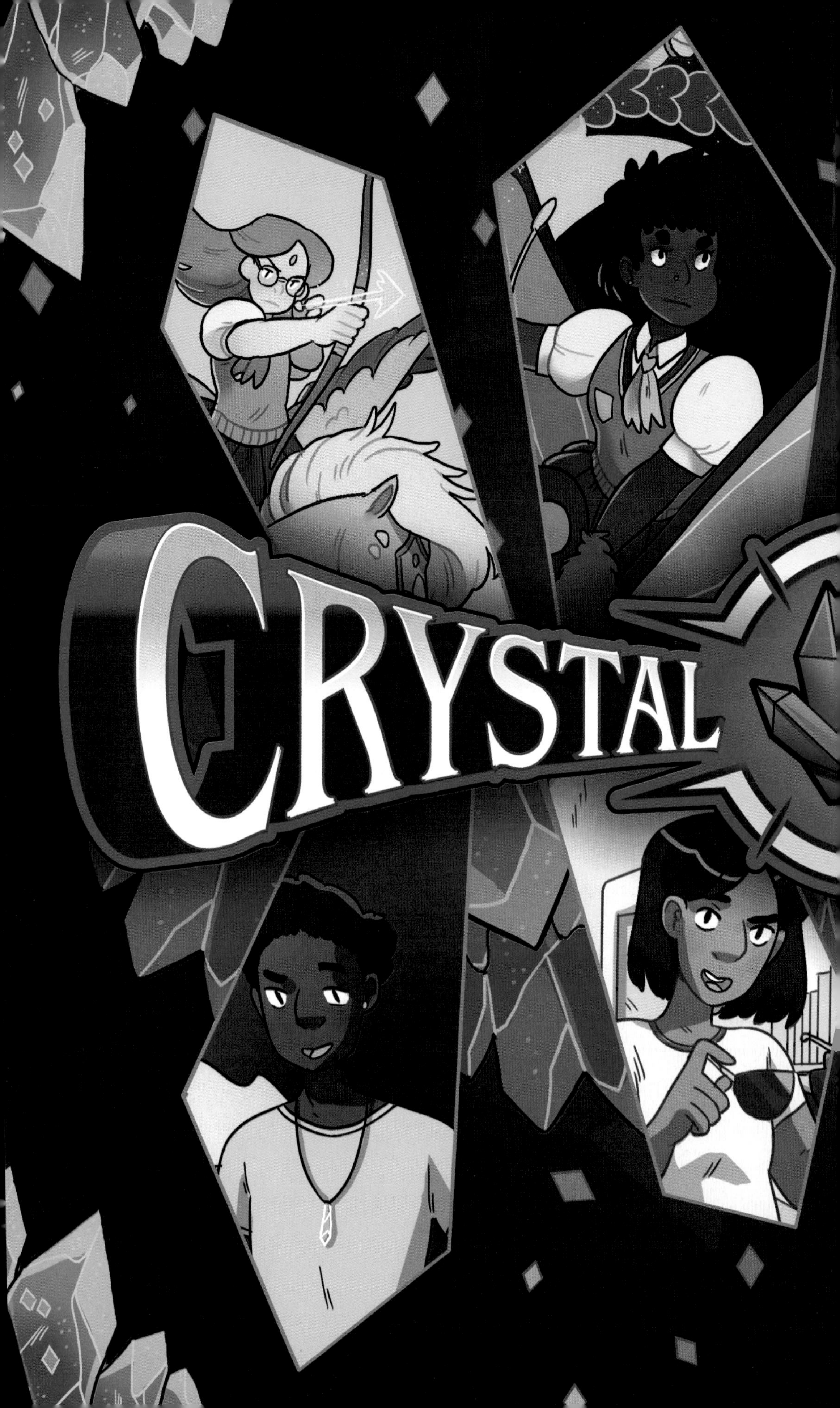
CRYSTAL

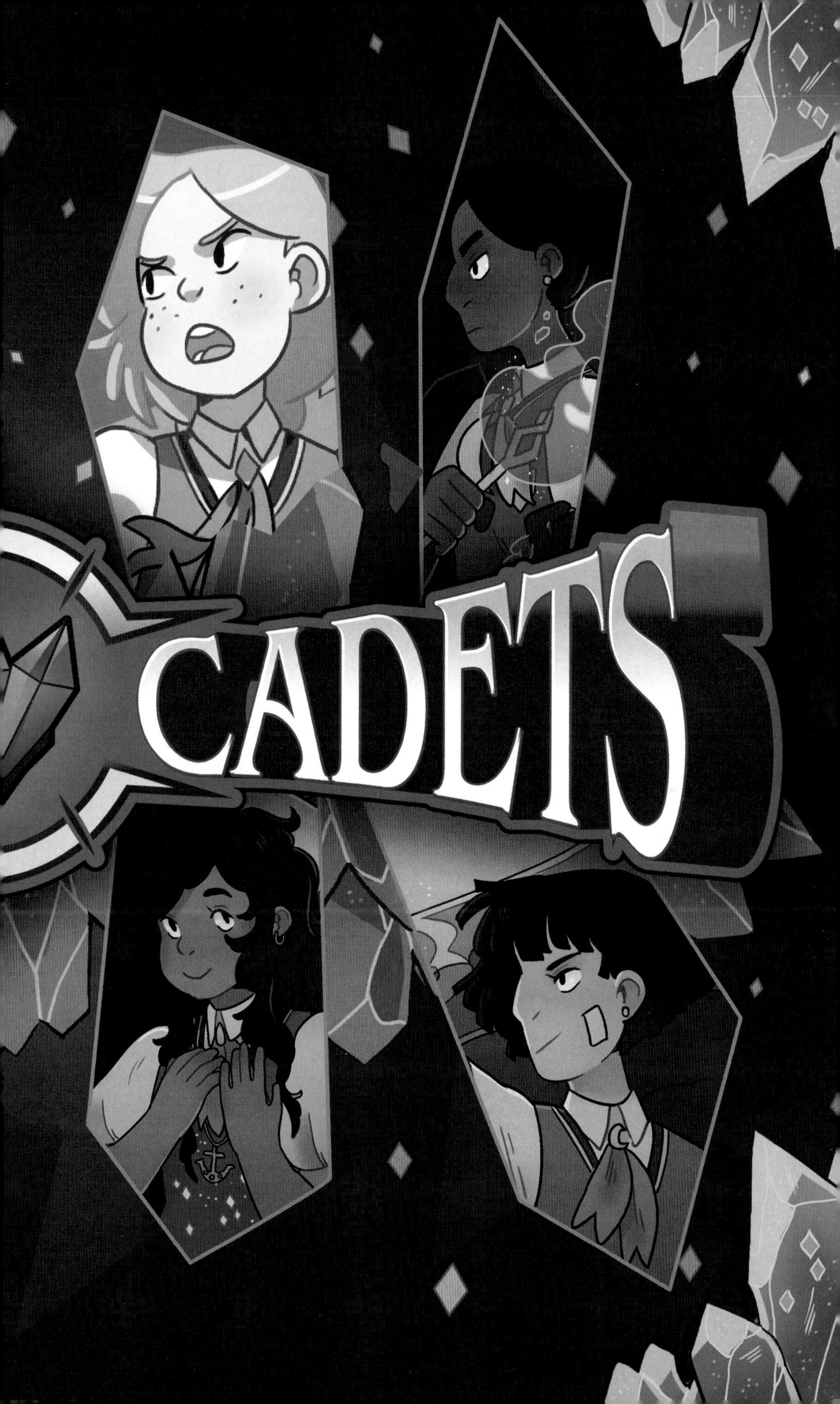
CADETS

CRYSTAL CADETS

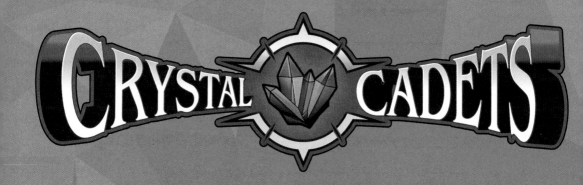

ANNE TOOLE ◊ Writer
KATIE O'NEILL ◊ Artist
PAULINA GANUCHEAU ◊ Colors

ERIKA TERRIQUEZ ▫ Letters **ANDWORLD DESIGN** ▫ Design

KATIE O'NEILL - Collection Cover, Covers 1-5 ◆ **PAULINA GANUCHEAU** - Covers 6-8

ADAM STAFFARONI - Editor
KATE WARDENBURG - Asst. Story Editor ◆ **HAZEL NEWLEVANT** - Asst. Collection Editor

---

Publisher's Cataloging-In-Publication Data
(Prepared by The Donohue Group, Inc.)

Names: Toole, Anne. | O'Neill, Katie, illustrator. | Ganucheau, Paulina, illustrator. | Terriquez, Erika, letterer. | AndWorld Design (Firm), designer.
Title: Crystal Cadets. Volume 1 / Anne Toole, writer ; Katie O'Neill, artist ; Paulina Ganucheau, colors ; Erika Terriquez, letters ; Andworld Design, design.
Description: Revised edition. | [St. Louis, Missouri] : Roar Comics, an imprint of Lion Forge Comics, 2016. | Interest age level: 004-008. | Summary: "Zoe is a shy girl struggling to fit in at her new school when she finds a mysterious gem left to her by her birth mother. All of a sudden, darkness-spewing dragons are chasing her down in the schoolyard, and a squad of crystal-wielding girls is there to save her!"--Provided by publisher.
Identifiers: ISBN 978-1-941302-16-3 | ISBN 978-1-5493-0070-7 (ebook)
Subjects: LCSH: Bashfulness in children--Comic books, strips, etc. | Girls--Comic books, strips, etc. | Gems--Comic books, strips, etc. | Superheroes--Comic books, strips, etc. | Superhero comic books, strips, etc. | LCGFT: Graphic novels.
Classification: LCC PN6728 .C79 2016 (print) | LCC PN6728 (ebook) | DDC 813/.6 [Fic]--dc23

ROAR COMICS is an imprint of Lion Forge Comics

Second printing.

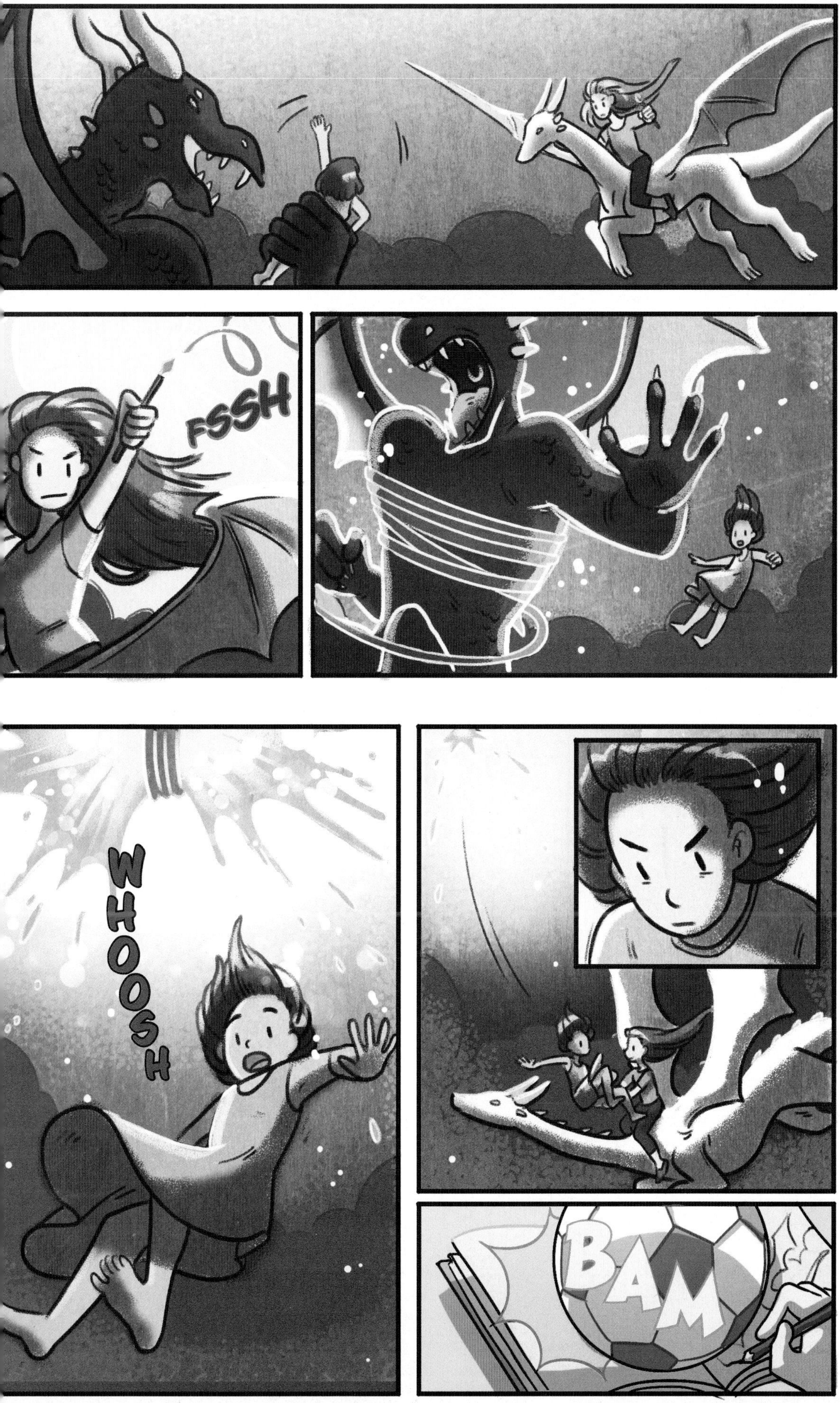
FSSH
WHOOSH
BAM

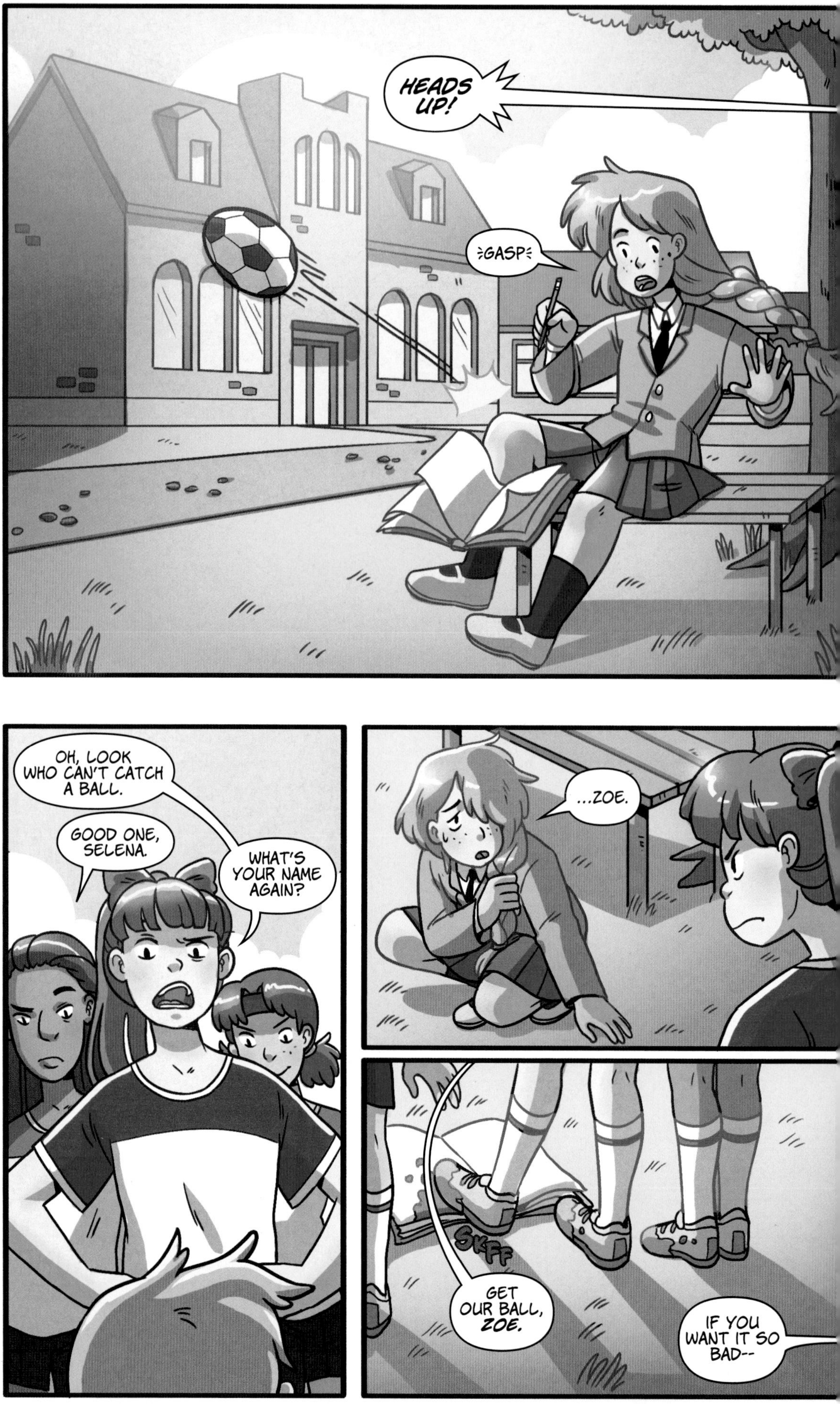
HEADS UP!
GASP
OH, LOOK WHO CAN'T CATCH A BALL.
GOOD ONE, SELENA.
WHAT'S YOUR NAME AGAIN?
...ZOE.
SKFF
GET OUR BALL, ZOE.
IF YOU WANT IT SO BAD--

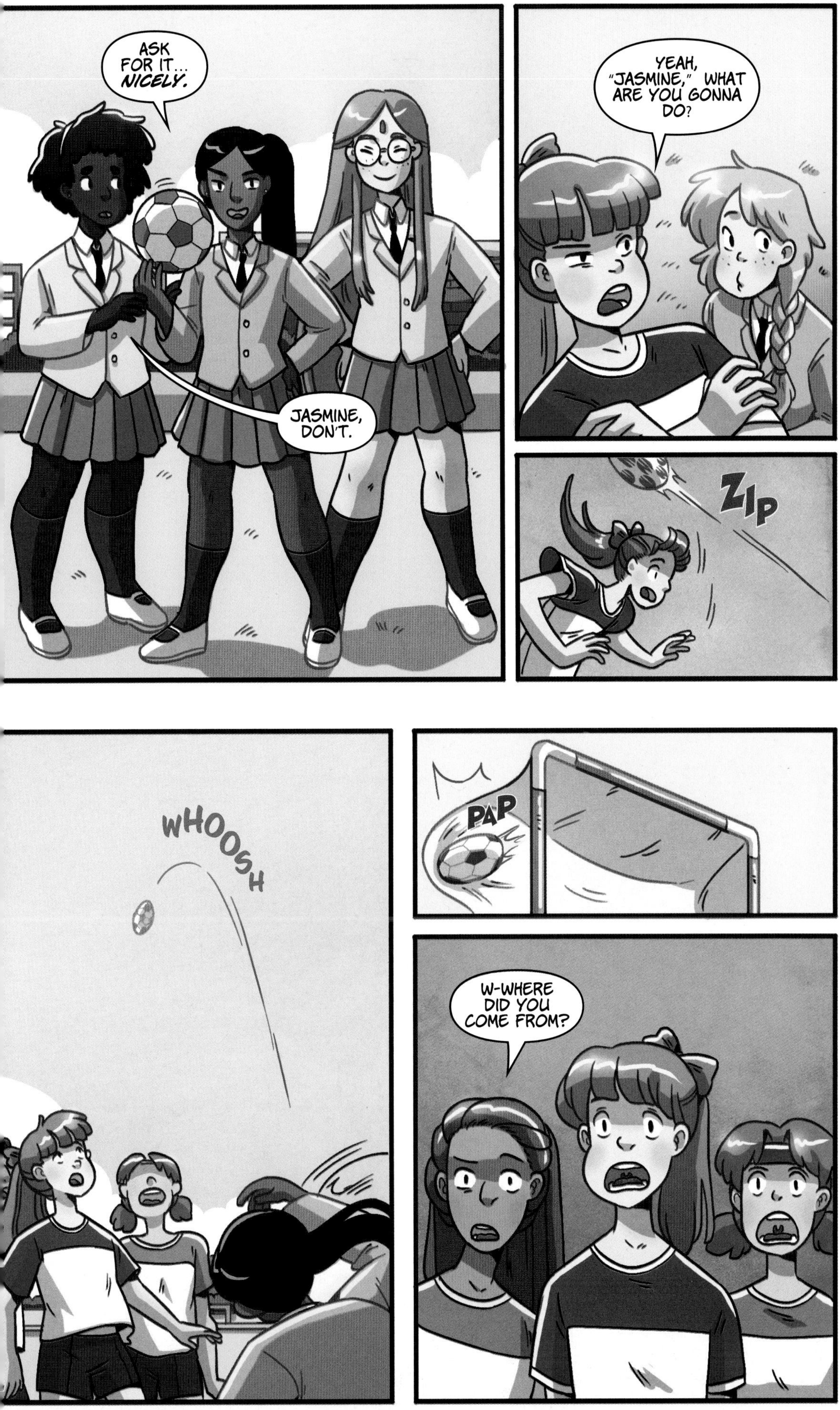
ASK FOR IT... *NICELY.*
JASMINE, DON'T.
YEAH, "JASMINE," WHAT ARE YOU GONNA DO?
ZIP
WHOOSH
PAP
W-WHERE DID YOU COME FROM?

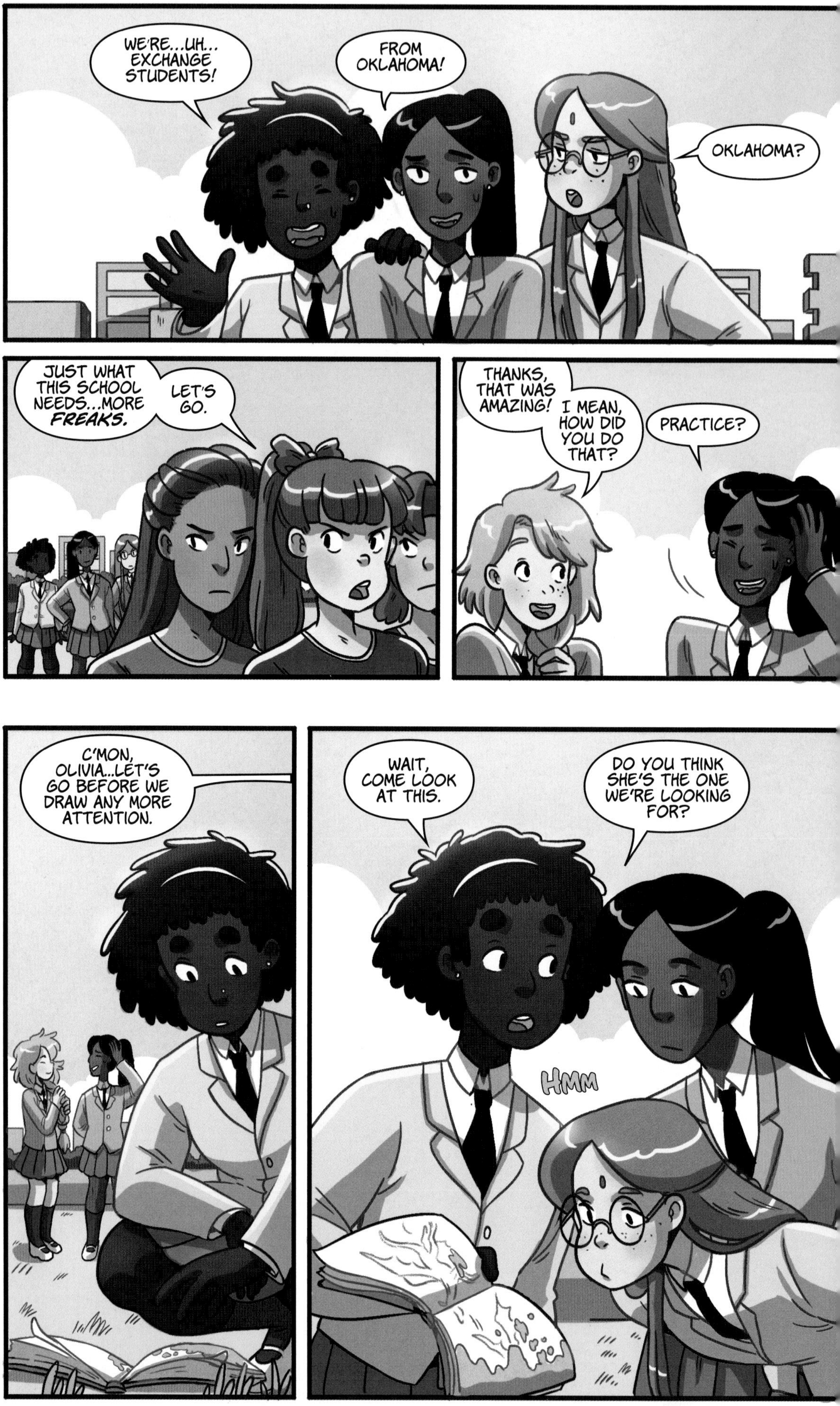

WE'RE...UH... EXCHANGE STUDENTS!
FROM OKLAHOMA!
OKLAHOMA?
JUST WHAT THIS SCHOOL NEEDS...MORE *FREAKS.*
LET'S GO.
THANKS, THAT WAS AMAZING!
I MEAN, HOW DID YOU DO THAT?
PRACTICE?
C'MON, OLIVIA...LET'S GO BEFORE WE DRAW ANY MORE ATTENTION.
WAIT, COME LOOK AT THIS.
DO YOU THINK SHE'S THE ONE WE'RE LOOKING FOR?
HMM

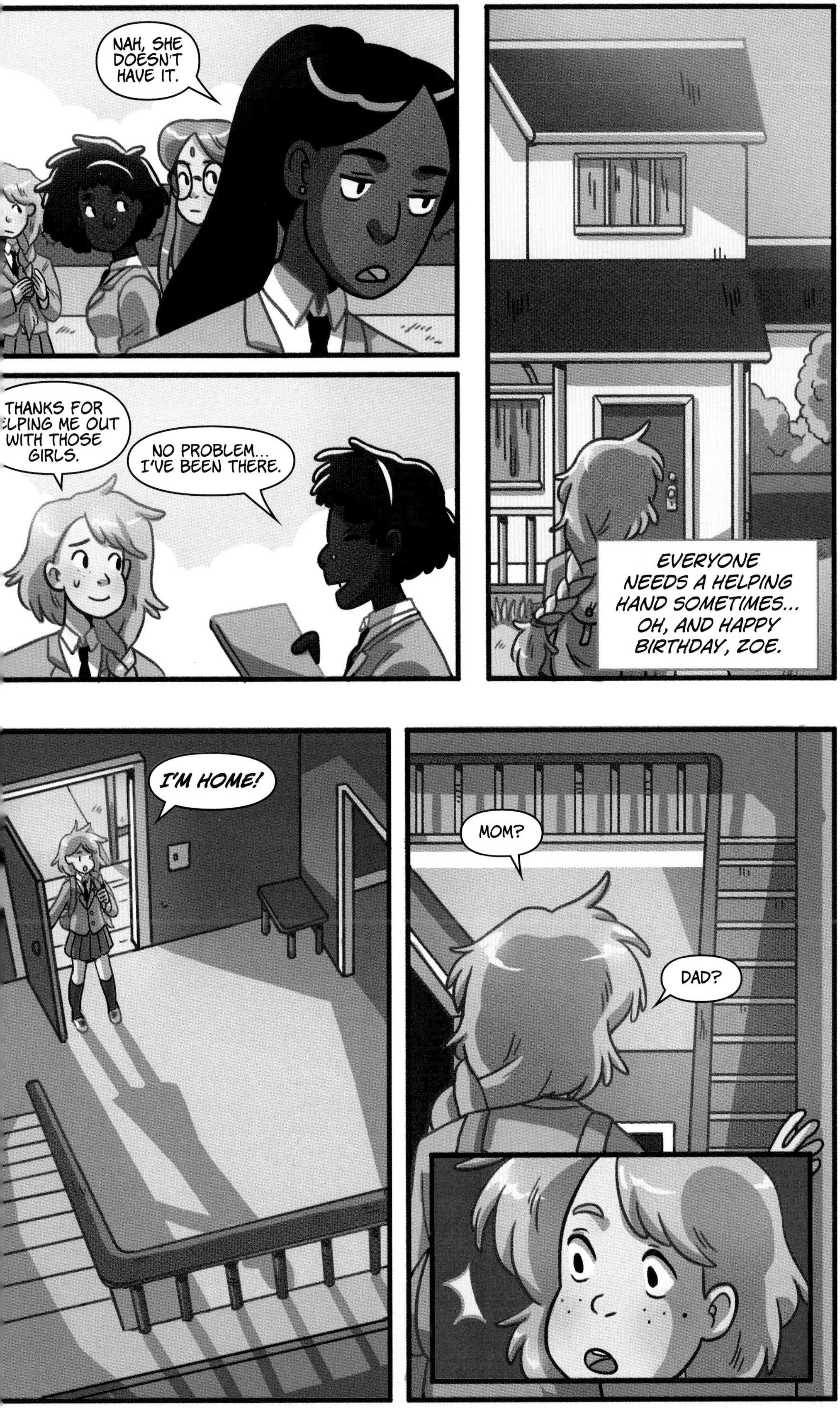
NAH, SHE DOESN'T HAVE IT.
THANKS FOR HELPING ME OUT WITH THOSE GIRLS.
NO PROBLEM... I'VE BEEN THERE.
EVERYONE NEEDS A HELPING HAND SOMETIMES... OH, AND HAPPY BIRTHDAY, ZOE.
I'M HOME!
MOM?
DAD?

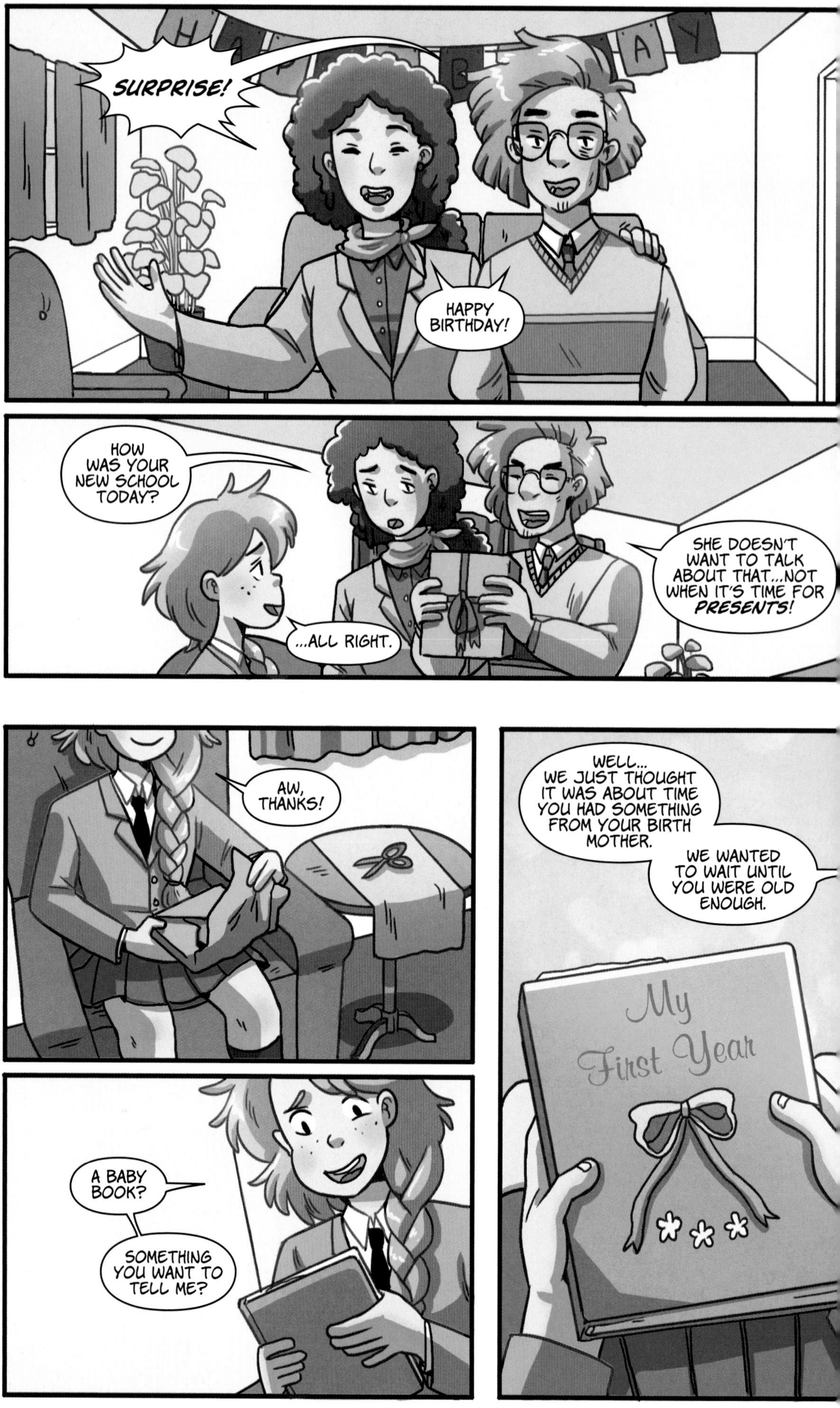

SURPRISE!
HAPPY BIRTHDAY!
HOW WAS YOUR NEW SCHOOL TODAY?
...ALL RIGHT.
SHE DOESN'T WANT TO TALK ABOUT THAT...NOT WHEN IT'S TIME FOR PRESENTS!
AW, THANKS!
A BABY BOOK?
SOMETHING YOU WANT TO TELL ME?
WELL... WE JUST THOUGHT IT WAS ABOUT TIME YOU HAD SOMETHING FROM YOUR BIRTH MOTHER.
WE WANTED TO WAIT UNTIL YOU WERE OLD ENOUGH.
My First Year

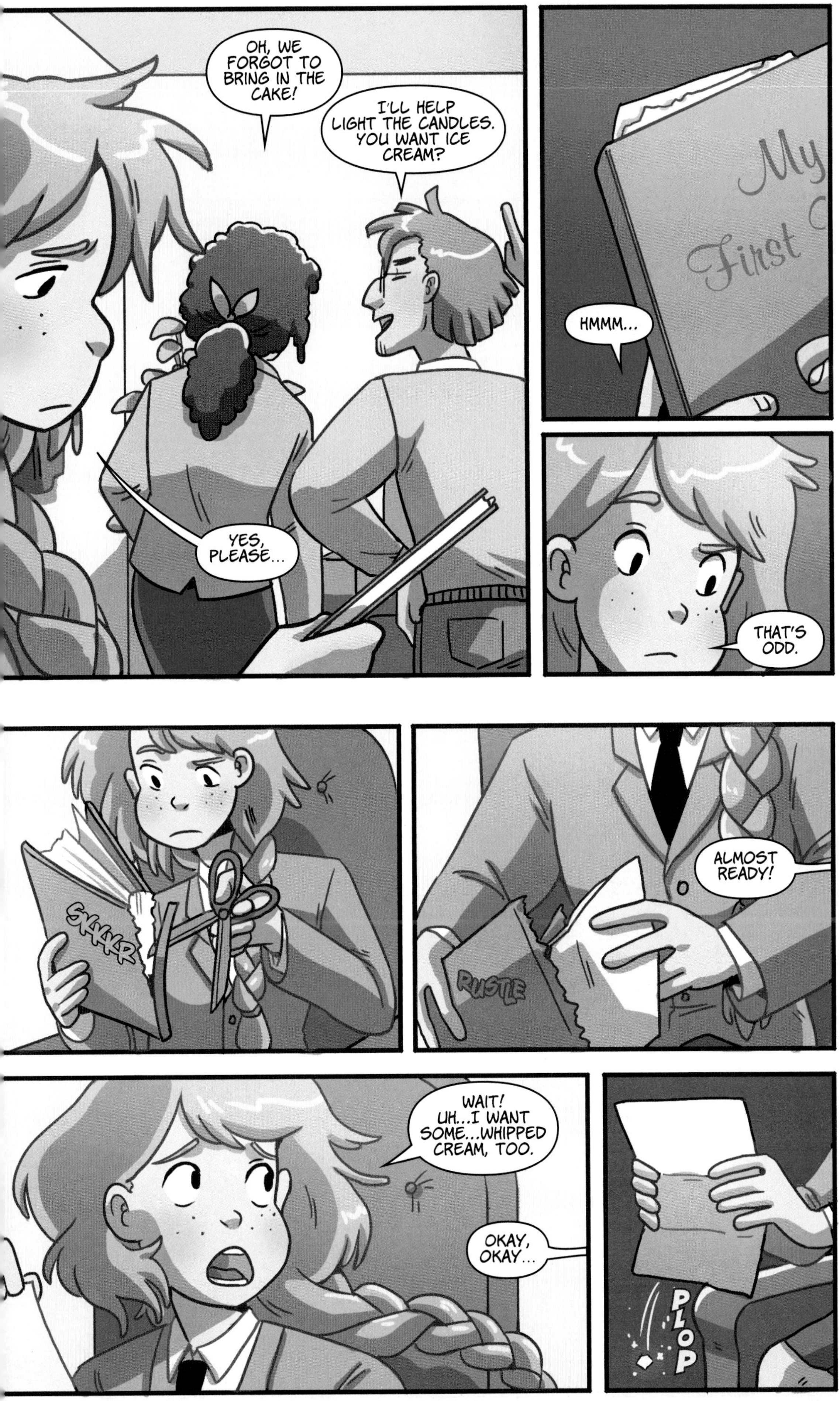
OH, WE FORGOT TO BRING IN THE CAKE!
I'LL HELP LIGHT THE CANDLES. YOU WANT ICE CREAM?
YES, PLEASE...
My First
HMMM...
THAT'S ODD.
SKKKR
ALMOST READY!
RUSTLE
WAIT! UH...I WANT SOME...WHIPPED CREAM, TOO.
OKAY, OKAY...
PLOP

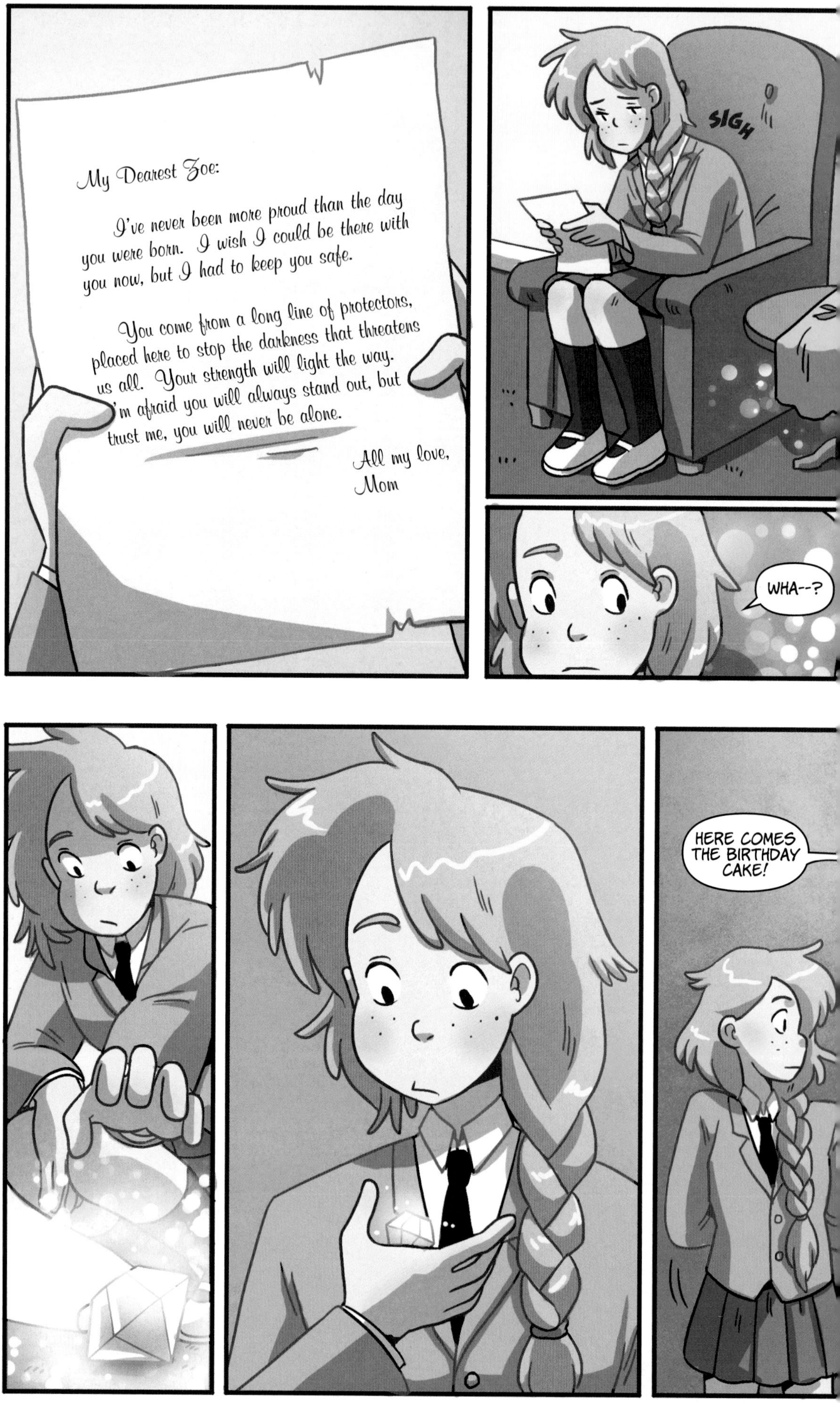
My Dearest Zoe:
I've never been more proud than the day you were born. I wish I could be there with you now, but I had to keep you safe.
You come from a long line of protectors, placed here to stop the darkness that threatens us all. Your strength will light the way. I'm afraid you will always stand out, but trust me, you will never be alone.
All my love,
Mom
SIGH
WHA--?
HERE COMES THE BIRTHDAY CAKE!

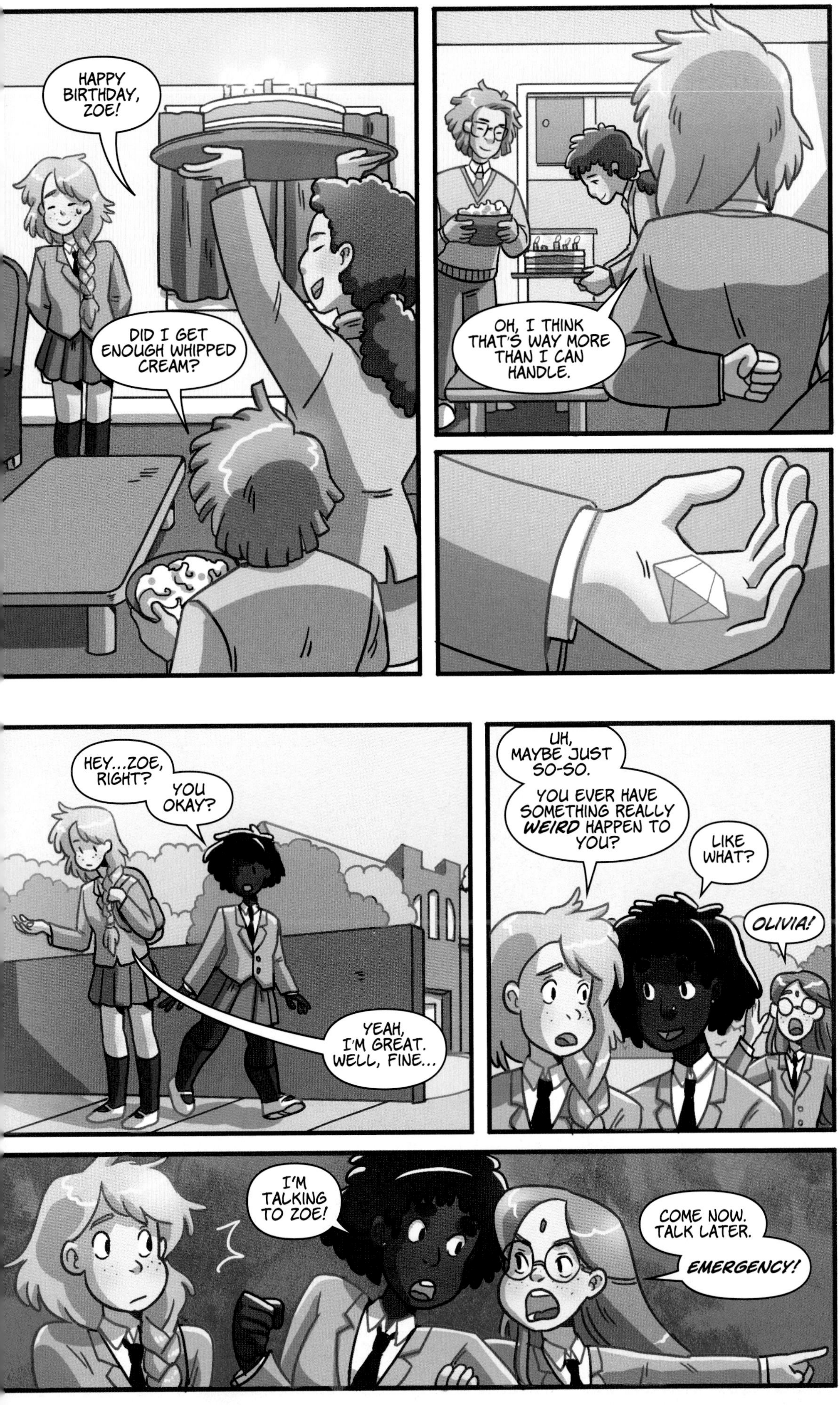
HAPPY BIRTHDAY, ZOE!
DID I GET ENOUGH WHIPPED CREAM?
OH, I THINK THAT'S WAY MORE THAN I CAN HANDLE.
HEY...ZOE, RIGHT?
YOU OKAY?
YEAH, I'M GREAT. WELL, FINE...
UH, MAYBE JUST SO-SO.
YOU EVER HAVE SOMETHING REALLY *WEIRD* HAPPEN TO YOU?
LIKE WHAT?
OLIVIA!
I'M TALKING TO ZOE!
COME NOW. TALK LATER.
EMERGENCY!

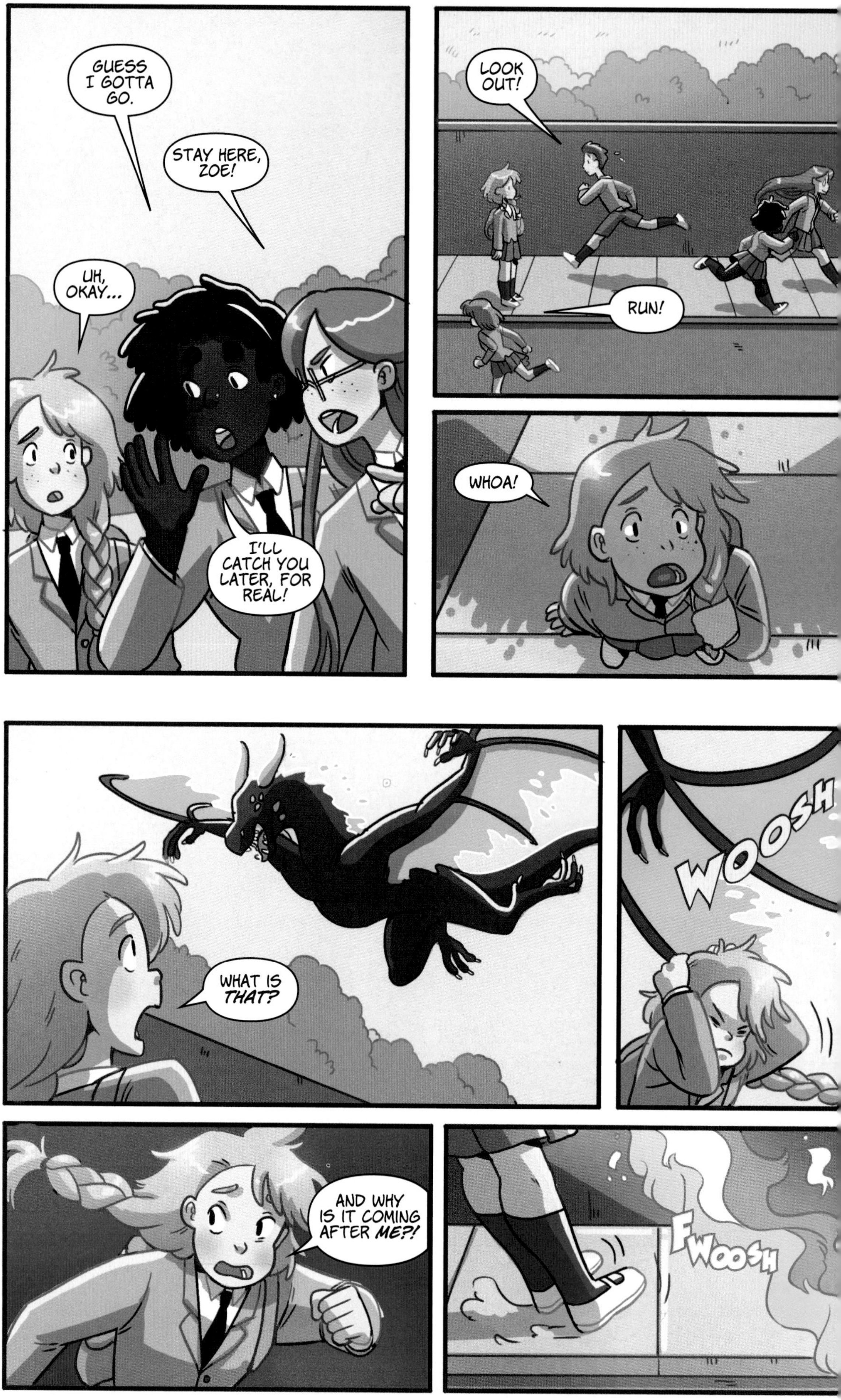
GUESS I GOTTA GO.
STAY HERE, ZOE!
UH, OKAY...
I'LL CATCH YOU LATER, FOR REAL!
LOOK OUT!
RUN!
WHOA!
WHAT IS *THAT?*
WOOSH
AND WHY IS IT COMING AFTER *ME?!*
FWOOSH

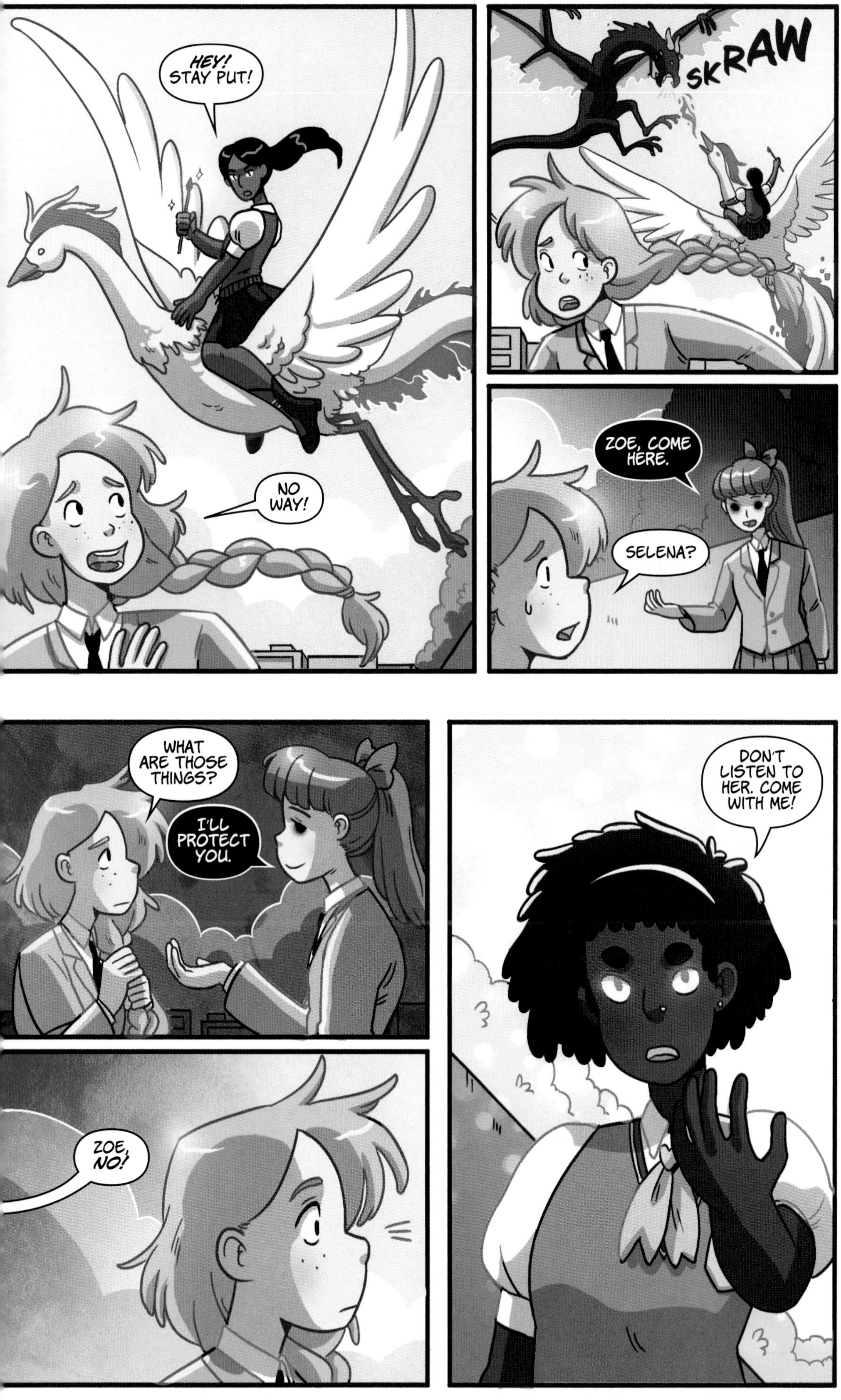
HEY! STAY PUT!
NO WAY!
SKRAW
ZOE, COME HERE.
SELENA?
WHAT ARE THOSE THINGS?
I'LL PROTECT YOU.
ZOE, NO!
DON'T LISTEN TO HER. COME WITH ME!

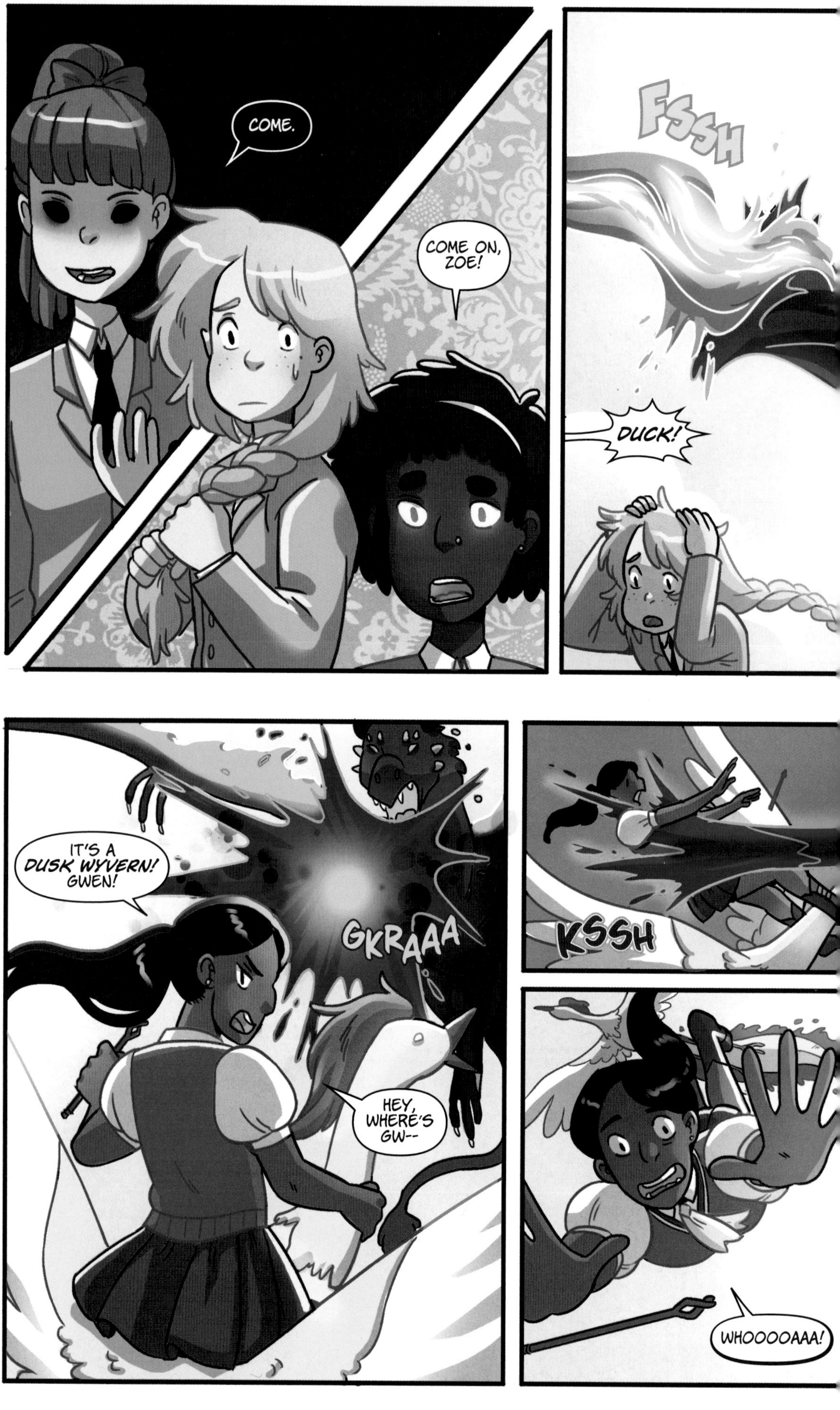
COME.
COME ON, ZOE!
FSSH
DUCK!
IT'S A DUSK WYVERN! GWEN!
GKRAAA
HEY, WHERE'S GW--
KSSH
WHOOOOAAA!

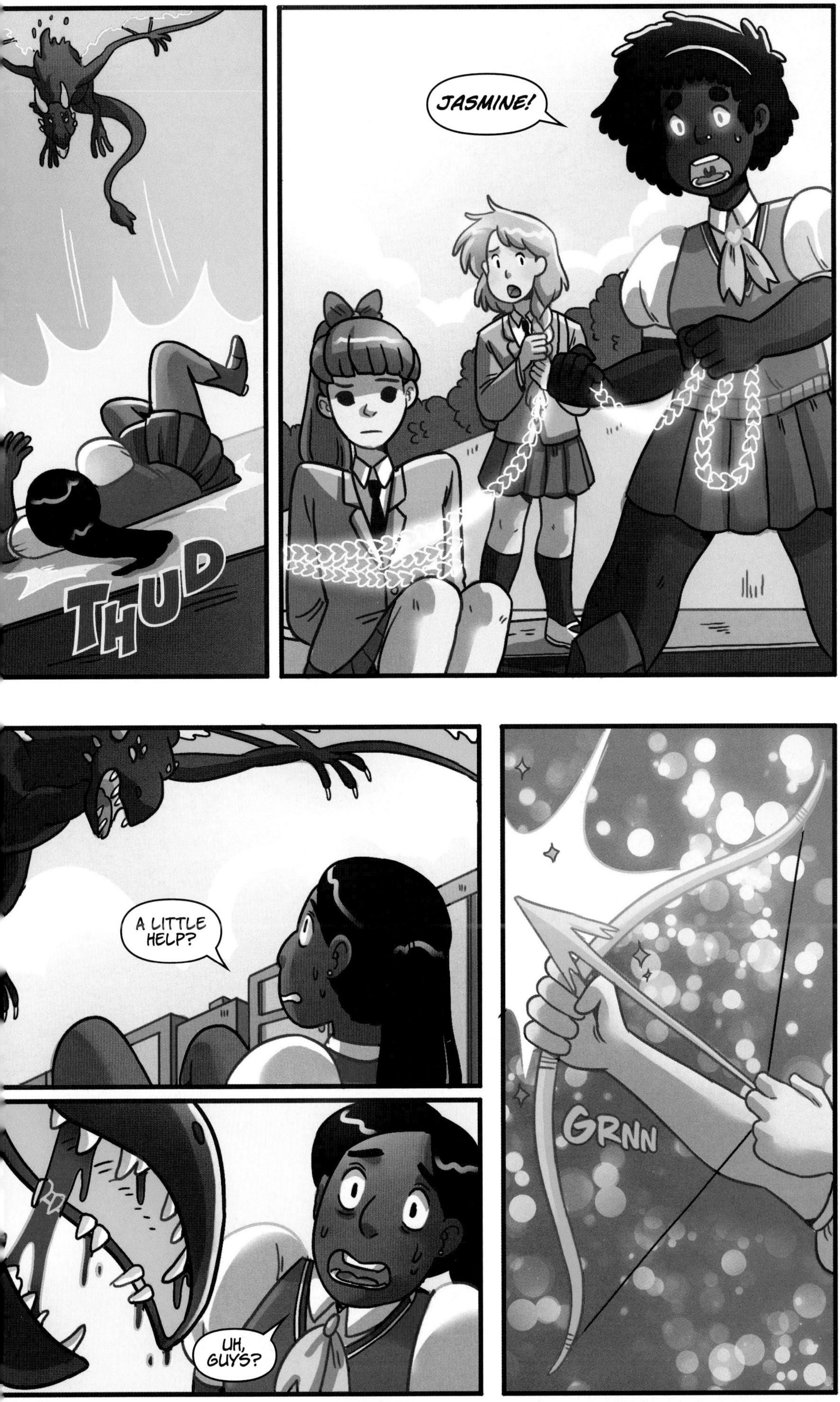
THUD
JASMINE!
A LITTLE HELP?
UH, GUYS?
GRNN

FWOOSH

WAAK!

CUTTING IT A BIT CLOSE, AREN'T YOU?

MY BOW WAS IN MY LOCKER!

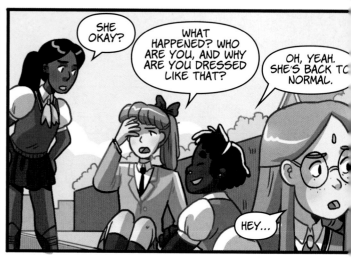

SHE OKAY?

WHAT HAPPENED? WHO ARE YOU, AND WHY ARE YOU DRESSED LIKE THAT?

OH, YEAH. SHE'S BACK TO NORMAL.

HEY...

"WHERE'S ZOE?"

MOM?

DAD?

YOU WILL *NOT* BELIEVE WHAT JUST HAPPENED. I REALLY NEED TO TALK TO YOU.

WE'RE IN HERE, HONEY.

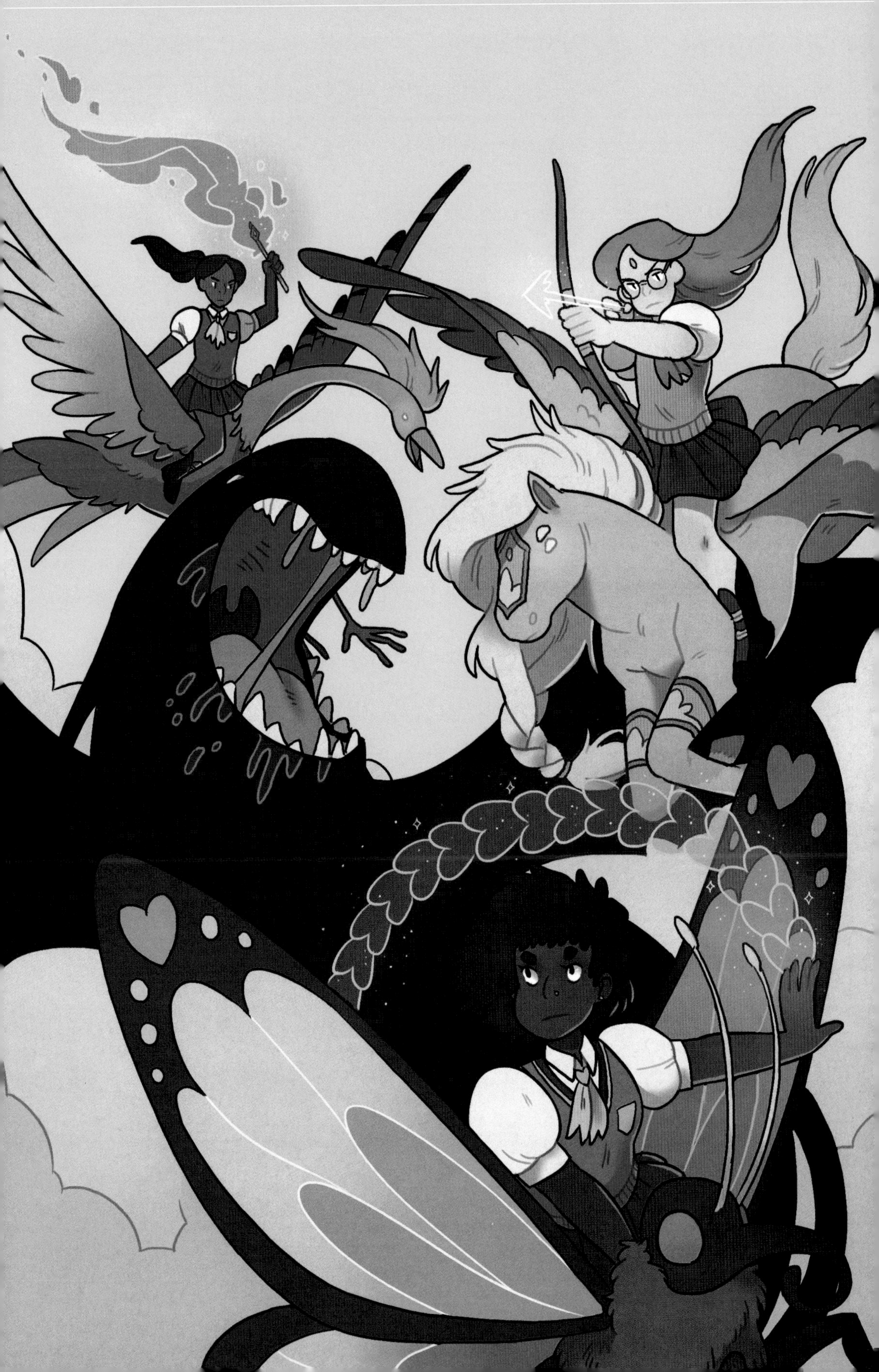

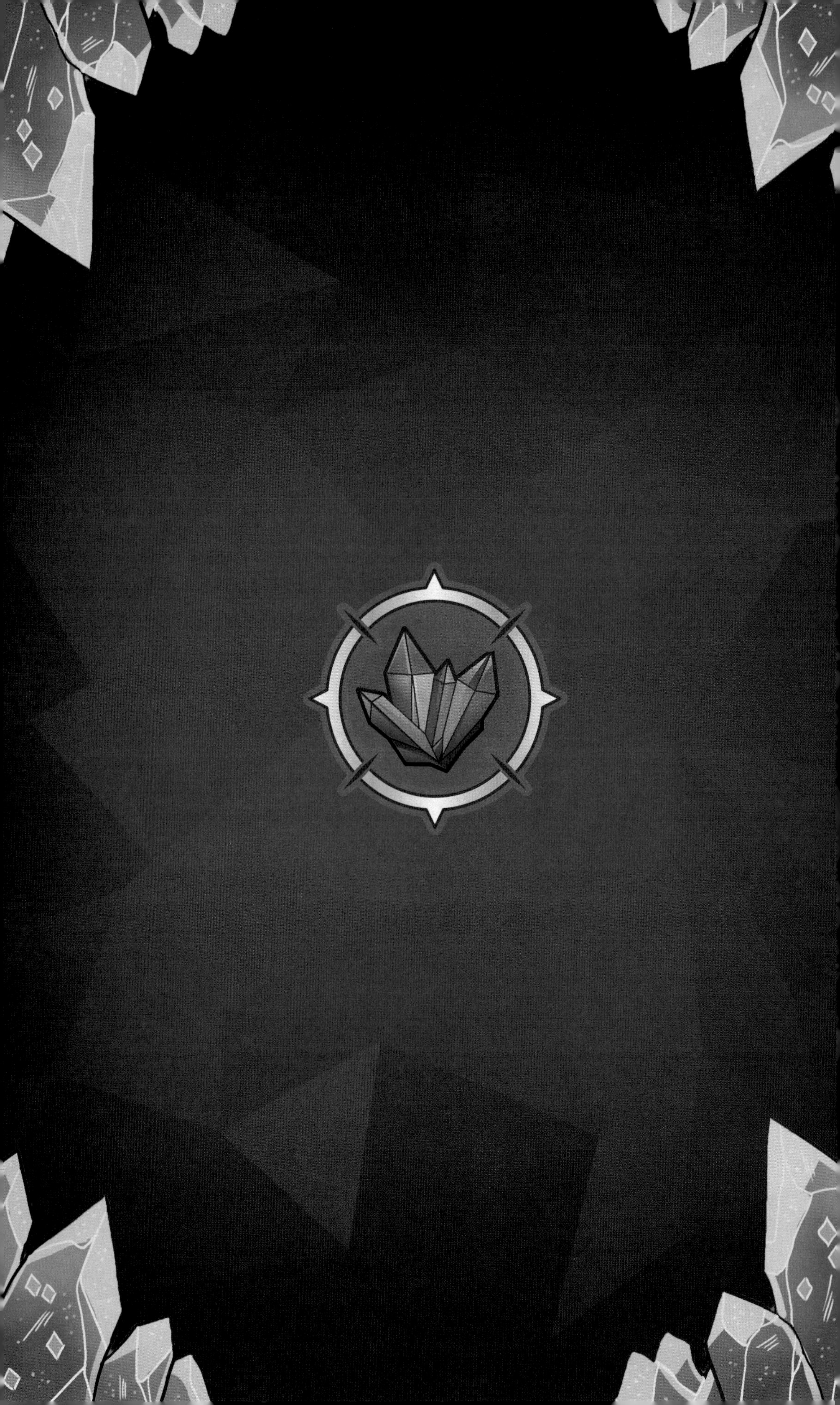

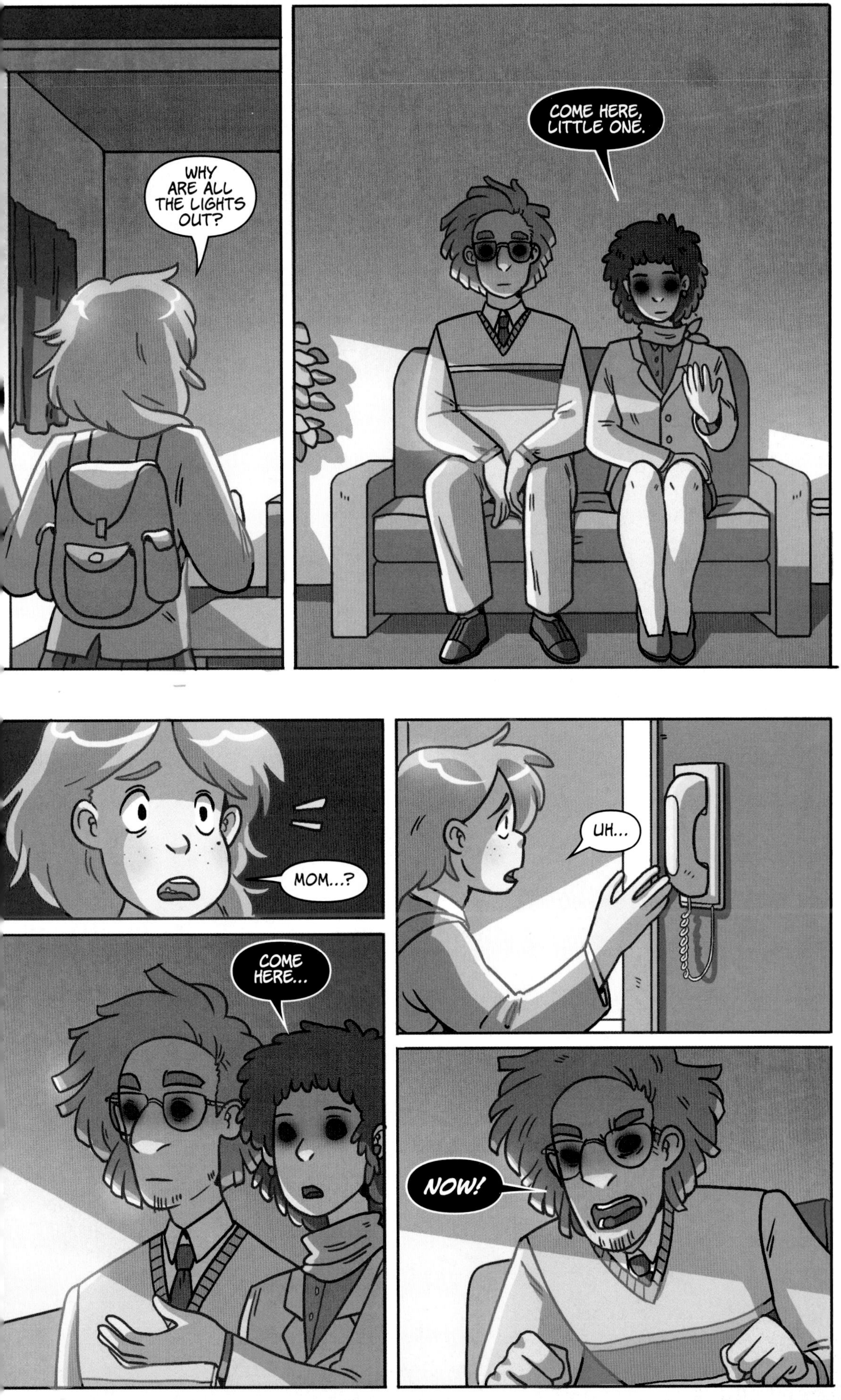
WHY ARE ALL THE LIGHTS OUT?
COME HERE, LITTLE ONE.
MOM...?
UH...
COME HERE...
NOW!

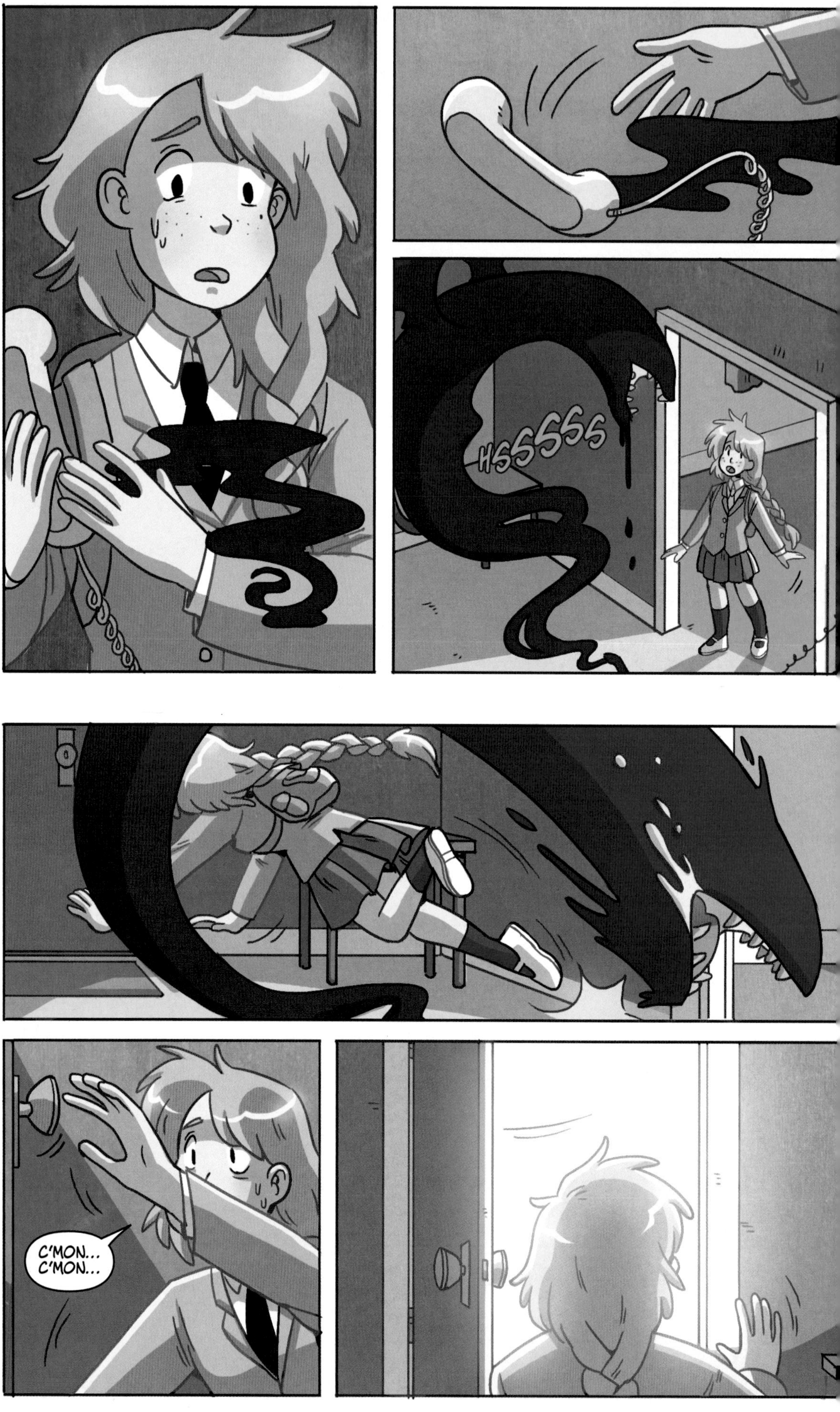
HSSSSSS
C'MON...
C'MON...

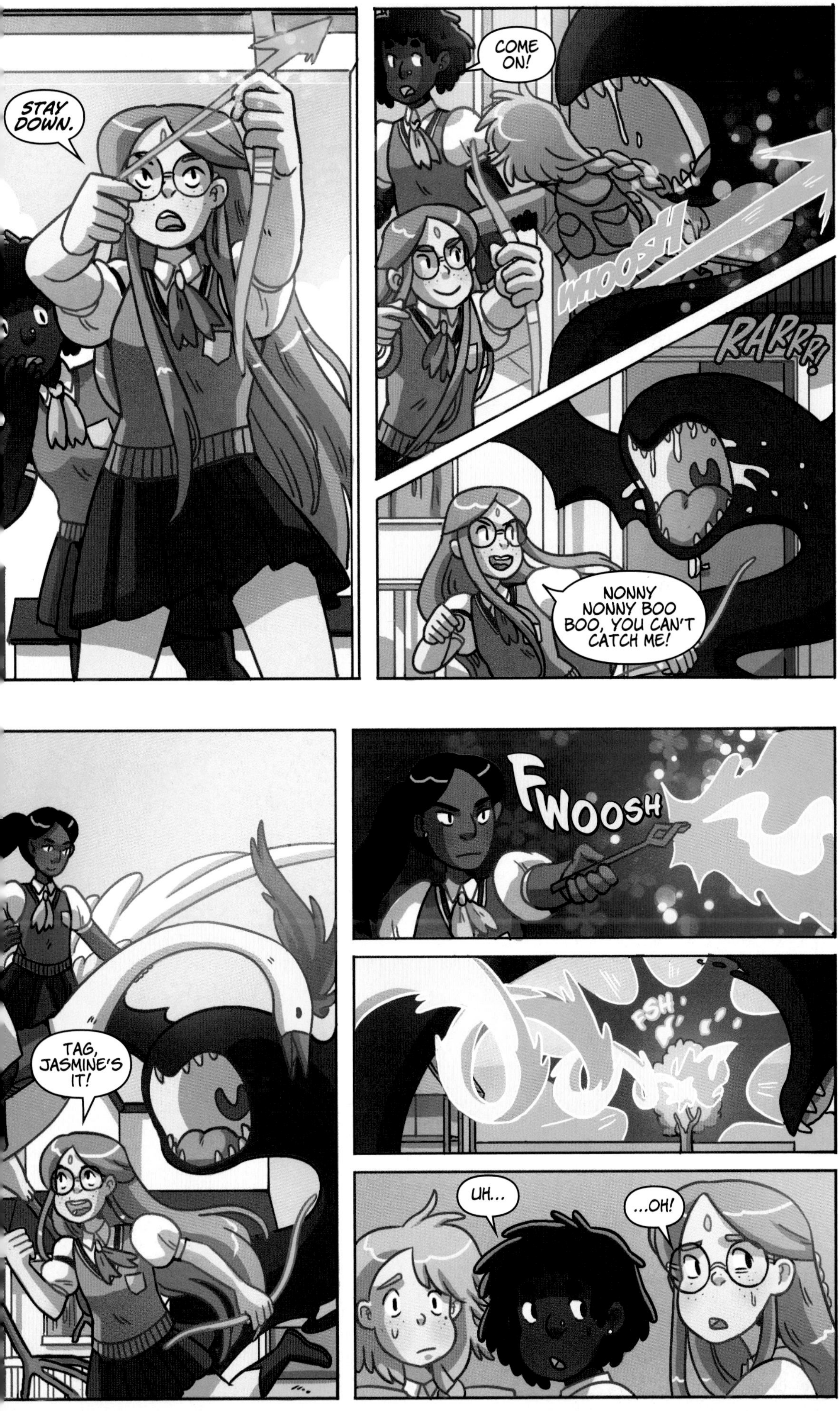
STAY DOWN.
COME ON!
WHOOSH
RARRR!
NONNY NONNY BOO BOO, YOU CAN'T CATCH ME!
TAG, JASMINE'S IT!
FWOOSH
FSH
UH...
...OH!

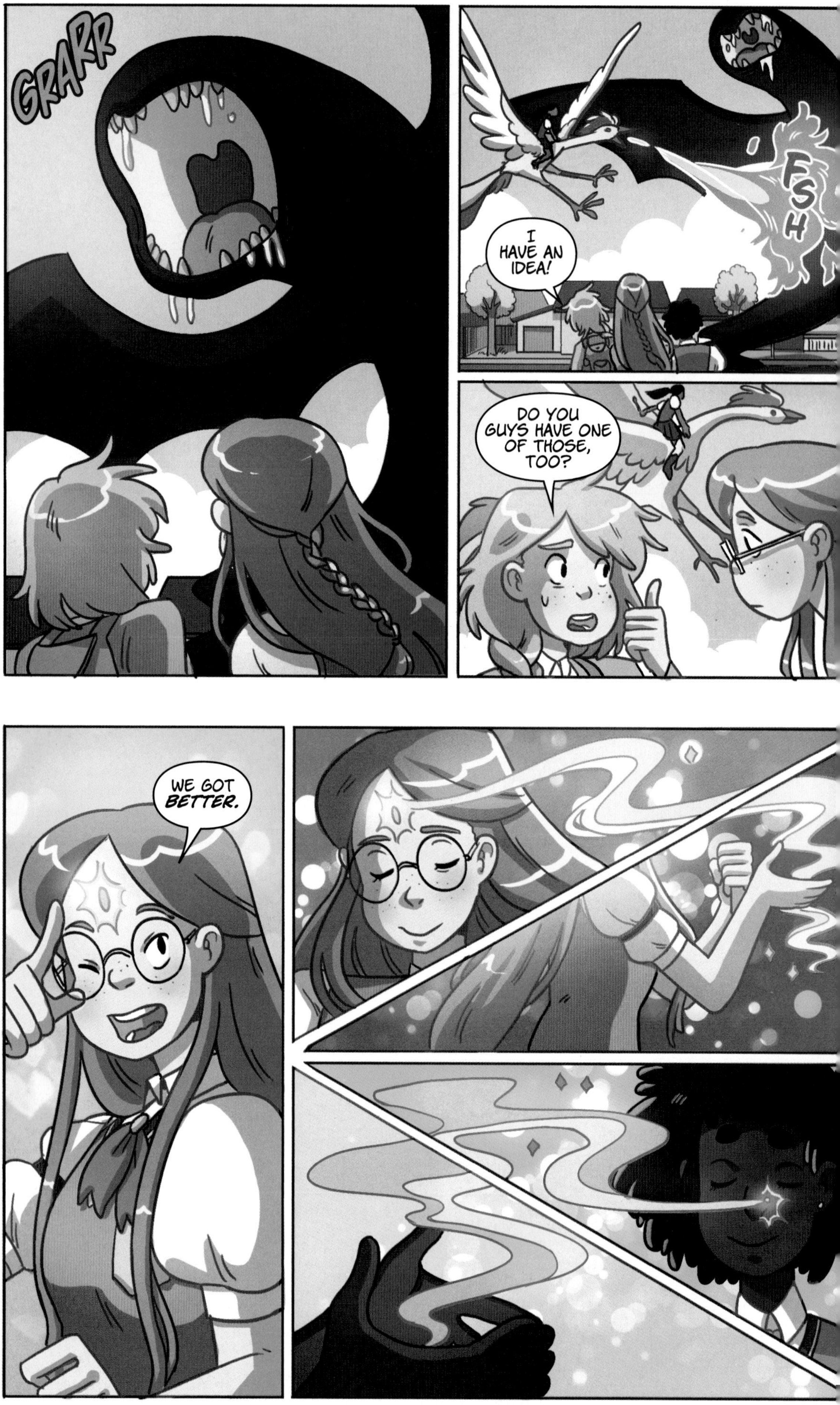
GRARR
FSH
I HAVE AN IDEA!
DO YOU GUYS HAVE ONE OF THOSE, TOO?
WE GOT BETTER.

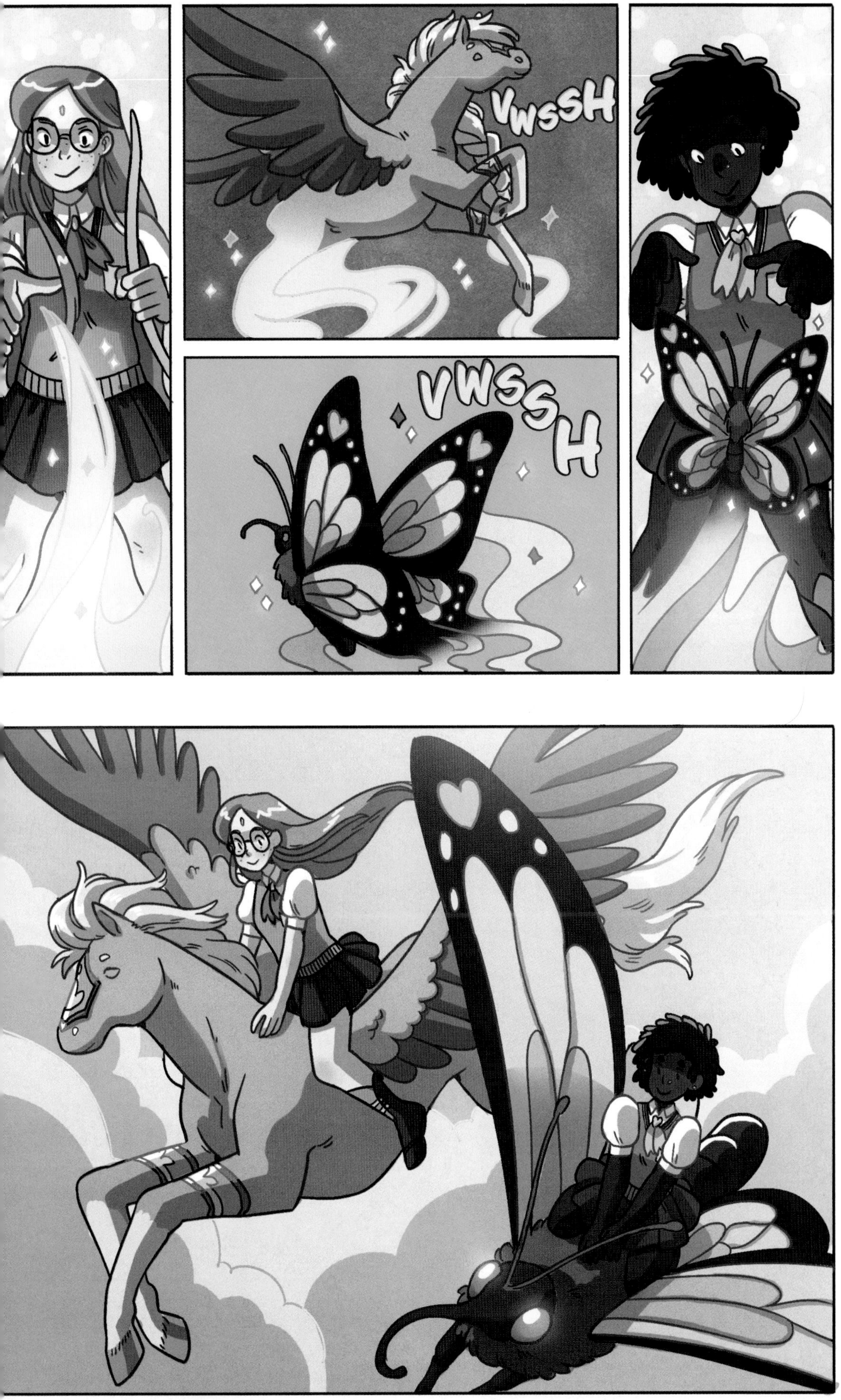
VWSSH
VWSSH

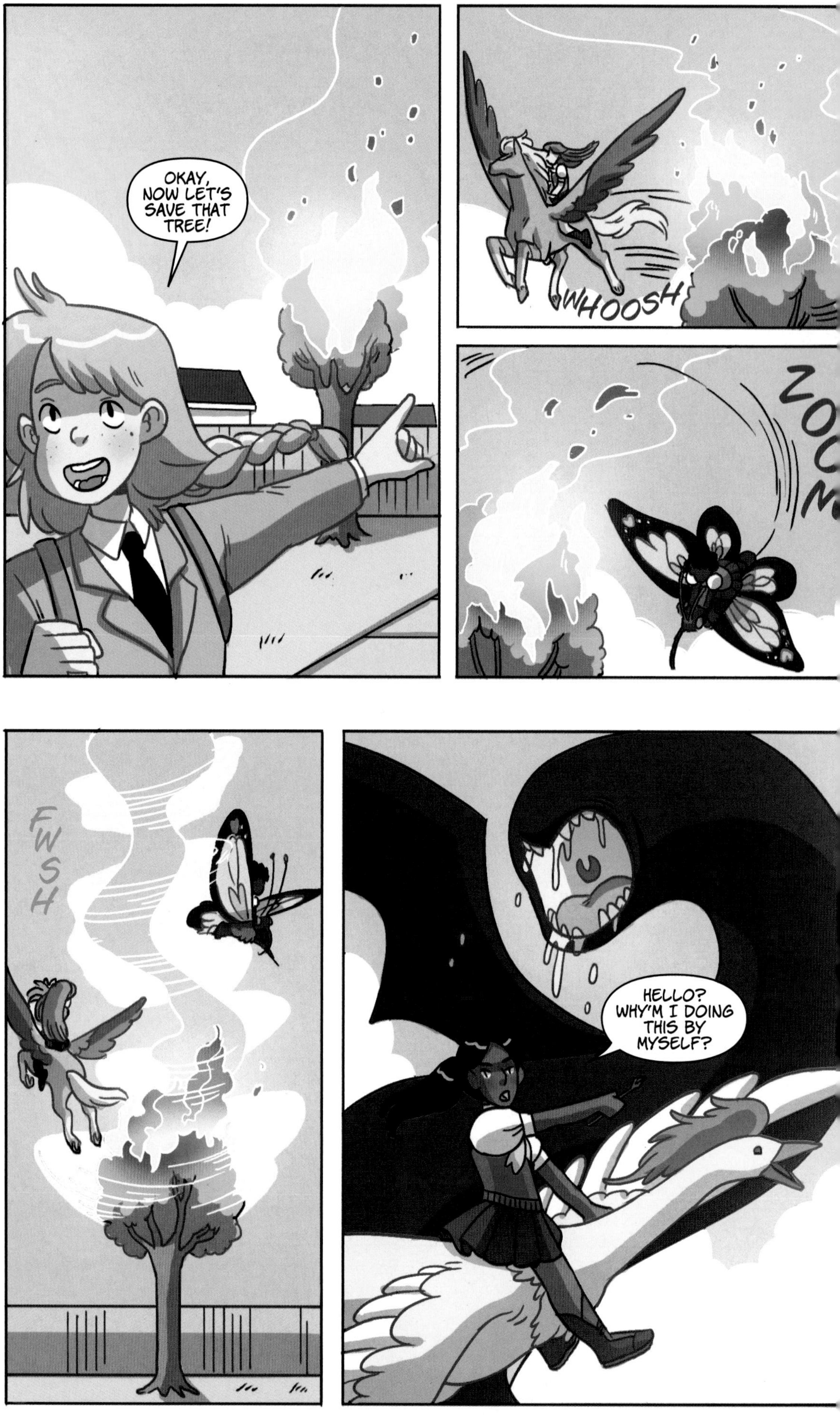
OKAY, NOW LET'S SAVE THAT TREE!
WHOOSH
ZOOM
FWSH
HELLO? WHY'M I DOING THIS BY MYSELF?

THEY'RE PUTTING OUT THE FIRE!

NOW LET'S TAKE THIS GUY OUT *TOGETHER!*

READY...

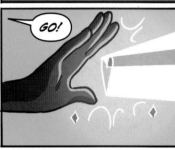

SET...

GO!

AAWWKKK!!

GO CADETS!

DON'T YOU MEAN...

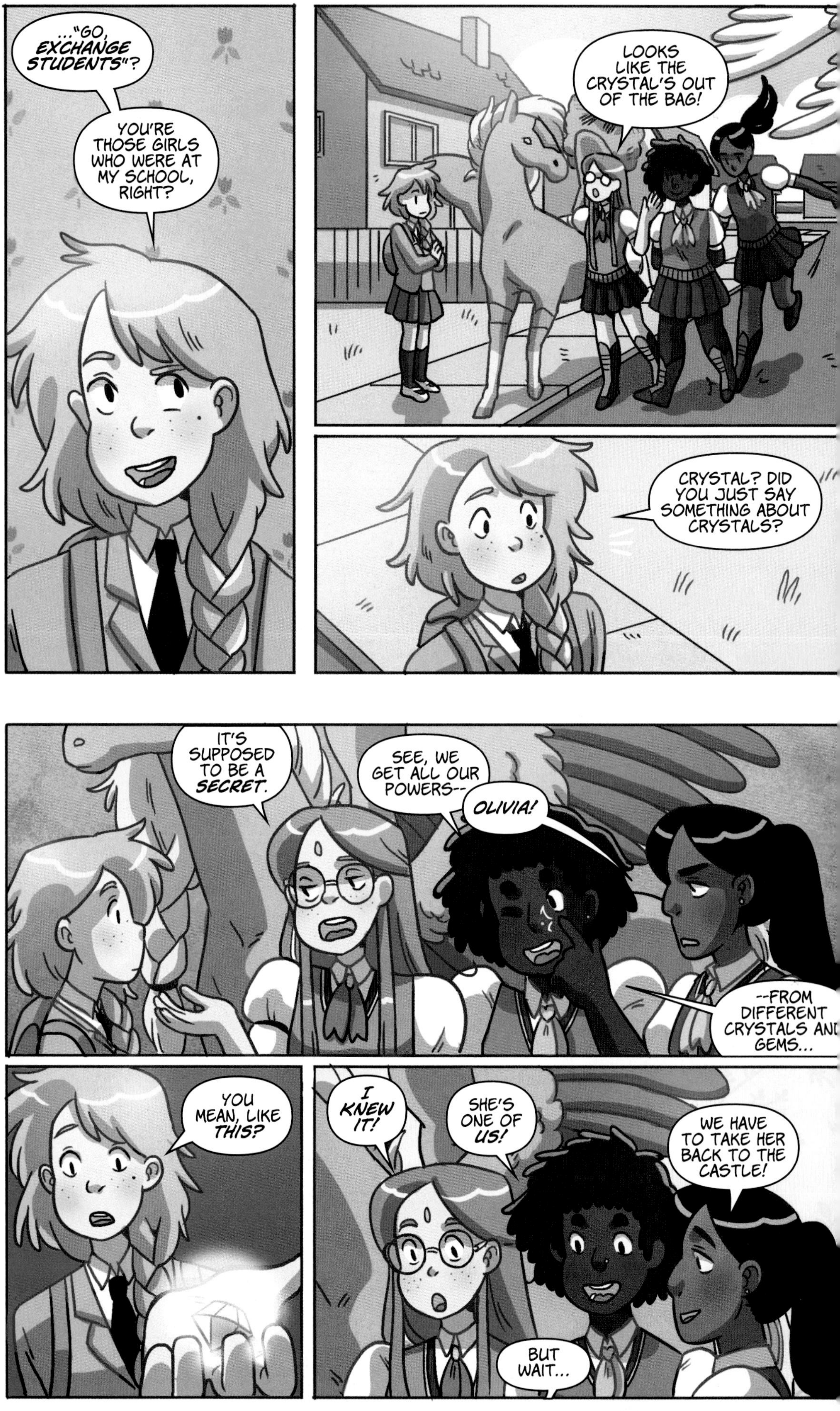

..."GO, EXCHANGE STUDENTS"?
YOU'RE THOSE GIRLS WHO WERE AT MY SCHOOL, RIGHT?
LOOKS LIKE THE CRYSTAL'S OUT OF THE BAG!
CRYSTAL? DID YOU JUST SAY SOMETHING ABOUT CRYSTALS?
IT'S SUPPOSED TO BE A SECRET.
SEE, WE GET ALL OUR POWERS--
OLIVIA!
--FROM DIFFERENT CRYSTALS AND GEMS...
YOU MEAN, LIKE THIS?
I KNEW IT!
SHE'S ONE OF US!
WE HAVE TO TAKE HER BACK TO THE CASTLE!
BUT WAIT...

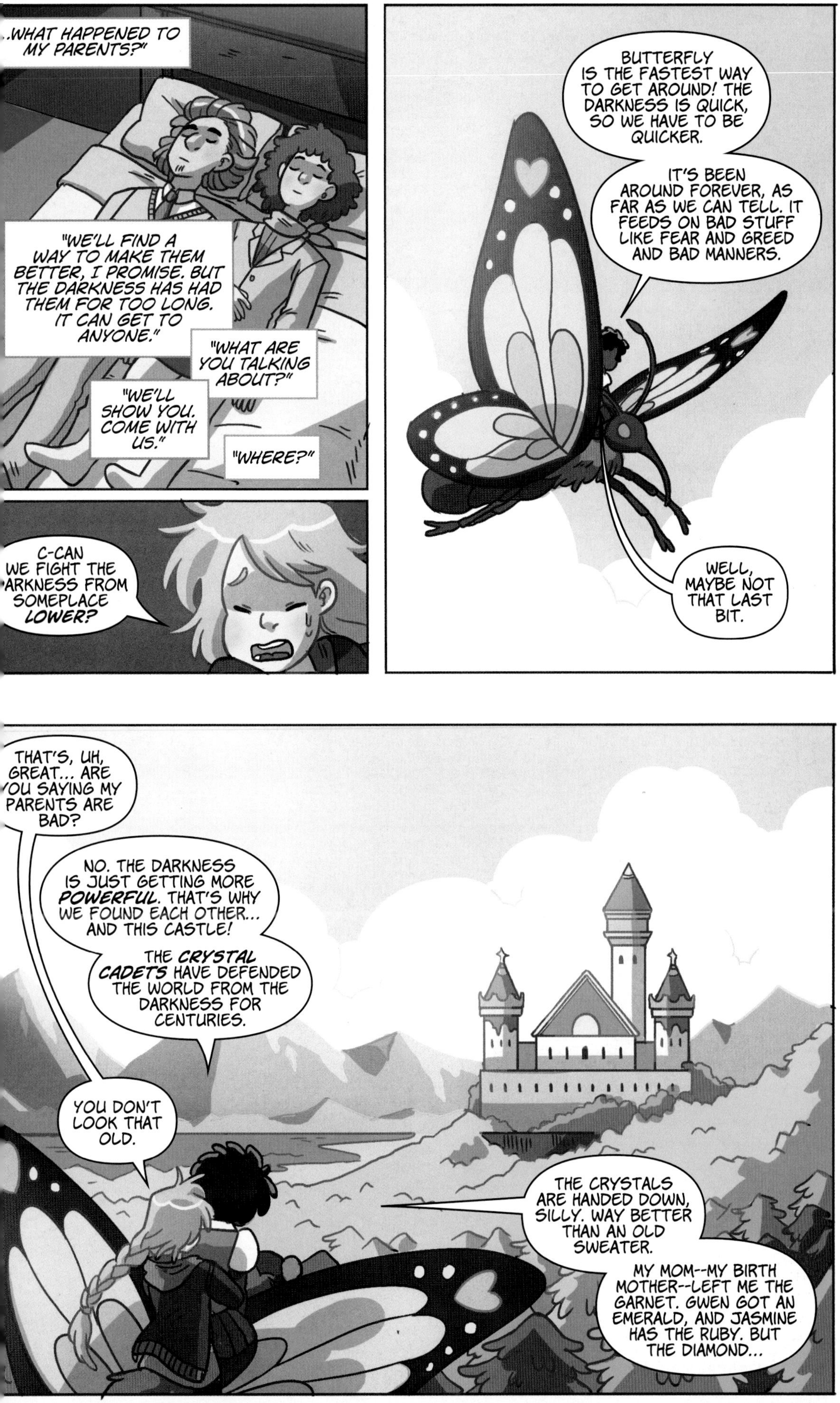

..WHAT HAPPENED TO MY PARENTS?"
"WE'LL FIND A WAY TO MAKE THEM BETTER, I PROMISE. BUT THE DARKNESS HAS HAD THEM FOR TOO LONG. IT CAN GET TO ANYONE."
"WHAT ARE YOU TALKING ABOUT?"
"WE'LL SHOW YOU. COME WITH US."
"WHERE?"
C-CAN WE FIGHT THE ARKNESS FROM SOMEPLACE LOWER?
BUTTERFLY IS THE FASTEST WAY TO GET AROUND! THE DARKNESS IS QUICK, SO WE HAVE TO BE QUICKER.
IT'S BEEN AROUND FOREVER, AS FAR AS WE CAN TELL. IT FEEDS ON BAD STUFF LIKE FEAR AND GREED AND BAD MANNERS.
WELL, MAYBE NOT THAT LAST BIT.
THAT'S, UH, GREAT... ARE OU SAYING MY PARENTS ARE BAD?
NO. THE DARKNESS IS JUST GETTING MORE POWERFUL. THAT'S WHY WE FOUND EACH OTHER... AND THIS CASTLE!
THE CRYSTAL CADETS HAVE DEFENDED THE WORLD FROM THE DARKNESS FOR CENTURIES.
YOU DON'T LOOK THAT OLD.
THE CRYSTALS ARE HANDED DOWN, SILLY. WAY BETTER THAN AN OLD SWEATER.
MY MOM--MY BIRTH MOTHER--LEFT ME THE GARNET. GWEN GOT AN EMERALD, AND JASMINE HAS THE RUBY. BUT THE DIAMOND...

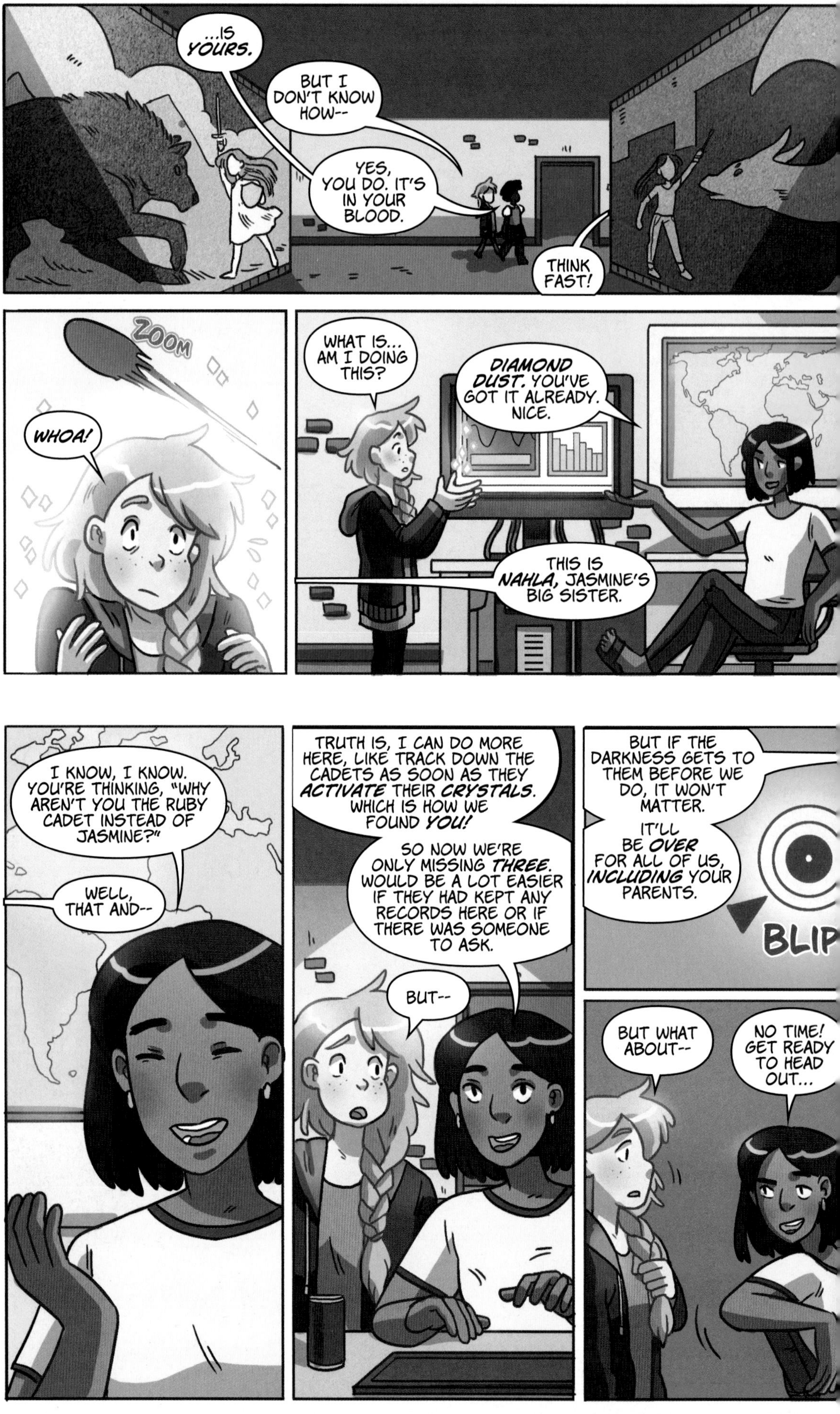
...IS YOURS.
BUT I DON'T KNOW HOW--
YES, YOU DO. IT'S IN YOUR BLOOD.
THINK FAST!
ZOOM
WHOA!
WHAT IS... AM I DOING THIS?
DIAMOND DUST. YOU'VE GOT IT ALREADY. NICE.
THIS IS NAHLA, JASMINE'S BIG SISTER.
I KNOW, I KNOW. YOU'RE THINKING, "WHY AREN'T YOU THE RUBY CADET INSTEAD OF JASMINE?"
WELL, THAT AND--
TRUTH IS, I CAN DO MORE HERE, LIKE TRACK DOWN THE CADETS AS SOON AS THEY ACTIVATE THEIR CRYSTALS. WHICH IS HOW WE FOUND YOU!
SO NOW WE'RE ONLY MISSING THREE. WOULD BE A LOT EASIER IF THEY HAD KEPT ANY RECORDS HERE OR IF THERE WAS SOMEONE TO ASK.
BUT--
BUT IF THE DARKNESS GETS TO THEM BEFORE WE DO, IT WON'T MATTER.
IT'LL BE OVER FOR ALL OF US, INCLUDING YOUR PARENTS.
BLIP
BUT WHAT ABOUT--
NO TIME! GET READY TO HEAD OUT...

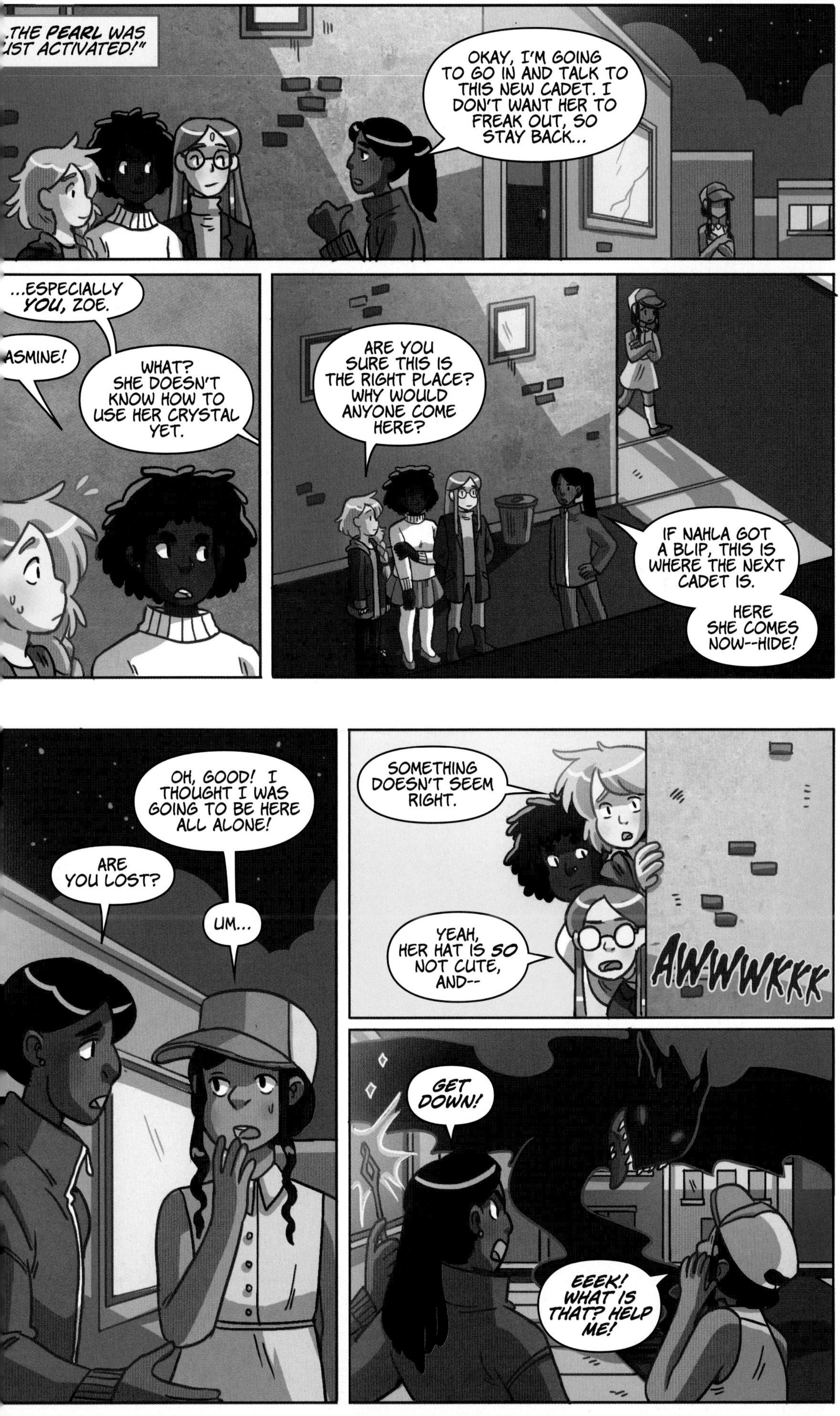

...THE PEARL WAS
...IST ACTIVATED!"
OKAY, I'M GOING TO GO IN AND TALK TO THIS NEW CADET. I DON'T WANT HER TO FREAK OUT, SO STAY BACK...
...ESPECIALLY YOU, ZOE.
...ASMINE!
WHAT? SHE DOESN'T KNOW HOW TO USE HER CRYSTAL YET.
ARE YOU SURE THIS IS THE RIGHT PLACE? WHY WOULD ANYONE COME HERE?
IF NAHLA GOT A BLIP, THIS IS WHERE THE NEXT CADET IS.
HERE SHE COMES NOW--HIDE!
OH, GOOD! I THOUGHT I WAS GOING TO BE HERE ALL ALONE!
ARE YOU LOST?
UM...
SOMETHING DOESN'T SEEM RIGHT.
YEAH, HER HAT IS SO NOT CUTE, AND--
AWWWKKK
GET DOWN!
EEEK! WHAT IS THAT? HELP ME!

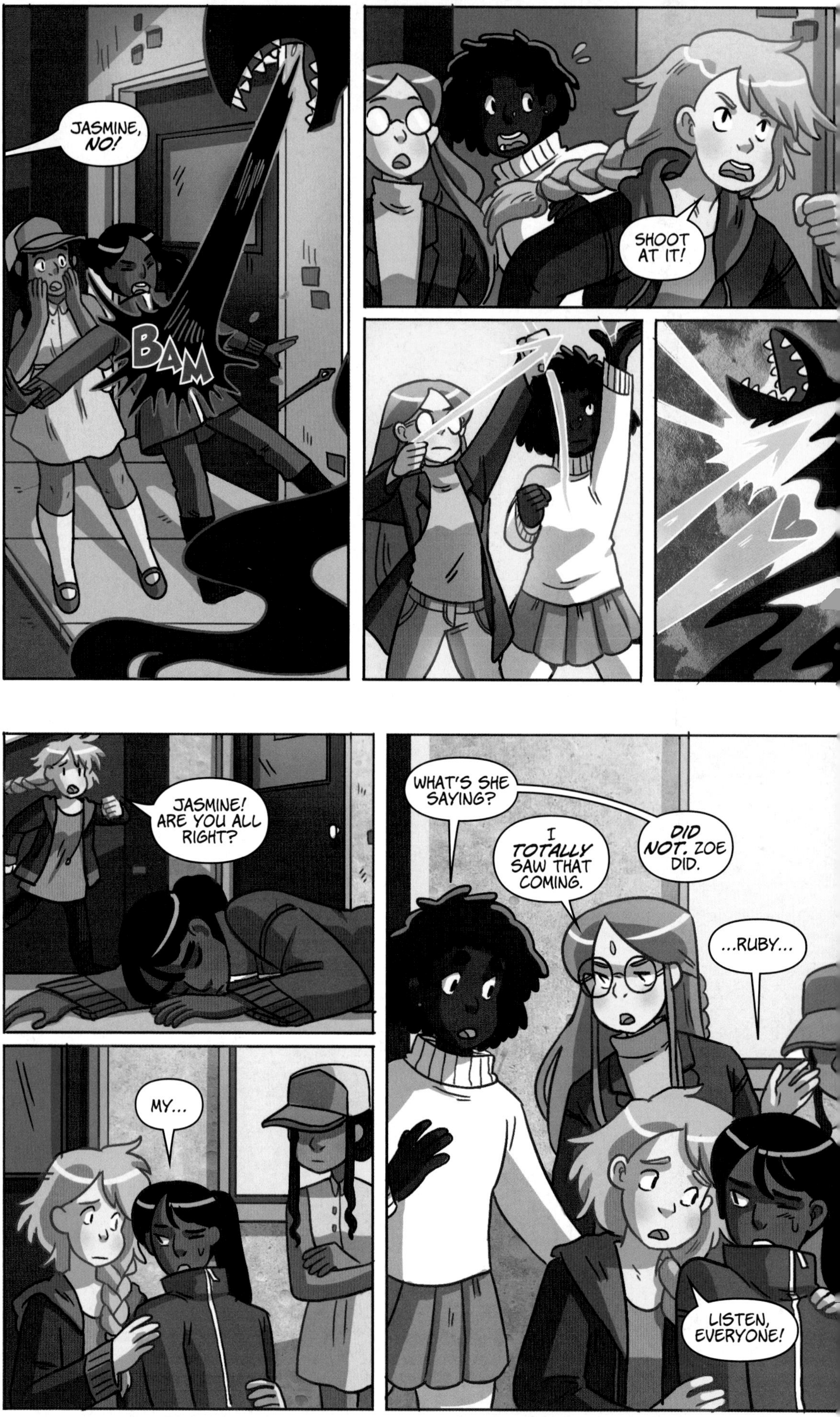
JASMINE, NO!
SHOOT AT IT!
BAM
JASMINE! ARE YOU ALL RIGHT?
MY...
WHAT'S SHE SAYING?
I TOTALLY SAW THAT COMING.
DID NOT. ZOE DID.
...RUBY...
LISTEN, EVERYONE!

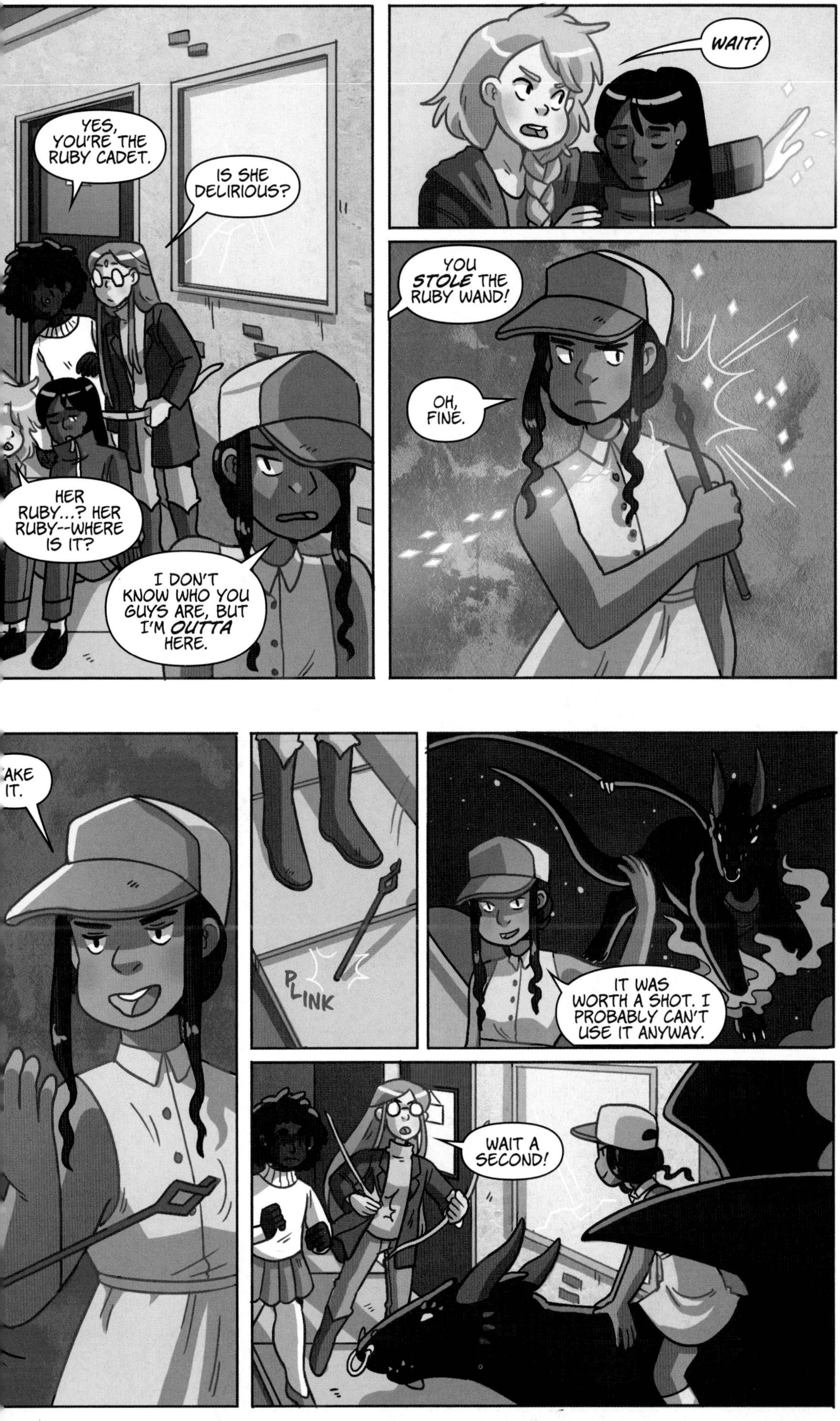
YES, YOU'RE THE RUBY CADET.
IS SHE DELIRIOUS?
HER RUBY...? HER RUBY--WHERE IS IT?
I DON'T KNOW WHO YOU GUYS ARE, BUT I'M *OUTTA* HERE.
WAIT!
YOU ***STOLE*** THE RUBY WAND!
OH, FINE.
AKE IT.
PLINK
IT WAS WORTH A SHOT. I PROBABLY CAN'T USE IT ANYWAY.
WAIT A SECOND!

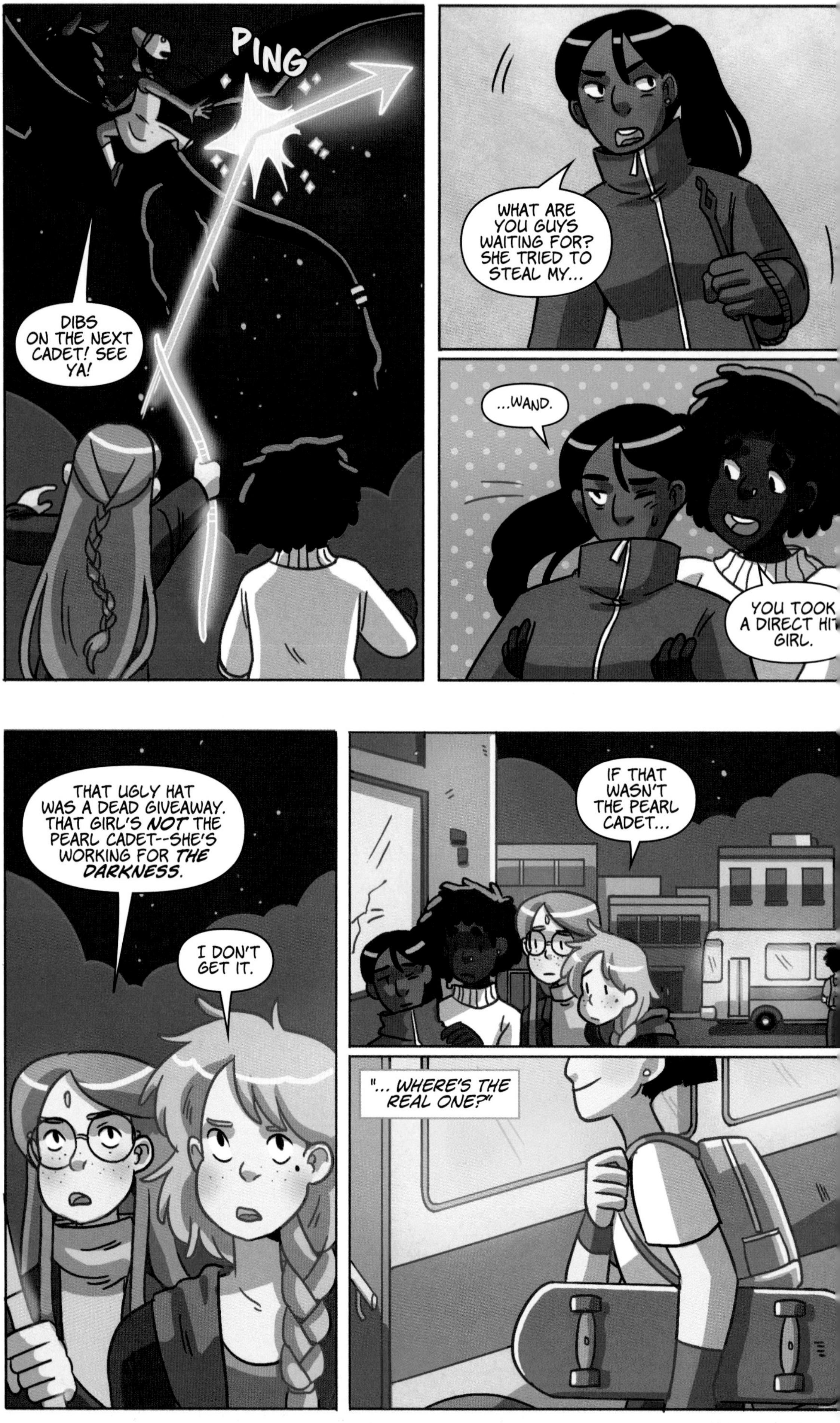
PING
DIBS ON THE NEXT CADET! SEE YA!
WHAT ARE YOU GUYS WAITING FOR? SHE TRIED TO STEAL MY...
...WAND.
YOU TOOK A DIRECT HIT GIRL.
THAT UGLY HAT WAS A DEAD GIVEAWAY. THAT GIRL'S *NOT* THE PEARL CADET--SHE'S WORKING FOR *THE DARKNESS*.
I DON'T GET IT.
IF THAT WASN'T THE PEARL CADET...
"... *WHERE'S THE REAL ONE?*"

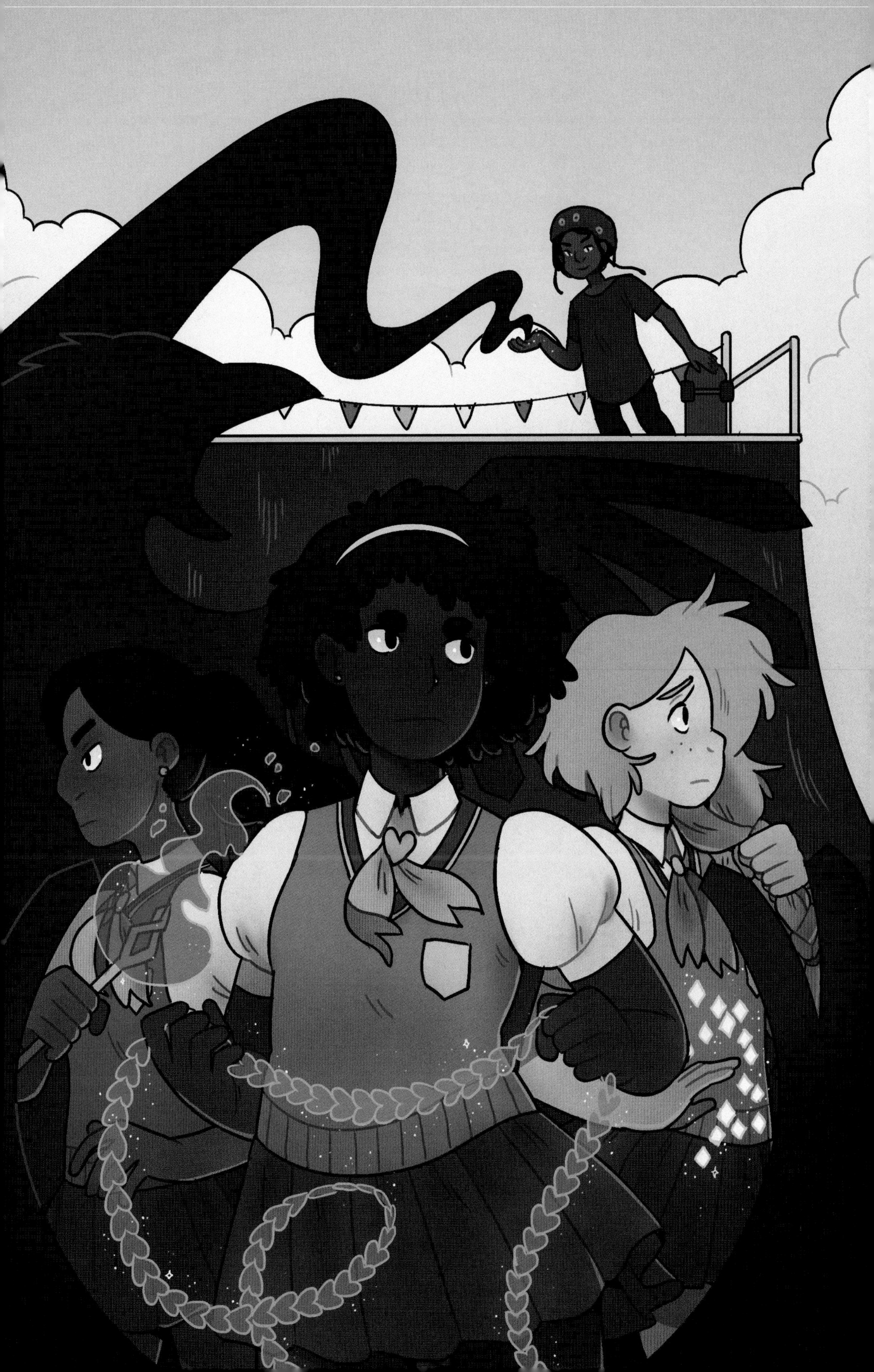

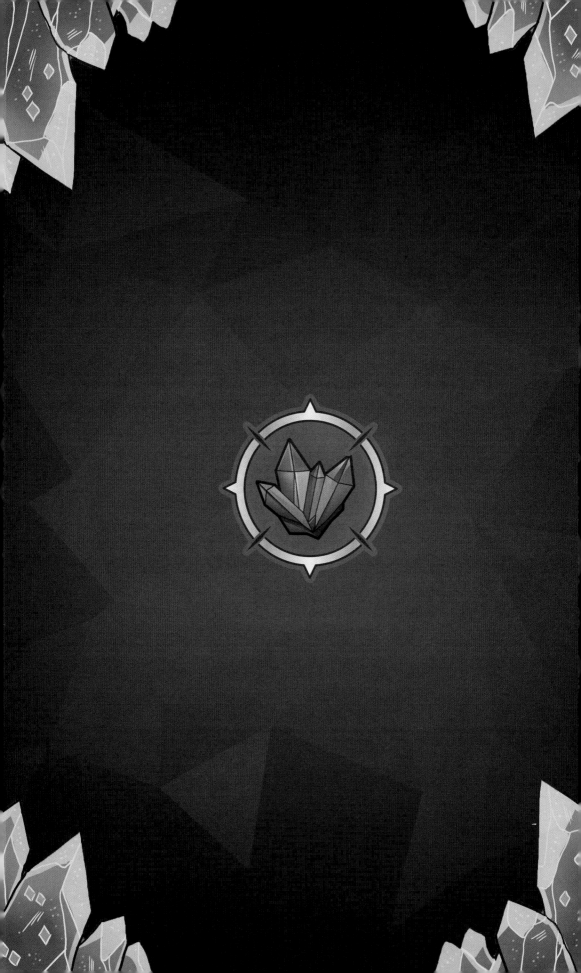

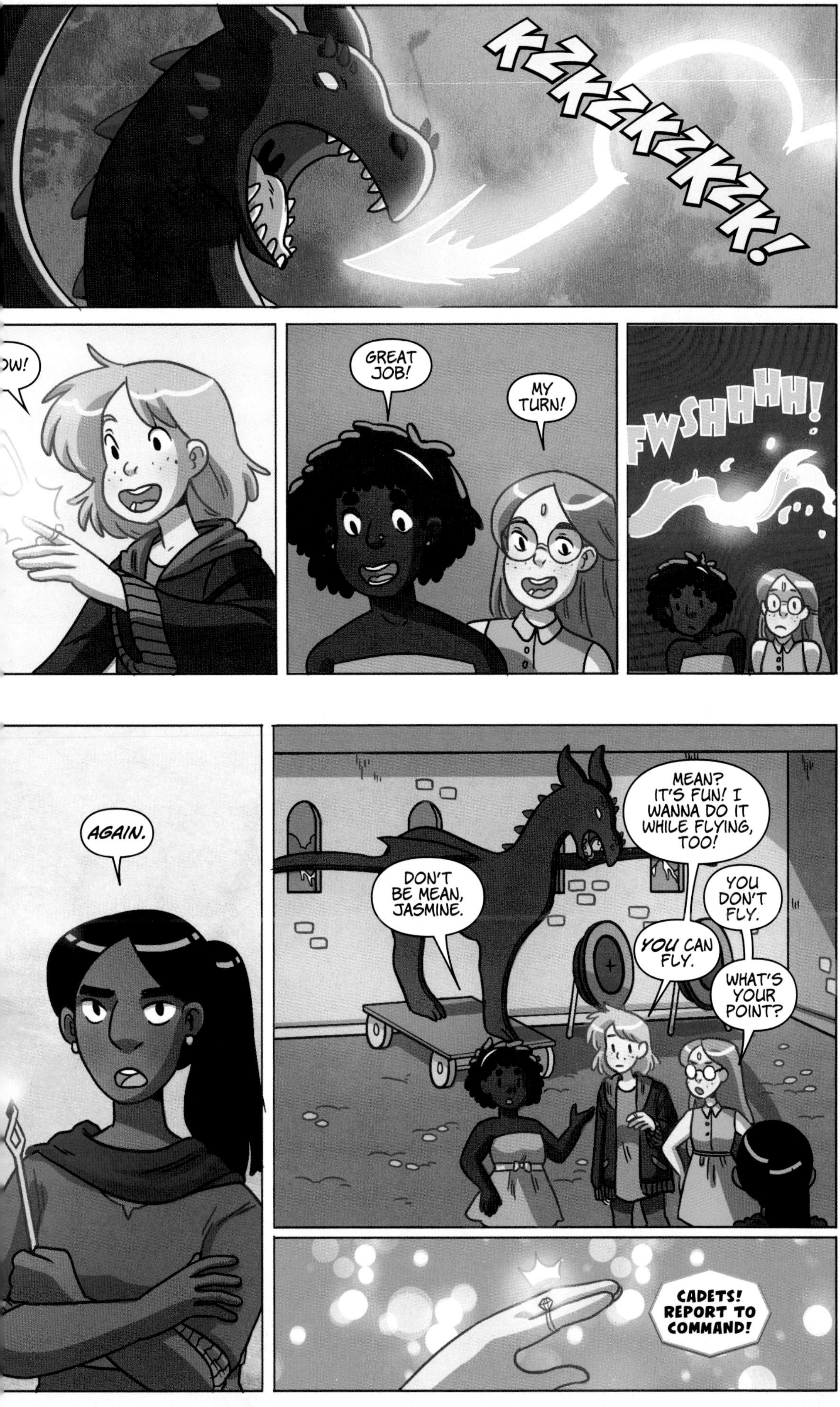
KZKZKZKZKZK!
OW!
GREAT JOB!
MY TURN!
FWSHHHHH!
AGAIN.
DON'T BE MEAN, JASMINE.
MEAN? IT'S FUN! I WANNA DO IT WHILE FLYING, TOO!
YOU DON'T FLY.
YOU CAN FLY.
WHAT'S YOUR POINT?
CADETS! REPORT TO COMMAND!

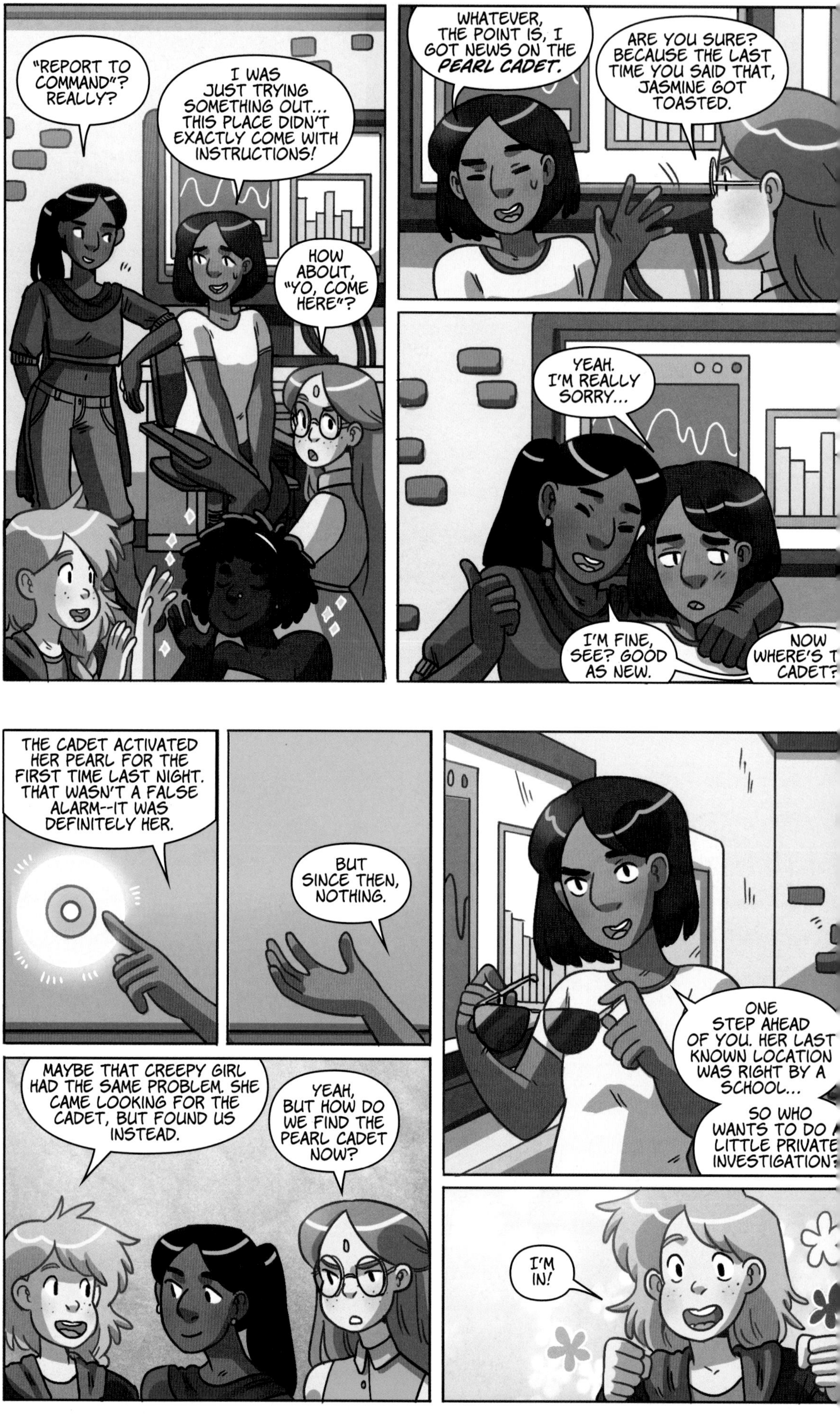

"REPORT TO COMMAND"? REALLY?
I WAS JUST TRYING SOMETHING OUT... THIS PLACE DIDN'T EXACTLY COME WITH INSTRUCTIONS!
HOW ABOUT, "YO, COME HERE"?
WHATEVER, THE POINT IS, I GOT NEWS ON THE PEARL CADET.
ARE YOU SURE? BECAUSE THE LAST TIME YOU SAID THAT, JASMINE GOT TOASTED.
YEAH. I'M REALLY SORRY...
I'M FINE, SEE? GOOD AS NEW.
NOW WHERE'S T CADET?
THE CADET ACTIVATED HER PEARL FOR THE FIRST TIME LAST NIGHT. THAT WASN'T A FALSE ALARM--IT WAS DEFINITELY HER.
BUT SINCE THEN, NOTHING.
ONE STEP AHEAD OF YOU. HER LAST KNOWN LOCATION WAS RIGHT BY A SCHOOL...
SO WHO WANTS TO DO A LITTLE PRIVATE INVESTIGATION?
MAYBE THAT CREEPY GIRL HAD THE SAME PROBLEM. SHE CAME LOOKING FOR THE CADET, BUT FOUND US INSTEAD.
YEAH, BUT HOW DO WE FIND THE PEARL CADET NOW?
I'M IN!

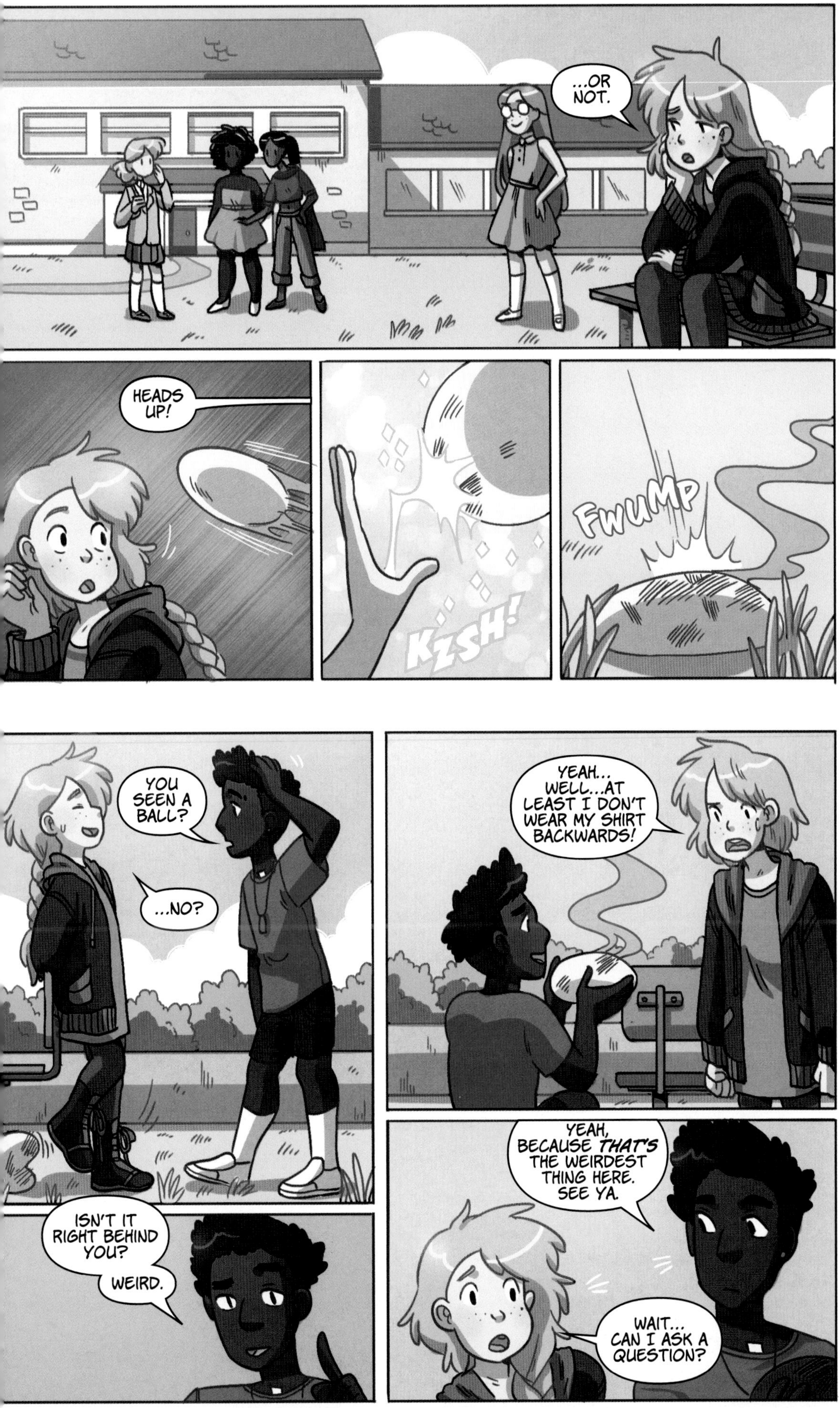
...OR NOT.
HEADS UP!
KZSH!
FWUMP
YOU SEEN A BALL?
...NO?
ISN'T IT RIGHT BEHIND YOU?
WEIRD.
YEAH... WELL...AT LEAST I DON'T WEAR MY SHIRT BACKWARDS!
YEAH, BECAUSE THAT'S THE WEIRDEST THING HERE. SEE YA.
WAIT... CAN I ASK A QUESTION?

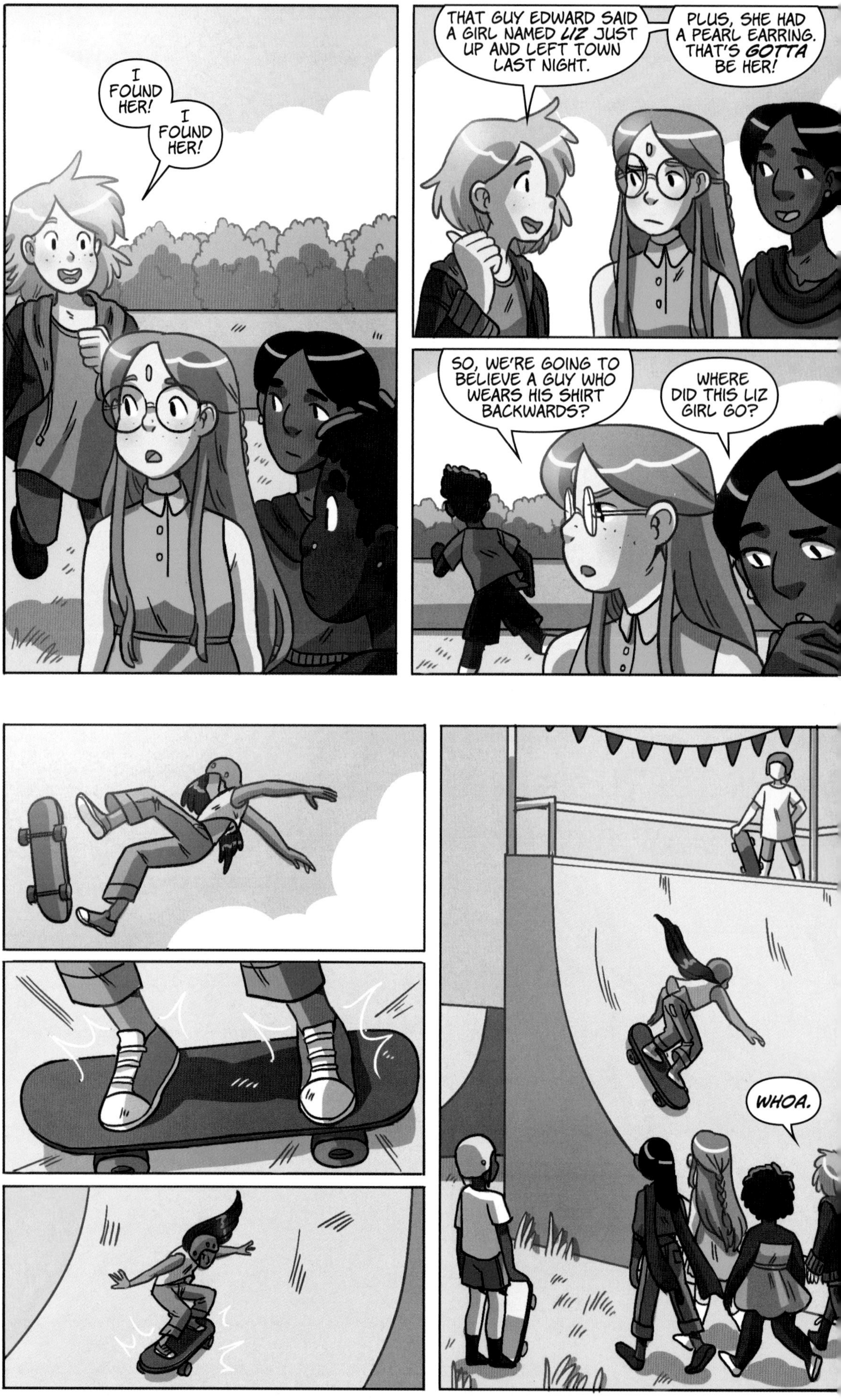
I FOUND HER!
I FOUND HER!
THAT GUY EDWARD SAID A GIRL NAMED *LIZ* JUST UP AND LEFT TOWN LAST NIGHT.
PLUS, SHE HAD A PEARL EARRING. THAT'S *GOTTA* BE HER!
SO, WE'RE GOING TO BELIEVE A GUY WHO WEARS HIS SHIRT BACKWARDS?
WHERE DID THIS LIZ GIRL GO?
WHOA.

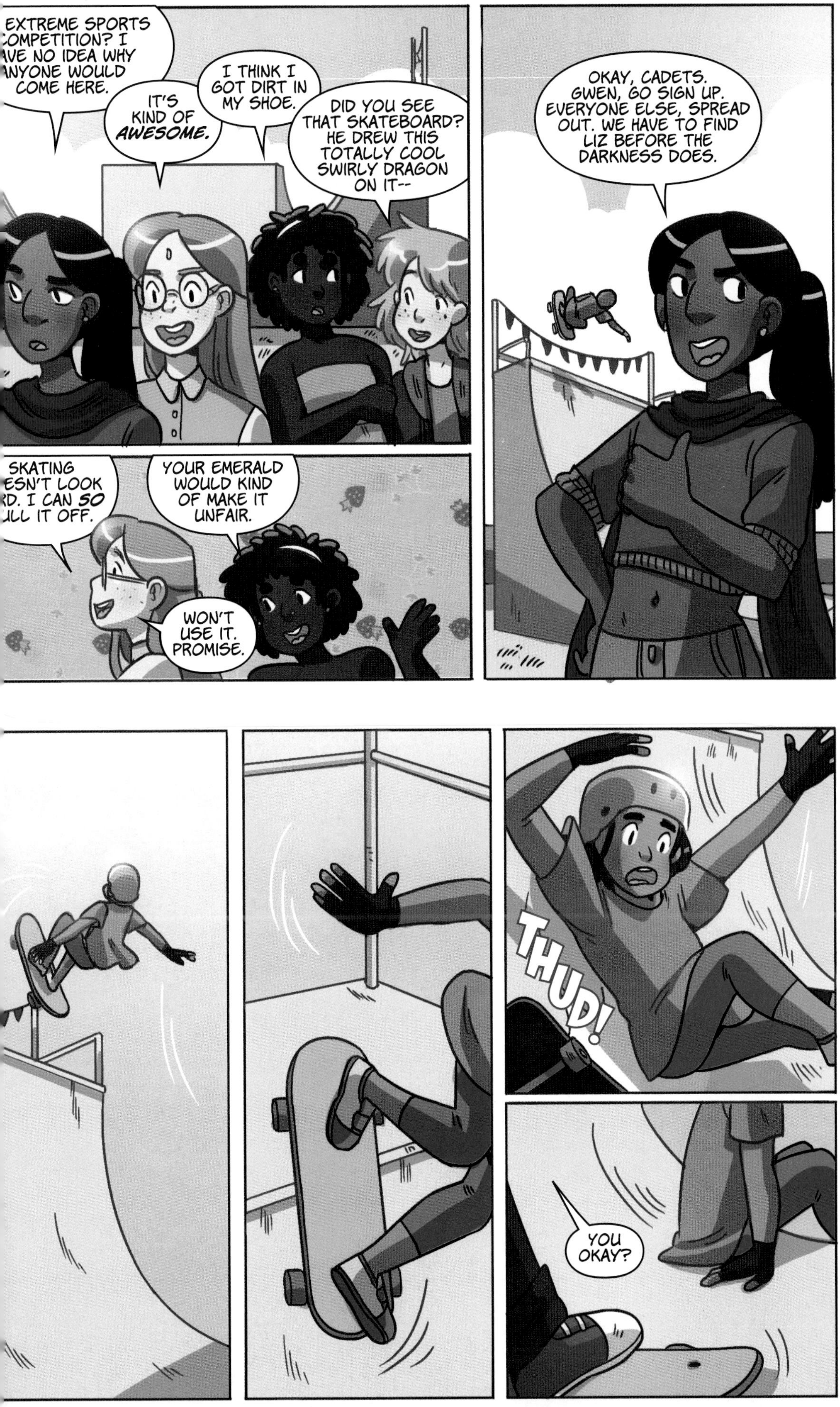

EXTREME SPORTS OMPETITION? I AVE NO IDEA WHY NYONE WOULD COME HERE.
IT'S KIND OF *AWESOME.*
I THINK I GOT DIRT IN MY SHOE.
DID YOU SEE THAT SKATEBOARD? HE DREW THIS TOTALLY COOL SWIRLY DRAGON ON IT--
SKATING ESN'T LOOK RD. I CAN *SO* ULL IT OFF.
YOUR EMERALD WOULD KIND OF MAKE IT UNFAIR.
WON'T USE IT. PROMISE.
OKAY, CADETS. GWEN, GO SIGN UP. EVERYONE ELSE, SPREAD OUT. WE HAVE TO FIND LIZ BEFORE THE DARKNESS DOES.
THUD!
YOU OKAY?

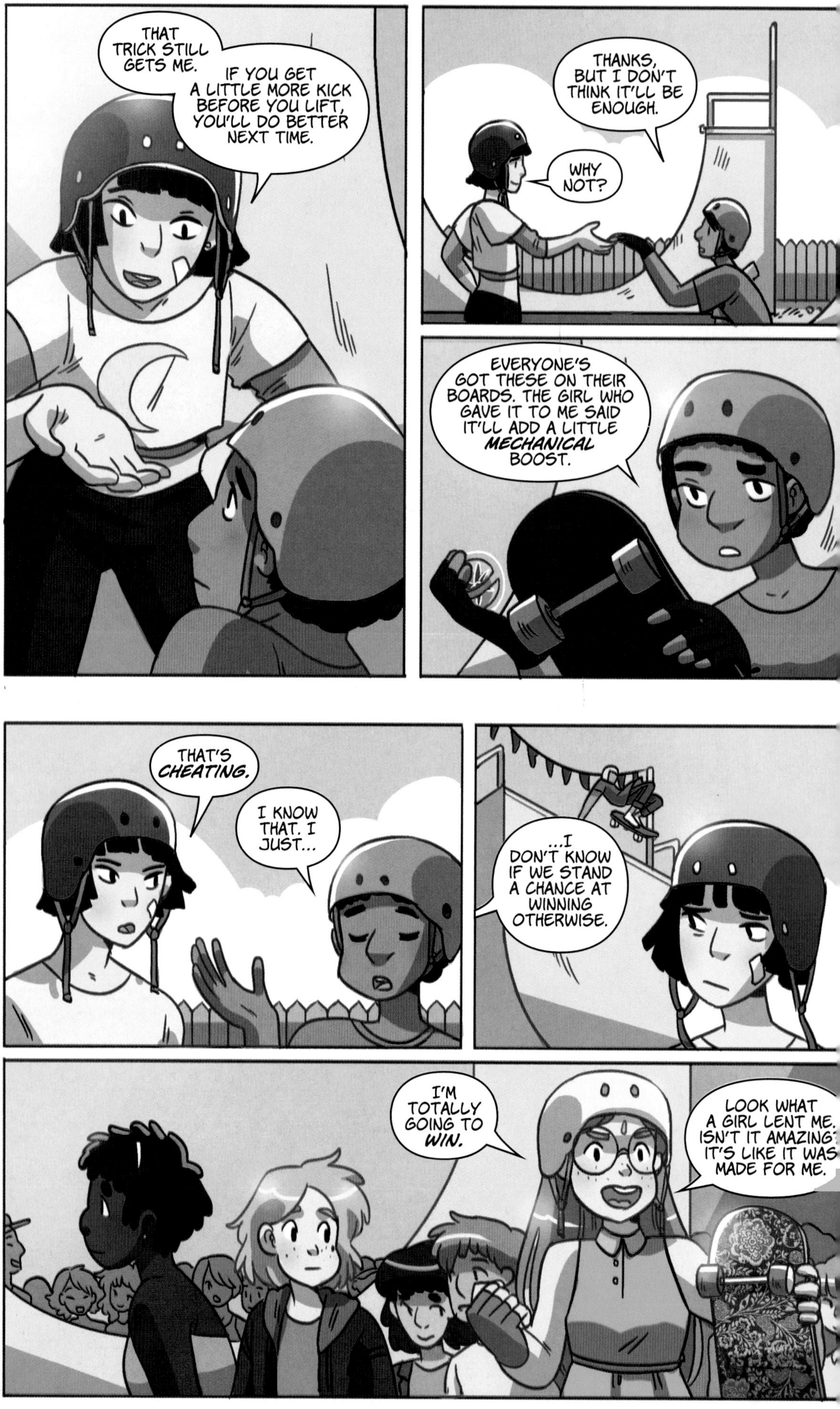
THAT TRICK STILL GETS ME.
IF YOU GET A LITTLE MORE KICK BEFORE YOU LIFT, YOU'LL DO BETTER NEXT TIME.
THANKS, BUT I DON'T THINK IT'LL BE ENOUGH.
WHY NOT?
EVERYONE'S GOT THESE ON THEIR BOARDS. THE GIRL WHO GAVE IT TO ME SAID IT'LL ADD A LITTLE ***MECHANICAL*** BOOST.
THAT'S ***CHEATING.***
I KNOW THAT. I JUST...
...I DON'T KNOW IF WE STAND A CHANCE AT WINNING OTHERWISE.
I'M TOTALLY GOING TO ***WIN.***
LOOK WHAT A GIRL LENT ME. ISN'T IT AMAZING? IT'S LIKE IT WAS MADE FOR ME.

I'VE ASKED EVERYONE IF THEY KNOW LIZ, BUT I ONLY FOUND A BETH. YOU KNOW--LIZ, BETH, ELIZABETH?

BUT IT WASN'T HER. YOU TURN UP ANYTHING?

NOTHING.

THE BIG COMPETITION IS NEXT. IF LIZ SHOWS UP, I'LL FIND HER.

LEAVE IT TO ME. I'VE BEEN DOING THIS A *LOT* LONGER THAN YOU.

"IF"?

I HEARD A RUMOR THAT SOME GIRLS ARE *CHEATING*. A REAL CADET WOULDN'T BE HERE FOR THAT.

WE HAVE TO STOP THEM!

WHY?

IT'S HOW THE *DARKNESS* SPREADS!

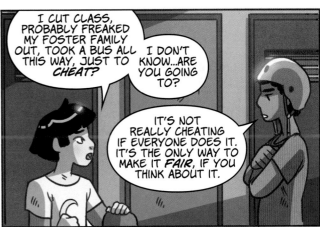

IF THEY CHEAT, THE DARKNESS WILL BE TOO STRONG!

WAIT, WHAT ABOUT MY COMPETITION? I'M SUPPOSED TO LINE UP!

THEN GO LINE UP!

YOU GOING TO USE THAT?

I CUT CLASS, PROBABLY FREAKED MY FOSTER FAMILY OUT, TOOK A BUS ALL THIS WAY, JUST TO *CHEAT?*

I DON'T KNOW...ARE YOU GOING TO?

IT'S NOT REALLY CHEATING IF EVERYONE DOES IT. IT'S THE ONLY WAY TO MAKE IT *FAIR*, IF YOU THINK ABOUT IT.

IT'S YOUR CHOICE. BUT I KNOW I WORKED REALLY HARD TO GET HERE, AND I'M NOT GIVING UP NOW.

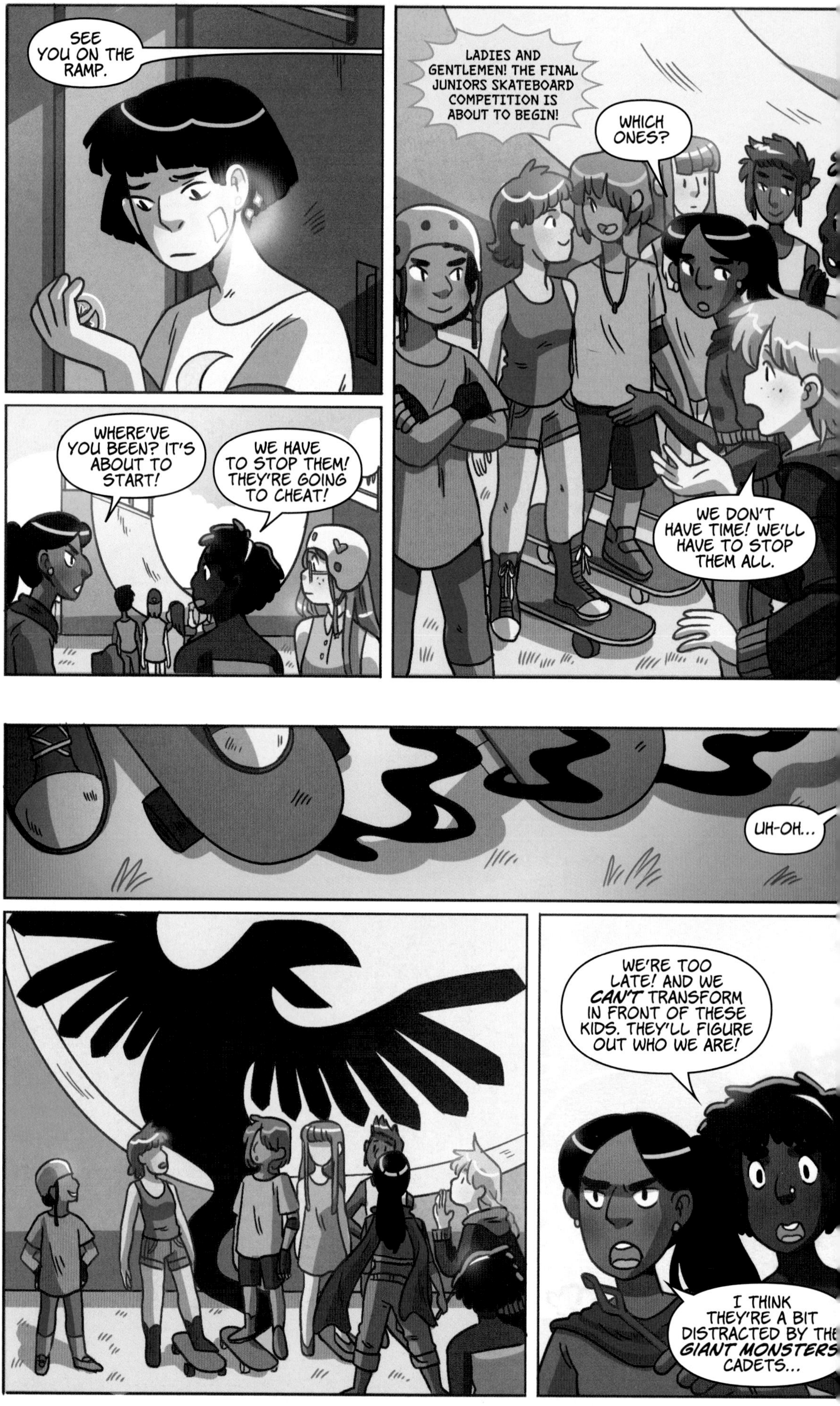
SEE YOU ON THE RAMP.
LADIES AND GENTLEMEN! THE FINAL JUNIORS SKATEBOARD COMPETITION IS ABOUT TO BEGIN!
WHICH ONES?
WHERE'VE YOU BEEN? IT'S ABOUT TO START!
WE HAVE TO STOP THEM! THEY'RE GOING TO CHEAT!
WE DON'T HAVE TIME! WE'LL HAVE TO STOP THEM ALL.
UH-OH...
WE'RE TOO LATE! AND WE *CAN'T* TRANSFORM IN FRONT OF THESE KIDS. THEY'LL FIGURE OUT WHO WE ARE!
I THINK THEY'RE A BIT DISTRACTED BY THE *GIANT MONSTERS*, CADETS...

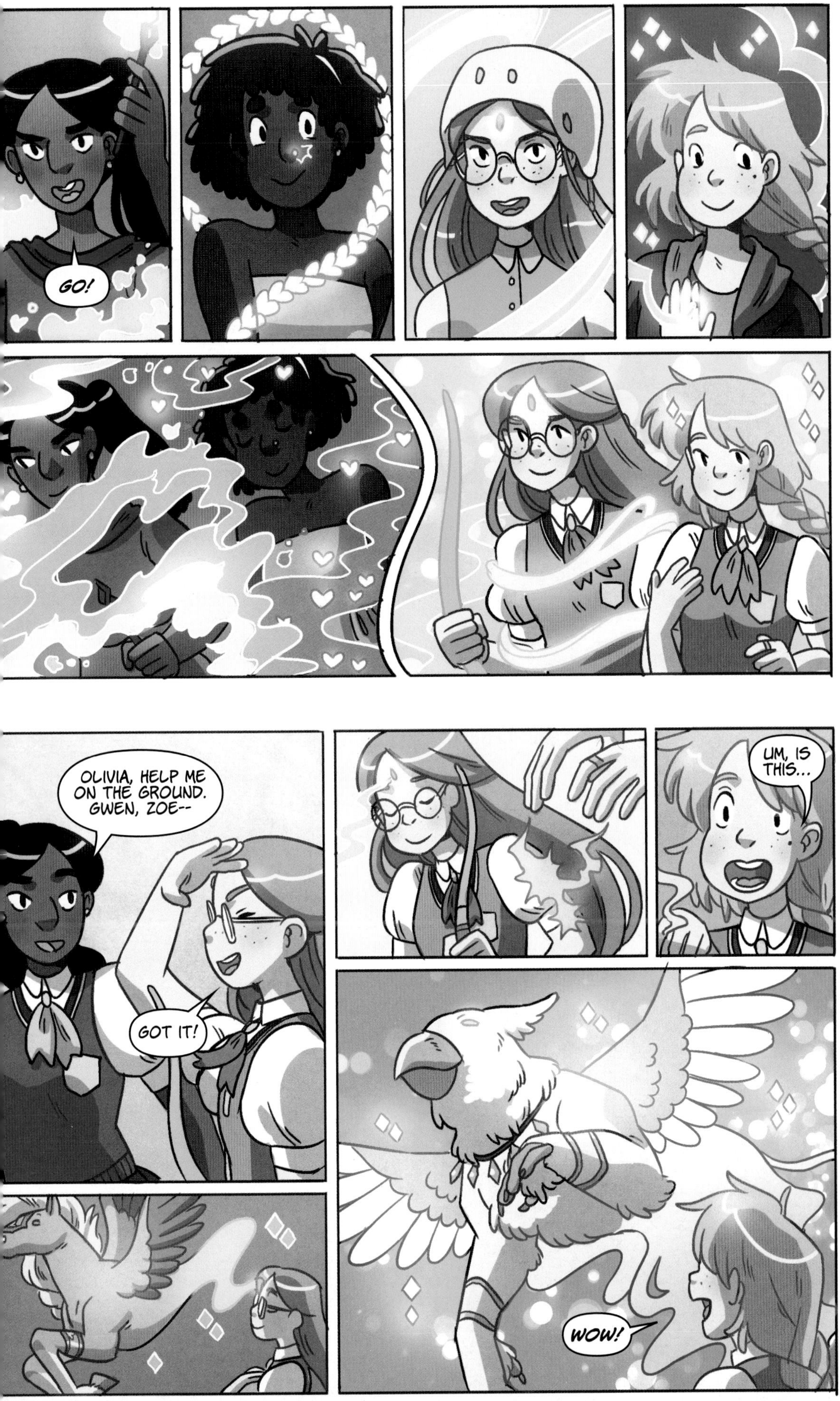
GO!
OLIVIA, HELP ME ON THE GROUND. GWEN, ZOE--
GOT IT!
UM, IS THIS...
WOW!

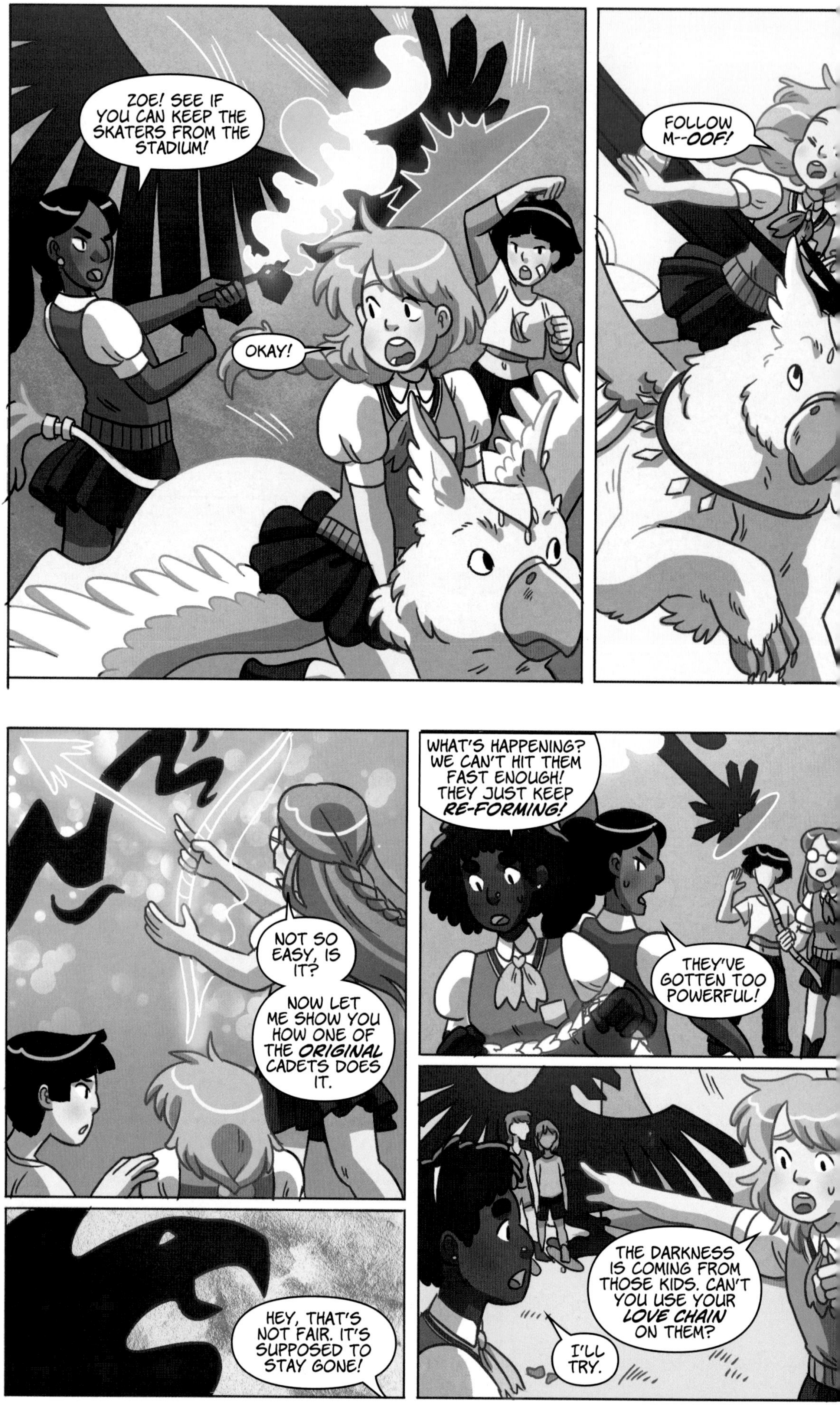

ZOE! SEE IF YOU CAN KEEP THE SKATERS FROM THE STADIUM!
OKAY!
FOLLOW M--OOF!
NOT SO EASY, IS IT?
NOW LET ME SHOW YOU HOW ONE OF THE ORIGINAL CADETS DOES IT.
WHAT'S HAPPENING? WE CAN'T HIT THEM FAST ENOUGH! THEY JUST KEEP RE-FORMING!
THEY'VE GOTTEN TOO POWERFUL!
HEY, THAT'S NOT FAIR. IT'S SUPPOSED TO STAY GONE!
THE DARKNESS IS COMING FROM THOSE KIDS. CAN'T YOU USE YOUR LOVE CHAIN ON THEM?
I'LL TRY.

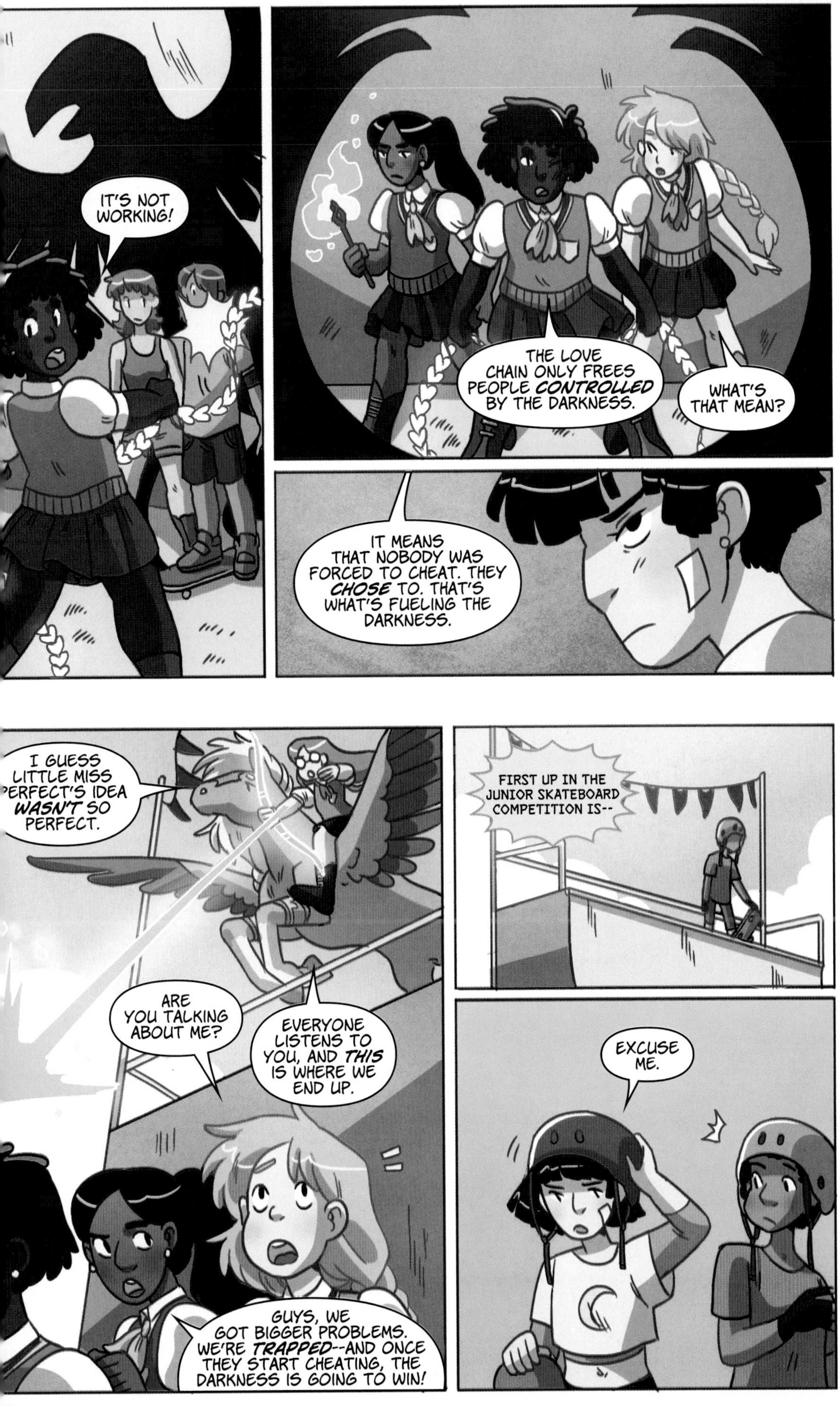

IT'S NOT WORKING!
THE LOVE CHAIN ONLY FREES PEOPLE *CONTROLLED* BY THE DARKNESS.
WHAT'S THAT MEAN?
IT MEANS THAT NOBODY WAS FORCED TO CHEAT. THEY *CHOSE* TO. THAT'S WHAT'S FUELING THE DARKNESS.
I GUESS LITTLE MISS PERFECT'S IDEA *WASN'T* SO PERFECT.
ARE YOU TALKING ABOUT ME?
EVERYONE LISTENS TO YOU, AND *THIS* IS WHERE WE END UP.
GUYS, WE GOT BIGGER PROBLEMS. WE'RE *TRAPPED*--AND ONCE THEY START CHEATING, THE DARKNESS IS GOING TO WIN!
FIRST UP IN THE JUNIOR SKATEBOARD COMPETITION IS--
EXCUSE ME.

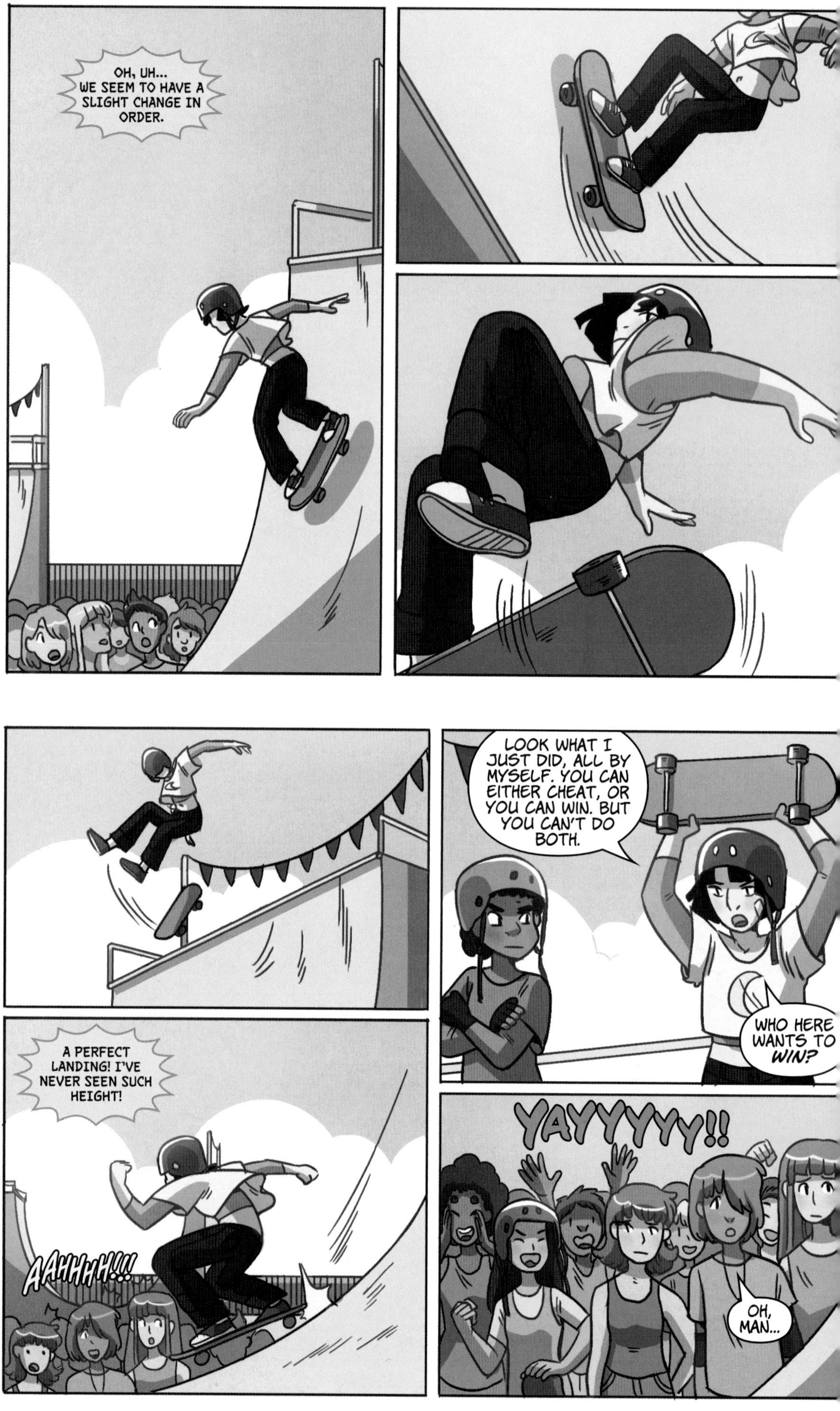

OH, UH... WE SEEM TO HAVE A SLIGHT CHANGE IN ORDER.
A PERFECT LANDING! I'VE NEVER SEEN SUCH HEIGHT!
AAHHHH!!!
LOOK WHAT I JUST DID, ALL BY MYSELF. YOU CAN EITHER CHEAT, OR YOU CAN WIN. BUT YOU CAN'T DO BOTH.
WHO HERE WANTS TO *WIN?*
YAYYYYY!!
OH, MAN...

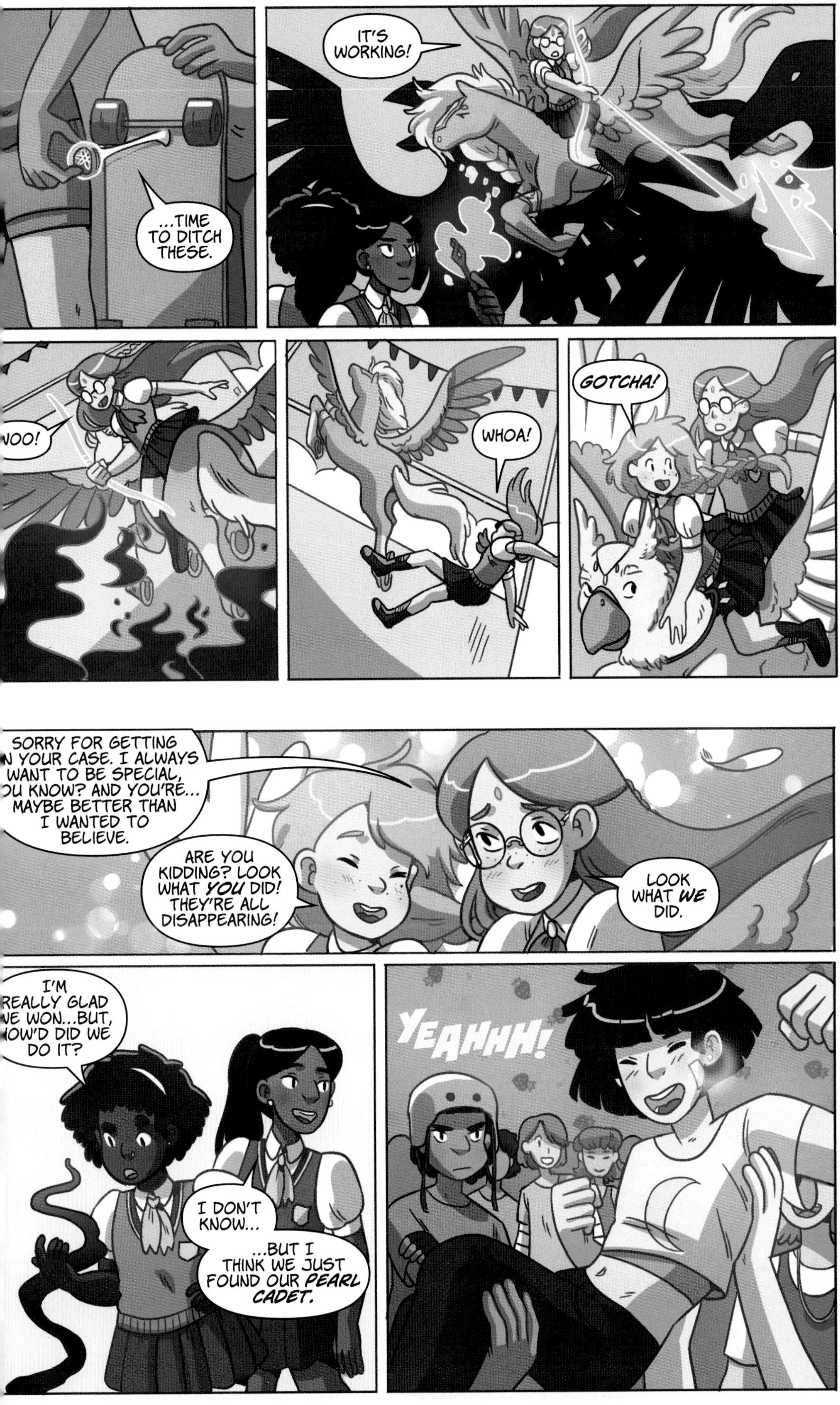
...TIME TO DITCH THESE.
IT'S WORKING!
NOO!
WHOA!
GOTCHA!
SORRY FOR GETTING N YOUR CASE. I ALWAYS WANT TO BE SPECIAL, OU KNOW? AND YOU'RE... MAYBE BETTER THAN I WANTED TO BELIEVE.
ARE YOU KIDDING? LOOK WHAT YOU DID! THEY'RE ALL DISAPPEARING!
LOOK WHAT WE DID.
I'M REALLY GLAD WE WON...BUT, HOW'D DID WE DO IT?
I DON'T KNOW...
...BUT I THINK WE JUST FOUND OUR PEARL CADET.
YEAHHH!

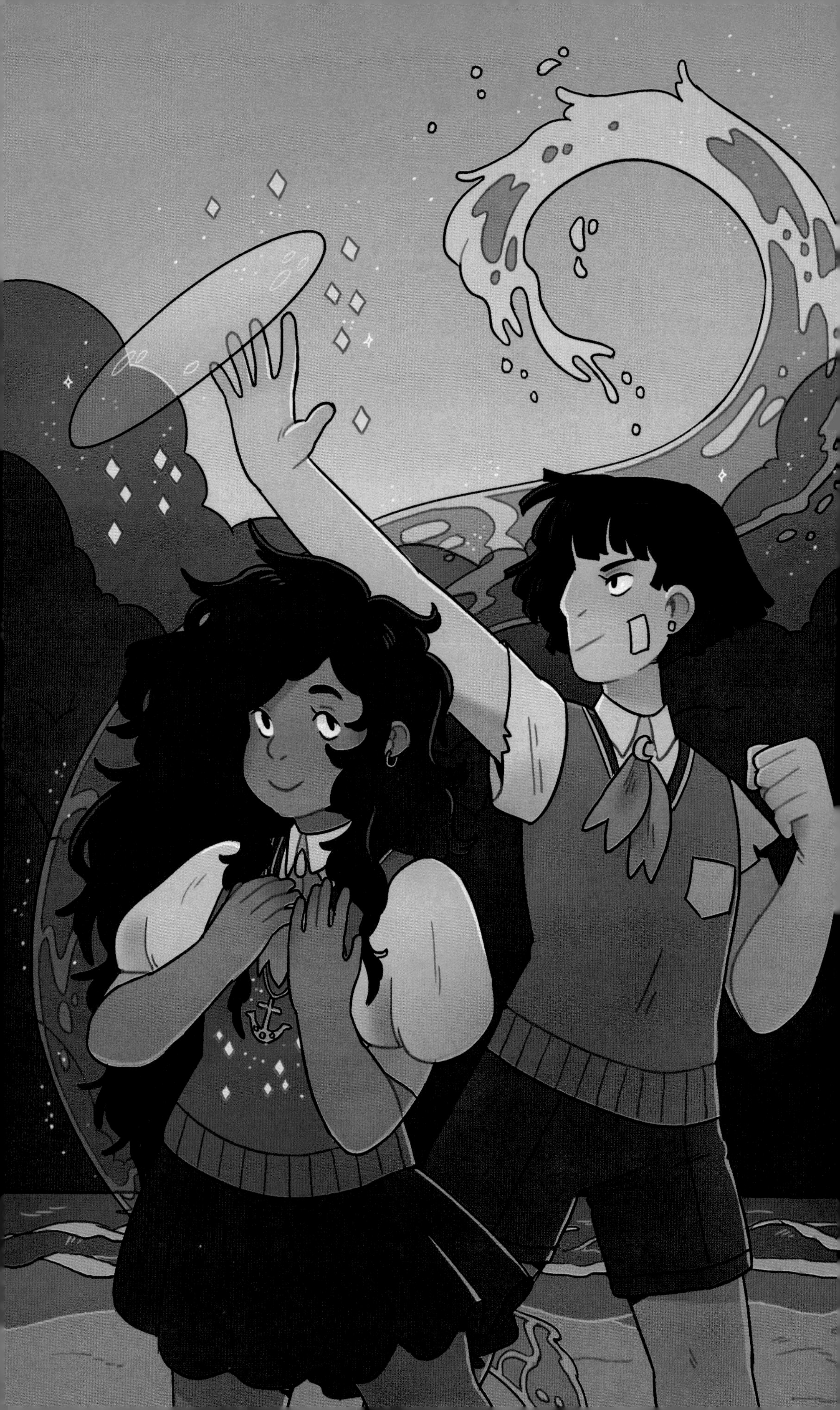

Winds are ramping up into a tropical storm. I suggest you change your heading due east.

THAT WILL COST US HOURS, AND WE'LL LOSE OUR BONUS MONEY.

Lose your bonus or lose your ship; it's up to you.

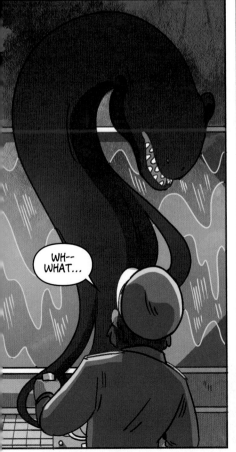

WH-- WHAT...

AHH!

HELP! SOMEBODY!

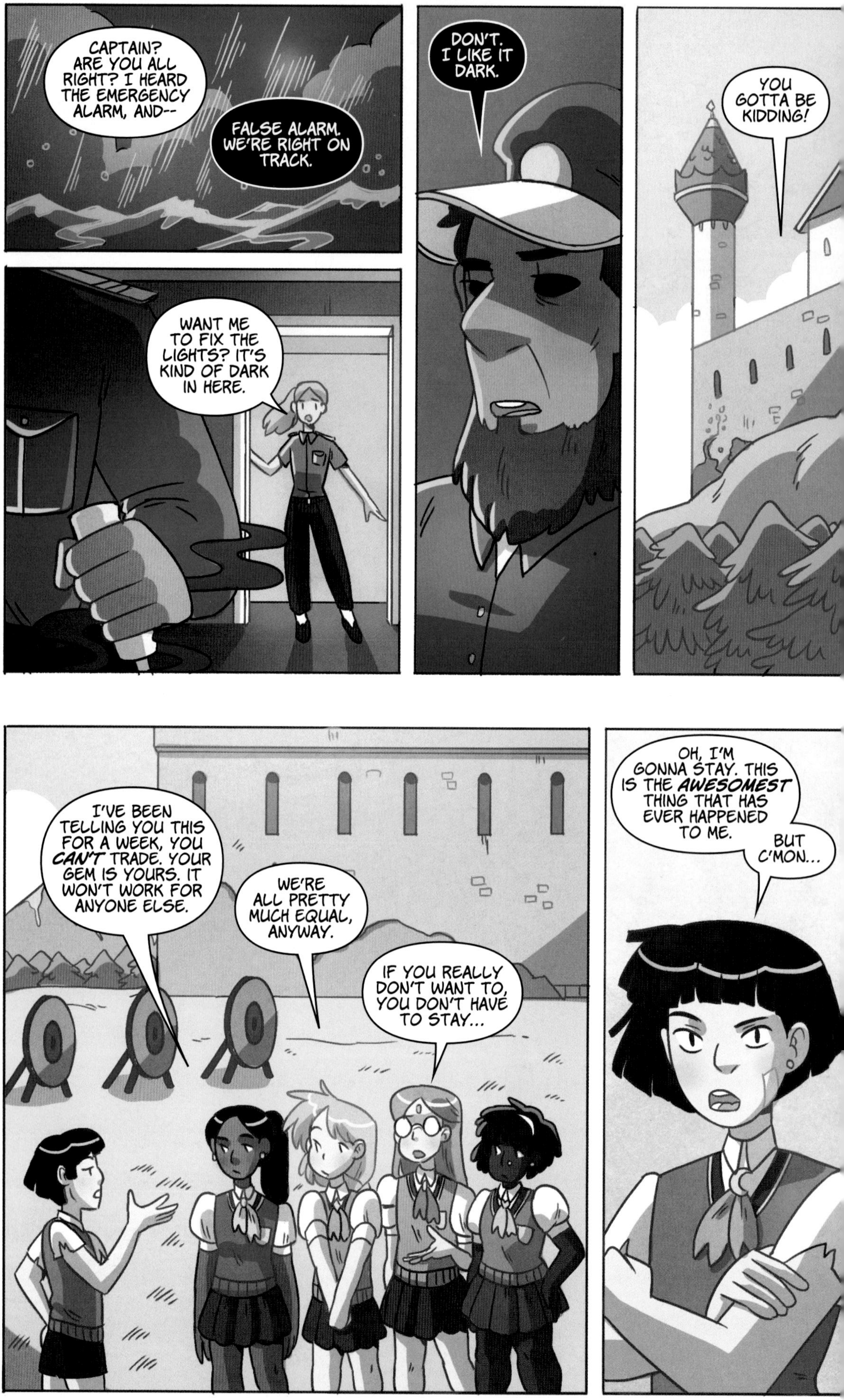
CAPTAIN? ARE YOU ALL RIGHT? I HEARD THE EMERGENCY ALARM, AND--
FALSE ALARM. WE'RE RIGHT ON TRACK.
WANT ME TO FIX THE LIGHTS? IT'S KIND OF DARK IN HERE.
DON'T. I LIKE IT DARK.
YOU GOTTA BE KIDDING!
I'VE BEEN TELLING YOU THIS FOR A WEEK, YOU *CAN'T* TRADE. YOUR GEM IS YOURS. IT WON'T WORK FOR ANYONE ELSE.
WE'RE ALL PRETTY MUCH EQUAL, ANYWAY.
IF YOU REALLY DON'T WANT TO, YOU DON'T HAVE TO STAY...
OH, I'M GONNA STAY. THIS IS THE ***AWESOMEST*** THING THAT HAS EVER HAPPENED TO ME.
BUT C'MON...

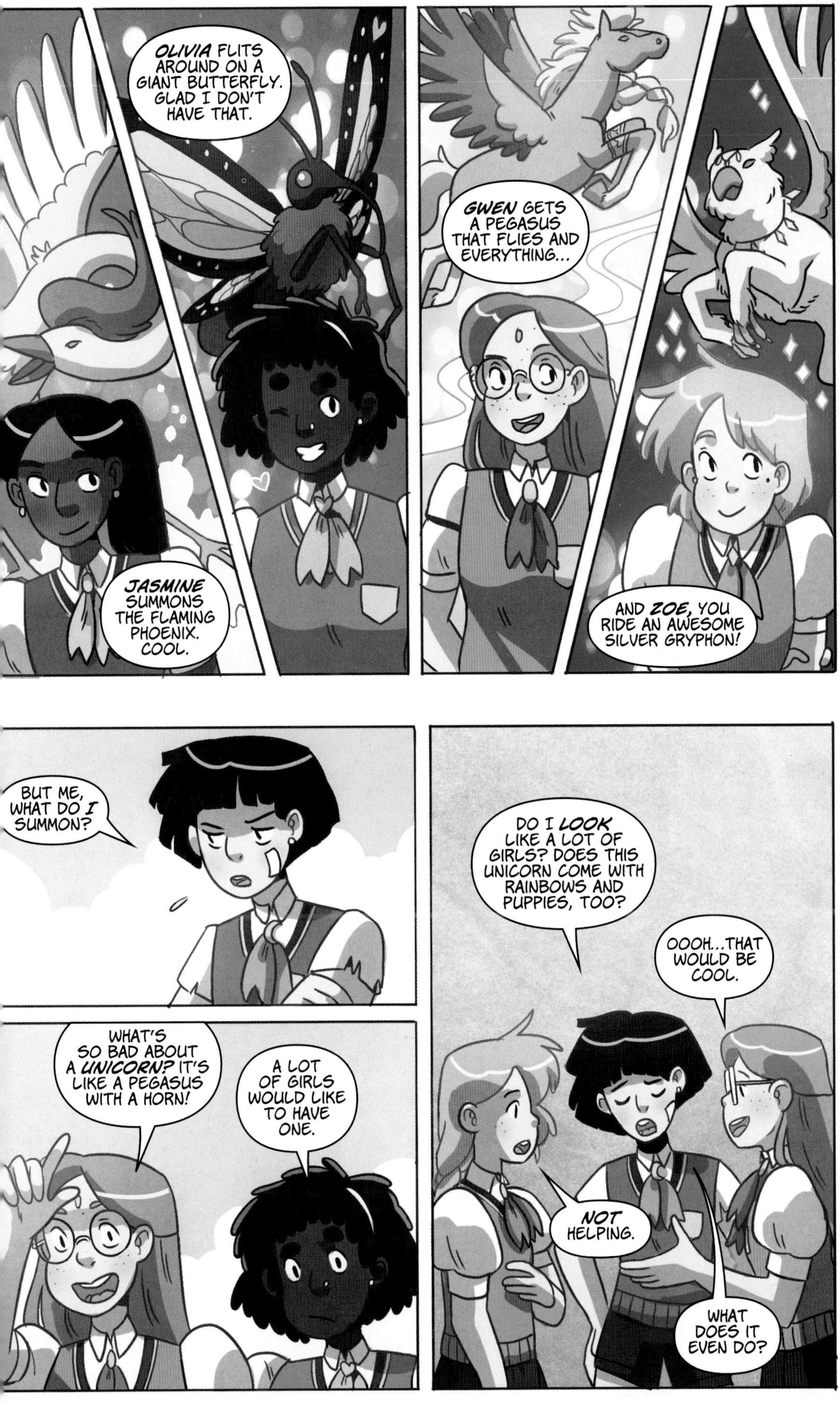

OLIVIA FLITS AROUND ON A GIANT BUTTERFLY. GLAD I DON'T HAVE THAT.
JASMINE SUMMONS THE FLAMING PHOENIX. COOL.
GWEN GETS A PEGASUS THAT FLIES AND EVERYTHING...
AND ZOE, YOU RIDE AN AWESOME SILVER GRYPHON!
BUT ME, WHAT DO I SUMMON?
WHAT'S SO BAD ABOUT A UNICORN? IT'S LIKE A PEGASUS WITH A HORN!
A LOT OF GIRLS WOULD LIKE TO HAVE ONE.
DO I LOOK LIKE A LOT OF GIRLS? DOES THIS UNICORN COME WITH RAINBOWS AND PUPPIES, TOO?
OOOH...THAT WOULD BE COOL.
NOT HELPING.
WHAT DOES IT EVEN DO?

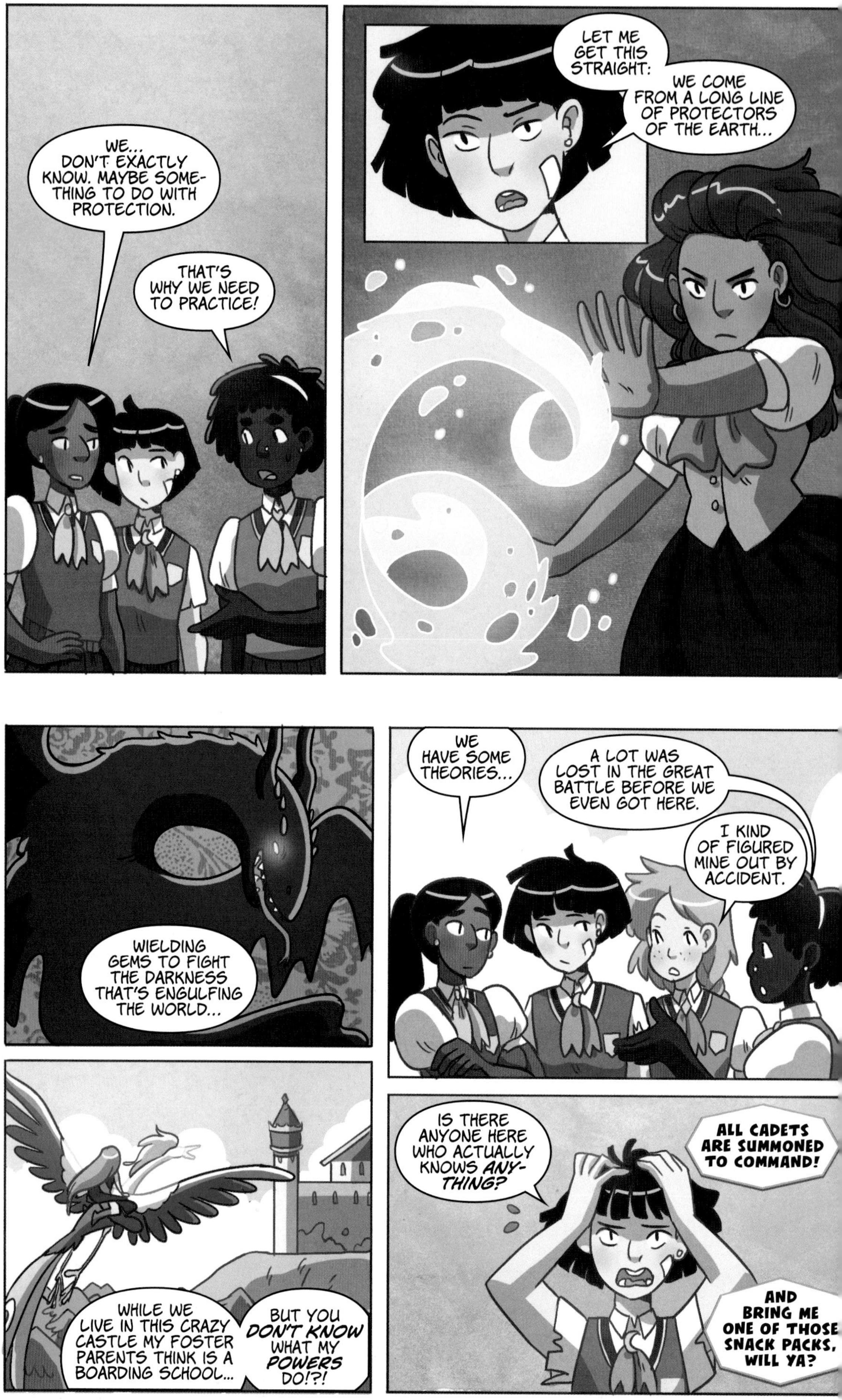
WE... DON'T EXACTLY KNOW. MAYBE SOME-THING TO DO WITH PROTECTION.
THAT'S WHY WE NEED TO PRACTICE!
LET ME GET THIS STRAIGHT:
WE COME FROM A LONG LINE OF PROTECTORS OF THE EARTH...
WIELDING GEMS TO FIGHT THE DARKNESS THAT'S ENGULFING THE WORLD...
WHILE WE LIVE IN THIS CRAZY CASTLE MY FOSTER PARENTS THINK IS A BOARDING SCHOOL...
BUT YOU *DON'T KNOW* WHAT MY *POWERS* DO!?!
WE HAVE SOME THEORIES...
A LOT WAS LOST IN THE GREAT BATTLE BEFORE WE EVEN GOT HERE.
I KIND OF FIGURED MINE OUT BY ACCIDENT.
IS THERE ANYONE HERE WHO ACTUALLY KNOWS *ANY-THING?*
ALL CADETS ARE SUMMONED TO COMMAND!
AND BRING ME ONE OF THOSE SNACK PACKS, WILL YA?

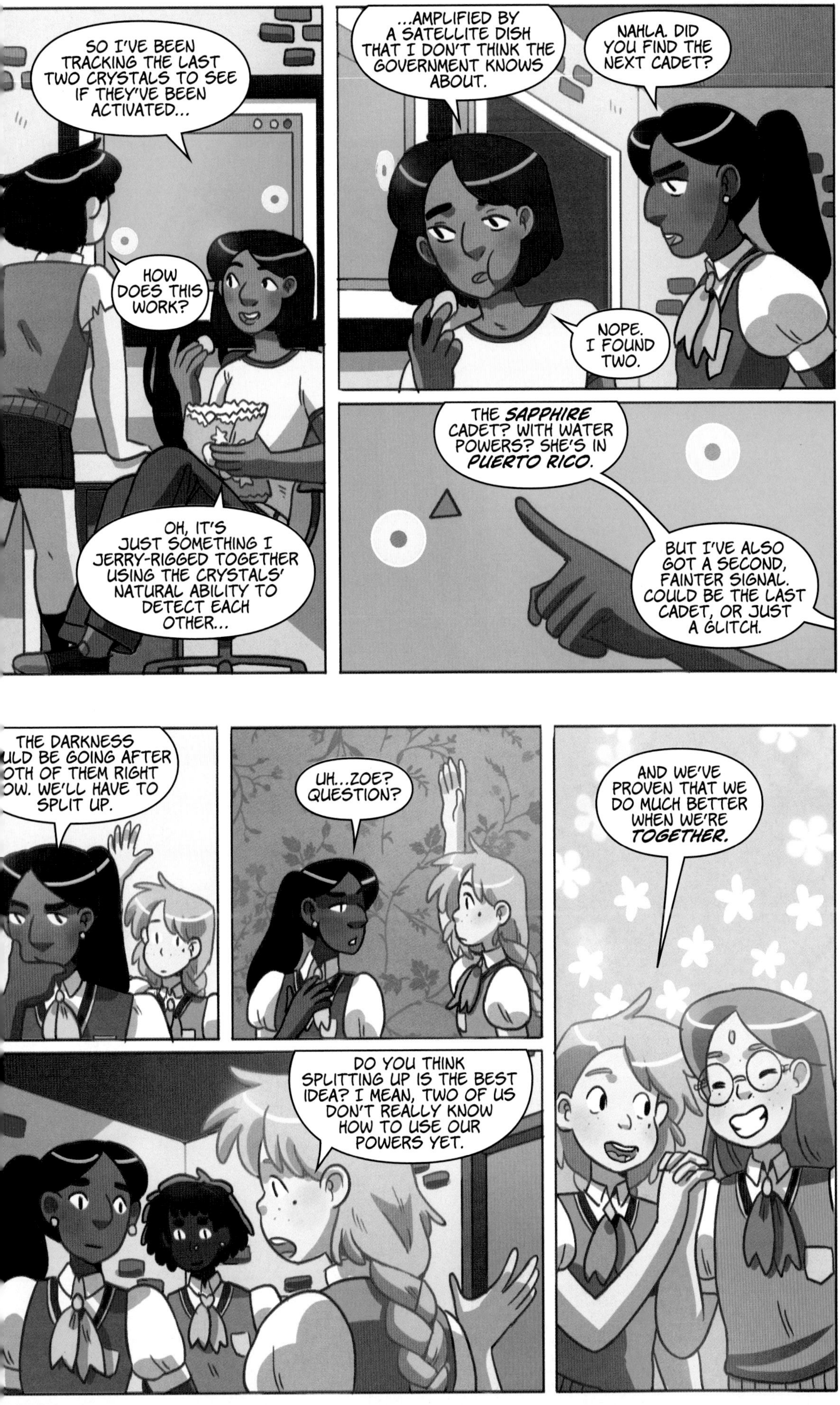
SO I'VE BEEN TRACKING THE LAST TWO CRYSTALS TO SEE IF THEY'VE BEEN ACTIVATED...
HOW DOES THIS WORK?
OH, IT'S JUST SOMETHING I JERRY-RIGGED TOGETHER USING THE CRYSTALS' NATURAL ABILITY TO DETECT EACH OTHER...
...AMPLIFIED BY A SATELLITE DISH THAT I DON'T THINK THE GOVERNMENT KNOWS ABOUT.
NAHLA. DID YOU FIND THE NEXT CADET?
NOPE. I FOUND TWO.
THE *SAPPHIRE* CADET? WITH WATER POWERS? SHE'S IN *PUERTO RICO*.
BUT I'VE ALSO GOT A SECOND, FAINTER SIGNAL. COULD BE THE LAST CADET, OR JUST A GLITCH.
THE DARKNESS ULD BE GOING AFTER OTH OF THEM RIGHT OW. WE'LL HAVE TO SPLIT UP.
UH...ZOE? QUESTION?
DO YOU THINK SPLITTING UP IS THE BEST IDEA? I MEAN, TWO OF US DON'T REALLY KNOW HOW TO USE OUR POWERS YET.
AND WE'VE PROVEN THAT WE DO MUCH BETTER WHEN WE'RE *TOGETHER.*

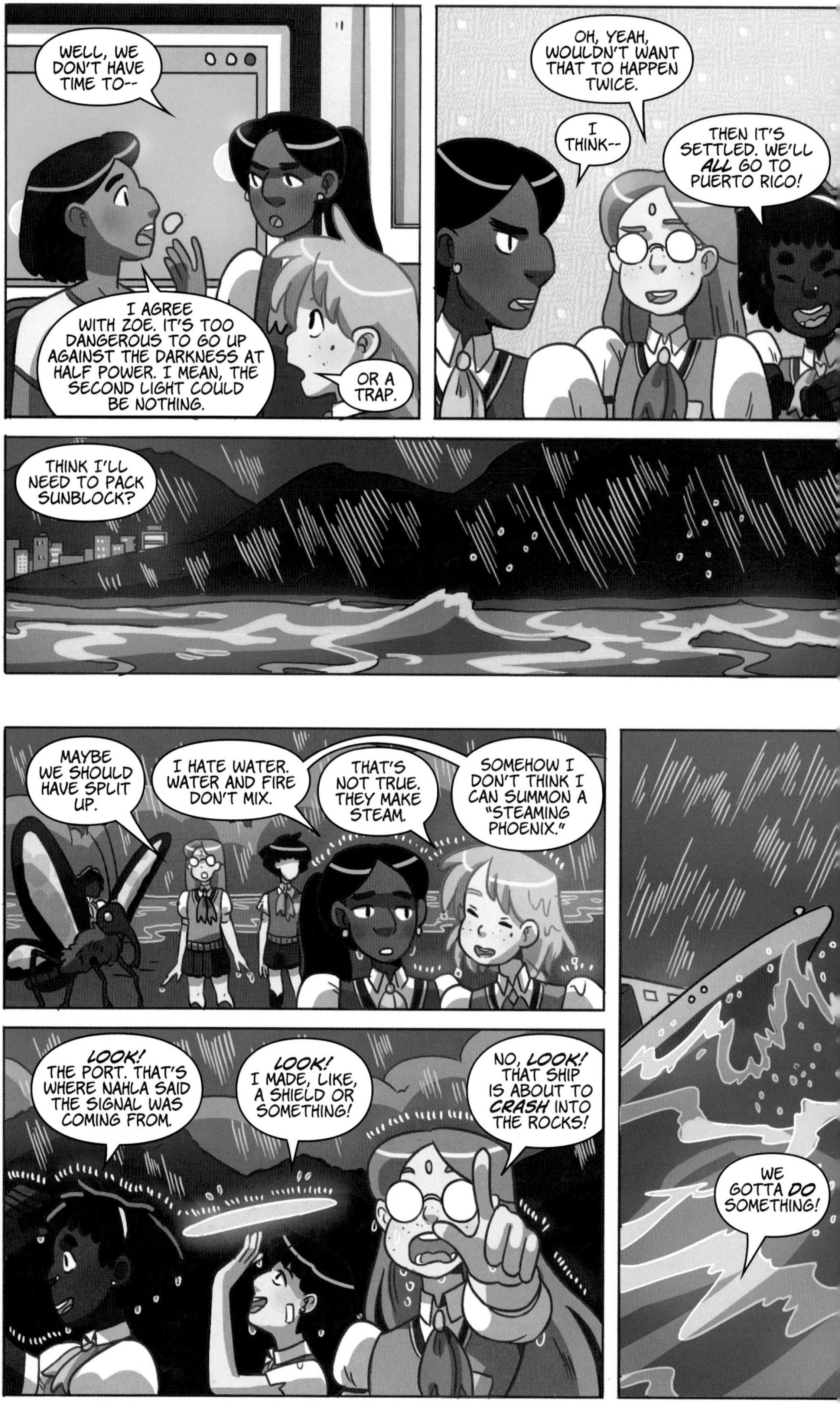
WELL, WE DON'T HAVE TIME TO--
I AGREE WITH ZOE. IT'S TOO DANGEROUS TO GO UP AGAINST THE DARKNESS AT HALF POWER. I MEAN, THE SECOND LIGHT COULD BE NOTHING.
OR A TRAP.
OH, YEAH, WOULDN'T WANT THAT TO HAPPEN TWICE.
I THINK--
THEN IT'S SETTLED. WE'LL ALL GO TO PUERTO RICO!
THINK I'LL NEED TO PACK SUNBLOCK?
MAYBE WE SHOULD HAVE SPLIT UP.
I HATE WATER. WATER AND FIRE DON'T MIX.
THAT'S NOT TRUE. THEY MAKE STEAM.
SOMEHOW I DON'T THINK I CAN SUMMON A "STEAMING PHOENIX."
LOOK! THE PORT. THAT'S WHERE NAHLA SAID THE SIGNAL WAS COMING FROM.
LOOK! I MADE, LIKE, A SHIELD OR SOMETHING!
NO, LOOK! THAT SHIP IS ABOUT TO CRASH INTO THE ROCKS!
WE GOTTA DO SOMETHING!

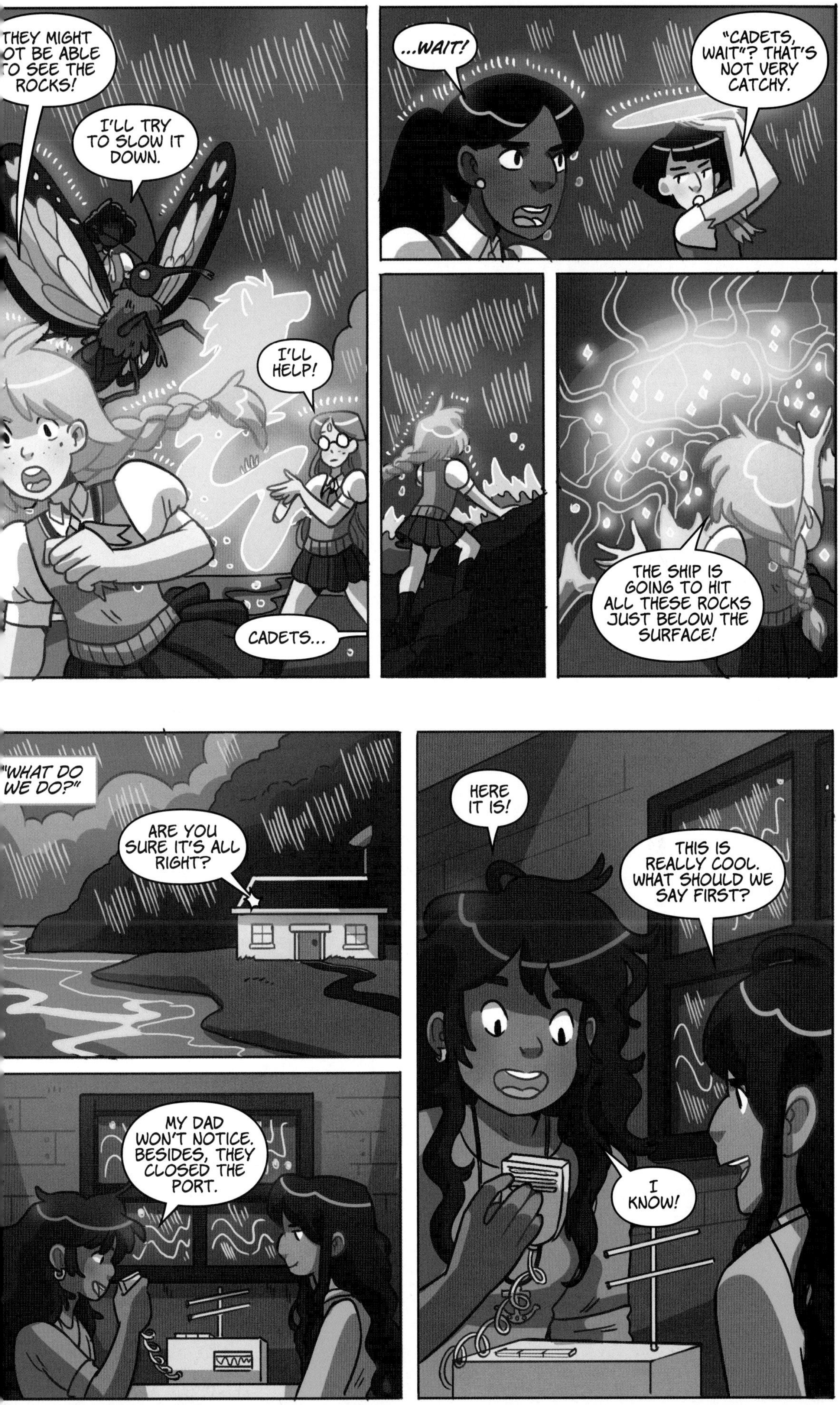
THEY MIGHT
OT BE ABLE
TO SEE THE
ROCKS!
I'LL TRY TO SLOW IT DOWN.
I'LL HELP!
CADETS...
...WAIT!
"CADETS, WAIT"? THAT'S NOT VERY CATCHY.
THE SHIP IS GOING TO HIT ALL THESE ROCKS JUST BELOW THE SURFACE!
"WHAT DO WE DO?"
ARE YOU SURE IT'S ALL RIGHT?
MY DAD WON'T NOTICE. BESIDES, THEY CLOSED THE PORT.
HERE IT IS!
THIS IS REALLY COOL. WHAT SHOULD WE SAY FIRST?
I KNOW!

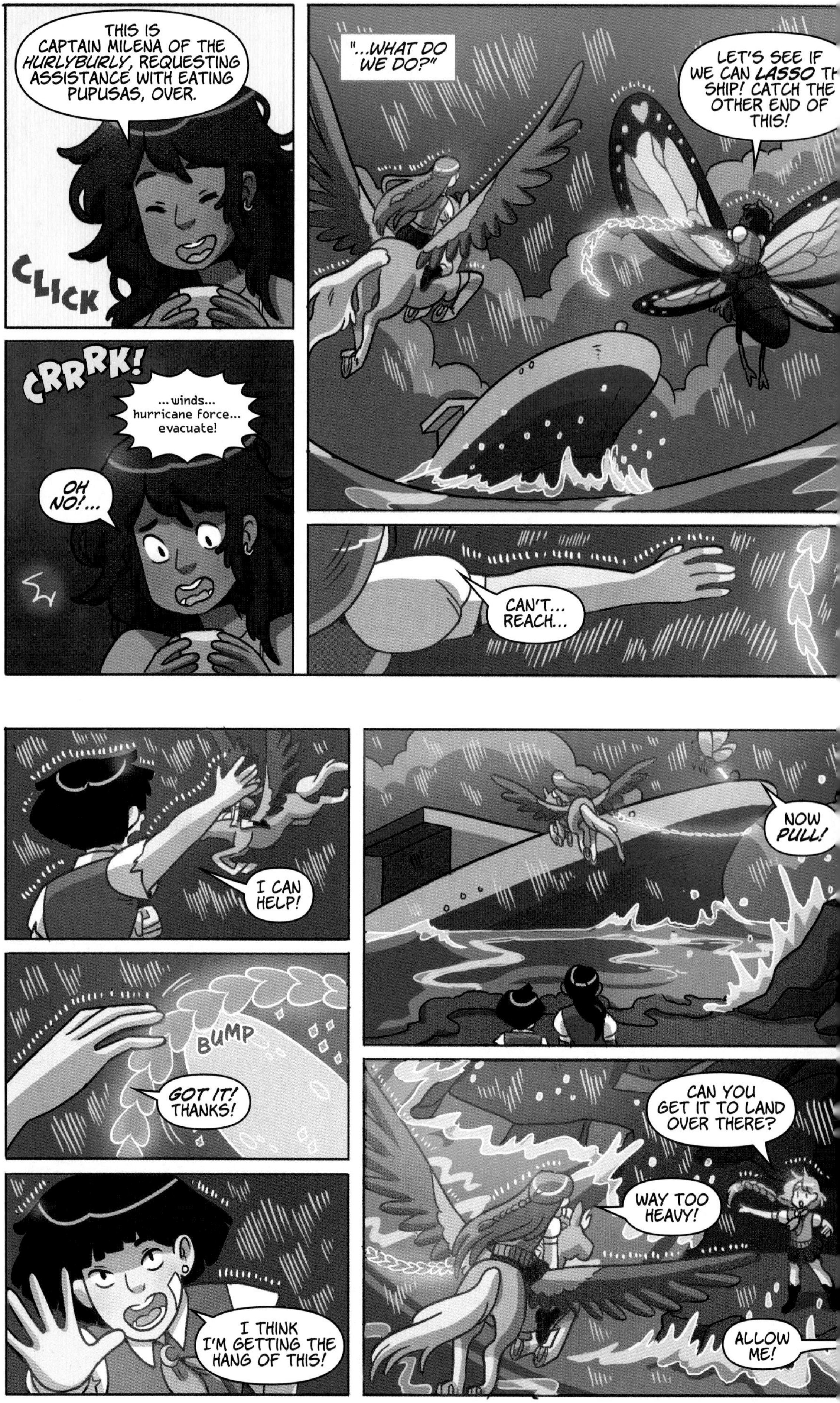
THIS IS CAPTAIN MILENA OF THE *HURLYBURLY*, REQUESTING ASSISTANCE WITH EATING PUPUSAS, OVER.
CLICK
CRRRK!
...winds... hurricane force... evacuate!
OH NO!...
"...WHAT DO WE DO?"
LET'S SEE IF WE CAN **LASSO** TH SHIP! CATCH THE OTHER END OF THIS!
CAN'T... REACH...
I CAN HELP!
BUMP
GOT IT! THANKS!
I THINK I'M GETTING THE HANG OF THIS!
NOW *PULL!*
CAN YOU GET IT TO LAND OVER THERE?
WAY TOO HEAVY!
ALLOW ME!

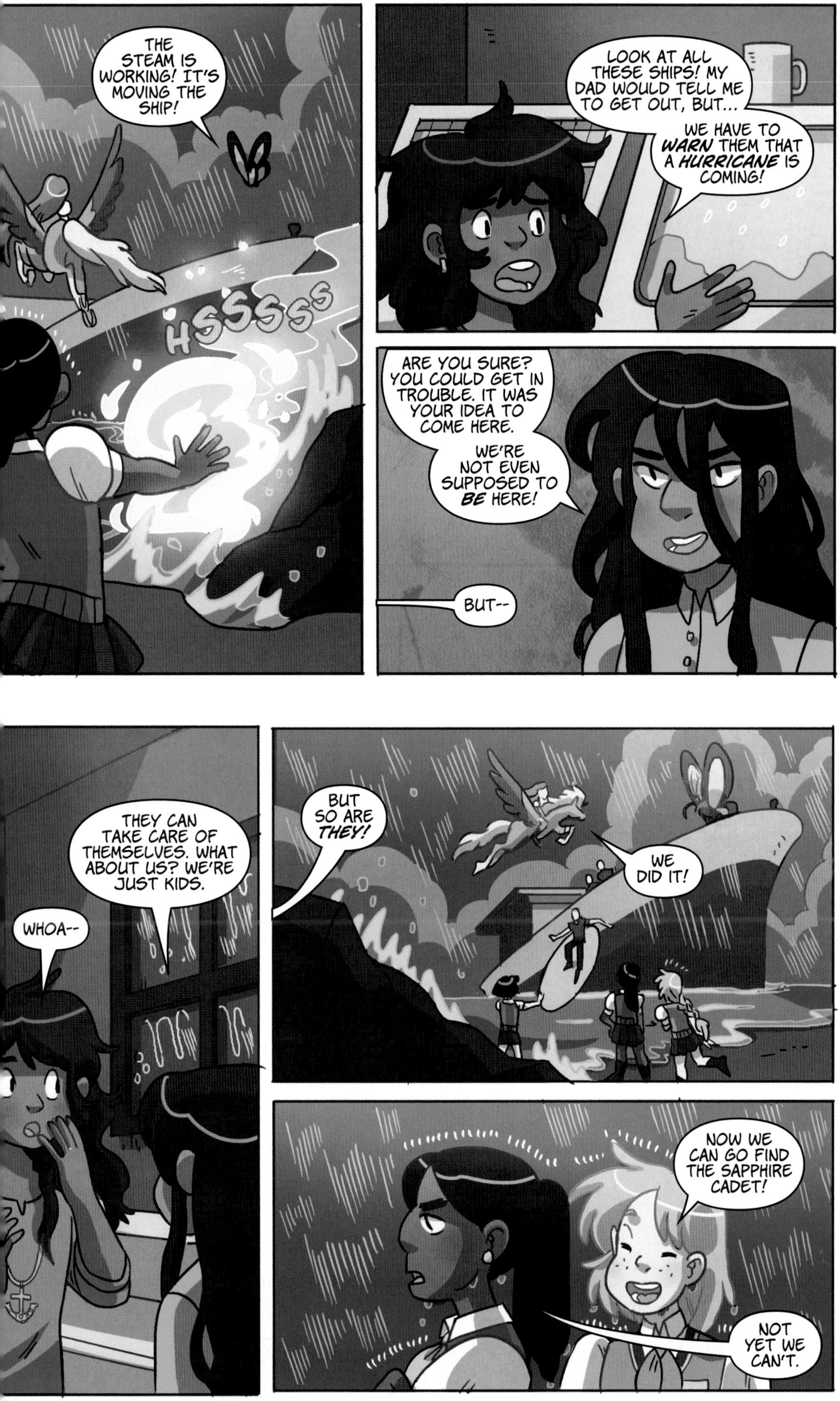
THE STEAM IS WORKING! IT'S MOVING THE SHIP!
HSSSSSS
LOOK AT ALL THESE SHIPS! MY DAD WOULD TELL ME TO GET OUT, BUT...
WE HAVE TO WARN THEM THAT A HURRICANE IS COMING!
ARE YOU SURE? YOU COULD GET IN TROUBLE. IT WAS YOUR IDEA TO COME HERE.
WE'RE NOT EVEN SUPPOSED TO BE HERE!
BUT--
THEY CAN TAKE CARE OF THEMSELVES. WHAT ABOUT US? WE'RE JUST KIDS.
WHOA--
BUT SO ARE THEY!
WE DID IT!
NOW WE CAN GO FIND THE SAPPHIRE CADET!
NOT YET WE CAN'T.

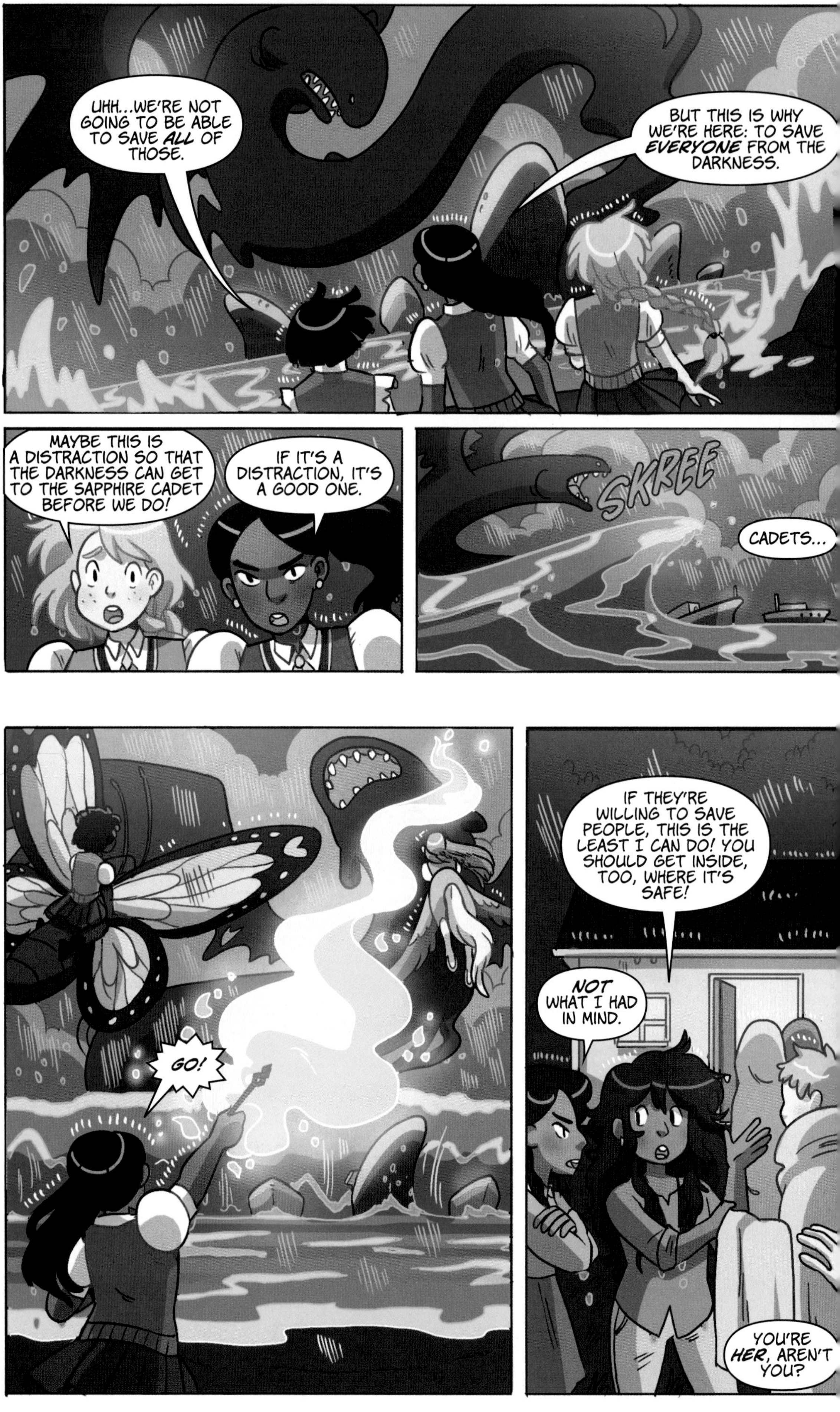
UHH...WE'RE NOT GOING TO BE ABLE TO SAVE *ALL* OF THOSE.
BUT THIS IS WHY WE'RE HERE: TO SAVE *EVERYONE* FROM THE DARKNESS.
MAYBE THIS IS A DISTRACTION SO THAT THE DARKNESS CAN GET TO THE SAPPHIRE CADET BEFORE WE DO!
IF IT'S A DISTRACTION, IT'S A GOOD ONE.
SKREE
CADETS...
GO!
IF THEY'RE WILLING TO SAVE PEOPLE, THIS IS THE LEAST I CAN DO! YOU SHOULD GET INSIDE, TOO, WHERE IT'S SAFE!
NOT WHAT I HAD IN MIND.
YOU'RE *HER*, AREN'T YOU?

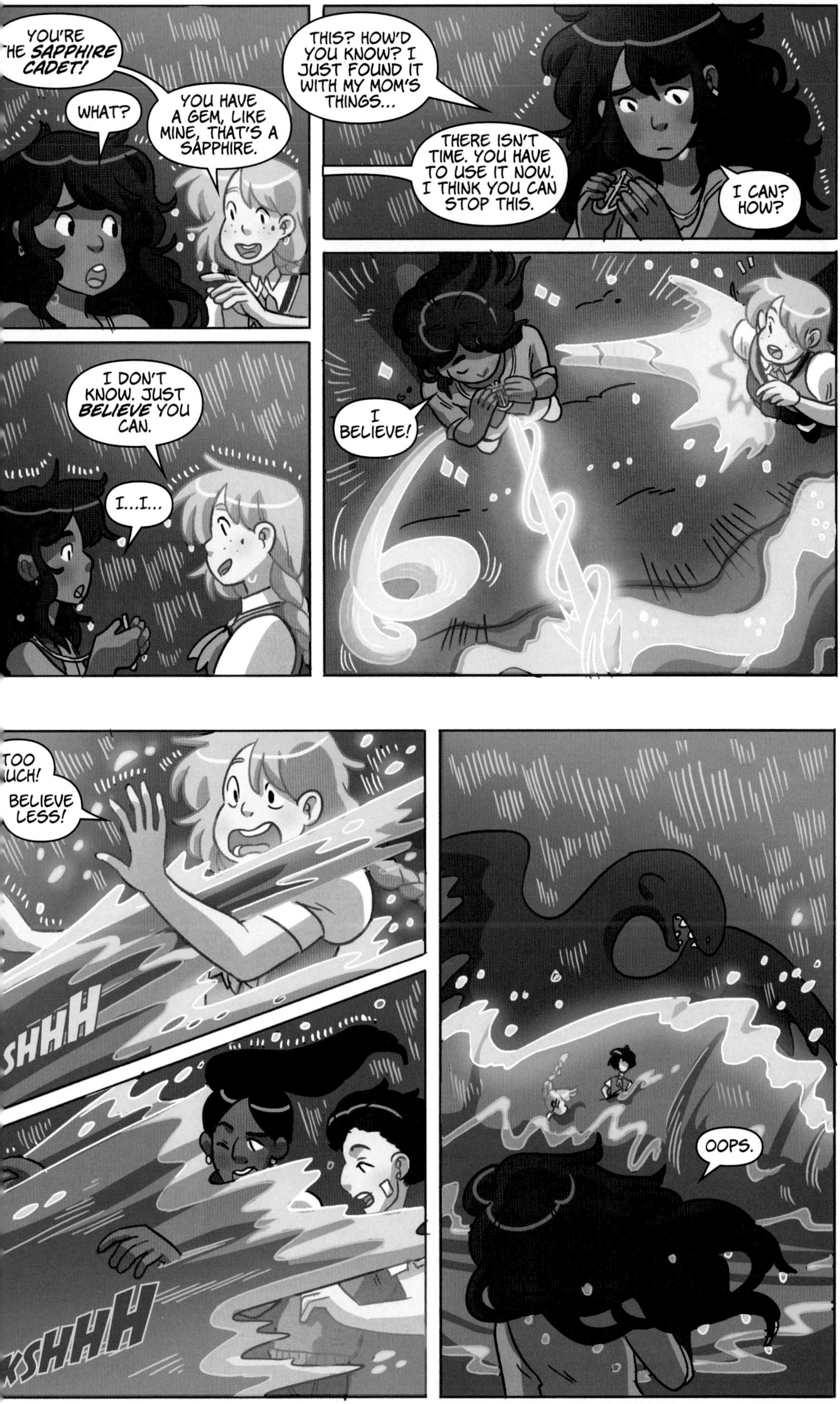
YOU'RE THE *SAPPHIRE CADET!*
WHAT?
YOU HAVE A GEM, LIKE MINE, THAT'S A SAPPHIRE.
THIS? HOW'D YOU KNOW? I JUST FOUND IT WITH MY MOM'S THINGS...
THERE ISN'T TIME. YOU HAVE TO USE IT NOW. I THINK YOU CAN STOP THIS.
I CAN? HOW?
I DON'T KNOW. JUST *BELIEVE* YOU CAN.
I...I...
I BELIEVE!
TOO MUCH!
BELIEVE LESS!
SHHH
KSHHHH
OOPS.

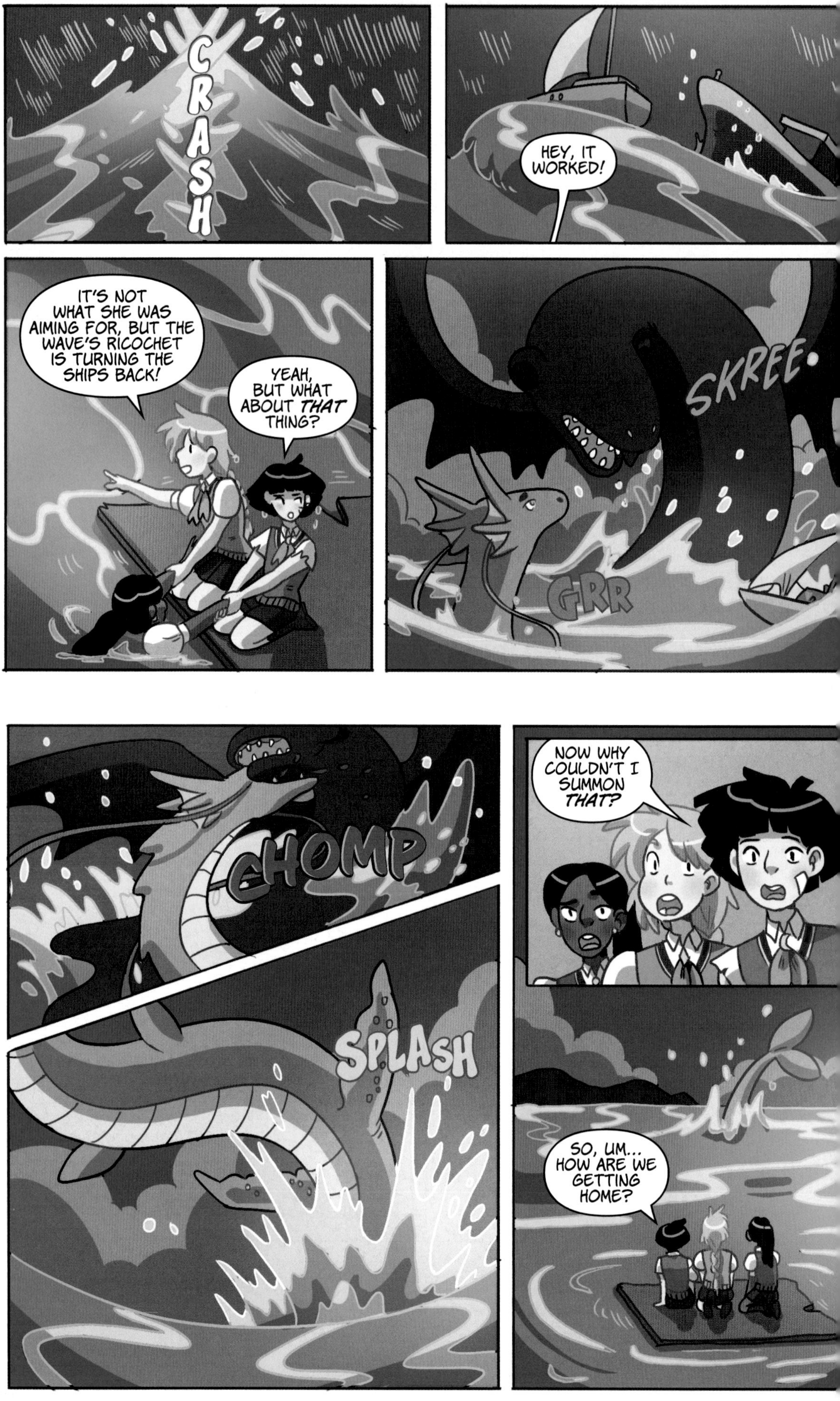
CRASH
HEY, IT WORKED!
IT'S NOT WHAT SHE WAS AIMING FOR, BUT THE WAVE'S RICOCHET IS TURNING THE SHIPS BACK!
YEAH, BUT WHAT ABOUT *THAT* THING?
SKREE
GRR
CHOMP
SPLASH
NOW WHY COULDN'T I SUMMON *THAT?*
SO, UM... HOW ARE WE GETTING HOME?

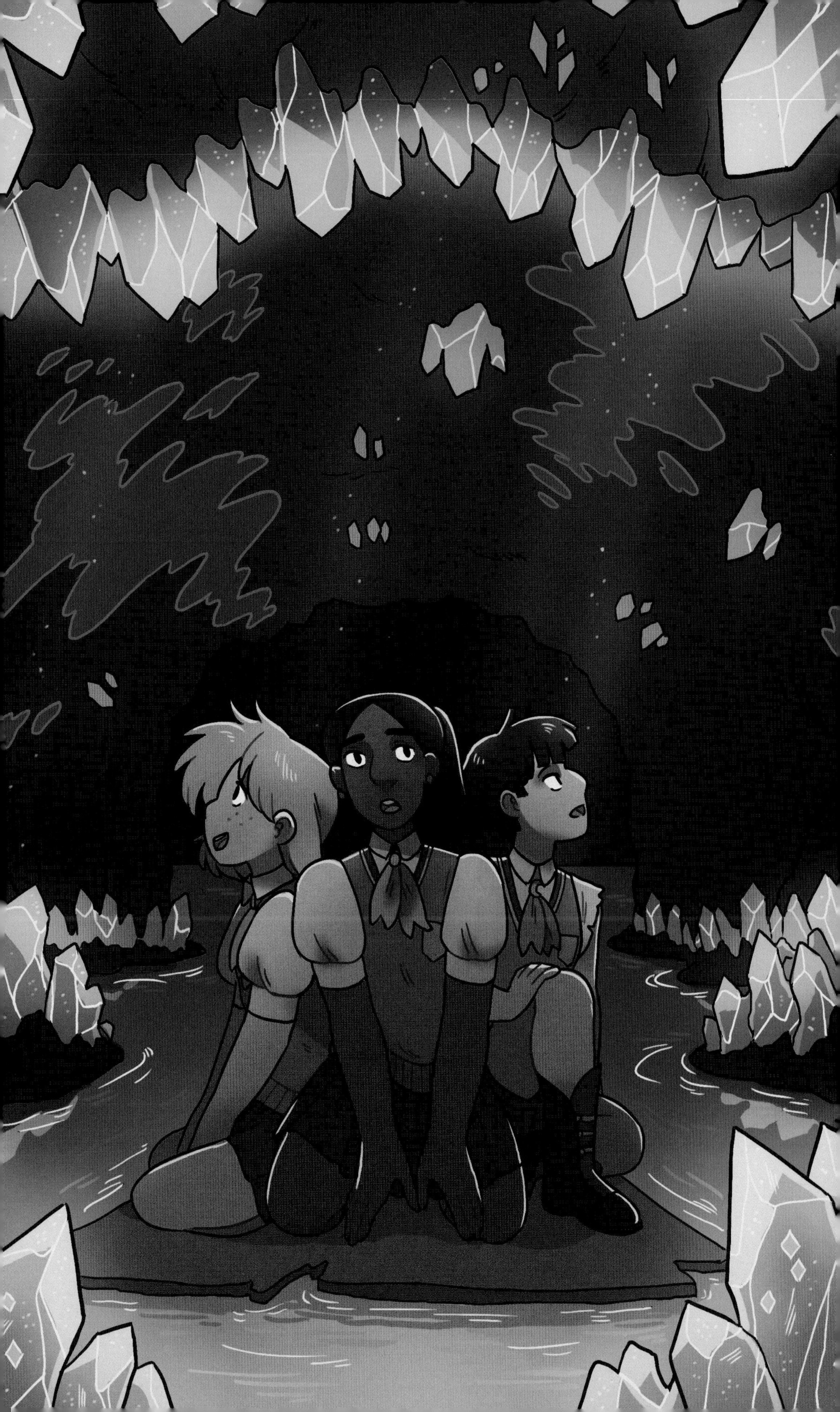

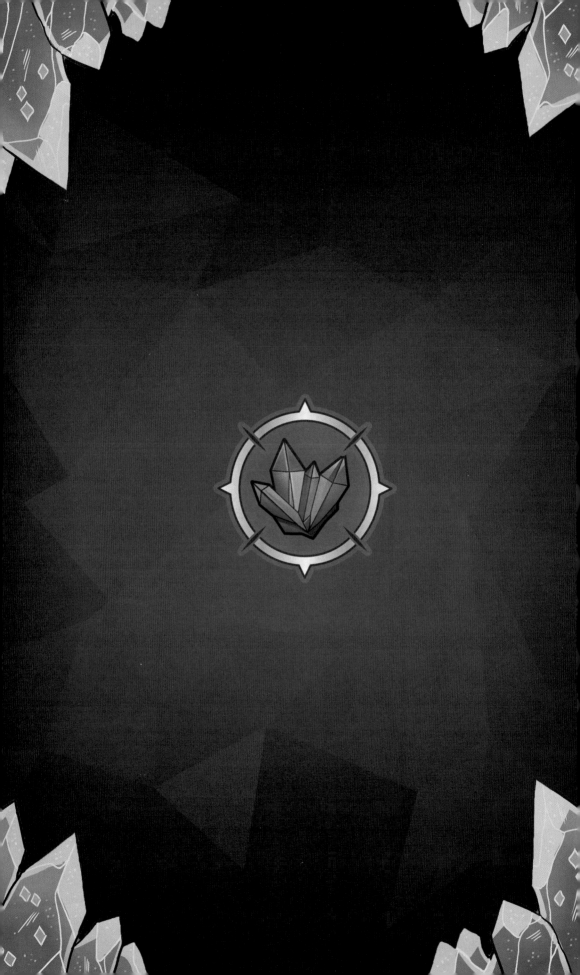

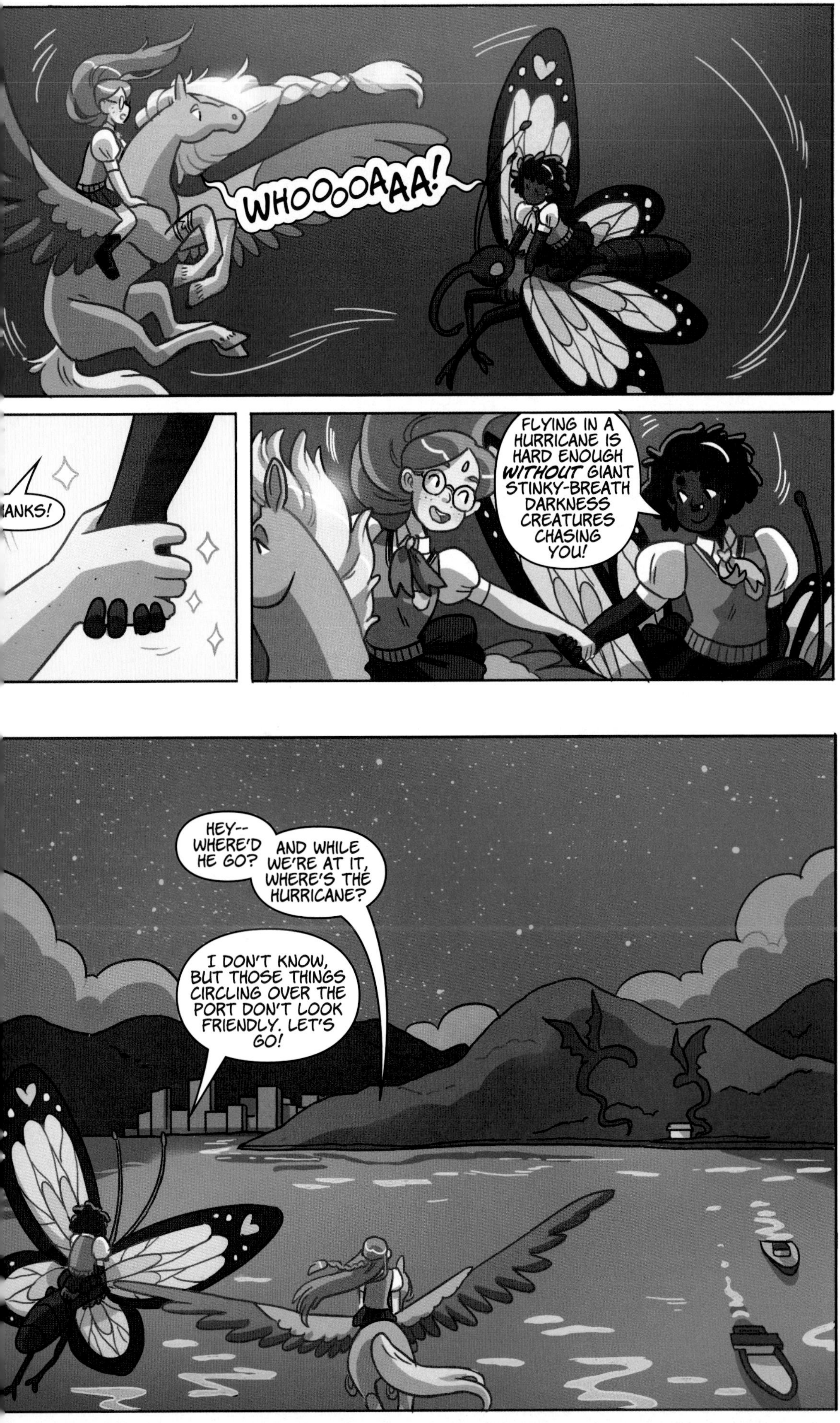
WHOOOOAAA!
ANKS!
FLYING IN A HURRICANE IS HARD ENOUGH *WITHOUT* GIANT STINKY-BREATH DARKNESS CREATURES CHASING YOU!
HEY-- WHERE'D HE GO?
AND WHILE WE'RE AT IT, WHERE'S THE HURRICANE?
I DON'T KNOW, BUT THOSE THINGS CIRCLING OVER THE PORT DON'T LOOK FRIENDLY. LET'S GO!

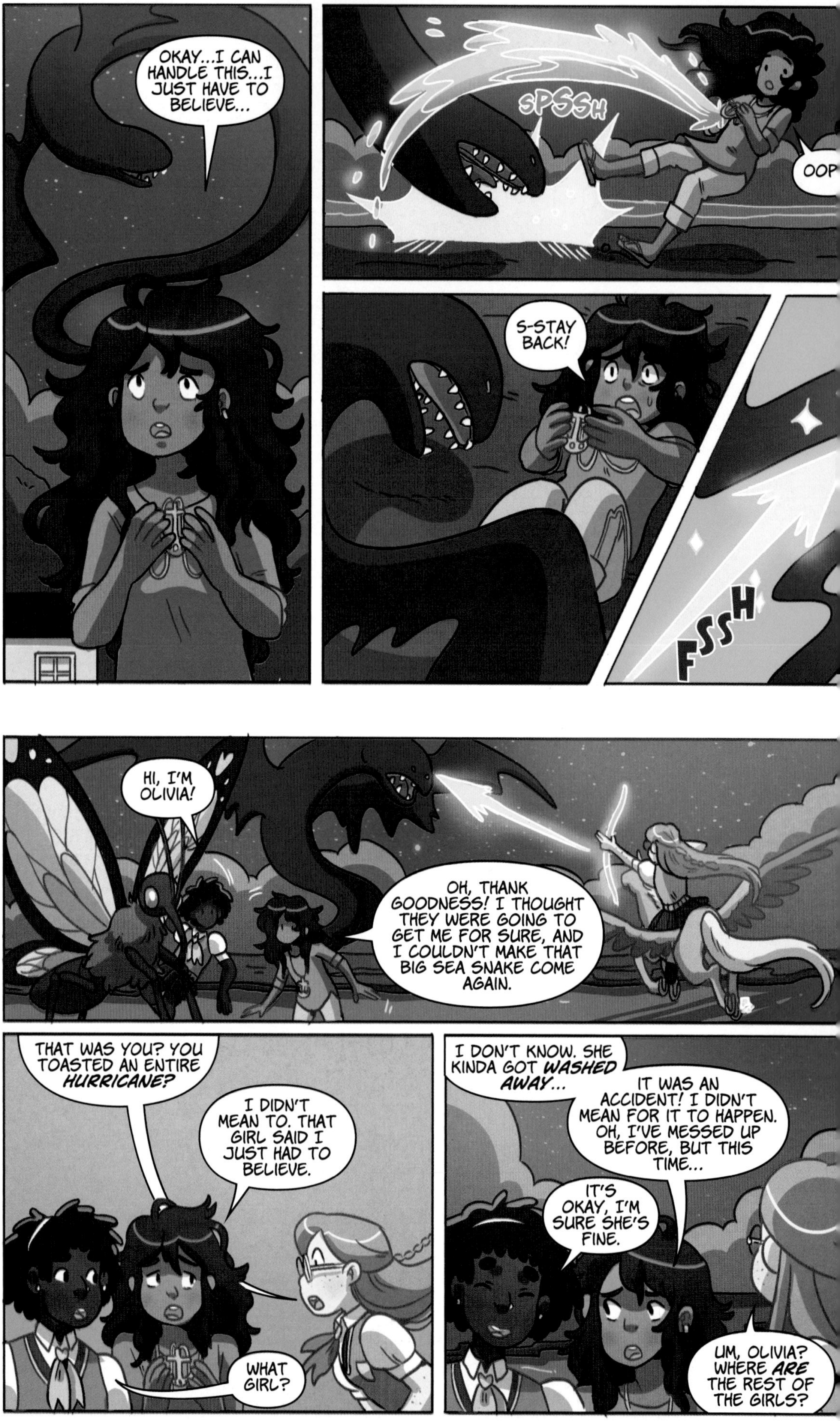

OKAY...I CAN HANDLE THIS...I JUST HAVE TO BELIEVE...
SPSSH
OOP
S-STAY BACK!
FSSH
HI, I'M OLIVIA!
OH, THANK GOODNESS! I THOUGHT THEY WERE GOING TO GET ME FOR SURE, AND I COULDN'T MAKE THAT BIG SEA SNAKE COME AGAIN.
THAT WAS YOU? YOU TOASTED AN ENTIRE *HURRICANE?*
I DIDN'T MEAN TO. THAT GIRL SAID I JUST HAD TO BELIEVE.
WHAT GIRL?
I DON'T KNOW. SHE KINDA GOT *WASHED AWAY...*
IT WAS AN ACCIDENT! I DIDN'T MEAN FOR IT TO HAPPEN. OH, I'VE MESSED UP BEFORE, BUT THIS TIME...
IT'S OKAY, I'M SURE SHE'S FINE.
UM, OLIVIA? WHERE *ARE* THE REST OF THE GIRLS?

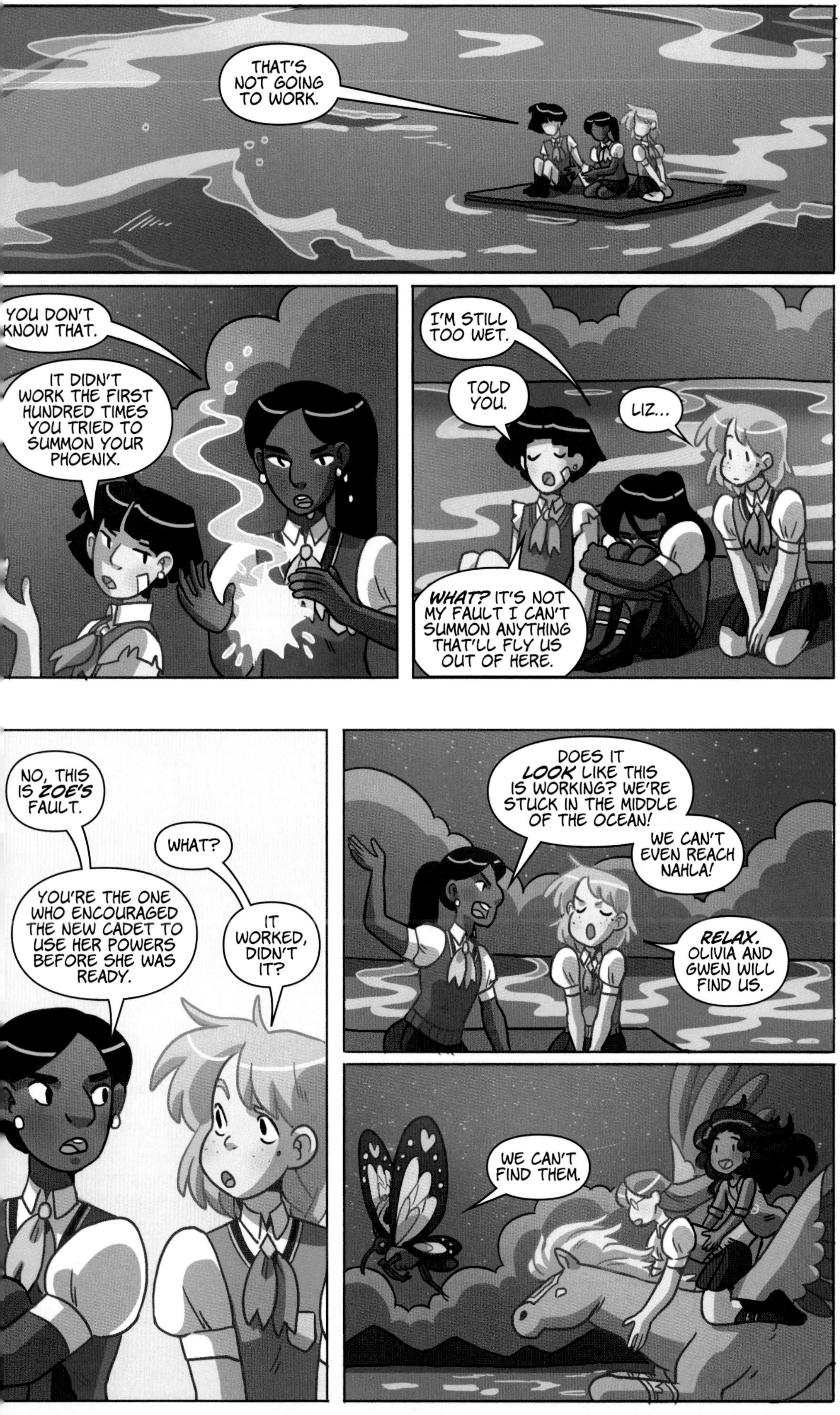
THAT'S NOT GOING TO WORK.
YOU DON'T KNOW THAT.
IT DIDN'T WORK THE FIRST HUNDRED TIMES YOU TRIED TO SUMMON YOUR PHOENIX.
I'M STILL TOO WET.
TOLD YOU.
LIZ...
WHAT? IT'S NOT MY FAULT I CAN'T SUMMON ANYTHING THAT'LL FLY US OUT OF HERE.
NO, THIS IS ZOE'S FAULT.
WHAT?
YOU'RE THE ONE WHO ENCOURAGED THE NEW CADET TO USE HER POWERS BEFORE SHE WAS READY.
IT WORKED, DIDN'T IT?
DOES IT LOOK LIKE THIS IS WORKING? WE'RE STUCK IN THE MIDDLE OF THE OCEAN!
WE CAN'T EVEN REACH NAHLA!
RELAX. OLIVIA AND GWEN WILL FIND US.
WE CAN'T FIND THEM.

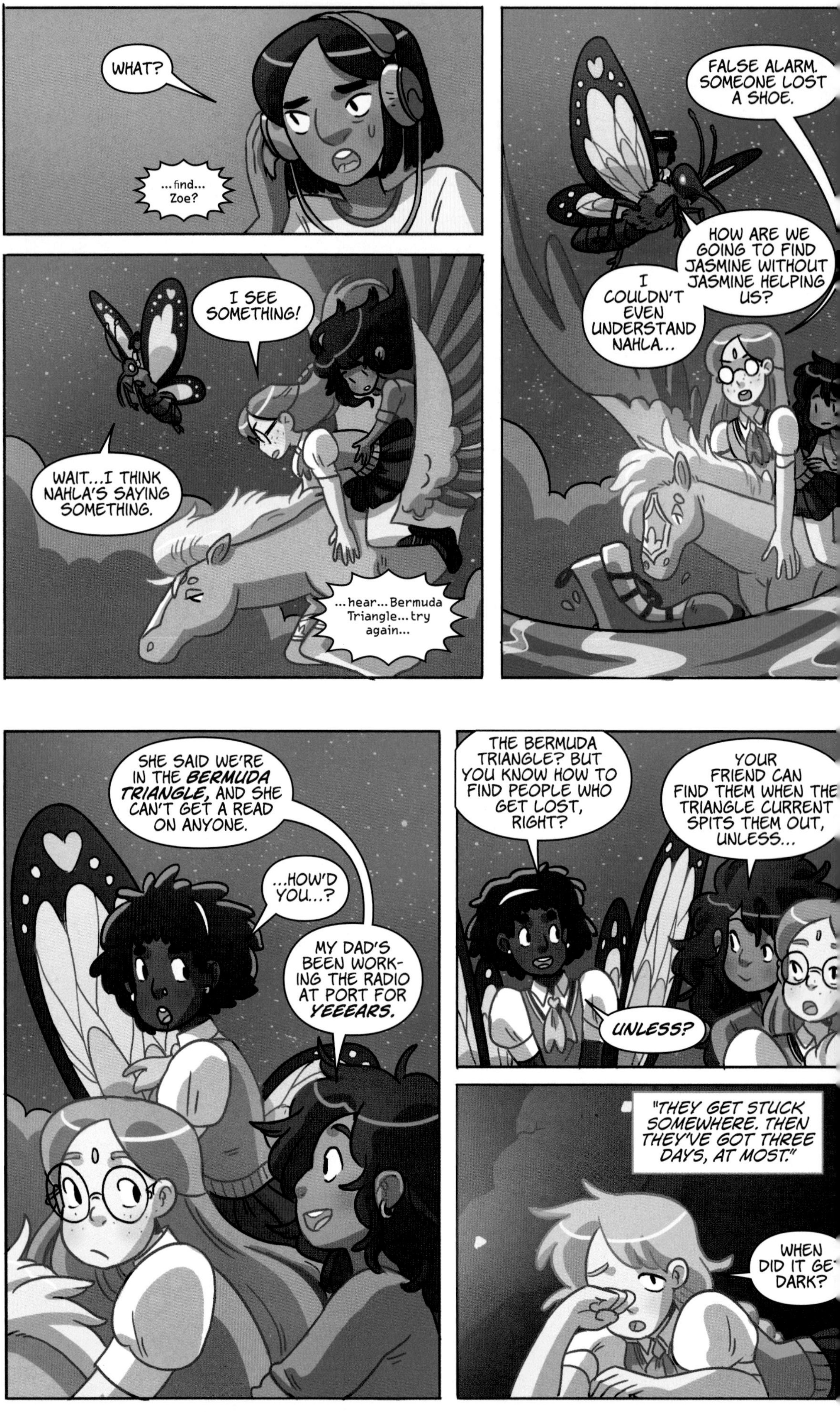
WHAT?
...find... Zoe?
I SEE SOMETHING!
WAIT...I THINK NAHLA'S SAYING SOMETHING.
...hear...Bermuda Triangle...try again...
FALSE ALARM. SOMEONE LOST A SHOE.
HOW ARE WE GOING TO FIND JASMINE WITHOUT JASMINE HELPING US?
I COULDN'T EVEN UNDERSTAND NAHLA...
SHE SAID WE'RE IN THE BERMUDA TRIANGLE, AND SHE CAN'T GET A READ ON ANYONE.
...HOW'D YOU...?
MY DAD'S BEEN WORKING THE RADIO AT PORT FOR YEEEARS.
THE BERMUDA TRIANGLE? BUT YOU KNOW HOW TO FIND PEOPLE WHO GET LOST, RIGHT?
YOUR FRIEND CAN FIND THEM WHEN THE TRIANGLE CURRENT SPITS THEM OUT, UNLESS...
UNLESS?
"THEY GET STUCK SOMEWHERE. THEN THEY'VE GOT THREE DAYS, AT MOST."
WHEN DID IT GET DARK?

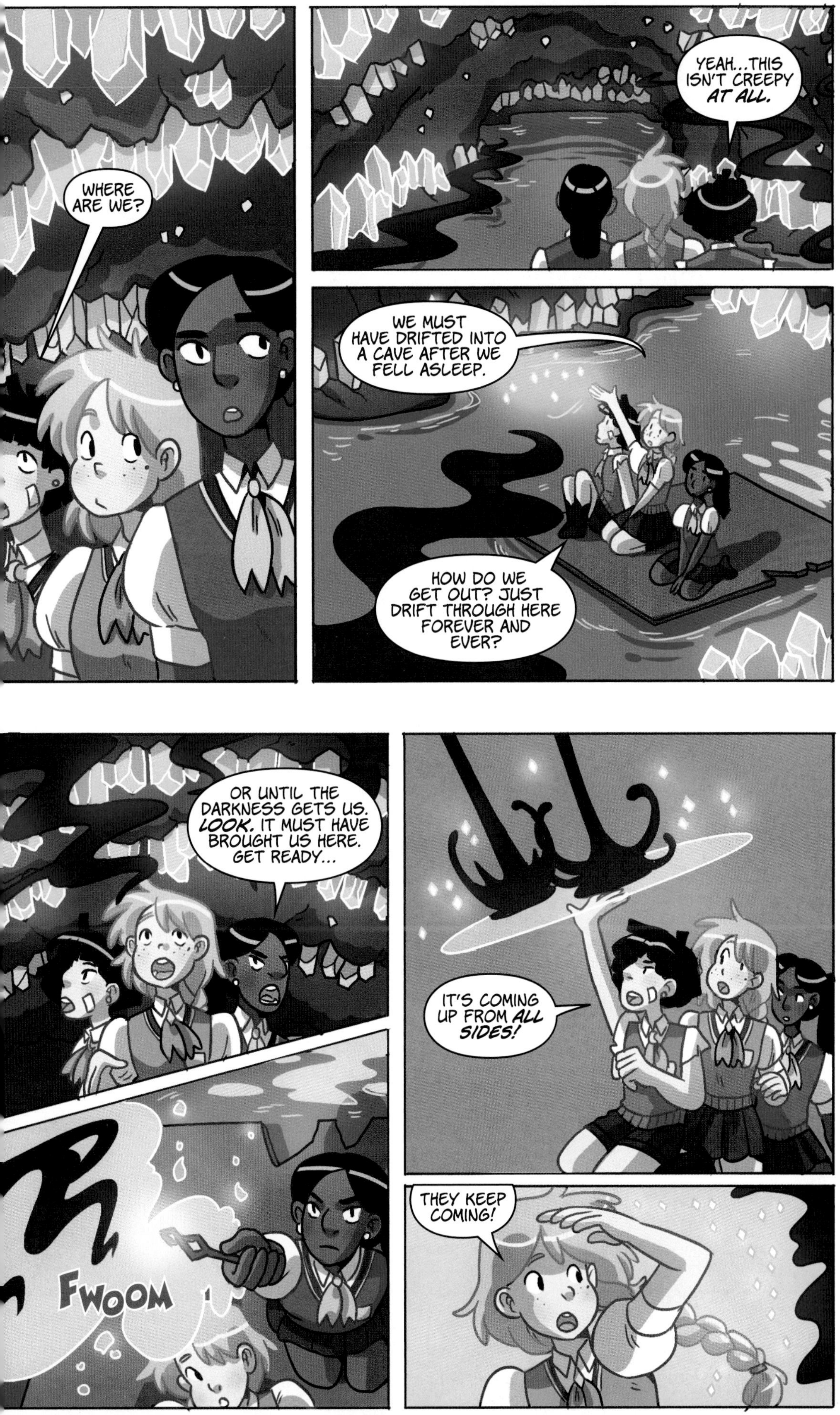
WHERE ARE WE?
YEAH...THIS ISN'T CREEPY AT ALL.
WE MUST HAVE DRIFTED INTO A CAVE AFTER WE FELL ASLEEP.
HOW DO WE GET OUT? JUST DRIFT THROUGH HERE FOREVER AND EVER?
OR UNTIL THE DARKNESS GETS US. LOOK. IT MUST HAVE BROUGHT US HERE. GET READY...
FWOOM
IT'S COMING UP FROM ALL SIDES!
THEY KEEP COMING!

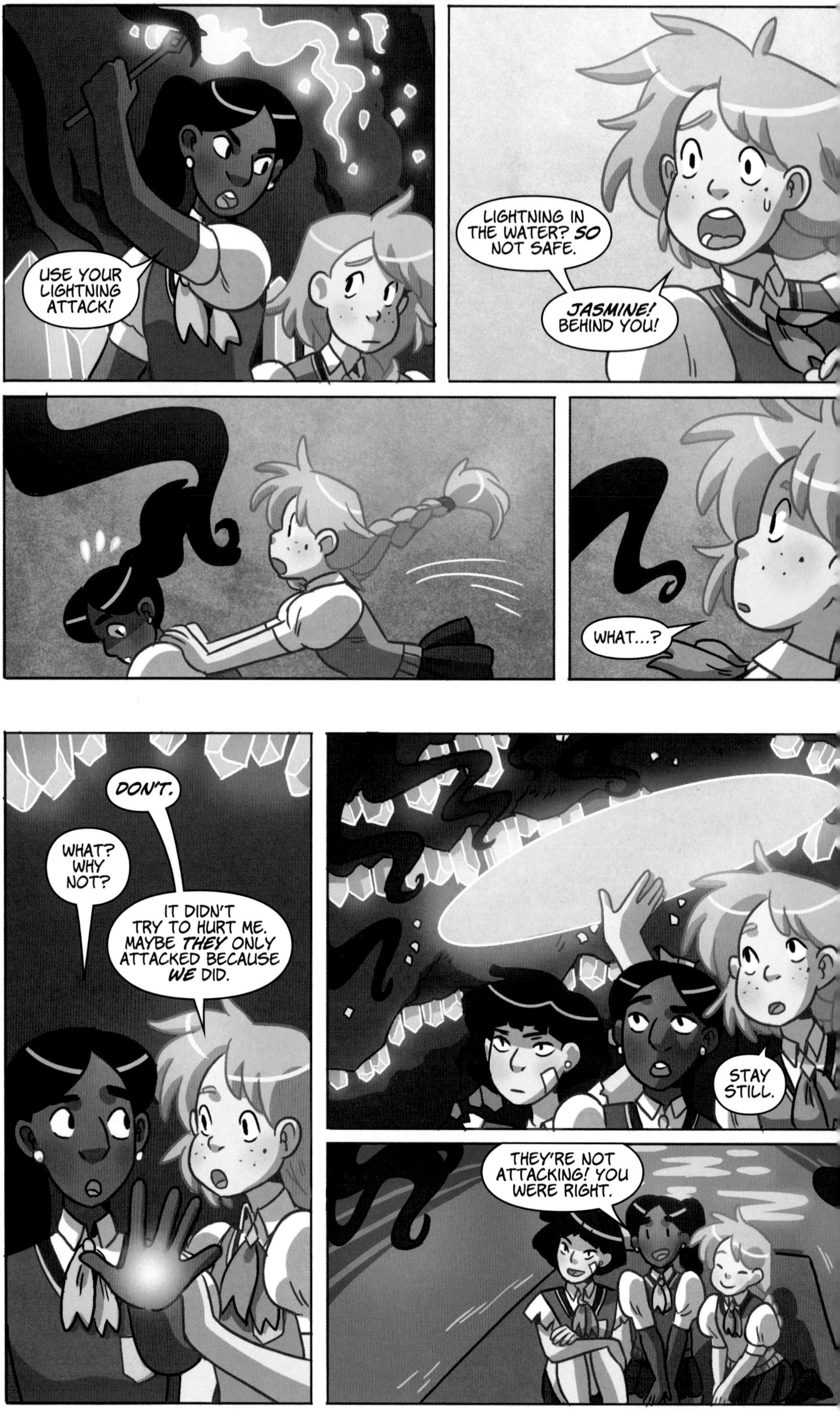

USE YOUR LIGHTNING ATTACK!
LIGHTNING IN THE WATER? SO NOT SAFE.
JASMINE! BEHIND YOU!
WHAT...?
DON'T.
WHAT? WHY NOT?
IT DIDN'T TRY TO HURT ME. MAYBE THEY ONLY ATTACKED BECAUSE WE DID.
STAY STILL.
THEY'RE NOT ATTACKING! YOU WERE RIGHT.

IT'S LIKE [TH]EY'RE RUNNING [FR]OM SOMETHING. [S]TAY CLOSE...

IT'S BEAUTIFUL!

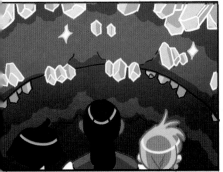

SO MANY CRYSTALS...

FZZ

I THINK MY DIAMOND THINKS IT'S HOME.

I SEE WHY.

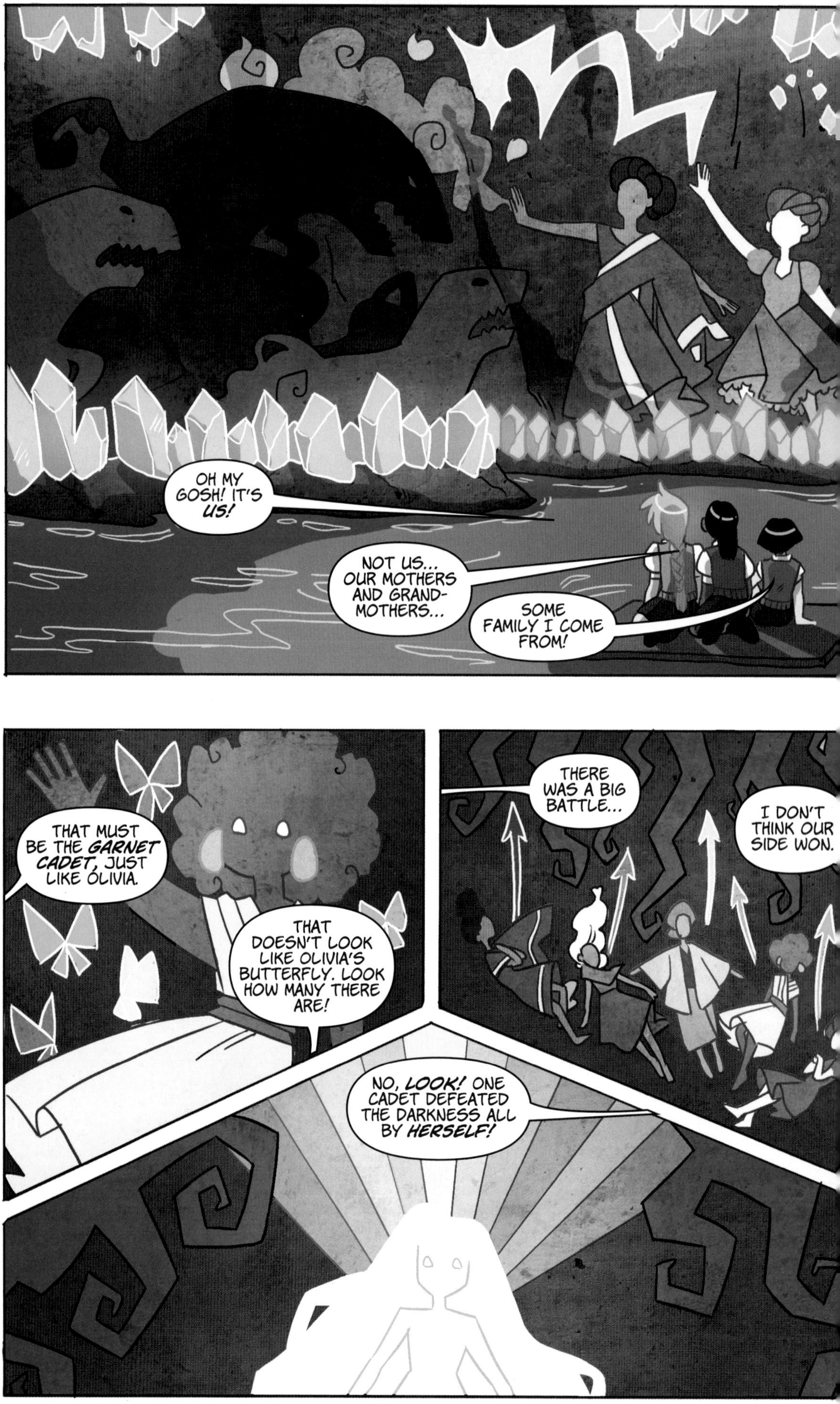

OH MY GOSH! IT'S *US!*
NOT US... OUR MOTHERS AND GRAND-MOTHERS...
SOME FAMILY I COME FROM!
THAT MUST BE THE *GARNET CADET*, JUST LIKE OLIVIA.
THAT DOESN'T LOOK LIKE OLIVIA'S BUTTERFLY. LOOK HOW MANY THERE ARE!
THERE WAS A BIG BATTLE...
I DON'T THINK OUR SIDE WON.
NO, *LOOK!* ONE CADET DEFEATED THE DARKNESS ALL BY *HERSELF!*

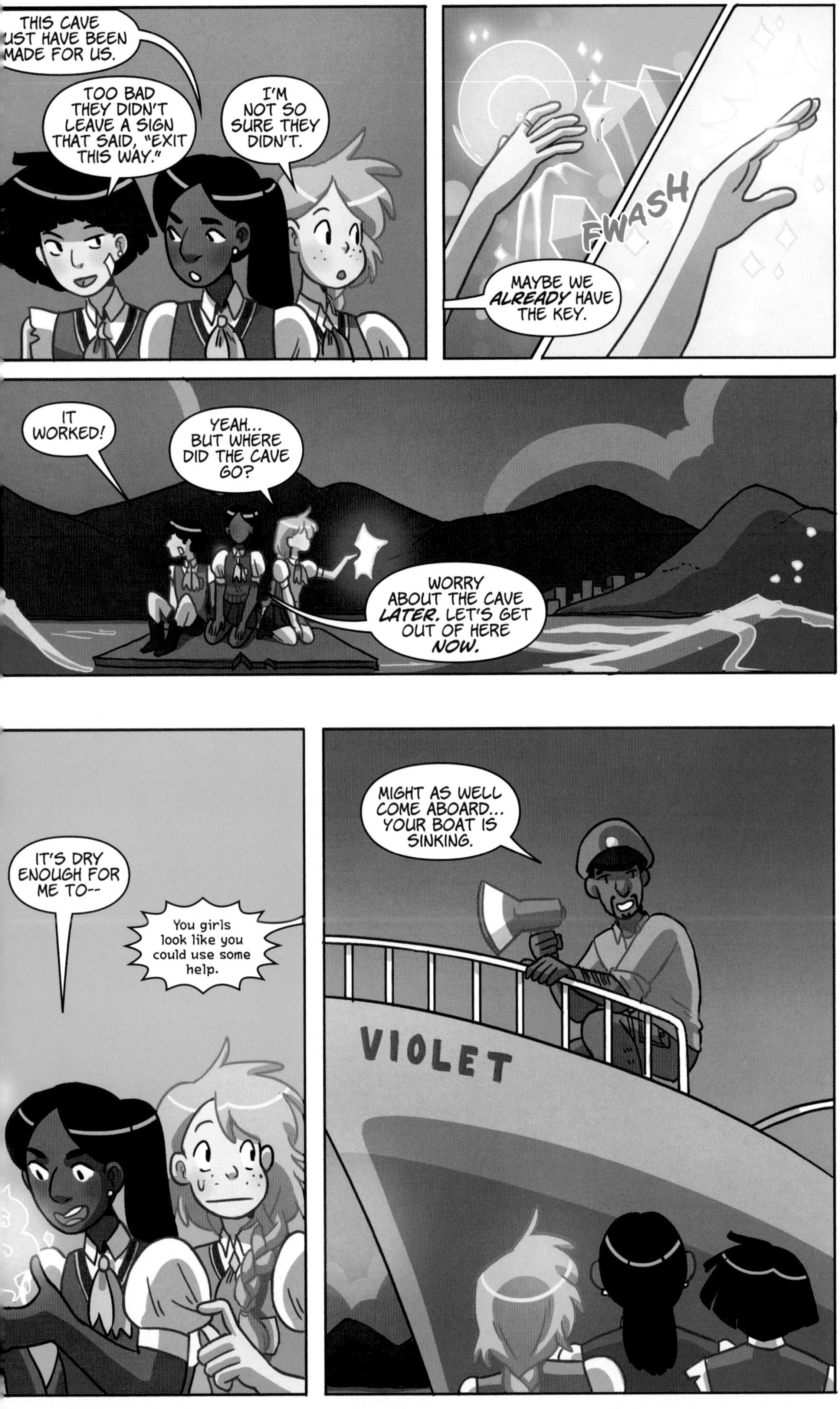

THIS CAVE UST HAVE BEEN MADE FOR US.
TOO BAD THEY DIDN'T LEAVE A SIGN THAT SAID, "EXIT THIS WAY."
I'M NOT SO SURE THEY DIDN'T.
FWASH
MAYBE WE *ALREADY* HAVE THE KEY.
IT WORKED!
YEAH... BUT WHERE DID THE CAVE GO?
WORRY ABOUT THE CAVE *LATER.* LET'S GET OUT OF HERE *NOW.*
IT'S DRY ENOUGH FOR ME TO--
You girls look like you could use some help.
MIGHT AS WELL COME ABOARD... YOUR BOAT IS SINKING.
VIOLET

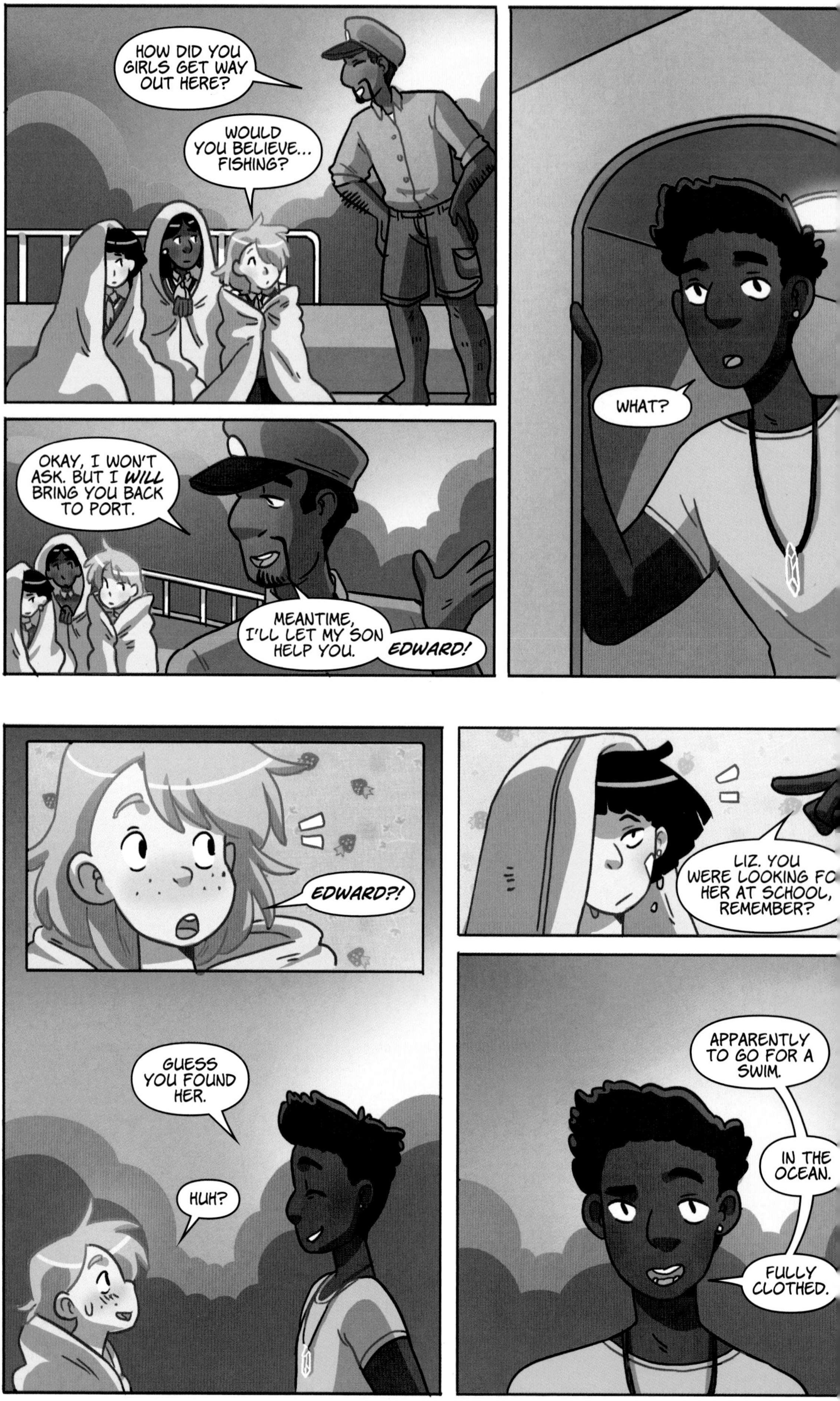
HOW DID YOU GIRLS GET WAY OUT HERE?
WOULD YOU BELIEVE... FISHING?
WHAT?
OKAY, I WON'T ASK. BUT I WILL BRING YOU BACK TO PORT.
MEANTIME, I'LL LET MY SON HELP YOU.
EDWARD!
EDWARD?!
LIZ. YOU WERE LOOKING FO
HER AT SCHOOL, REMEMBER?
GUESS YOU FOUND HER.
HUH?
APPARENTLY TO GO FOR A SWIM.
IN THE OCEAN.
FULLY CLOTHED.

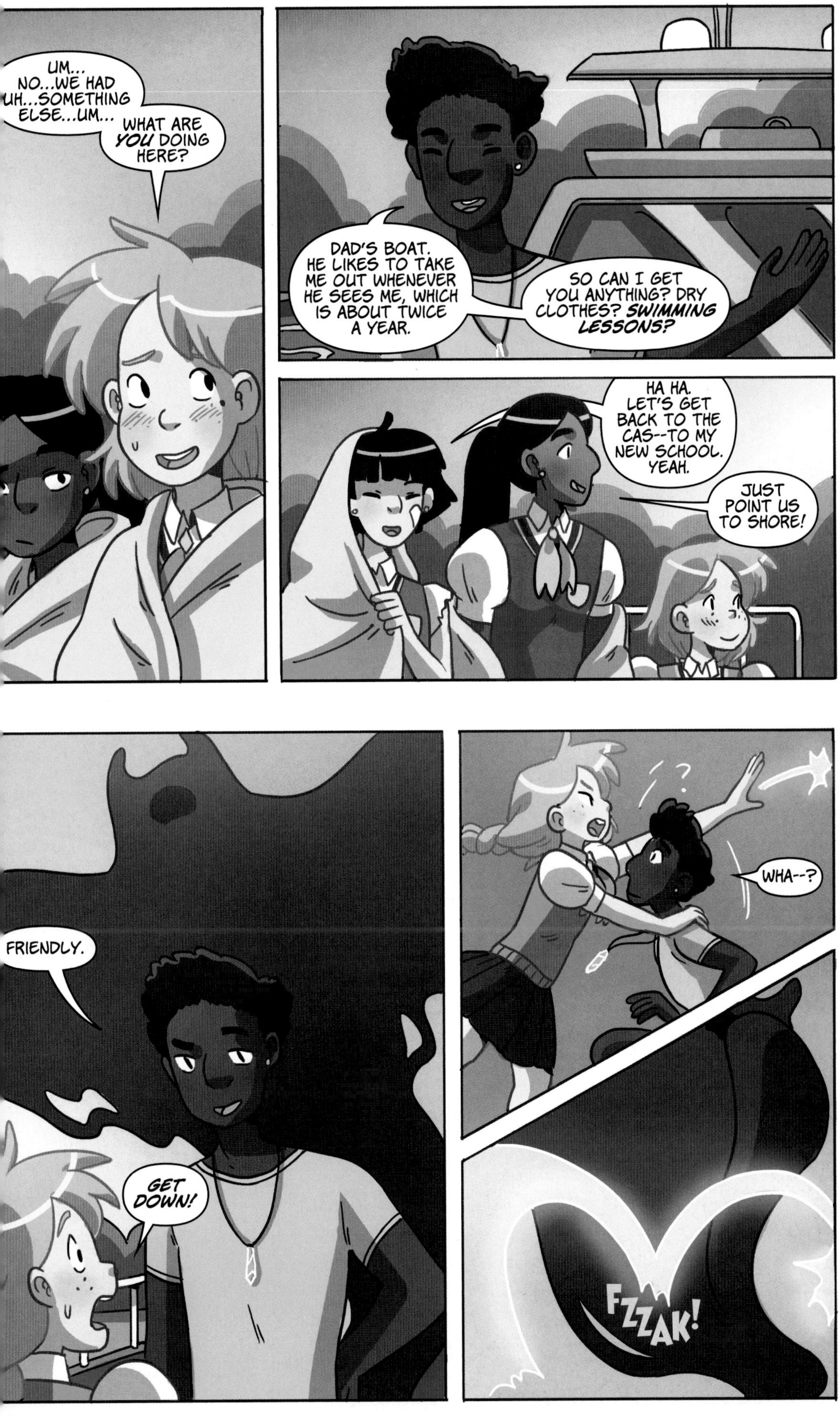
UM... NO...WE HAD UH...SOMETHING ELSE...UM...
WHAT ARE YOU DOING HERE?
DAD'S BOAT. HE LIKES TO TAKE ME OUT WHENEVER HE SEES ME, WHICH IS ABOUT TWICE A YEAR.
SO CAN I GET YOU ANYTHING? DRY CLOTHES? SWIMMING LESSONS?
HA HA. LET'S GET BACK TO THE CAS--TO MY NEW SCHOOL. YEAH.
JUST POINT US TO SHORE!
FRIENDLY.
GET DOWN!
WHA--?
FZZZAK!

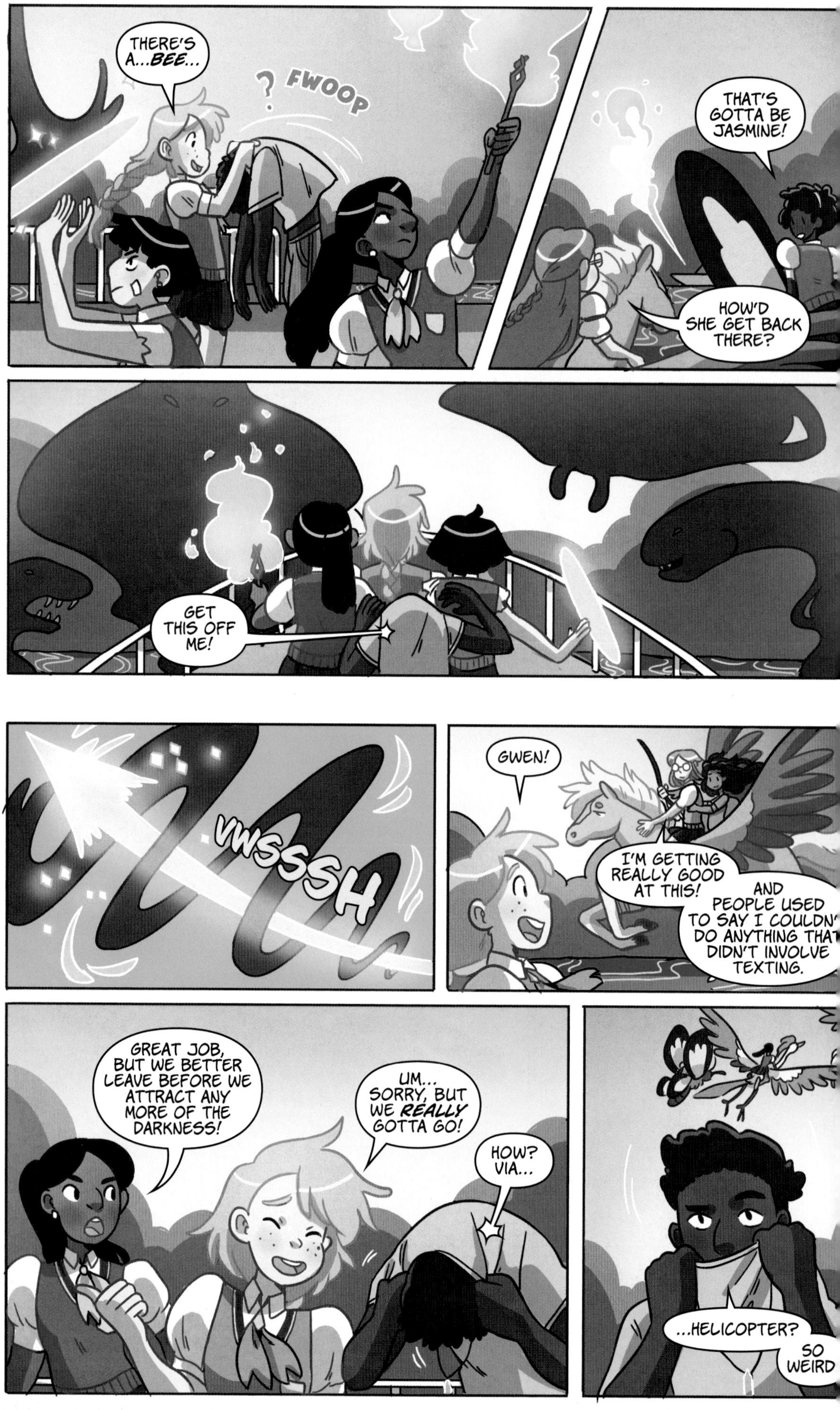
THERE'S A...BEE...
?
FWOOP
THAT'S GOTTA BE JASMINE!
HOW'D SHE GET BACK THERE?
GET THIS OFF ME!
VWSSSH
GWEN!
I'M GETTING REALLY GOOD AT THIS!
AND PEOPLE USED TO SAY I COULDN' DO ANYTHING THAT DIDN'T INVOLVE TEXTING.
GREAT JOB, BUT WE BETTER LEAVE BEFORE WE ATTRACT ANY MORE OF THE DARKNESS!
UM... SORRY, BUT WE REALLY GOTTA GO!
HOW? VIA...
...HELICOPTER?
SO WEIRD

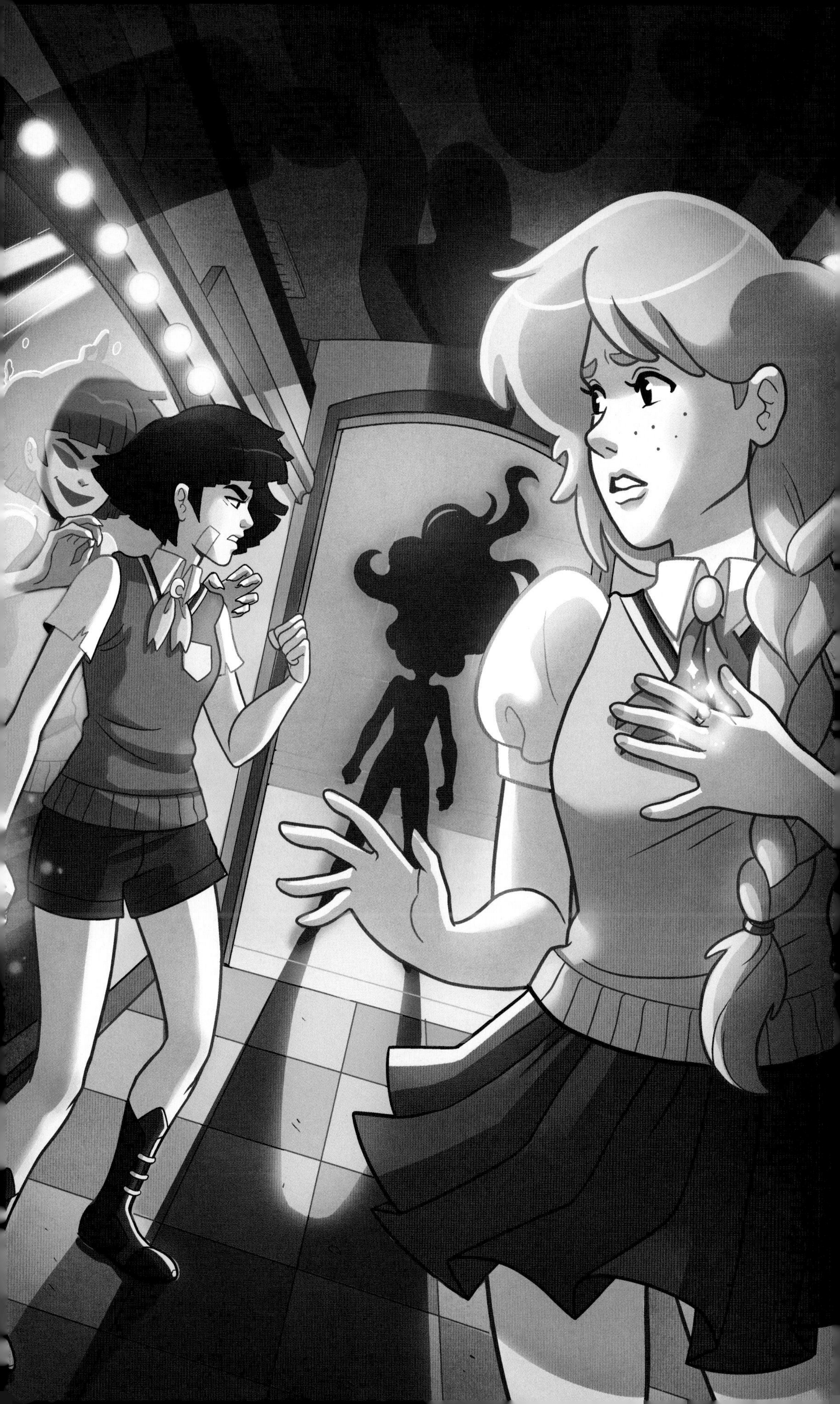

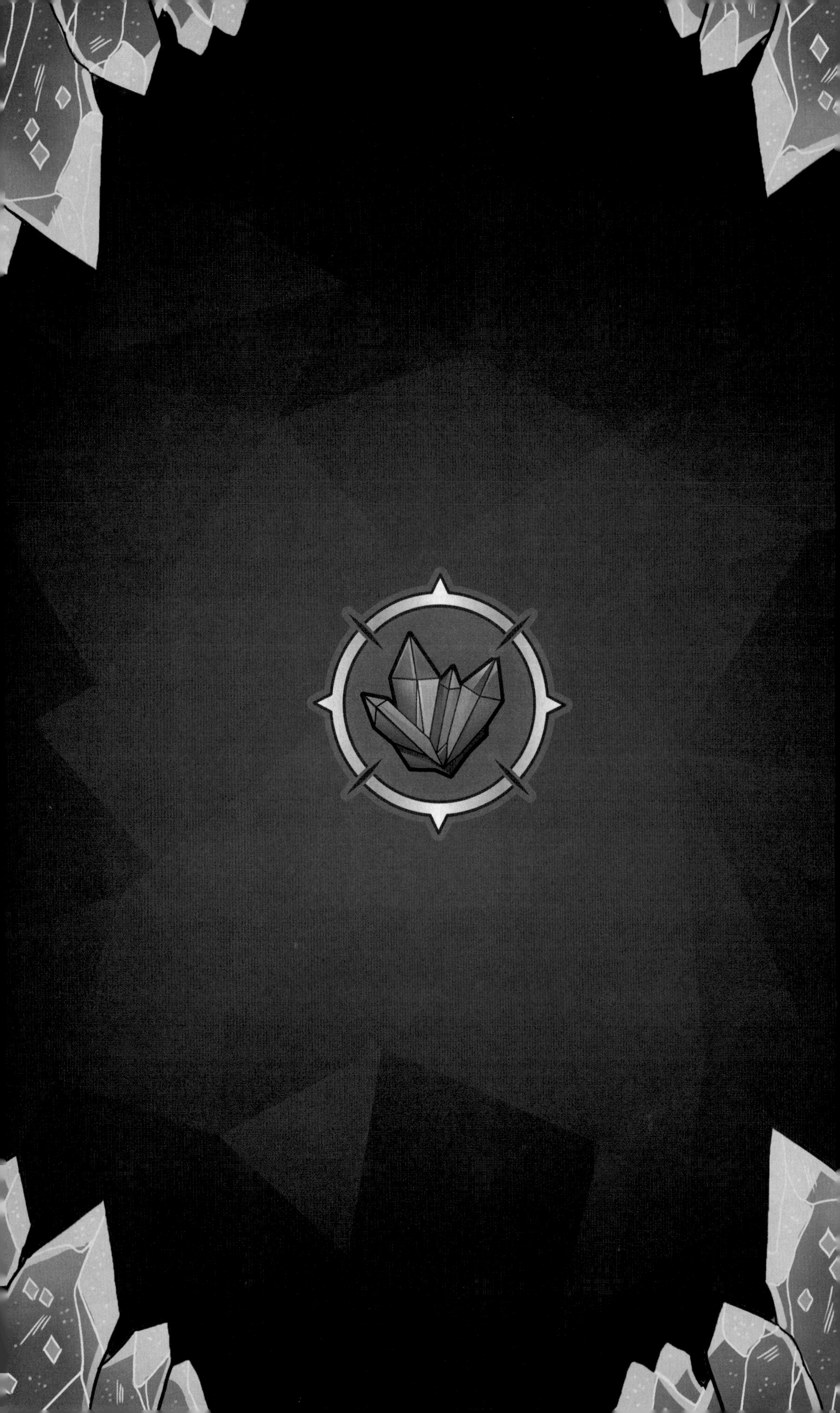

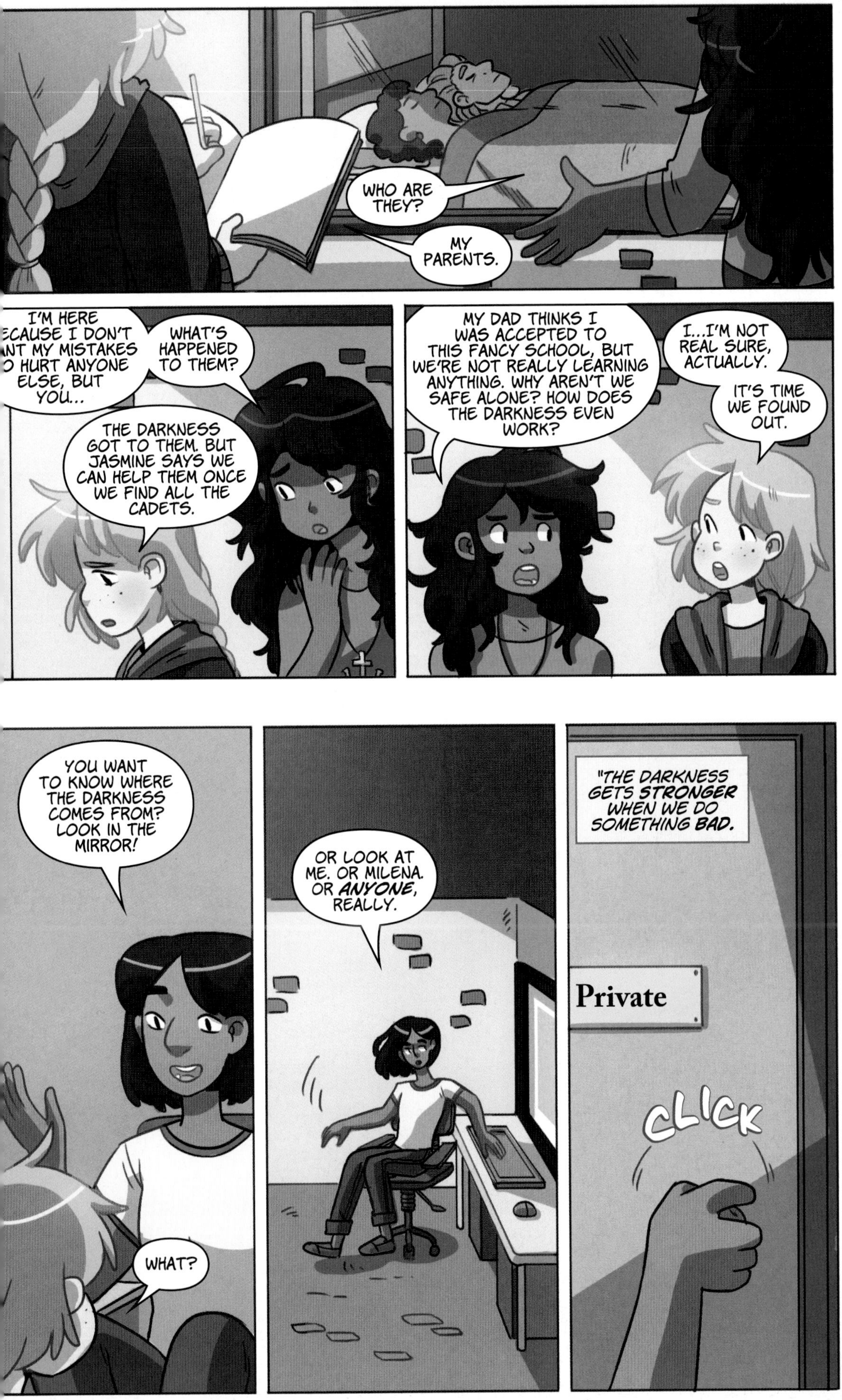
WHO ARE THEY?
MY PARENTS.
I'M HERE ECAUSE I DON'T NT MY MISTAKES O HURT ANYONE ELSE, BUT YOU...
WHAT'S HAPPENED TO THEM?
THE DARKNESS GOT TO THEM. BUT JASMINE SAYS WE CAN HELP THEM ONCE WE FIND ALL THE CADETS.
MY DAD THINKS I WAS ACCEPTED TO THIS FANCY SCHOOL, BUT WE'RE NOT REALLY LEARNING ANYTHING. WHY AREN'T WE SAFE ALONE? HOW DOES THE DARKNESS EVEN WORK?
I...I'M NOT REAL SURE, ACTUALLY.
IT'S TIME WE FOUND OUT.
YOU WANT TO KNOW WHERE THE DARKNESS COMES FROM? LOOK IN THE MIRROR!
WHAT?
OR LOOK AT ME. OR MILENA. OR *ANYONE*, REALLY.
"THE DARKNESS GETS **STRONGER** WHEN WE DO SOMETHING **BAD**.
Private
CLICK

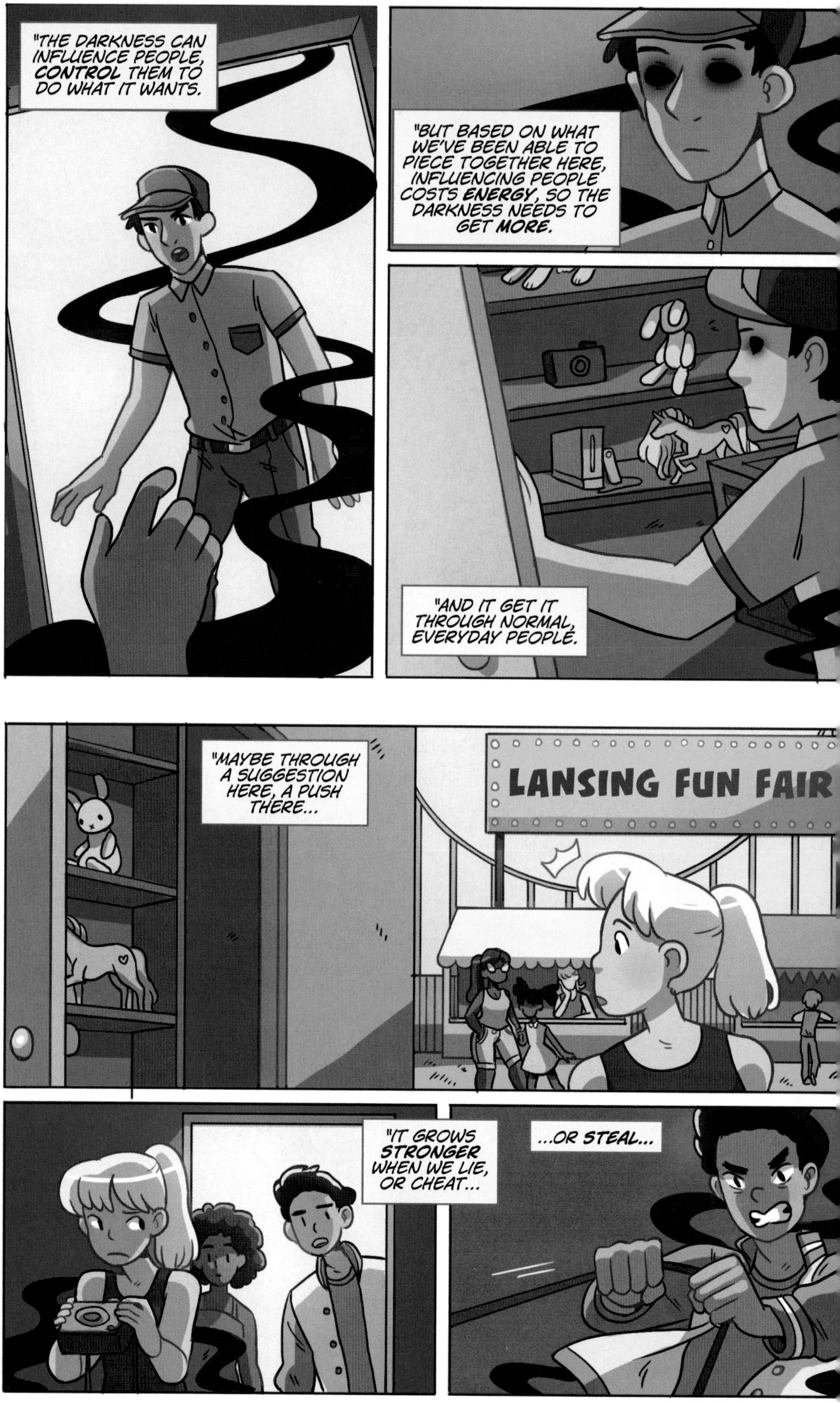
"THE DARKNESS CAN INFLUENCE PEOPLE, CONTROL THEM TO DO WHAT IT WANTS.
"BUT BASED ON WHAT WE'VE BEEN ABLE TO PIECE TOGETHER HERE, INFLUENCING PEOPLE COSTS ENERGY, SO THE DARKNESS NEEDS TO GET MORE.
"AND IT GET IT THROUGH NORMAL, EVERYDAY PEOPLE.
"MAYBE THROUGH A SUGGESTION HERE, A PUSH THERE...
LANSING FUN FAIR
"IT GROWS STRONGER WHEN WE LIE, OR CHEAT...
...OR STEAL...

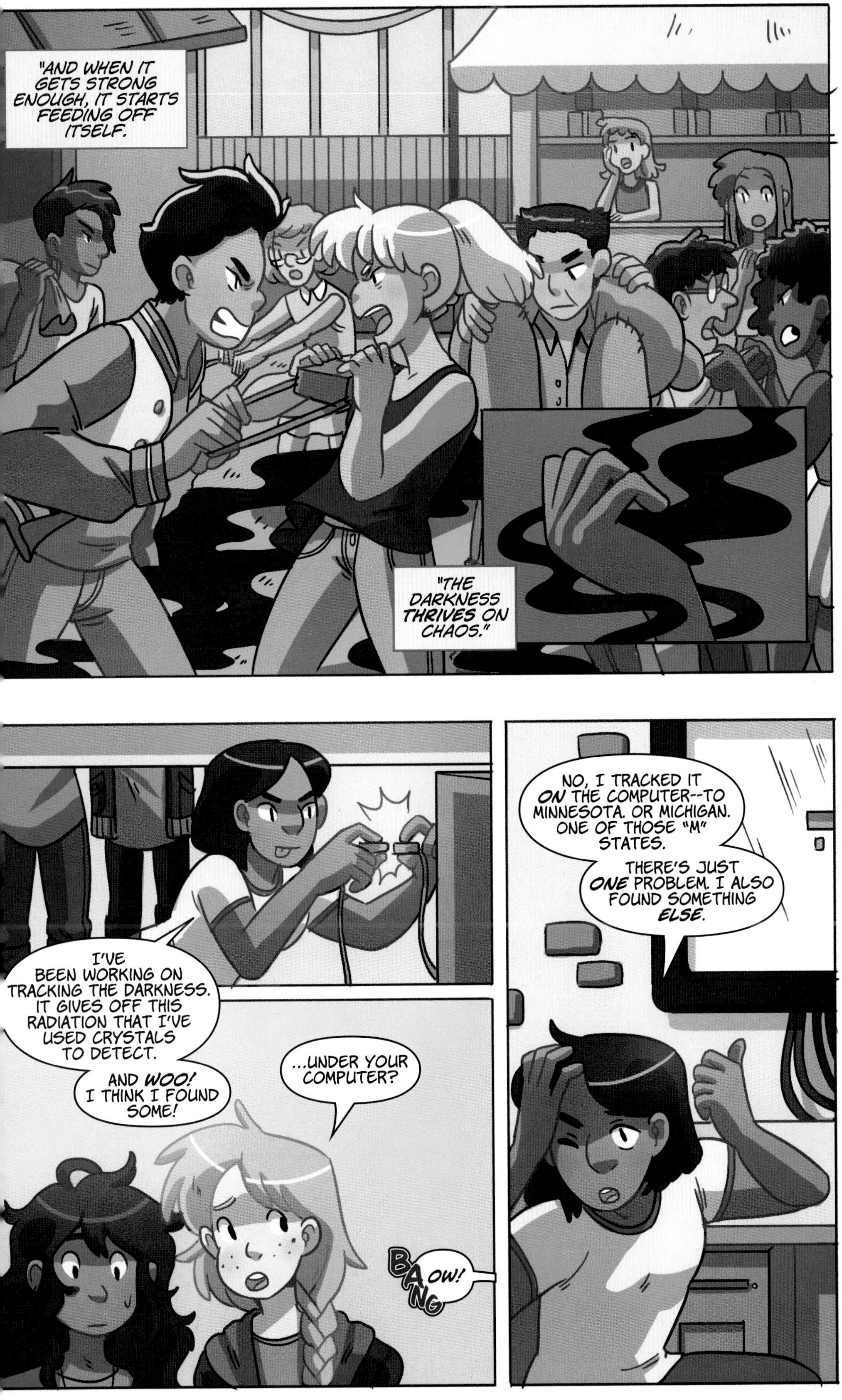
"AND WHEN IT GETS STRONG ENOUGH, IT STARTS FEEDING OFF ITSELF.
"THE DARKNESS THRIVES ON CHAOS."
I'VE BEEN WORKING ON TRACKING THE DARKNESS. IT GIVES OFF THIS RADIATION THAT I'VE USED CRYSTALS TO DETECT.
AND WOO! I THINK I FOUND SOME!
...UNDER YOUR COMPUTER?
BANG
OW!
NO, I TRACKED IT ON THE COMPUTER--TO MINNESOTA. OR MICHIGAN. ONE OF THOSE "M" STATES.
THERE'S JUST ONE PROBLEM. I ALSO FOUND SOMETHING ELSE.

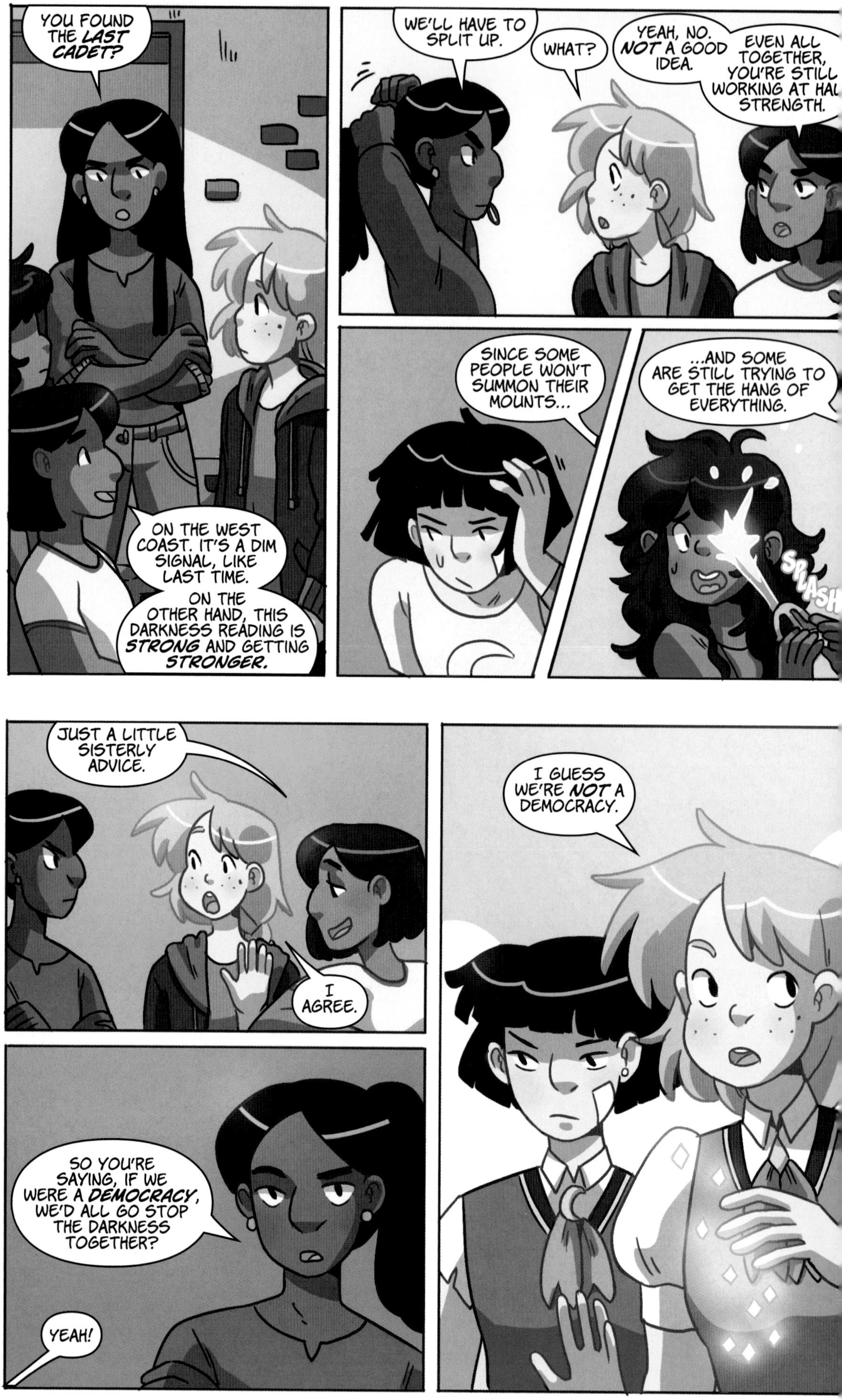

YOU FOUND THE *LAST CADET?*
ON THE WEST COAST. IT'S A DIM SIGNAL, LIKE LAST TIME.
ON THE OTHER HAND, THIS DARKNESS READING IS *STRONG* AND GETTING *STRONGER.*
WE'LL HAVE TO SPLIT UP.
WHAT?
YEAH, NO. *NOT* A GOOD IDEA.
EVEN ALL TOGETHER, YOU'RE STILL WORKING AT HAL
STRENGTH.
SINCE SOME PEOPLE WON'T SUMMON THEIR MOUNTS...
...AND SOME ARE STILL TRYING TO GET THE HANG OF EVERYTHING.
SPLASH
JUST A LITTLE SISTERLY ADVICE.
I AGREE.
SO YOU'RE SAYING, IF WE WERE A *DEMOCRACY*, WE'D ALL GO STOP THE DARKNESS TOGETHER?
YEAH!
I GUESS WE'RE *NOT* A DEMOCRACY.

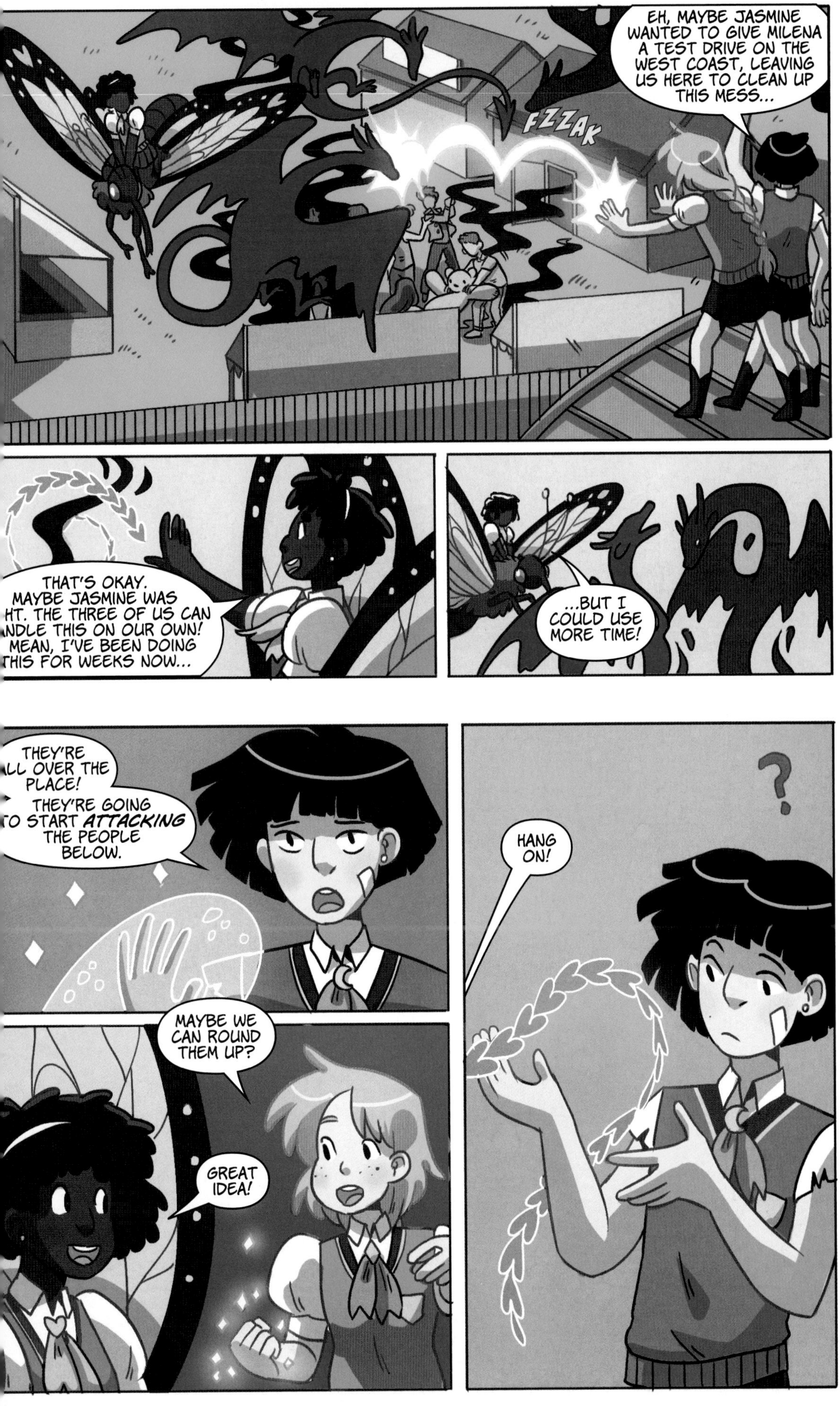
EH, MAYBE JASMINE WANTED TO GIVE MILENA A TEST DRIVE ON THE WEST COAST, LEAVING US HERE TO CLEAN UP THIS MESS...
FZZZAK
THAT'S OKAY. MAYBE JASMINE WAS HT. THE THREE OF US CAN NDLE THIS ON OUR OWN! MEAN, I'VE BEEN DOING THIS FOR WEEKS NOW...
...BUT I COULD USE MORE TIME!
THEY'RE LL OVER THE PLACE!
THEY'RE GOING O START ATTACKING THE PEOPLE BELOW.
MAYBE WE CAN ROUND THEM UP?
GREAT IDEA!
?
HANG ON!

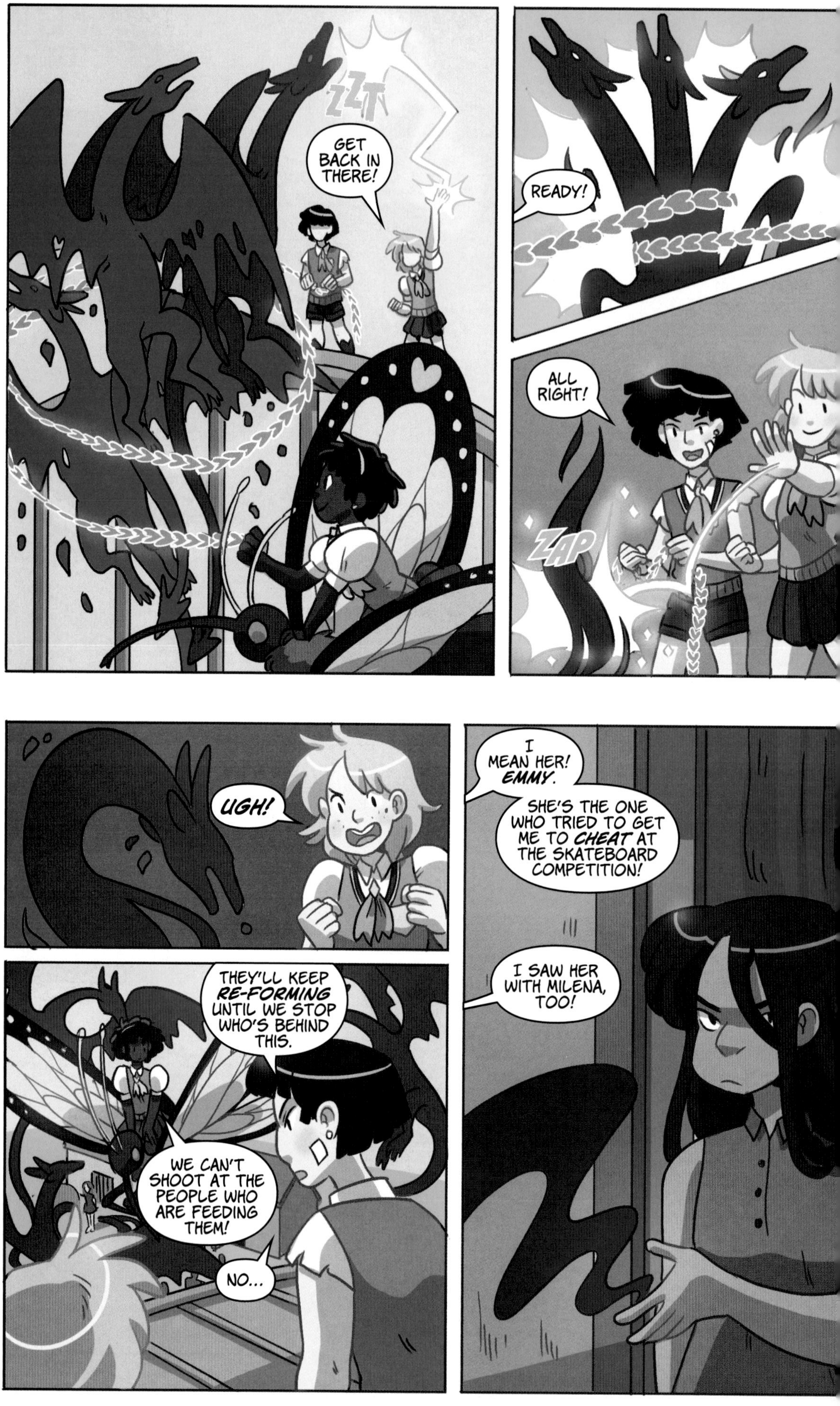
ZZZT
GET BACK IN THERE!
READY!
ALL RIGHT!
ZAP
UGH!
I MEAN HER! EMMY.
SHE'S THE ONE WHO TRIED TO GET ME TO CHEAT AT THE SKATEBOARD COMPETITION!
I SAW HER WITH MILENA, TOO!
THEY'LL KEEP RE-FORMING UNTIL WE STOP WHO'S BEHIND THIS.
WE CAN'T SHOOT AT THE PEOPLE WHO ARE FEEDING THEM!
NO...

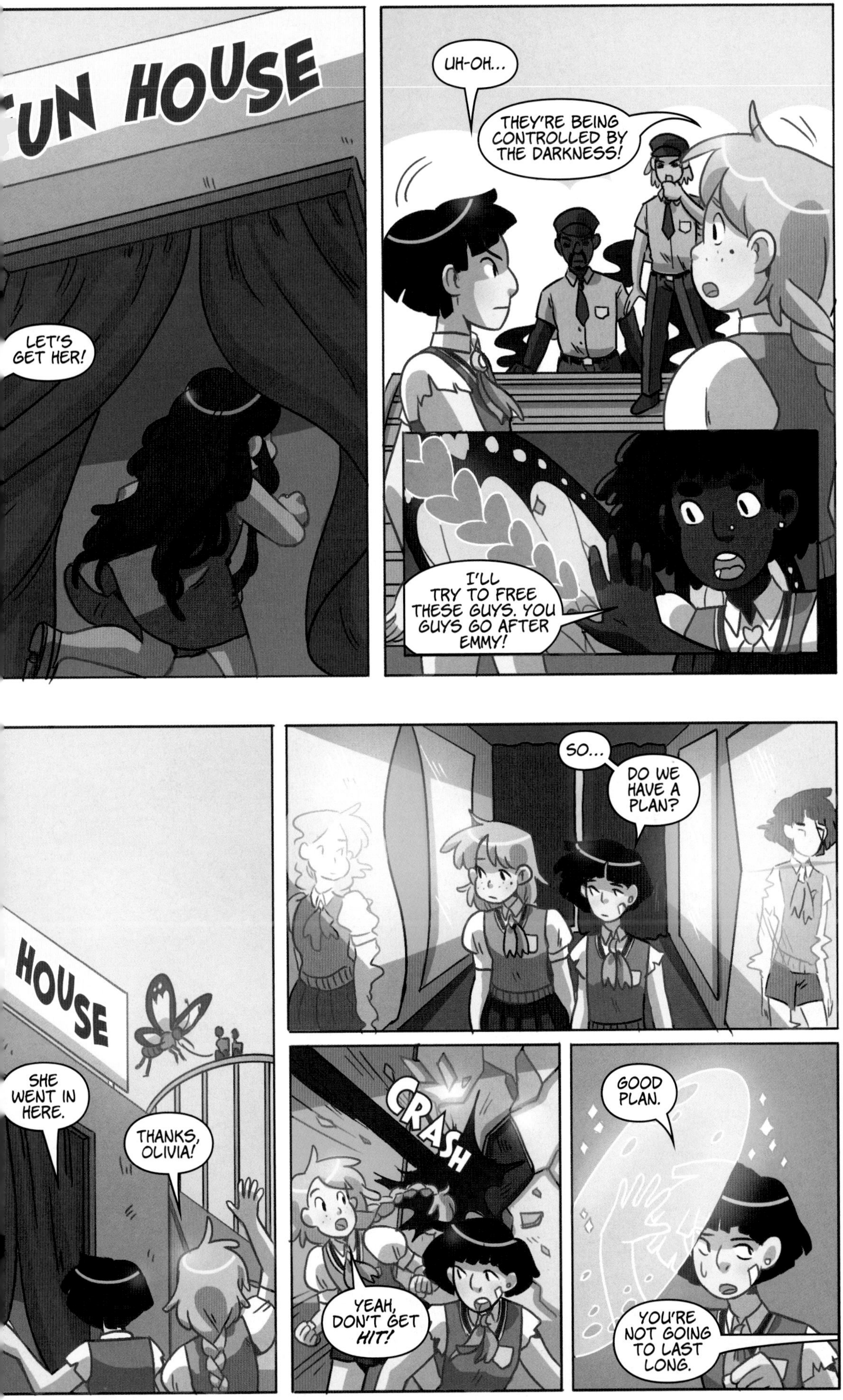
FUN HOUSE
LET'S GET HER!
UH-OH...
THEY'RE BEING CONTROLLED BY THE DARKNESS!
I'LL TRY TO FREE THESE GUYS. YOU GUYS GO AFTER EMMY!
HOUSE
SHE WENT IN HERE.
THANKS, OLIVIA!
SO...
DO WE HAVE A PLAN?
CRASH
YEAH, DON'T GET *HIT*!
GOOD PLAN.
YOU'RE NOT GOING TO LAST LONG.

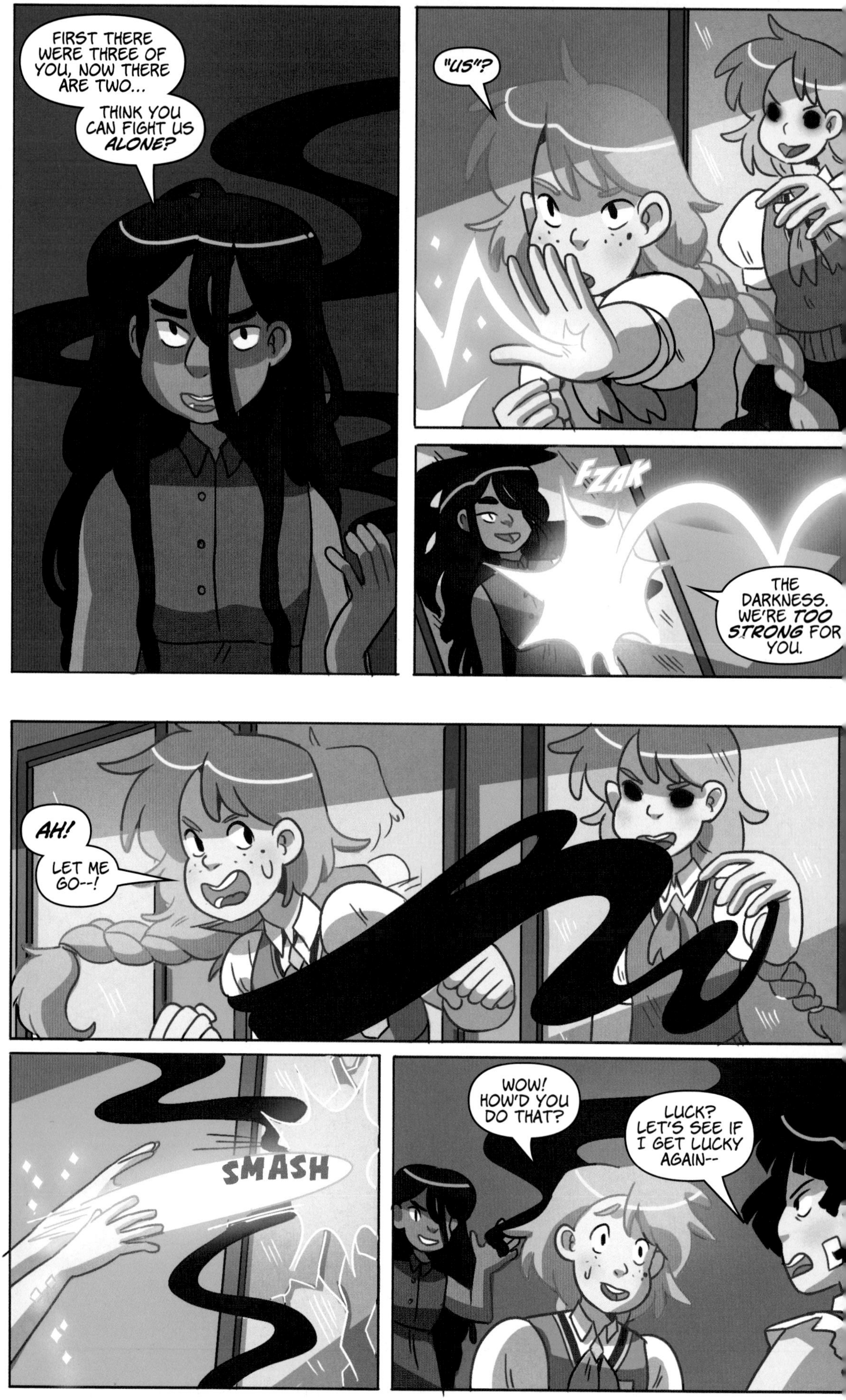
FIRST THERE WERE THREE OF YOU, NOW THERE ARE TWO...
THINK YOU CAN FIGHT US ALONE?
"US"?
FZAK
THE DARKNESS. WE'RE TOO STRONG FOR YOU.
AH!
LET ME GO--!
SMASH
WOW! HOW'D YOU DO THAT?
LUCK? LET'S SEE IF I GET LUCKY AGAIN--

THUD

IT WORKED!

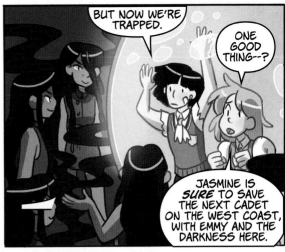

BUT NOW WE'RE TRAPPED.

ONE GOOD THING--?

JASMINE IS *SURE* TO SAVE THE NEXT CADET ON THE WEST COAST, WITH EMMY AND THE DARKNESS HERE.

WEST COAST, USA

FWASH

THE DARKNESS MUST HAVE GOTTEN HERE FIRST!

LOOK! THAT MUST BE THE LAST CADET!

HELP!

I GOT THIS.

MILENA, NO--

WAIT, THAT WAS SUPPOSED TO--

WHOOSH

AY, ME.

I'M REALLY SORRY.

AT LEAST THE DARKNESS IS GONE!

TRY HOLDING IT...

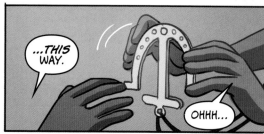

...THIS WAY.

OHHH...

WE'D BETTER GET HER BACK HOME. THE DARKNESS DOESN'T GIVE UP EASILY.

UGH...

YOU CAN'T STAY LIKE THIS FOREVER.

SHE'S RIGHT. I'LL NEED TO *PEE* EVENTUALLY.

WHY NOT *JOIN* ME? YOU COULD DO *WHATEVER* YOU WANTED.

GOOD, BECAUSE I WANT TO DO *THIS!*

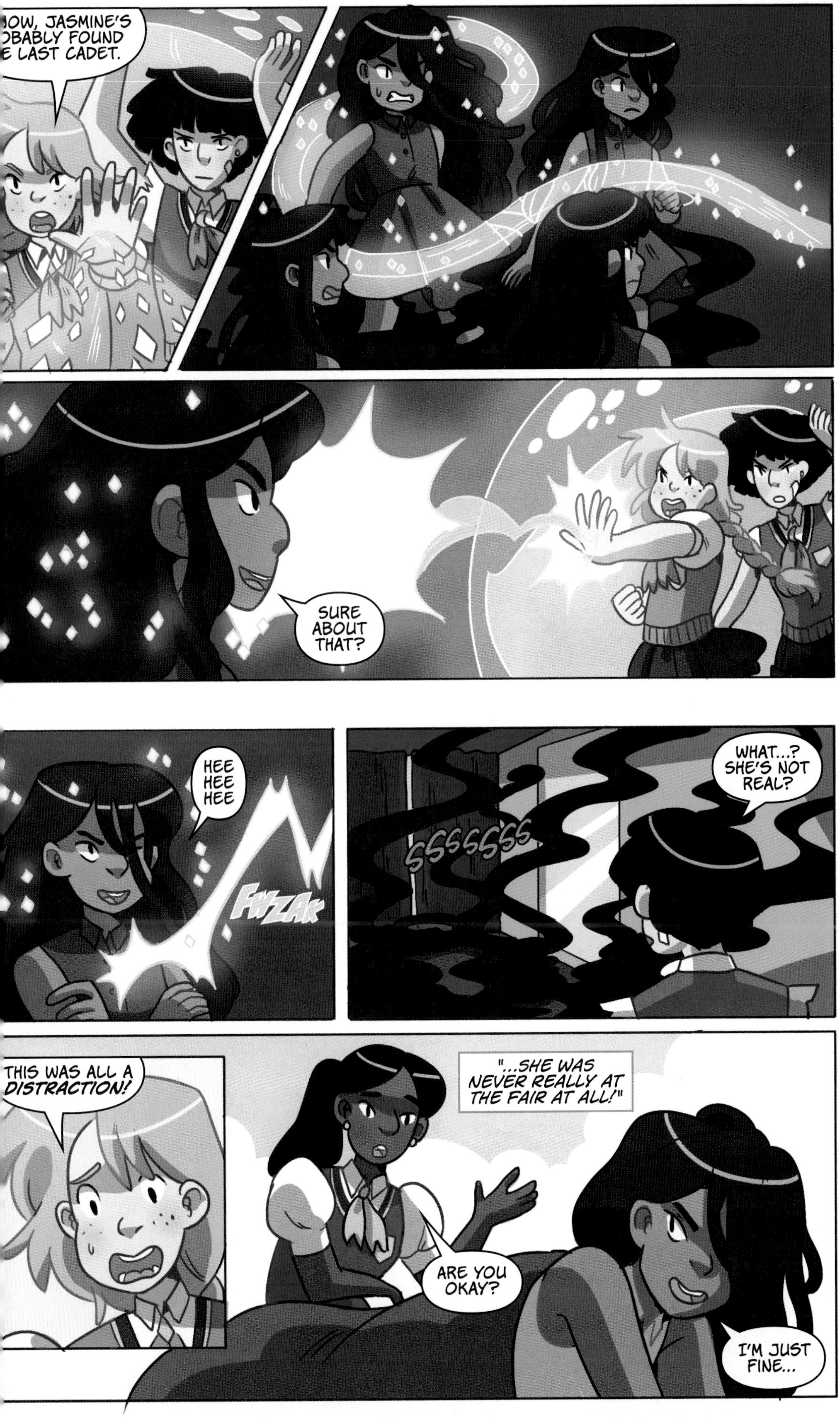

OW, JASMINE'S
OBABLY FOUND
E LAST CADET.
SURE ABOUT THAT?
HEE HEE HEE
FWZAK
SSSSSSS
WHAT...? SHE'S NOT REAL?
THIS WAS ALL A DISTRACTION!
"...SHE WAS NEVER REALLY AT THE FAIR AT ALL!"
ARE YOU OKAY?
I'M JUST FINE...

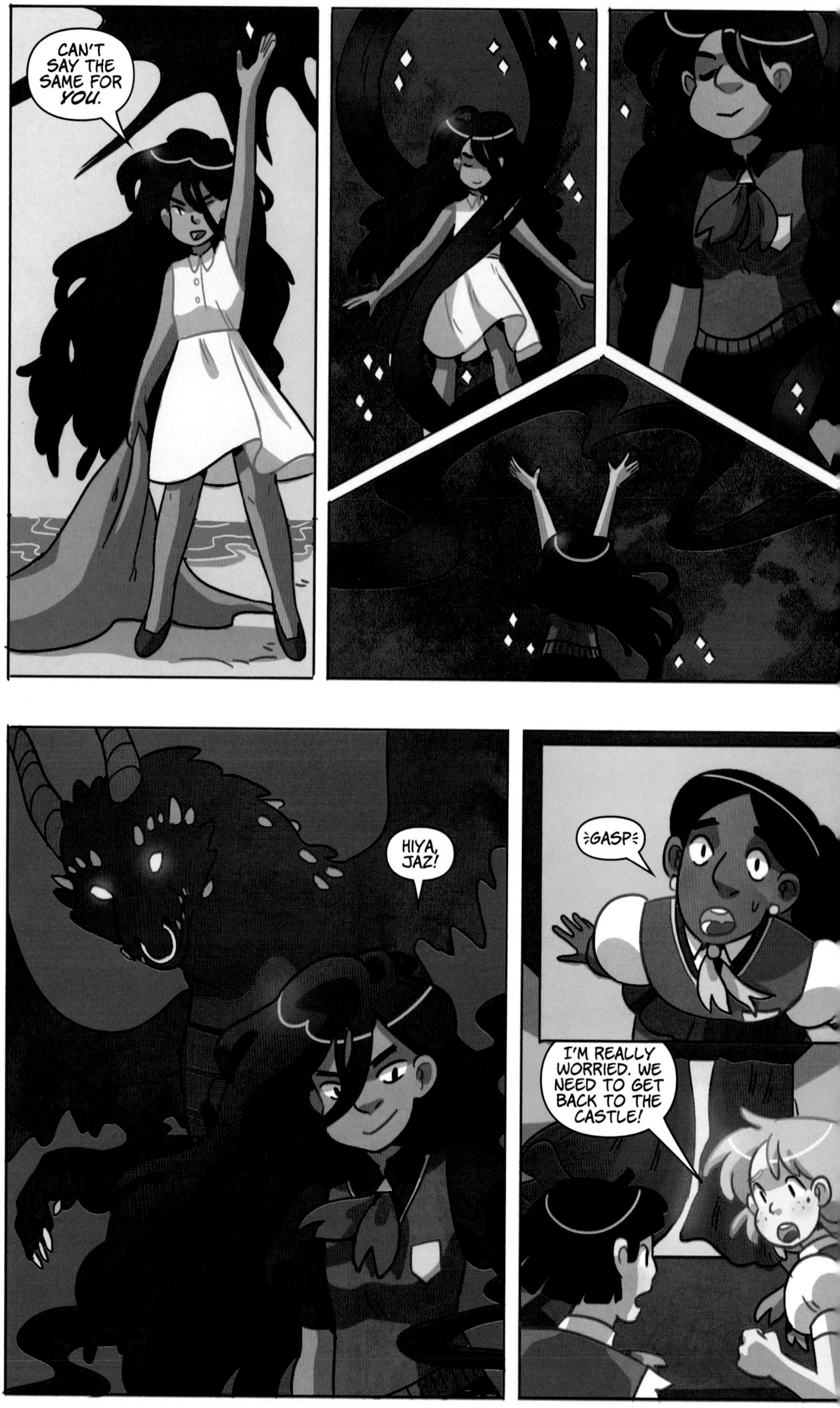
CAN'T SAY THE SAME FOR YOU.
HIYA, JAZ!
GASP
I'M REALLY WORRIED. WE NEED TO GET BACK TO THE CASTLE!

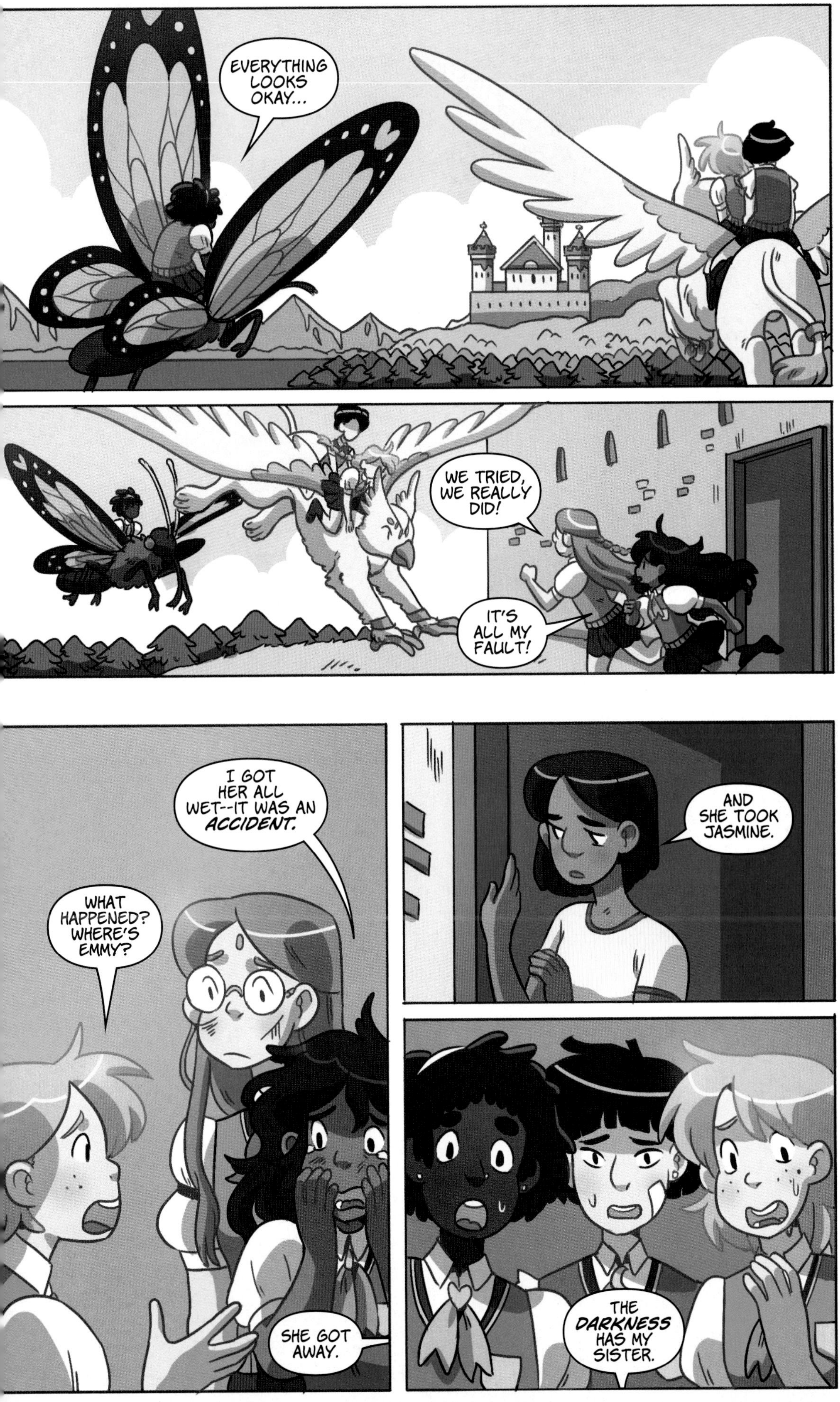
EVERYTHING LOOKS OKAY...
WE TRIED, WE REALLY DID!
IT'S ALL MY FAULT!
I GOT HER ALL WET--IT WAS AN *ACCIDENT.*
WHAT HAPPENED? WHERE'S EMMY?
SHE GOT AWAY.
AND SHE TOOK JASMINE.
THE *DARKNESS* HAS MY SISTER.

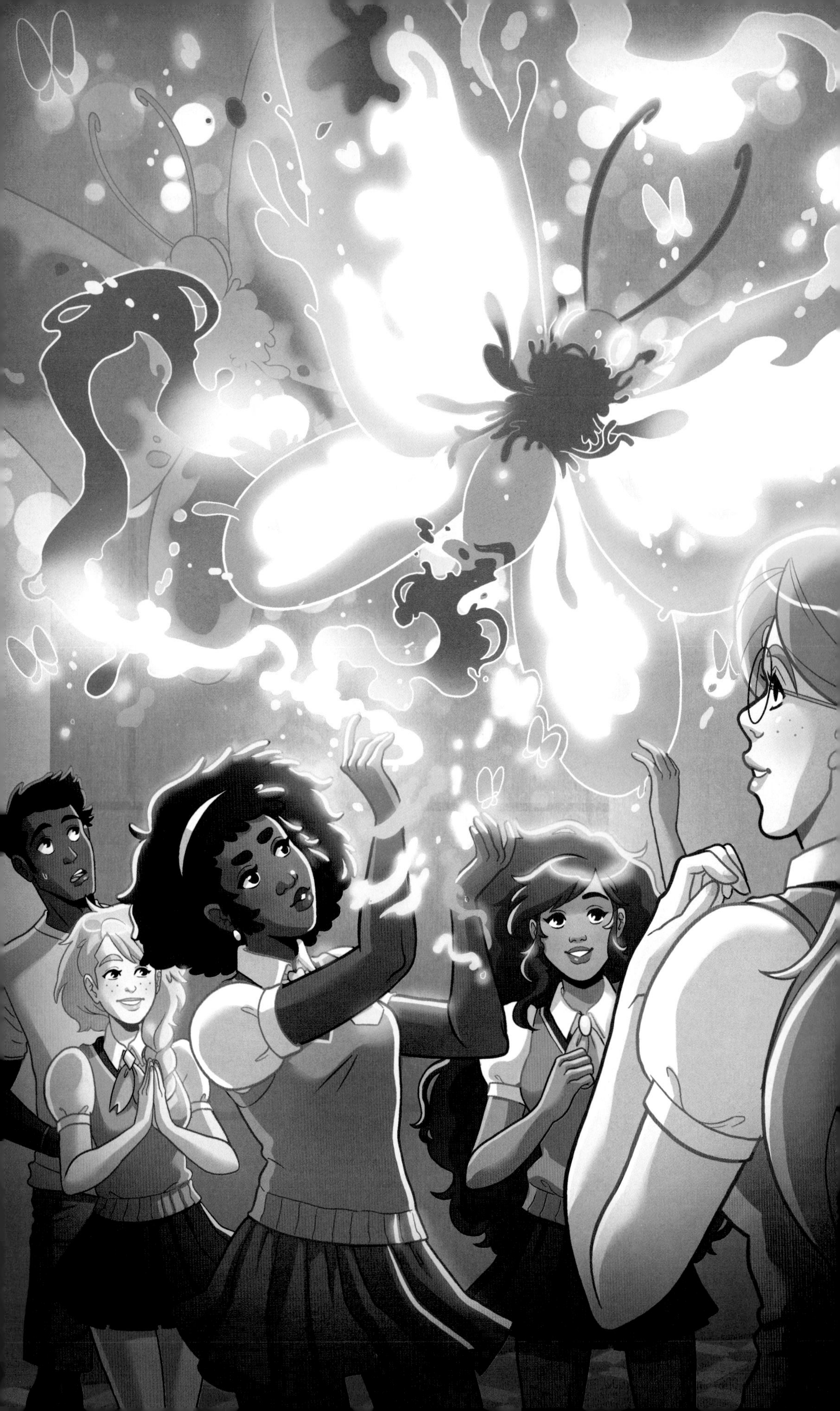

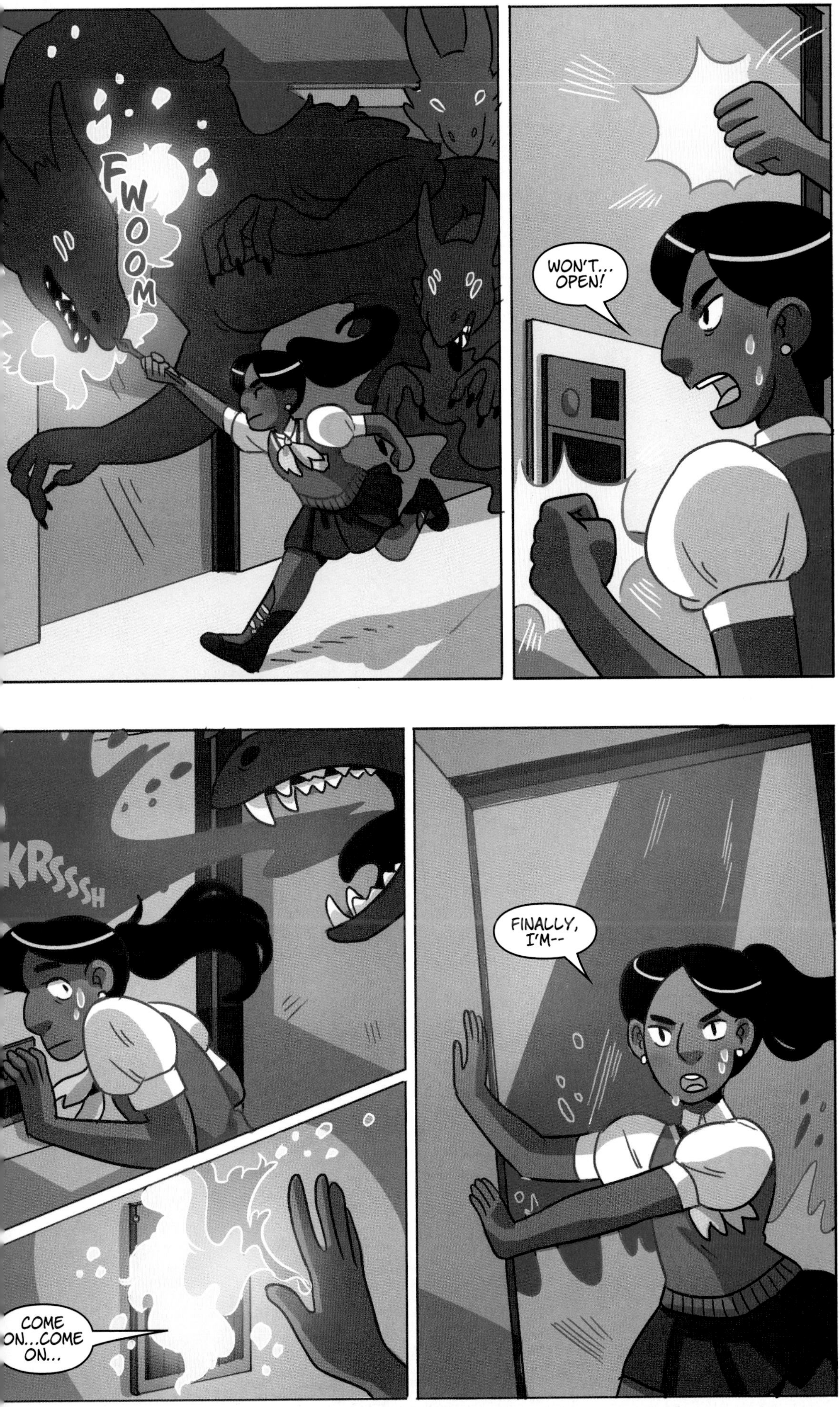
FWOOM
WON'T... OPEN!
KRSSSH
COME ON...COME ON...
FINALLY, I'M--

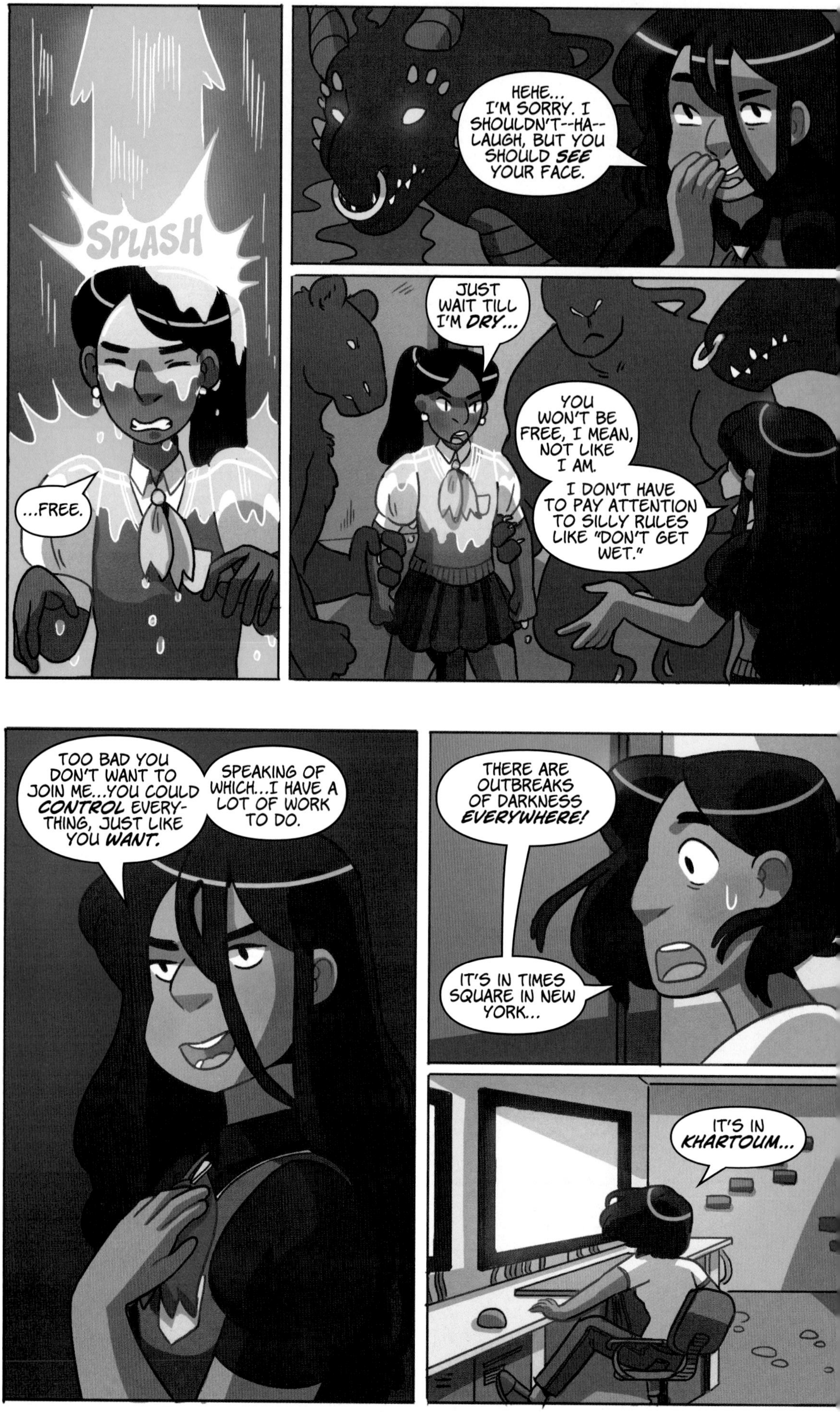
SPLASH
...FREE.
HEHE... I'M SORRY. I SHOULDN'T--HA--LAUGH, BUT YOU SHOULD SEE YOUR FACE.
JUST WAIT TILL I'M DRY...
YOU WON'T BE FREE, I MEAN, NOT LIKE I AM.
I DON'T HAVE TO PAY ATTENTION TO SILLY RULES LIKE "DON'T GET WET."
TOO BAD YOU DON'T WANT TO JOIN ME...YOU COULD CONTROL EVERYTHING, JUST LIKE YOU WANT.
SPEAKING OF WHICH...I HAVE A LOT OF WORK TO DO.
THERE ARE OUTBREAKS OF DARKNESS EVERYWHERE!
IT'S IN TIMES SQUARE IN NEW YORK...
IT'S IN KHARTOUM...

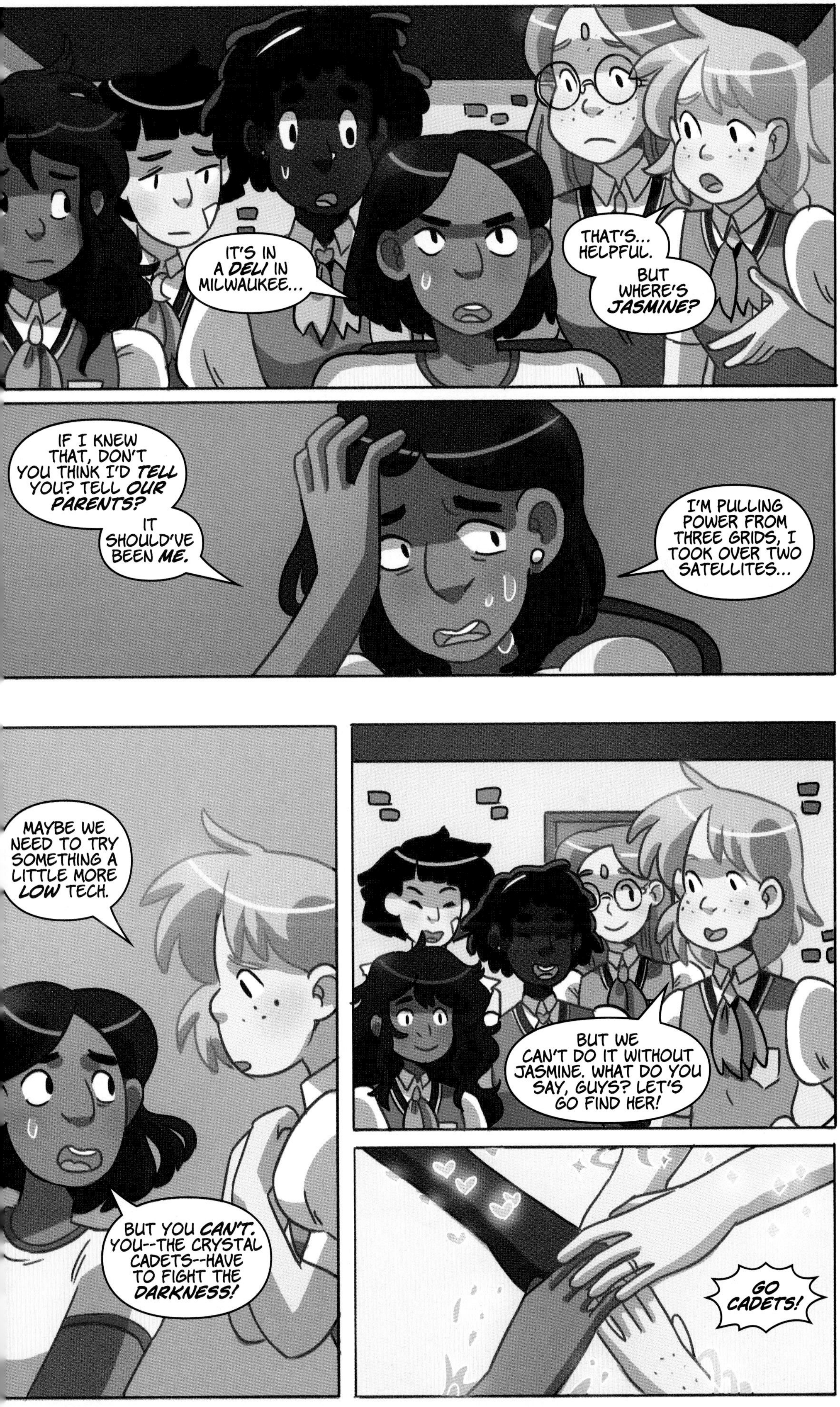
IT'S IN A DELI IN MILWAUKEE...
THAT'S... HELPFUL.
BUT WHERE'S JASMINE?
IF I KNEW THAT, DON'T YOU THINK I'D TELL YOU? TELL OUR PARENTS?
IT SHOULD'VE BEEN ME.
I'M PULLING POWER FROM THREE GRIDS, I TOOK OVER TWO SATELLITES...
MAYBE WE NEED TO TRY SOMETHING A LITTLE MORE LOW TECH.
BUT YOU CAN'T. YOU--THE CRYSTAL CADETS--HAVE TO FIGHT THE DARKNESS!
BUT WE CAN'T DO IT WITHOUT JASMINE. WHAT DO YOU SAY, GUYS? LET'S GO FIND HER!
GO CADETS!

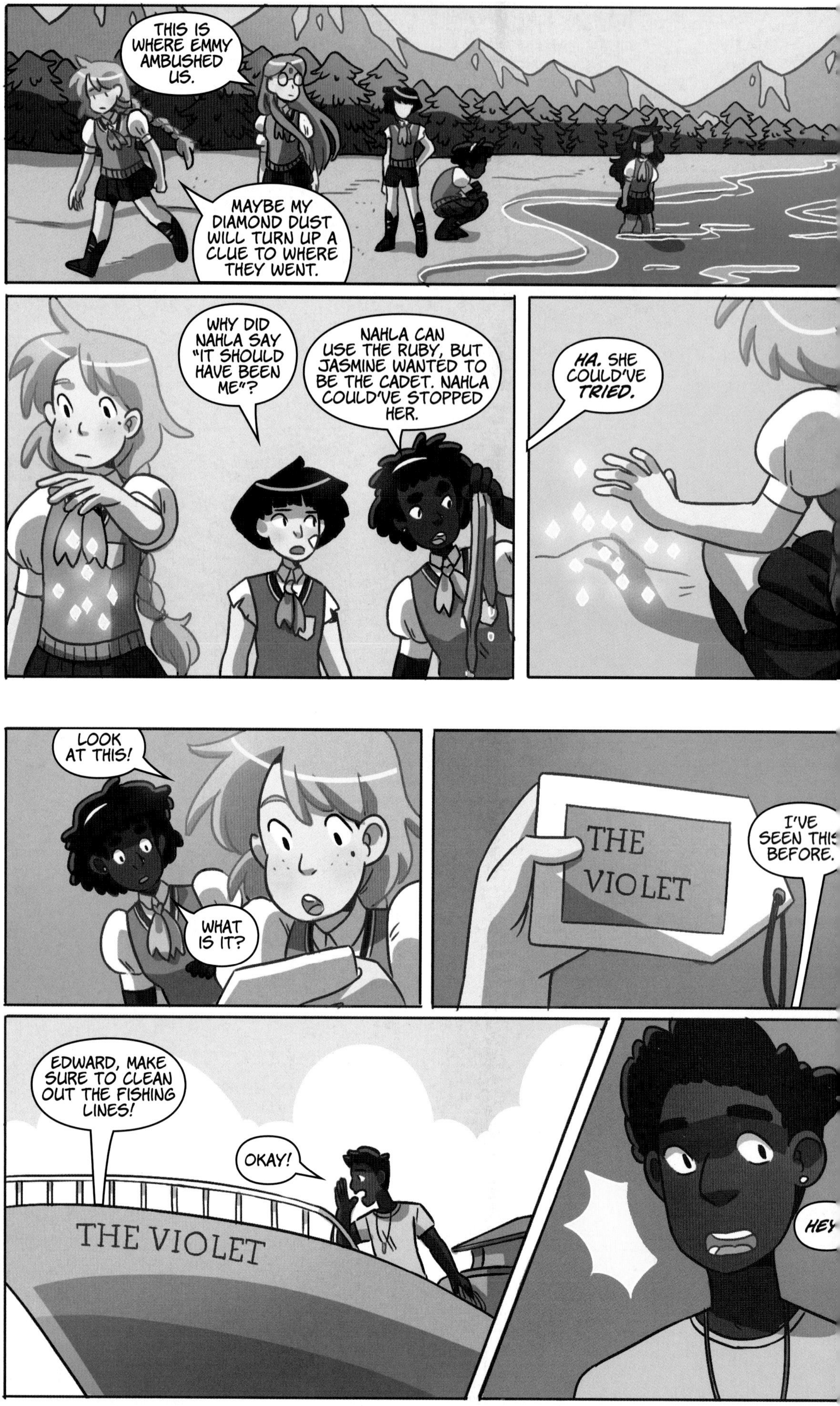
THIS IS WHERE EMMY AMBUSHED US.
MAYBE MY DIAMOND DUST WILL TURN UP A CLUE TO WHERE THEY WENT.
WHY DID NAHLA SAY "IT SHOULD HAVE BEEN ME"?
NAHLA CAN USE THE RUBY, BUT JASMINE WANTED TO BE THE CADET. NAHLA COULD'VE STOPPED HER.
HA. SHE COULD'VE TRIED.
LOOK AT THIS!
WHAT IS IT?
THE VIOLET
I'VE SEEN THIS BEFORE.
EDWARD, MAKE SURE TO CLEAN OUT THE FISHING LINES!
OKAY!
THE VIOLET

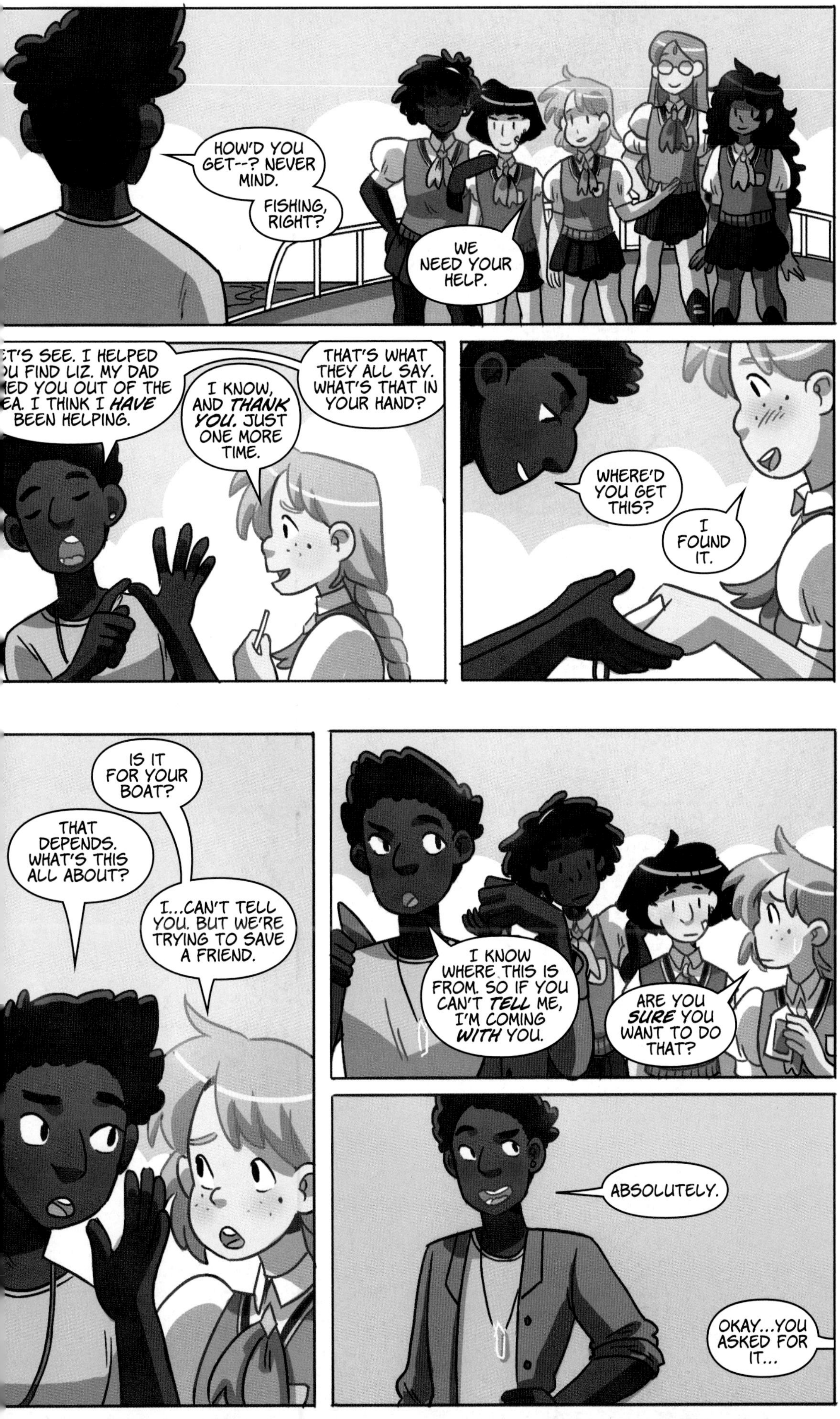
HOW'D YOU GET--? NEVER MIND.
FISHING, RIGHT?
WE NEED YOUR HELP.
T'S SEE. I HELPED U FIND LIZ. MY DAD ED YOU OUT OF THE EA. I THINK I HAVE BEEN HELPING.
I KNOW, AND THANK YOU. JUST ONE MORE TIME.
THAT'S WHAT THEY ALL SAY. WHAT'S THAT IN YOUR HAND?
WHERE'D YOU GET THIS?
I FOUND IT.
IS IT FOR YOUR BOAT?
THAT DEPENDS. WHAT'S THIS ALL ABOUT?
I...CAN'T TELL YOU. BUT WE'RE TRYING TO SAVE A FRIEND.
I KNOW WHERE THIS IS FROM. SO IF YOU CAN'T TELL ME, I'M COMING WITH YOU.
ARE YOU SURE YOU WANT TO DO THAT?
ABSOLUTELY.
OKAY...YOU ASKED FOR IT...

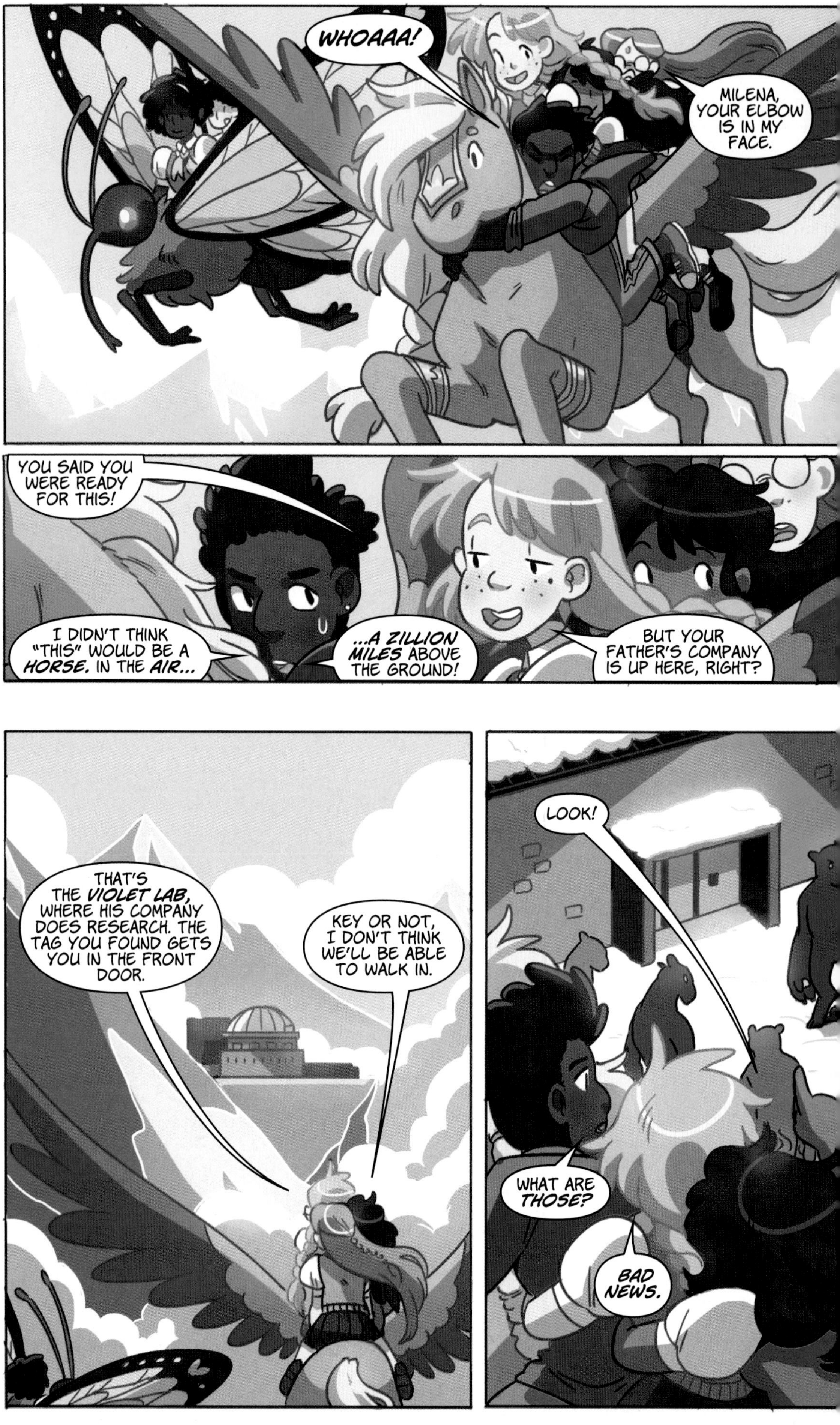

WHOAAA!
MILENA, YOUR ELBOW IS IN MY FACE.
YOU SAID YOU WERE READY FOR THIS!
I DIDN'T THINK "THIS" WOULD BE A HORSE. IN THE AIR...
...A ZILLION MILES ABOVE THE GROUND!
BUT YOUR FATHER'S COMPANY IS UP HERE, RIGHT?
THAT'S THE VIOLET LAB, WHERE HIS COMPANY DOES RESEARCH. THE TAG YOU FOUND GETS YOU IN THE FRONT DOOR.
KEY OR NOT, I DON'T THINK WE'LL BE ABLE TO WALK IN.
LOOK!
WHAT ARE THOSE?
BAD NEWS.

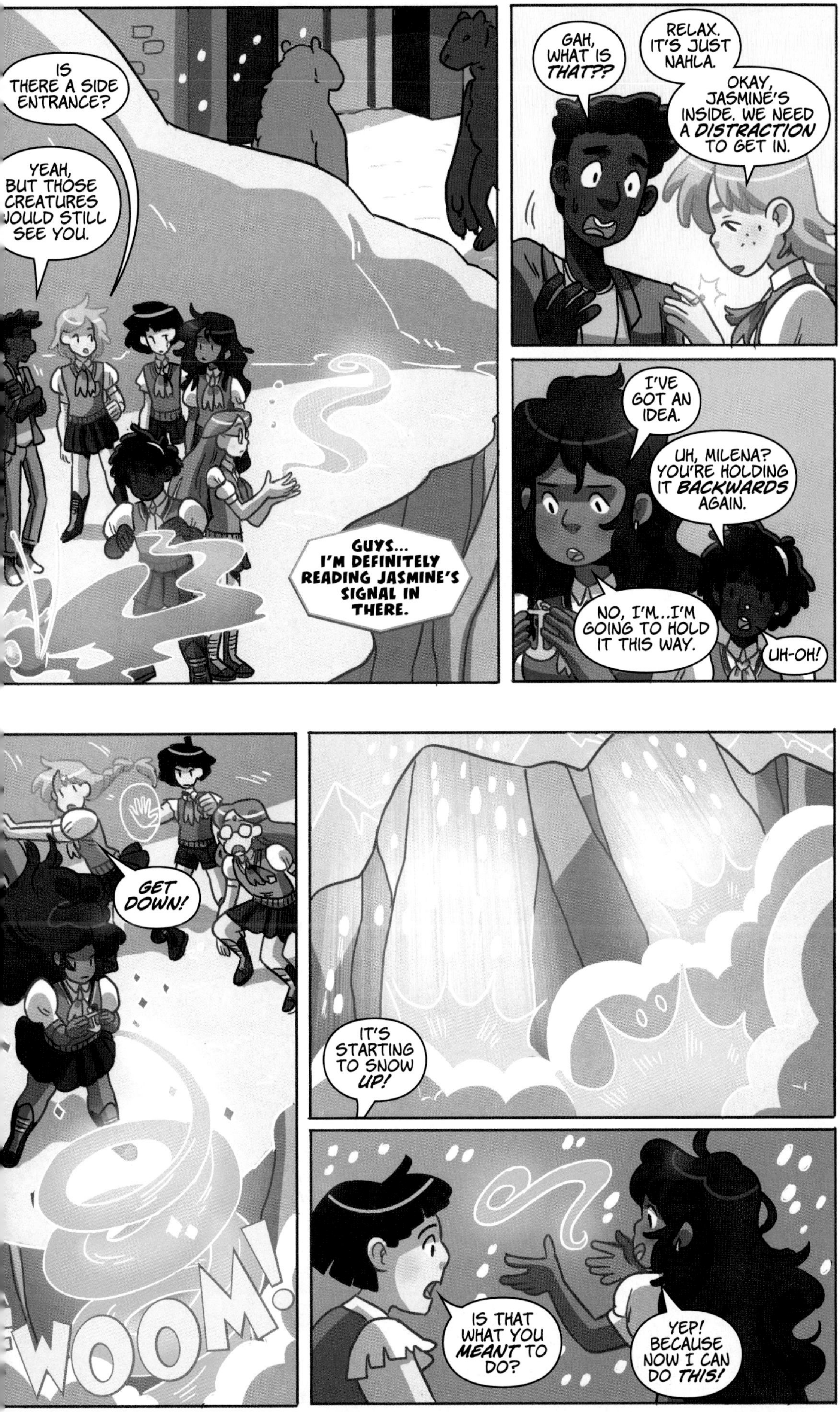
IS THERE A SIDE ENTRANCE?
YEAH, BUT THOSE CREATURES WOULD STILL SEE YOU.
GUYS... I'M DEFINITELY READING JASMINE'S SIGNAL IN THERE.
GAH, WHAT IS *THAT??*
RELAX. IT'S JUST NAHLA.
OKAY, JASMINE'S INSIDE. WE NEED A *DISTRACTION* TO GET IN.
I'VE GOT AN IDEA.
UH, MILENA? YOU'RE HOLDING IT *BACKWARDS* AGAIN.
NO, I'M...I'M GOING TO HOLD IT THIS WAY.
UH-OH!
GET DOWN!
WOOM!
IT'S STARTING TO SNOW *UP!*
IS THAT WHAT YOU *MEANT* TO DO?
YEP! BECAUSE NOW I CAN DO *THIS!*

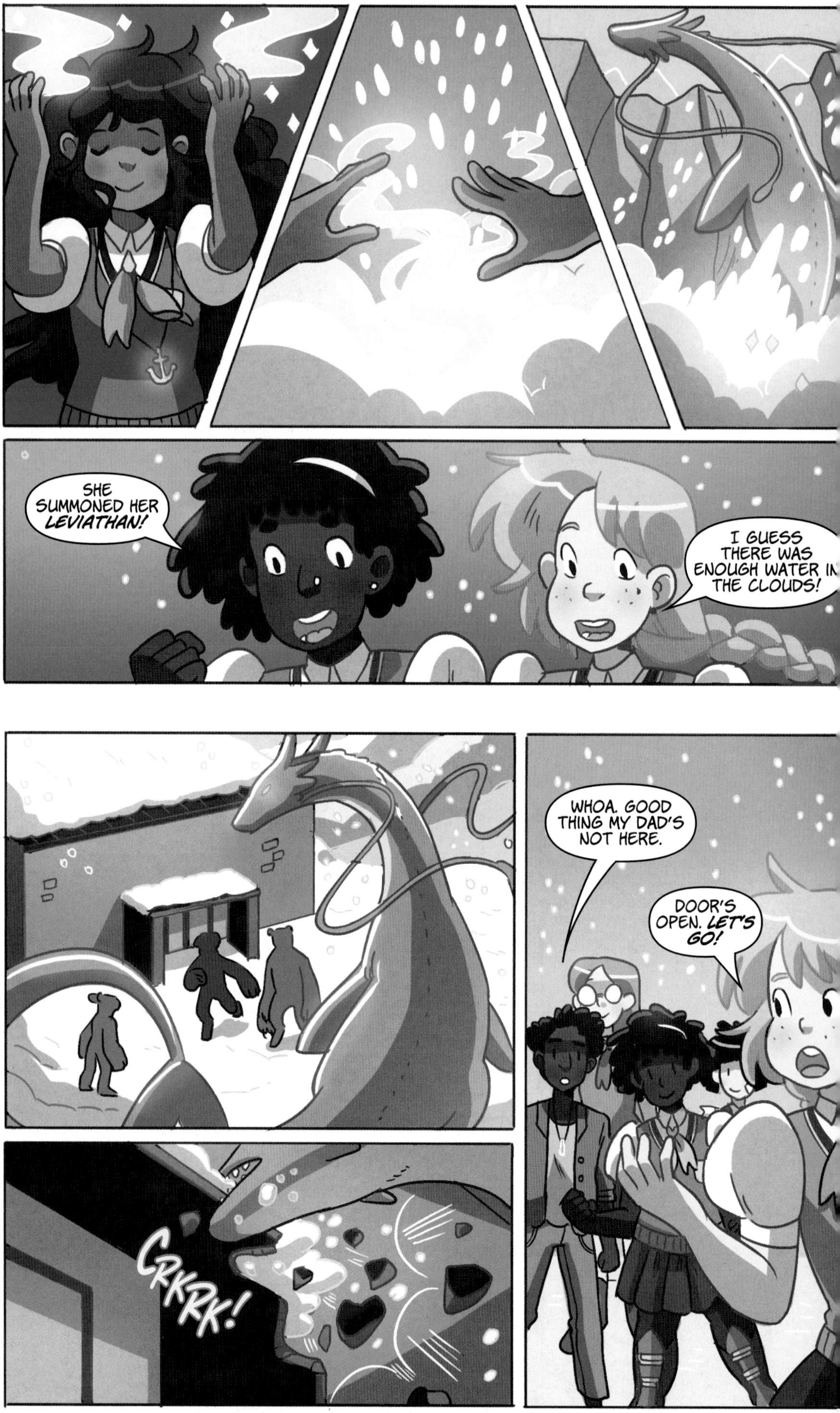
SHE SUMMONED HER LEVIATHAN!
I GUESS THERE WAS ENOUGH WATER IN THE CLOUDS!
CRKRK!
WHOA. GOOD THING MY DAD'S NOT HERE.
DOOR'S OPEN. LET'S GO!

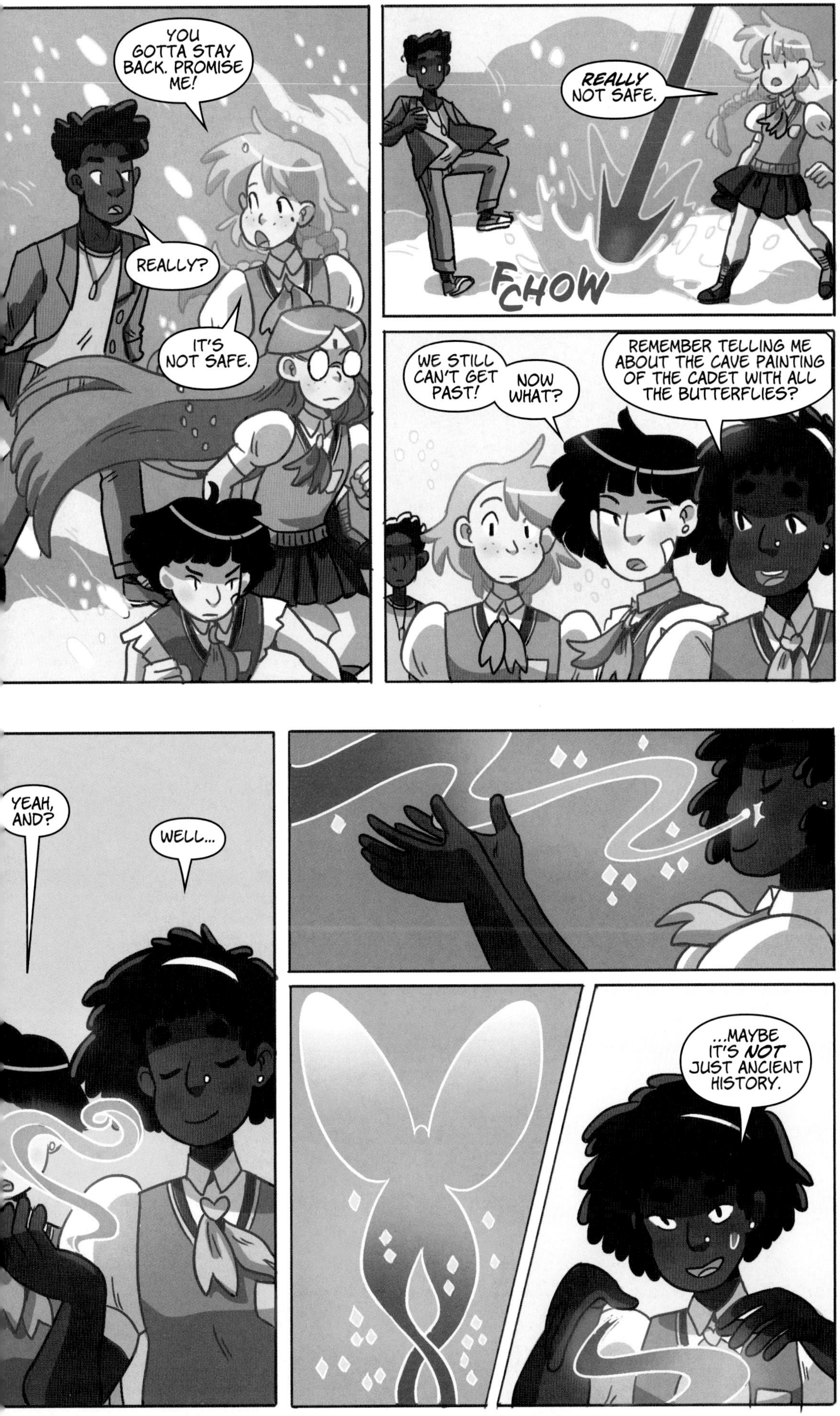
YOU GOTTA STAY BACK. PROMISE ME!
REALLY?
IT'S NOT SAFE.
REALLY NOT SAFE.
FCHOW
WE STILL CAN'T GET PAST!
NOW WHAT?
REMEMBER TELLING ME ABOUT THE CAVE PAINTING OF THE CADET WITH ALL THE BUTTERFLIES?
YEAH, AND?
WELL...
...MAYBE IT'S *NOT* JUST ANCIENT HISTORY.

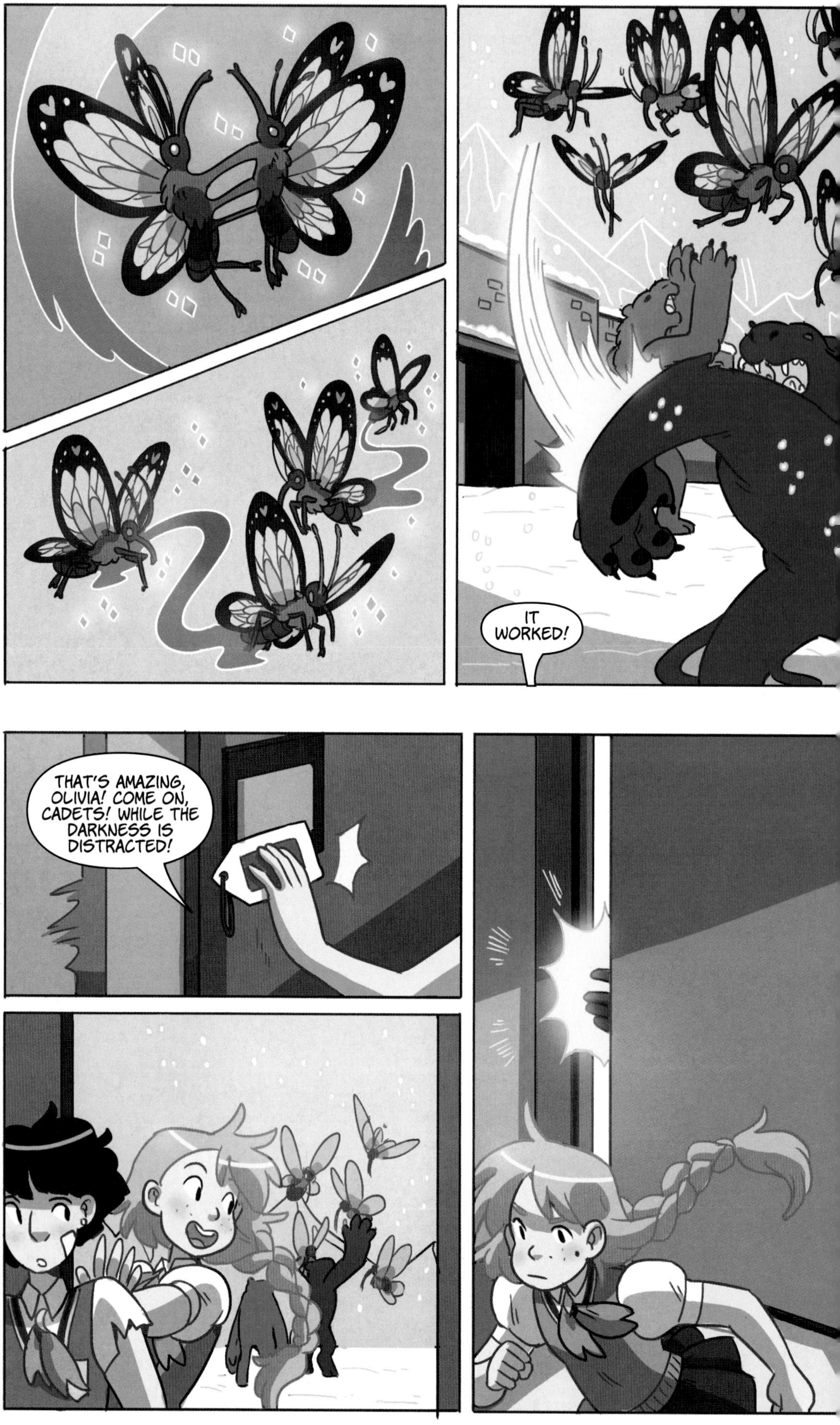
IT WORKED!
THAT'S AMAZING, OLIVIA! COME ON, CADETS! WHILE THE DARKNESS IS DISTRACTED!

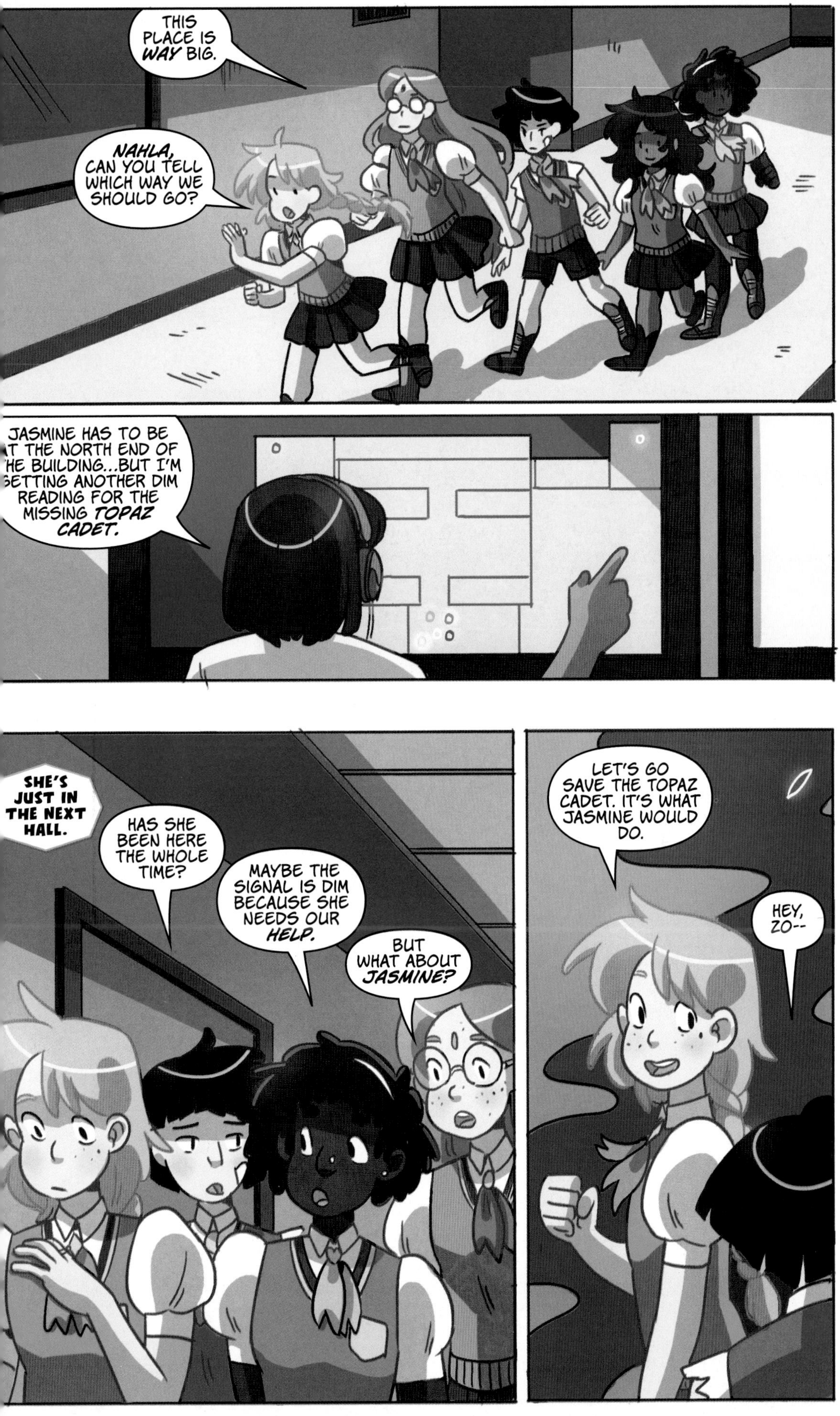

THIS PLACE IS WAY BIG.
NAHLA, CAN YOU TELL WHICH WAY WE SHOULD GO?
JASMINE HAS TO BE AT THE NORTH END OF THE BUILDING...BUT I'M GETTING ANOTHER DIM READING FOR THE MISSING TOPAZ CADET.
SHE'S JUST IN THE NEXT HALL.
HAS SHE BEEN HERE THE WHOLE TIME?
MAYBE THE SIGNAL IS DIM BECAUSE SHE NEEDS OUR HELP.
BUT WHAT ABOUT JASMINE?
LET'S GO SAVE THE TOPAZ CADET. IT'S WHAT JASMINE WOULD DO.
HEY, ZO--

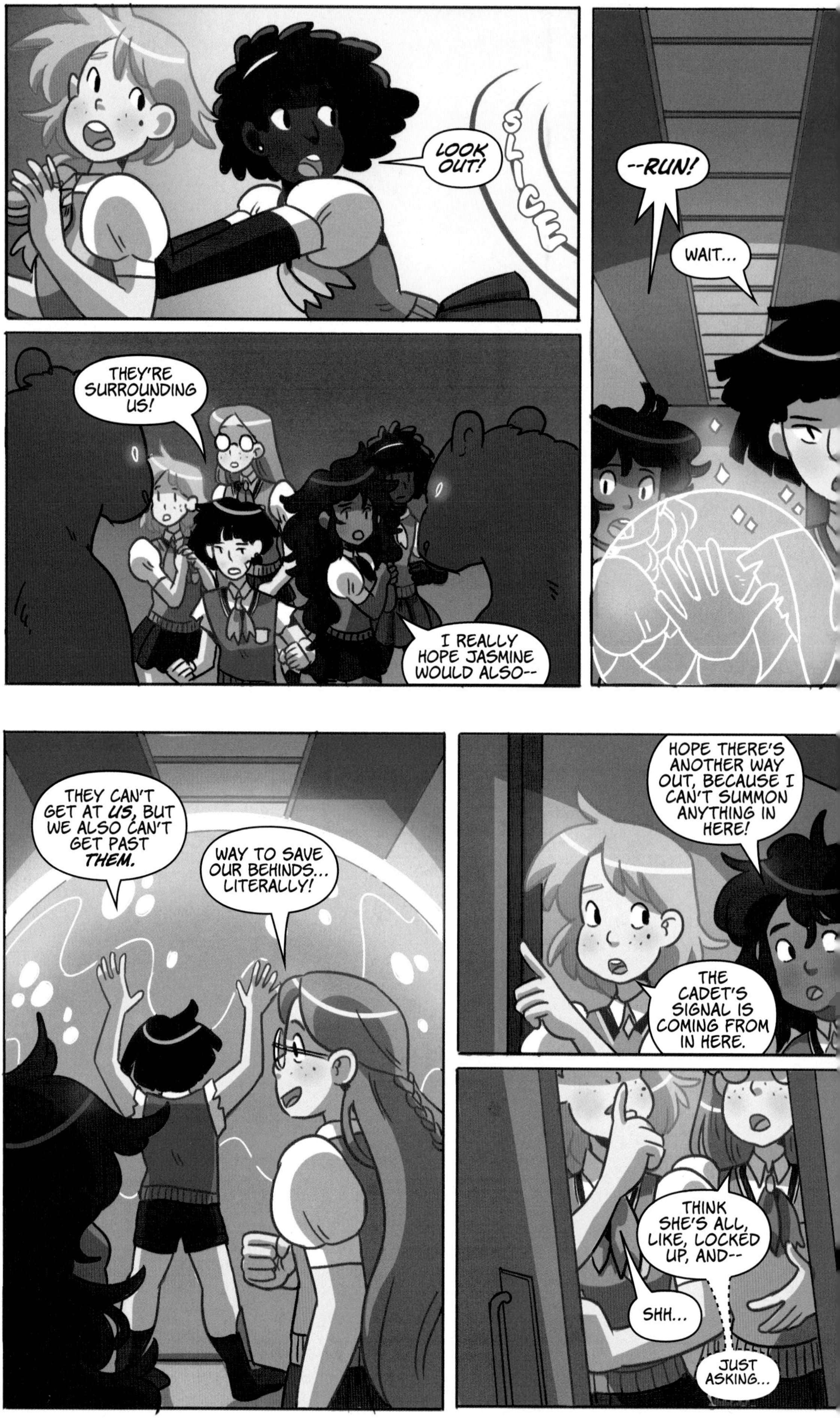
LOOK OUT!
SLICE
--RUN!
WAIT...
THEY'RE SURROUNDING US!
I REALLY HOPE JASMINE WOULD ALSO--
THEY CAN'T GET AT *US*, BUT WE ALSO CAN'T GET PAST *THEM.*
WAY TO SAVE OUR BEHINDS... LITERALLY!
HOPE THERE'S ANOTHER WAY OUT, BECAUSE I CAN'T SUMMON ANYTHING IN HERE!
THE CADET'S SIGNAL IS COMING FROM IN HERE.
THINK SHE'S ALL, LIKE, LOCKED UP, AND--
SHH...
JUST ASKING...

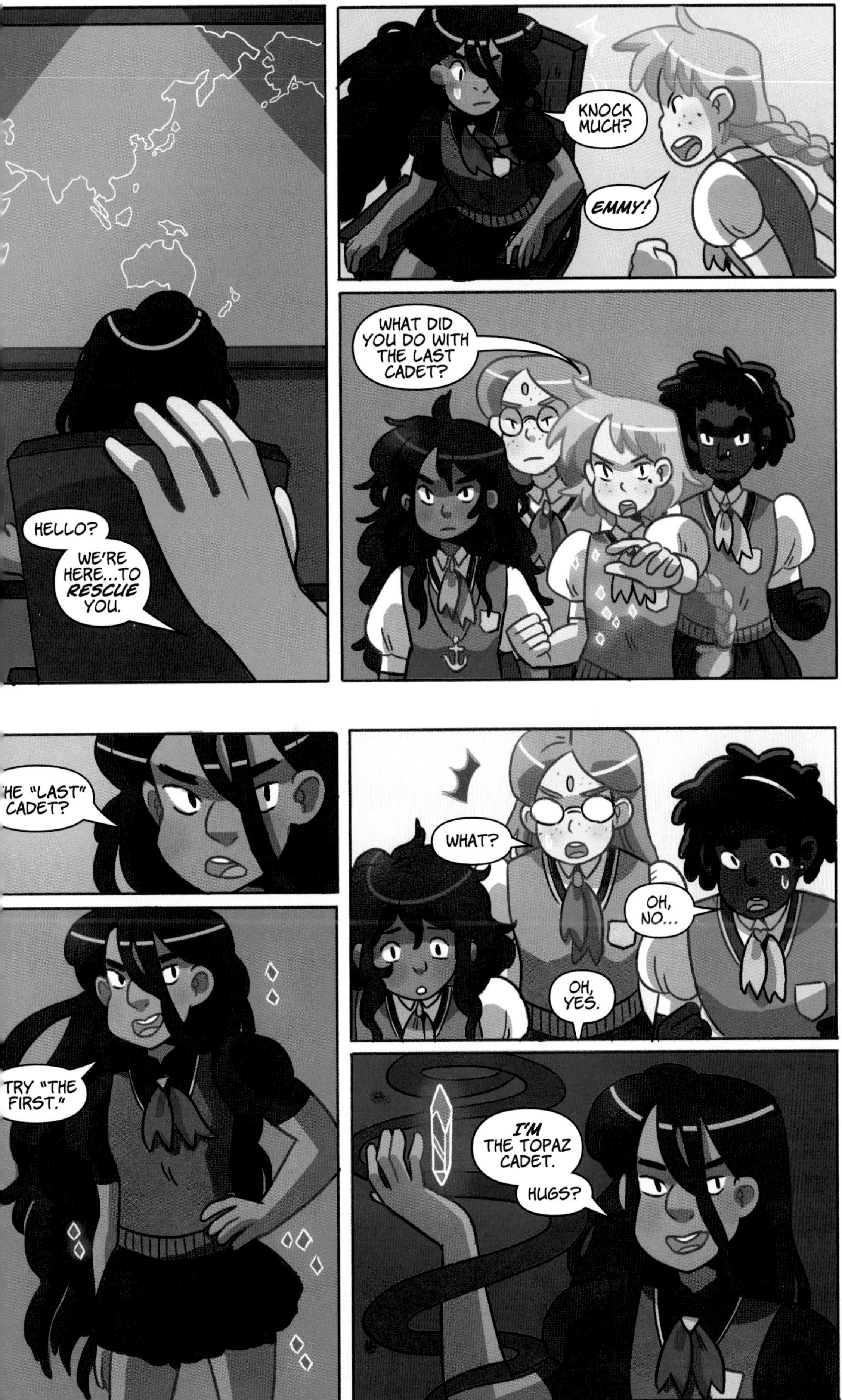
HELLO?
WE'RE HERE...TO RESCUE YOU.
KNOCK MUCH?
EMMY!
WHAT DID YOU DO WITH THE LAST CADET?
HE "LAST" CADET?
TRY "THE FIRST."
WHAT?
OH, NO...
OH, YES.
I'M THE TOPAZ CADET.
HUGS?

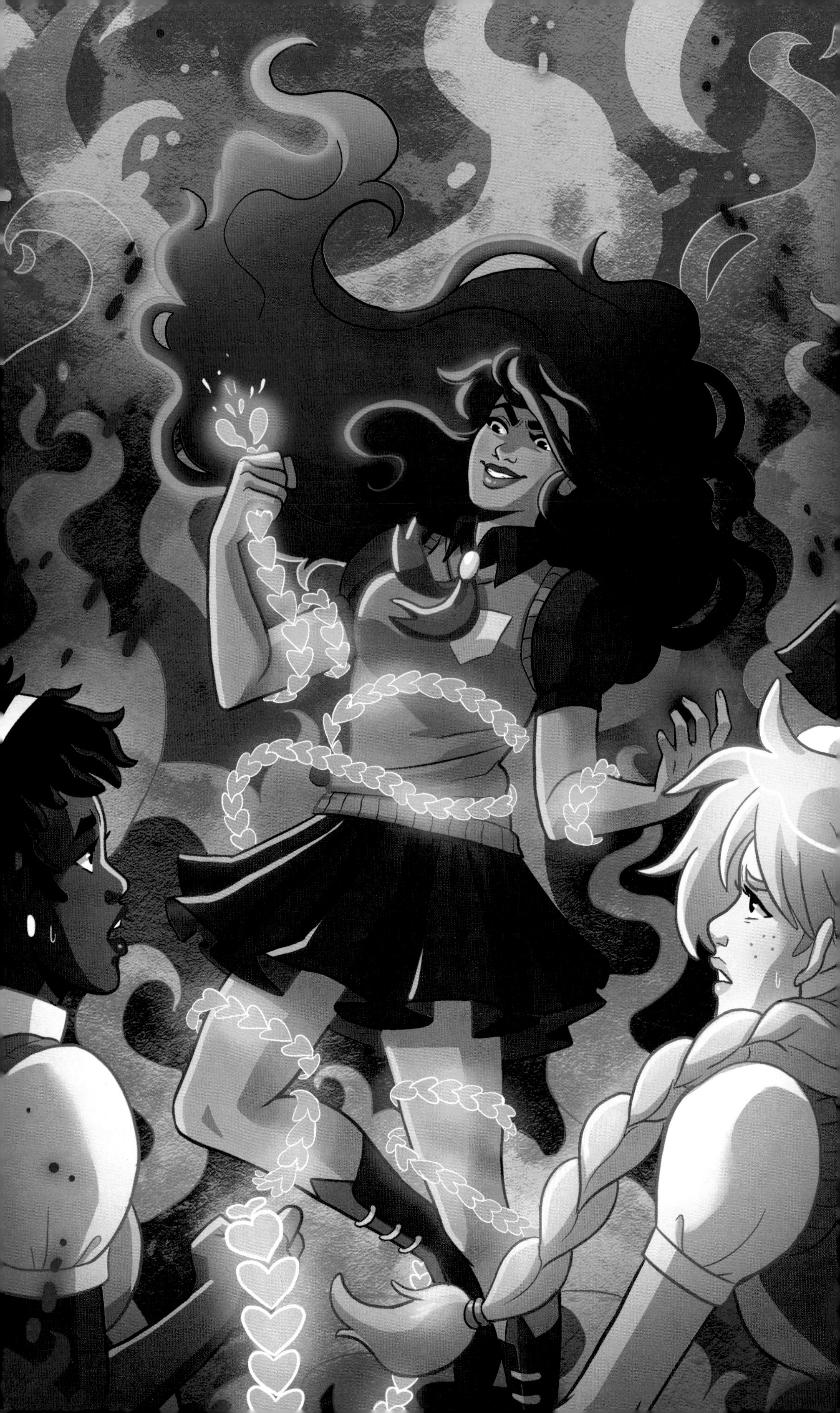

BUT... YOU **CAN'T** BE THE TOPAZ CADET. YOU CONTROL THE DARKNESS.

I KNOW. *COOL, HUH?*

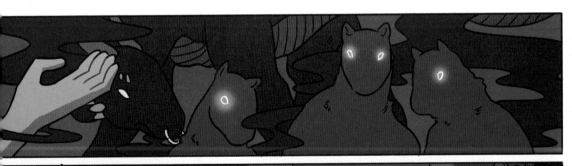

AND *YOU* CAN ONLY SUMMON ONE OF YOURS AT A TIME. *JEALOUS?*

ON MY MARK, CADETS...

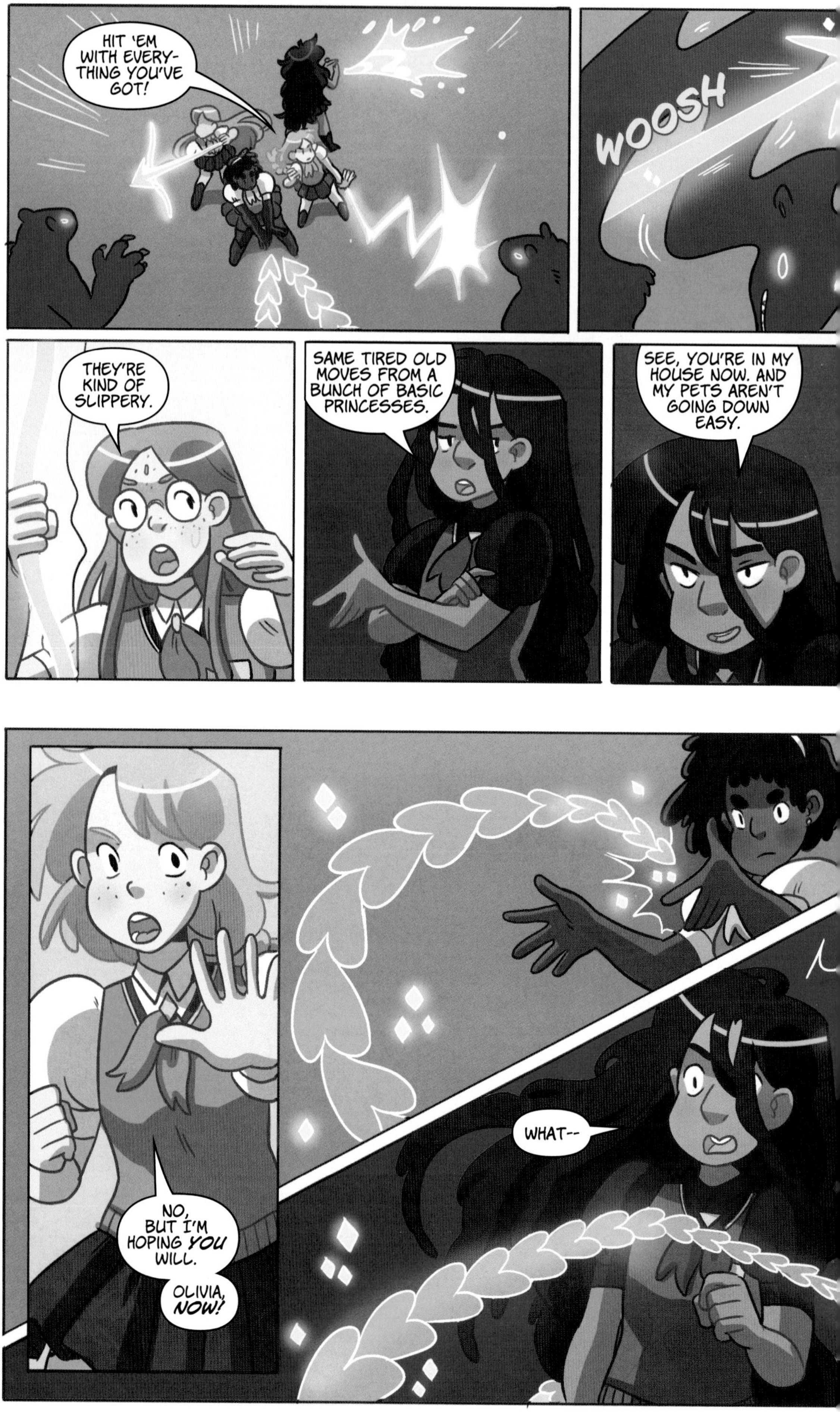
HIT 'EM WITH EVERY-THING YOU'VE GOT!
WOOSH
THEY'RE KIND OF SLIPPERY.
SAME TIRED OLD MOVES FROM A BUNCH OF BASIC PRINCESSES.
SEE, YOU'RE IN MY HOUSE NOW. AND MY PETS AREN'T GOING DOWN EASY.
NO, BUT I'M HOPING *YOU* WILL.
OLIVIA, *NOW!*
WHAT--

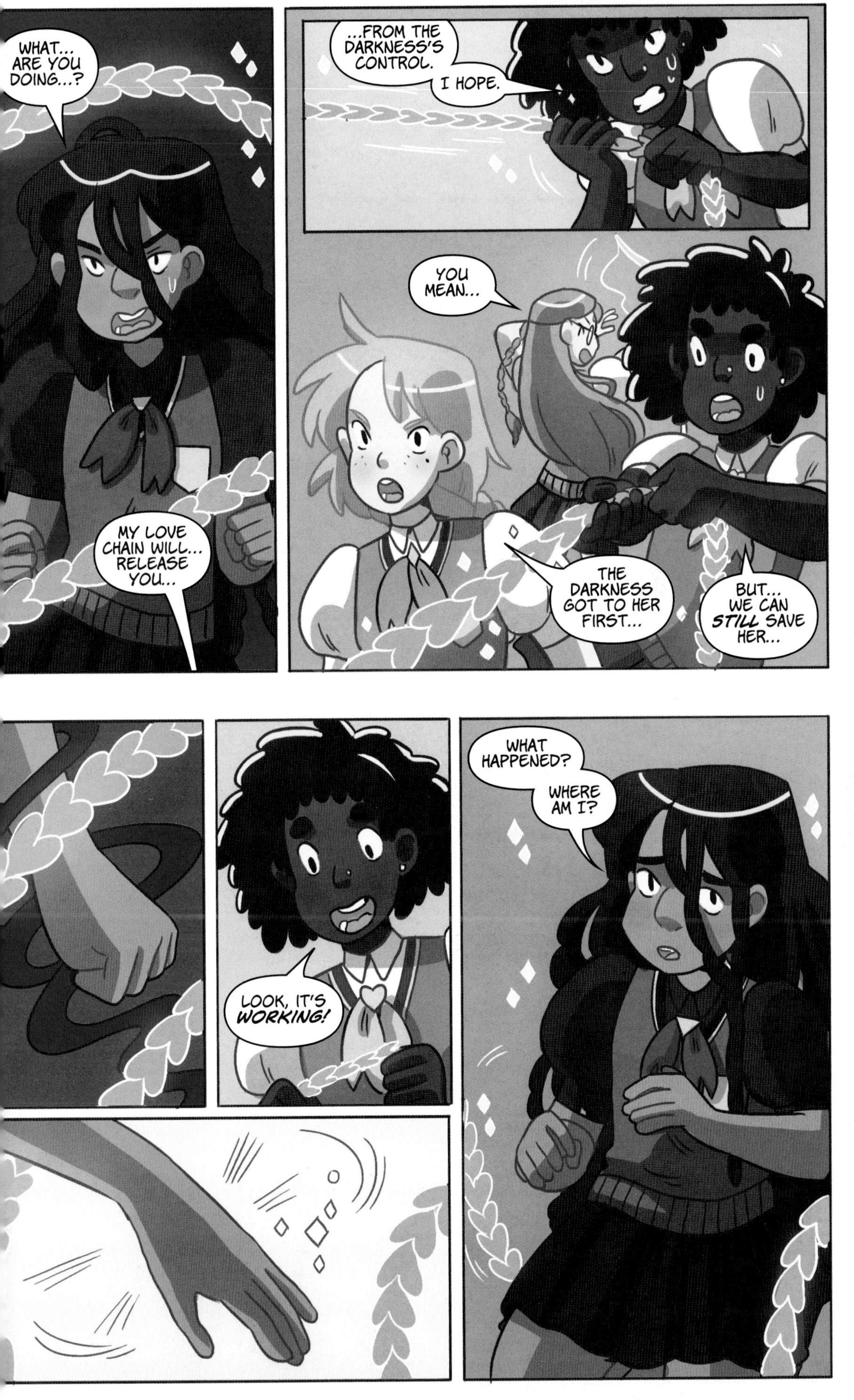
WHAT... ARE YOU DOING...?
MY LOVE CHAIN WILL... RELEASE YOU...
...FROM THE DARKNESS'S CONTROL.
I HOPE.
YOU MEAN...
THE DARKNESS GOT TO HER FIRST...
BUT... WE CAN *STILL* SAVE HER...
LOOK, IT'S *WORKING!*
WHAT HAPPENED?
WHERE AM I?

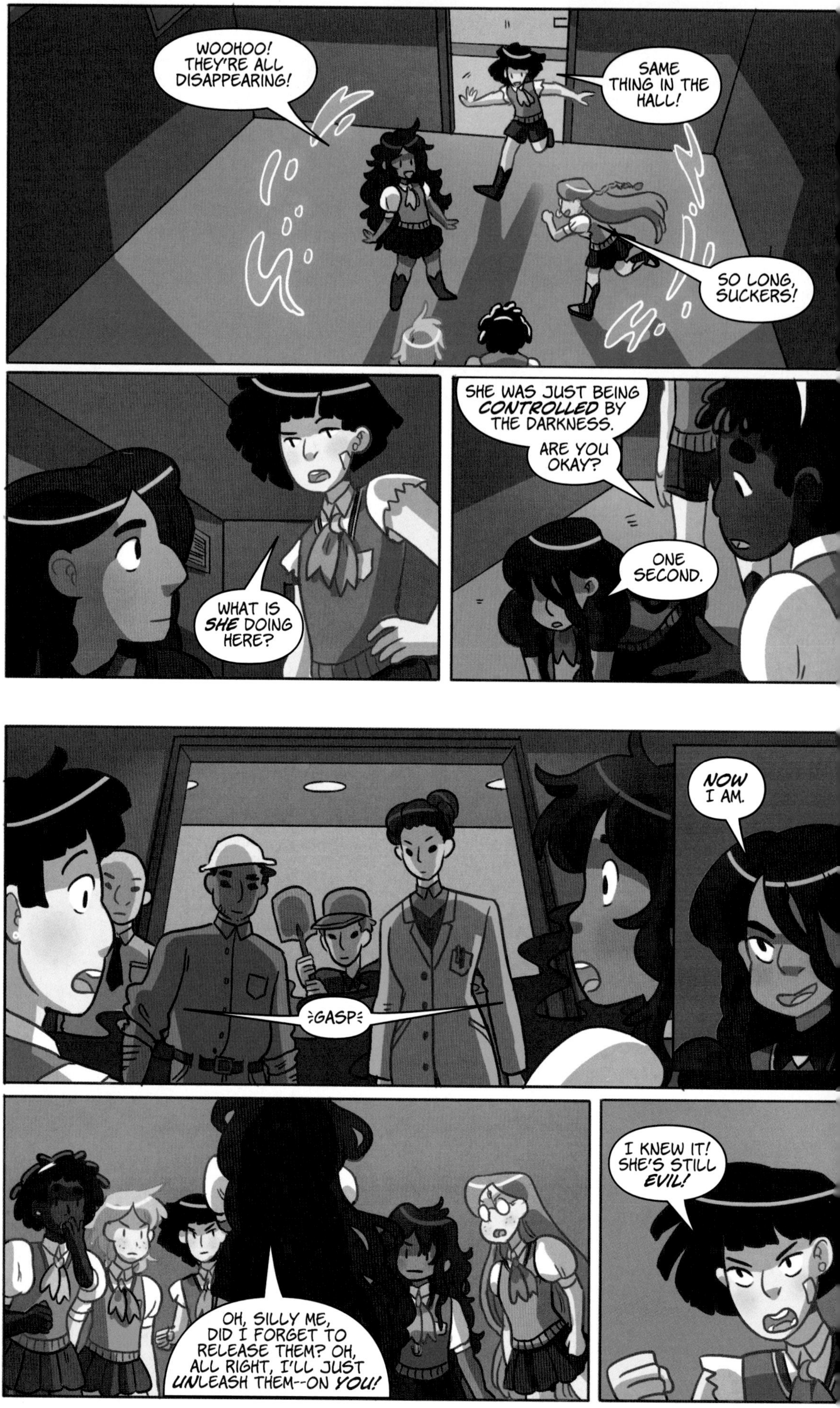
WOOHOO! THEY'RE ALL DISAPPEARING!
SAME THING IN THE HALL!
SO LONG, SUCKERS!
WHAT IS SHE DOING HERE?
SHE WAS JUST BEING CONTROLLED BY THE DARKNESS.
ARE YOU OKAY?
ONE SECOND.
GASP
NOW I AM.
OH, SILLY ME, DID I FORGET TO RELEASE THEM? OH, ALL RIGHT, I'LL JUST UNLEASH THEM--ON YOU!
I KNEW IT! SHE'S STILL EVIL!

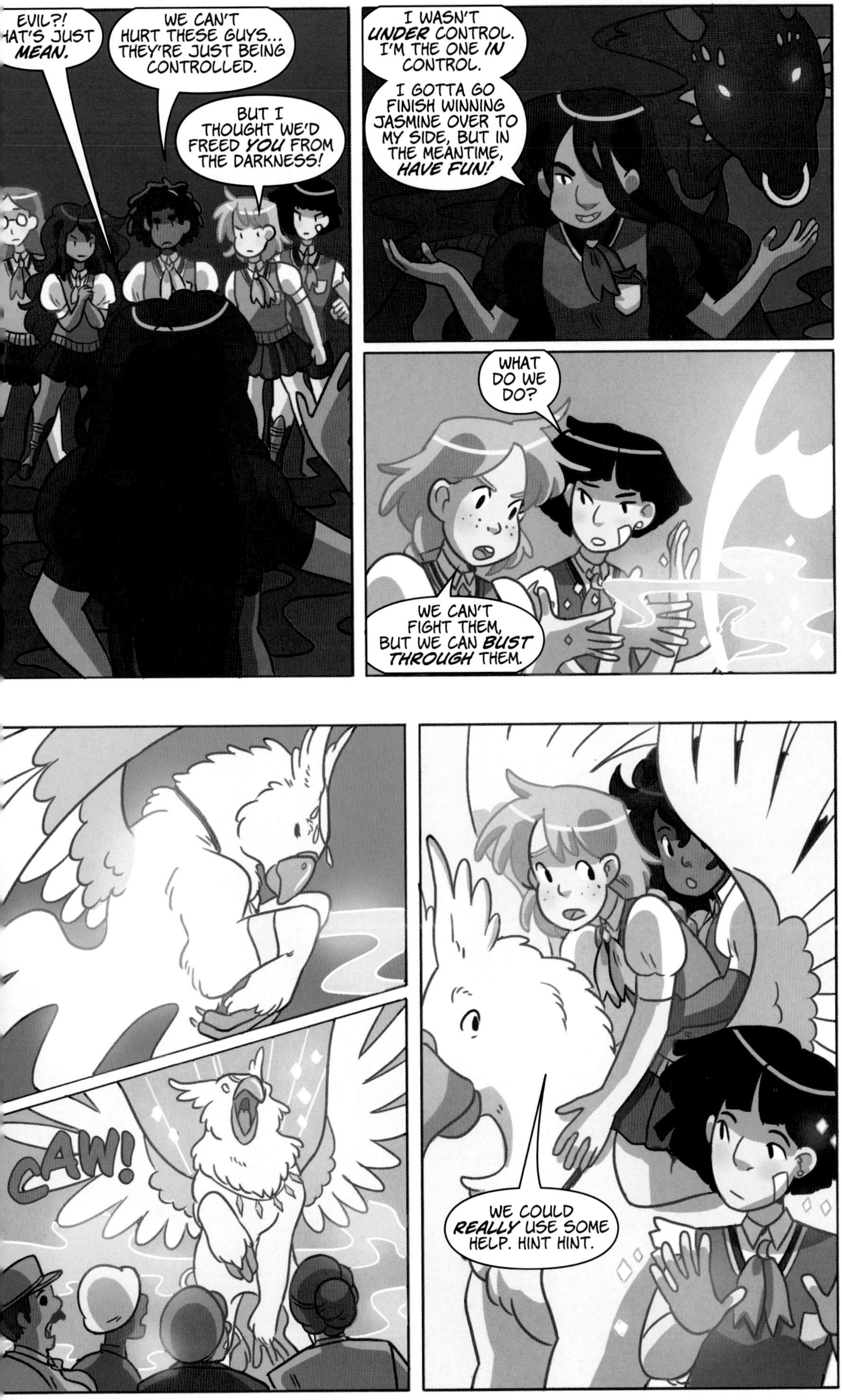
EVIL?! HAT'S JUST MEAN.
WE CAN'T HURT THESE GUYS... THEY'RE JUST BEING CONTROLLED.
BUT I THOUGHT WE'D FREED YOU FROM THE DARKNESS!
I WASN'T UNDER CONTROL. I'M THE ONE IN CONTROL.
I GOTTA GO FINISH WINNING JASMINE OVER TO MY SIDE, BUT IN THE MEANTIME, HAVE FUN!
WHAT DO WE DO?
WE CAN'T FIGHT THEM, BUT WE CAN BUST THROUGH THEM.
CAW!
WE COULD REALLY USE SOME HELP. HINT HINT.

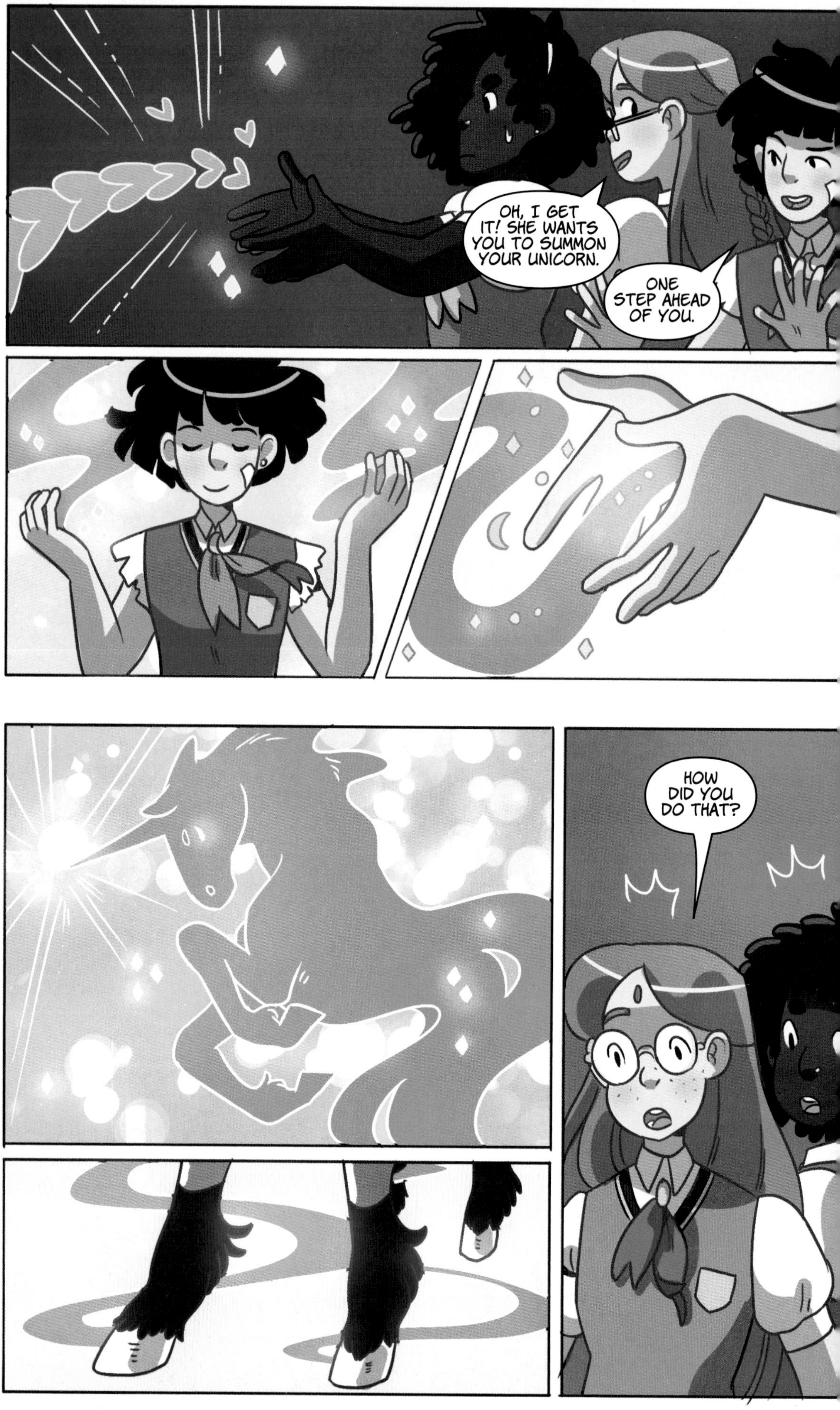
OH, I GET IT! SHE WANTS YOU TO SUMMON YOUR UNICORN.
ONE STEP AHEAD OF YOU.
HOW DID YOU DO THAT?

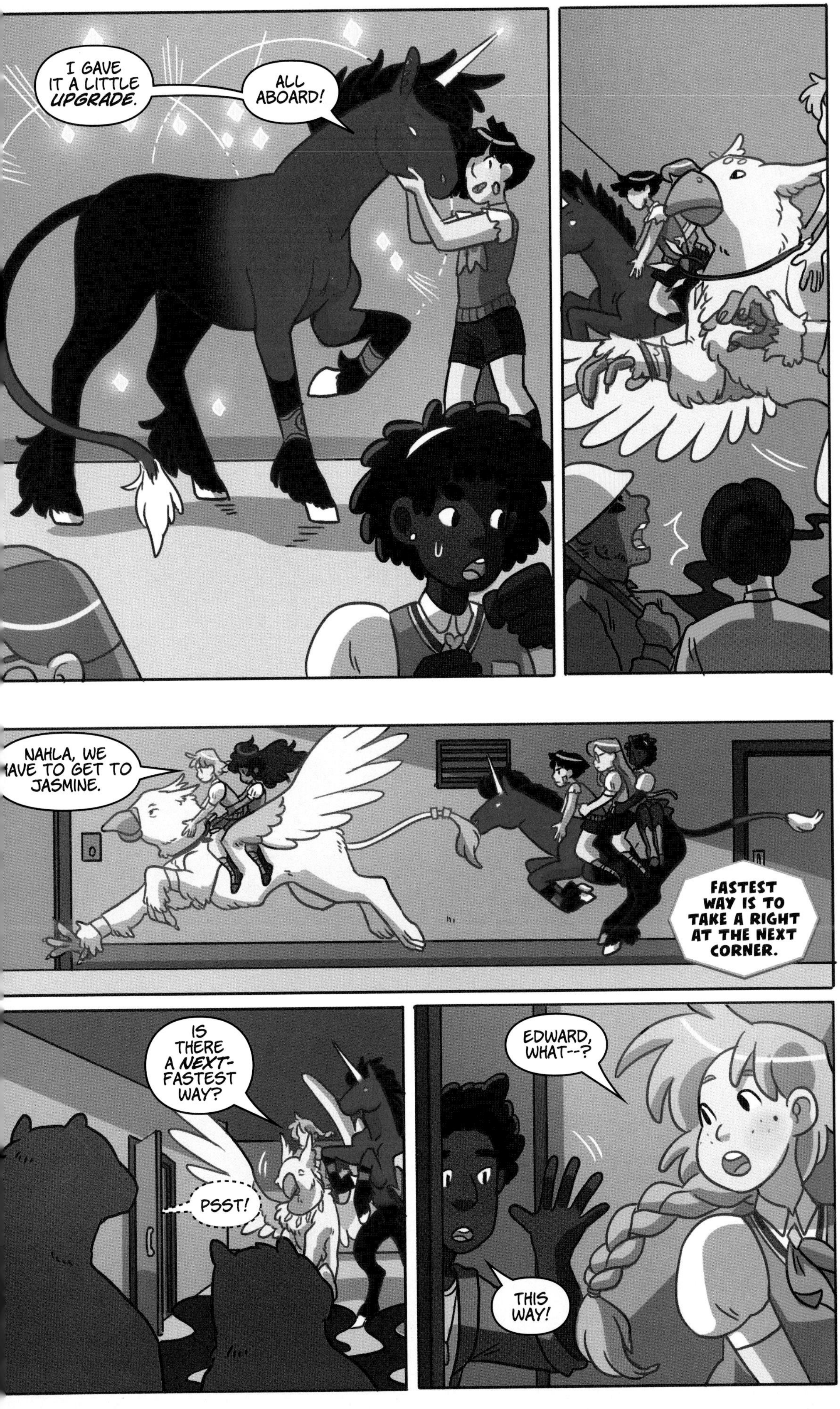
I GAVE IT A LITTLE *UPGRADE*.
ALL ABOARD!
NAHLA, WE HAVE TO GET TO JASMINE.
FASTEST WAY IS TO TAKE A RIGHT AT THE NEXT CORNER.
IS THERE A *NEXT*-FASTEST WAY?
PSST!
EDWARD, WHAT--?
THIS WAY!

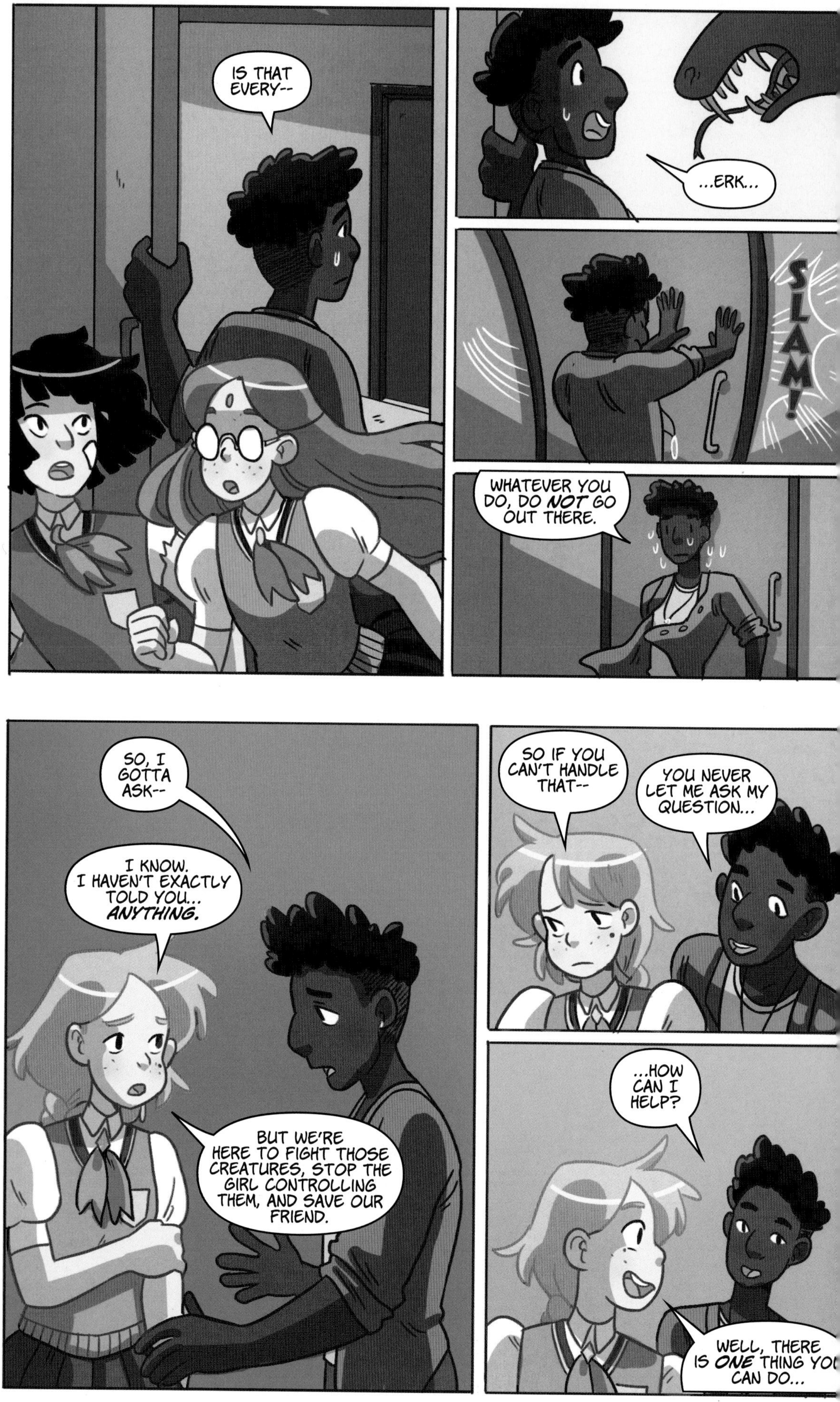
IS THAT EVERY--
...ERK...
SLAM!
WHATEVER YOU DO, DO NOT GO OUT THERE.
SO, I GOTTA ASK--
I KNOW. I HAVEN'T EXACTLY TOLD YOU... ANYTHING.
BUT WE'RE HERE TO FIGHT THOSE CREATURES, STOP THE GIRL CONTROLLING THEM, AND SAVE OUR FRIEND.
SO IF YOU CAN'T HANDLE THAT--
YOU NEVER LET ME ASK MY QUESTION...
...HOW CAN I HELP?
WELL, THERE IS ONE THING YO CAN DO...

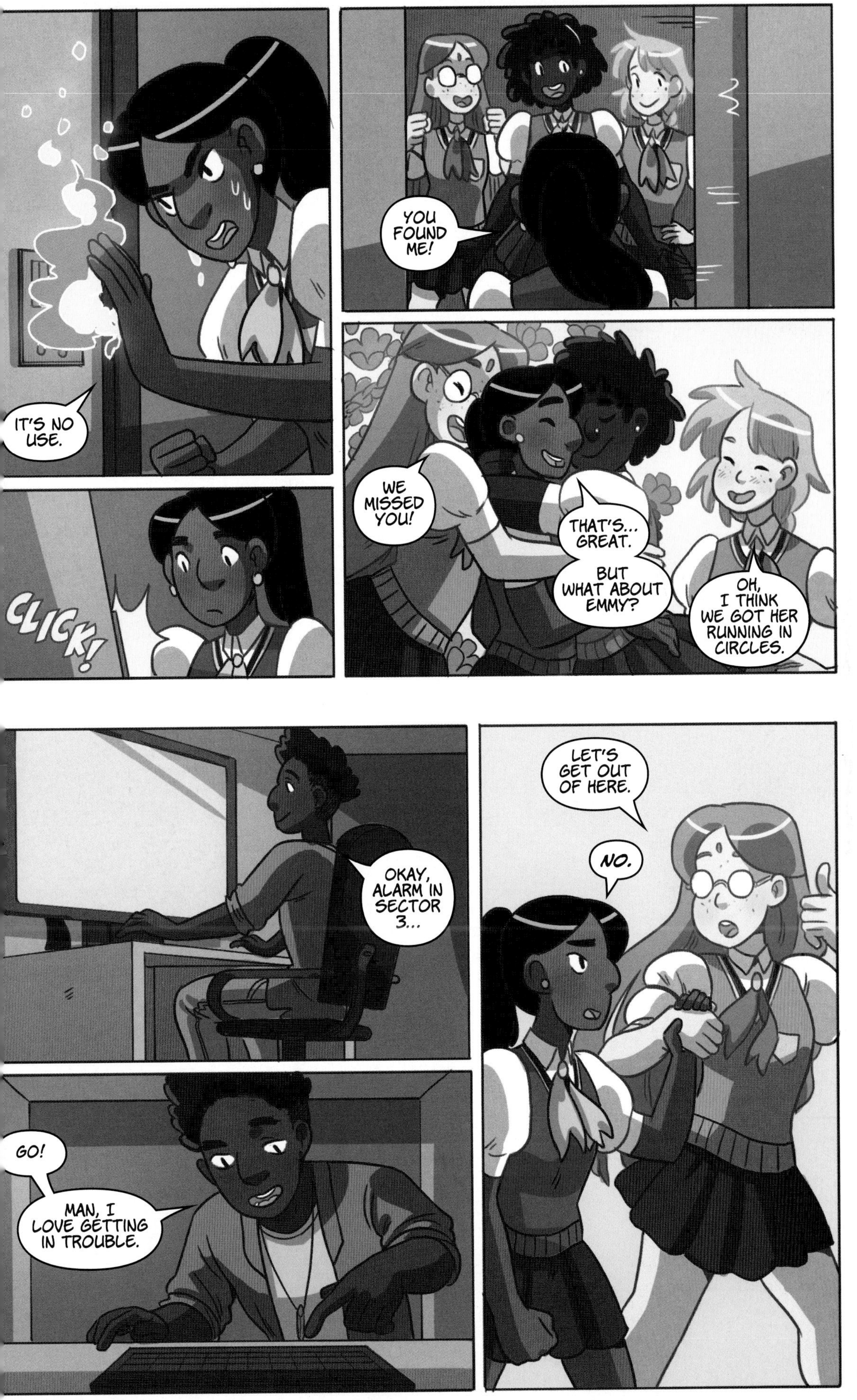
IT'S NO USE.
YOU FOUND ME!
CLICK!
WE MISSED YOU!
THAT'S... GREAT.
BUT WHAT ABOUT EMMY?
OH, I THINK WE GOT HER RUNNING IN CIRCLES.
OKAY, ALARM IN SECTOR 3...
GO!
MAN, I LOVE GETTING IN TROUBLE.
LET'S GET OUT OF HERE.
NO.

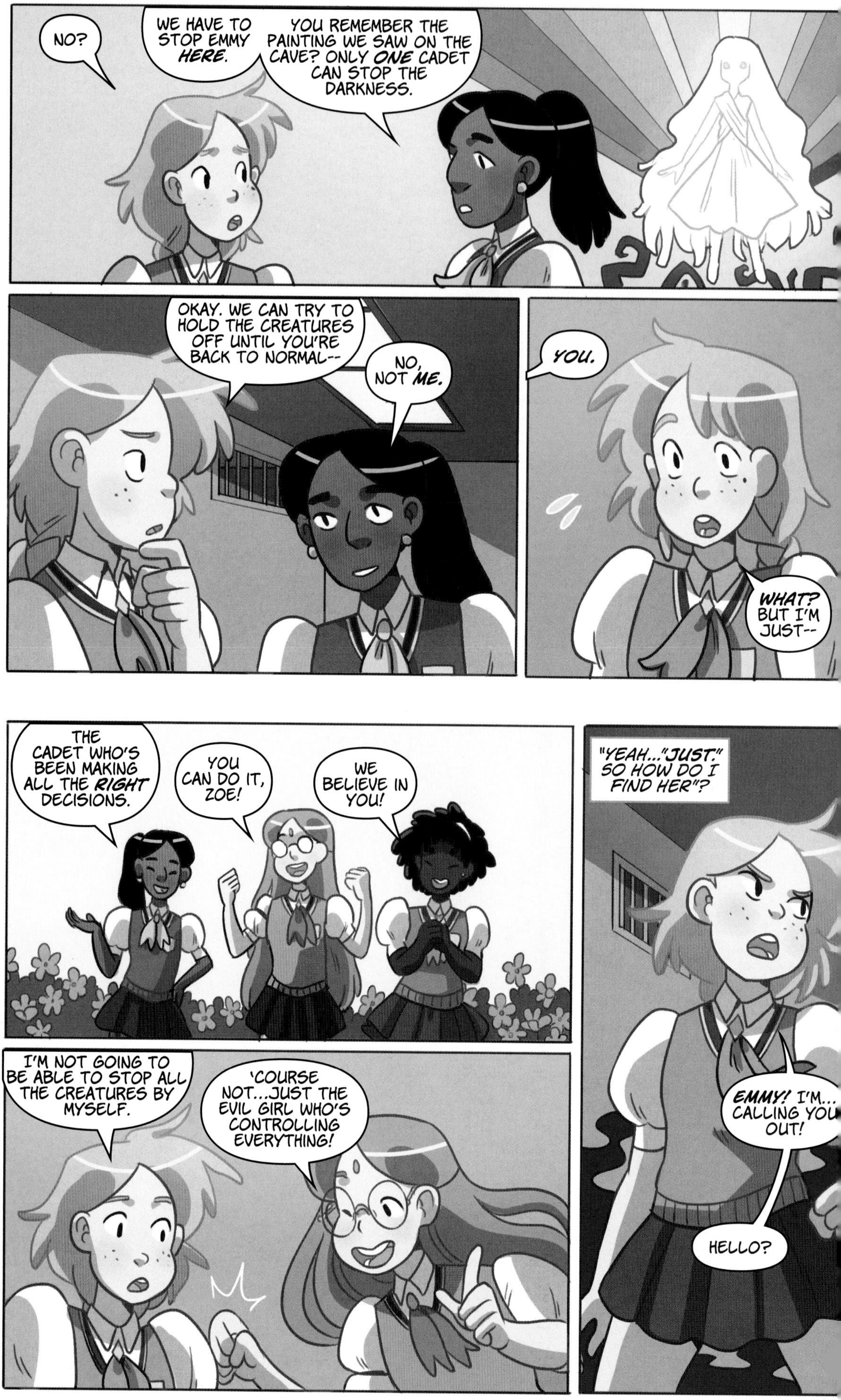
NO?
WE HAVE TO STOP EMMY *HERE*.
YOU REMEMBER THE PAINTING WE SAW ON THE CAVE? ONLY *ONE* CADET CAN STOP THE DARKNESS.
OKAY. WE CAN TRY TO HOLD THE CREATURES OFF UNTIL YOU'RE BACK TO NORMAL--
NO, NOT *ME.*
YOU.
WHAT? BUT I'M JUST--
THE CADET WHO'S BEEN MAKING ALL THE *RIGHT* DECISIONS.
YOU CAN DO IT, ZOE!
WE BELIEVE IN YOU!
I'M NOT GOING TO BE ABLE TO STOP ALL THE CREATURES BY MYSELF.
'COURSE NOT...JUST THE EVIL GIRL WHO'S CONTROLLING EVERYTHING!
"YEAH..."JUST." SO HOW DO I FIND HER"?
EMMY! I'M... CALLING YOU OUT!
HELLO?

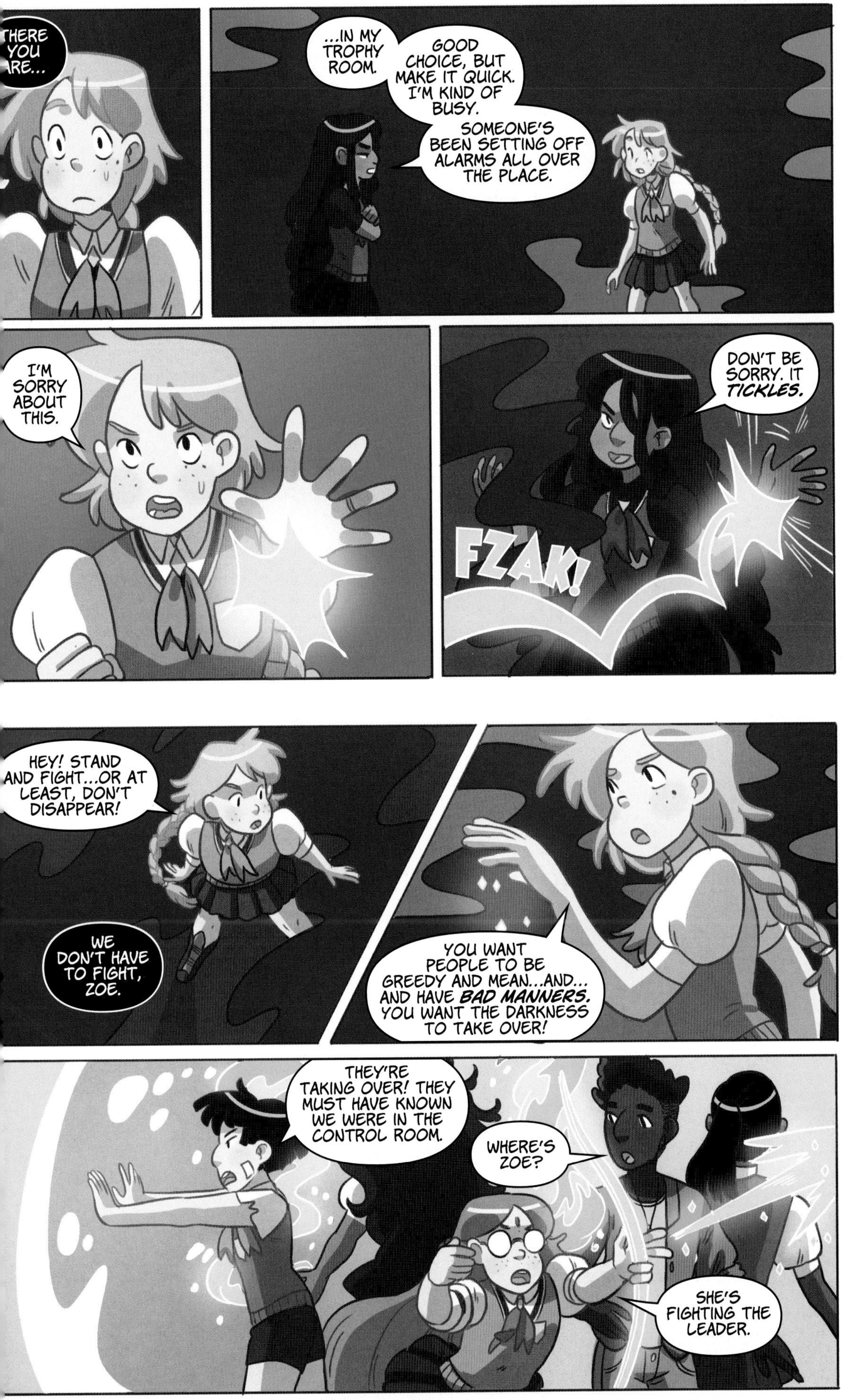
THERE YOU ARE...
...IN MY TROPHY ROOM.
GOOD CHOICE, BUT MAKE IT QUICK. I'M KIND OF BUSY.
SOMEONE'S BEEN SETTING OFF ALARMS ALL OVER THE PLACE.
I'M SORRY ABOUT THIS.
DON'T BE SORRY. IT *TICKLES.*
FZAK!
HEY! STAND AND FIGHT...OR AT LEAST, DON'T DISAPPEAR!
WE DON'T HAVE TO FIGHT, ZOE.
YOU WANT PEOPLE TO BE GREEDY AND MEAN...AND... AND HAVE *BAD MANNERS.* YOU WANT THE DARKNESS TO TAKE OVER!
THEY'RE TAKING OVER! THEY MUST HAVE KNOWN WE WERE IN THE CONTROL ROOM.
WHERE'S ZOE?
SHE'S FIGHTING THE LEADER.

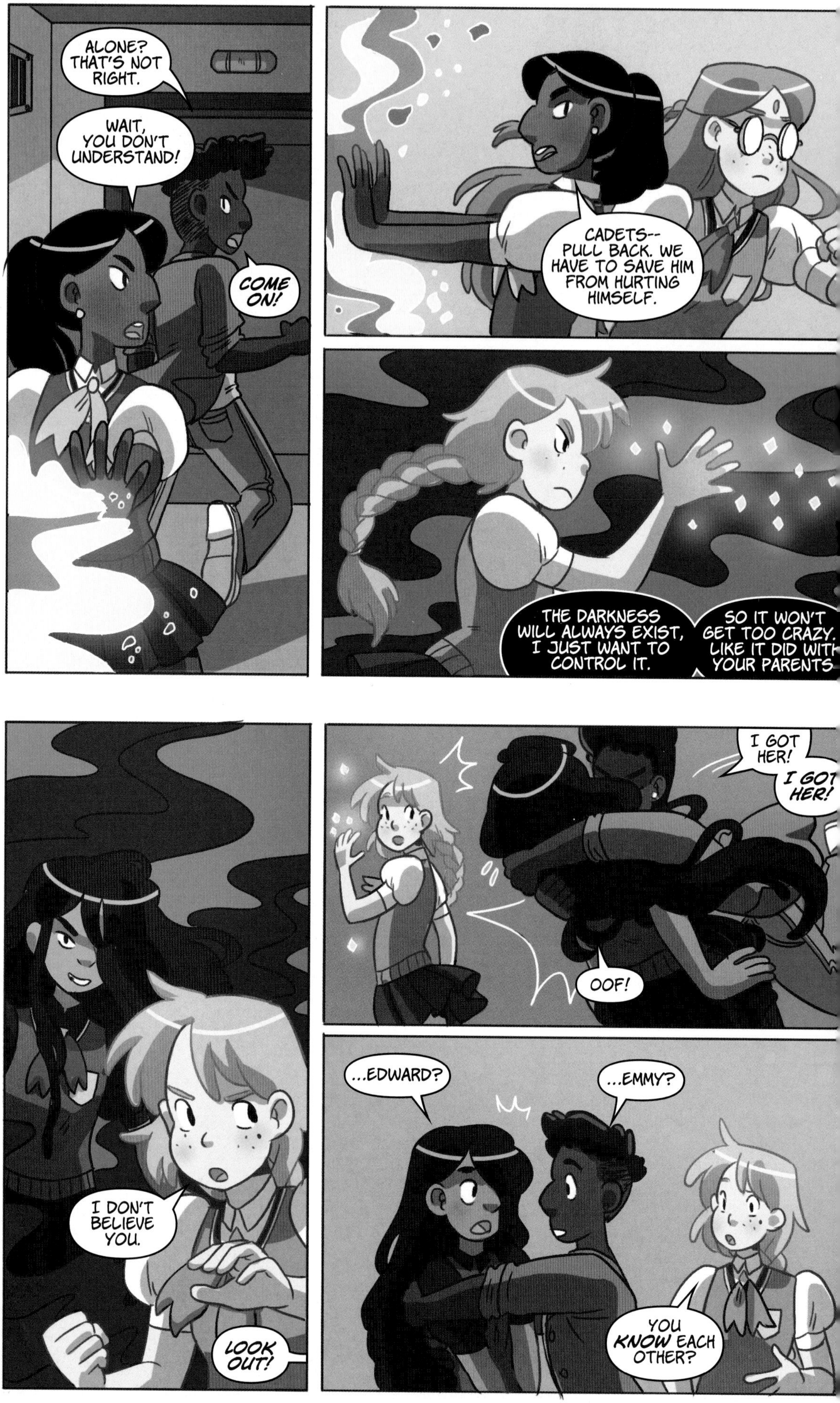
ALONE? THAT'S NOT RIGHT.
WAIT, YOU DON'T UNDERSTAND!
COME ON!
CADETS-- PULL BACK. WE HAVE TO SAVE HIM FROM HURTING HIMSELF.
THE DARKNESS WILL ALWAYS EXIST, I JUST WANT TO CONTROL IT.
SO IT WON'T GET TOO CRAZY. LIKE IT DID WITH YOUR PARENTS.
I DON'T BELIEVE YOU.
LOOK OUT!
I GOT HER!
I GOT HER!
OOF!
...EDWARD?
...EMMY?
YOU KNOW EACH OTHER?

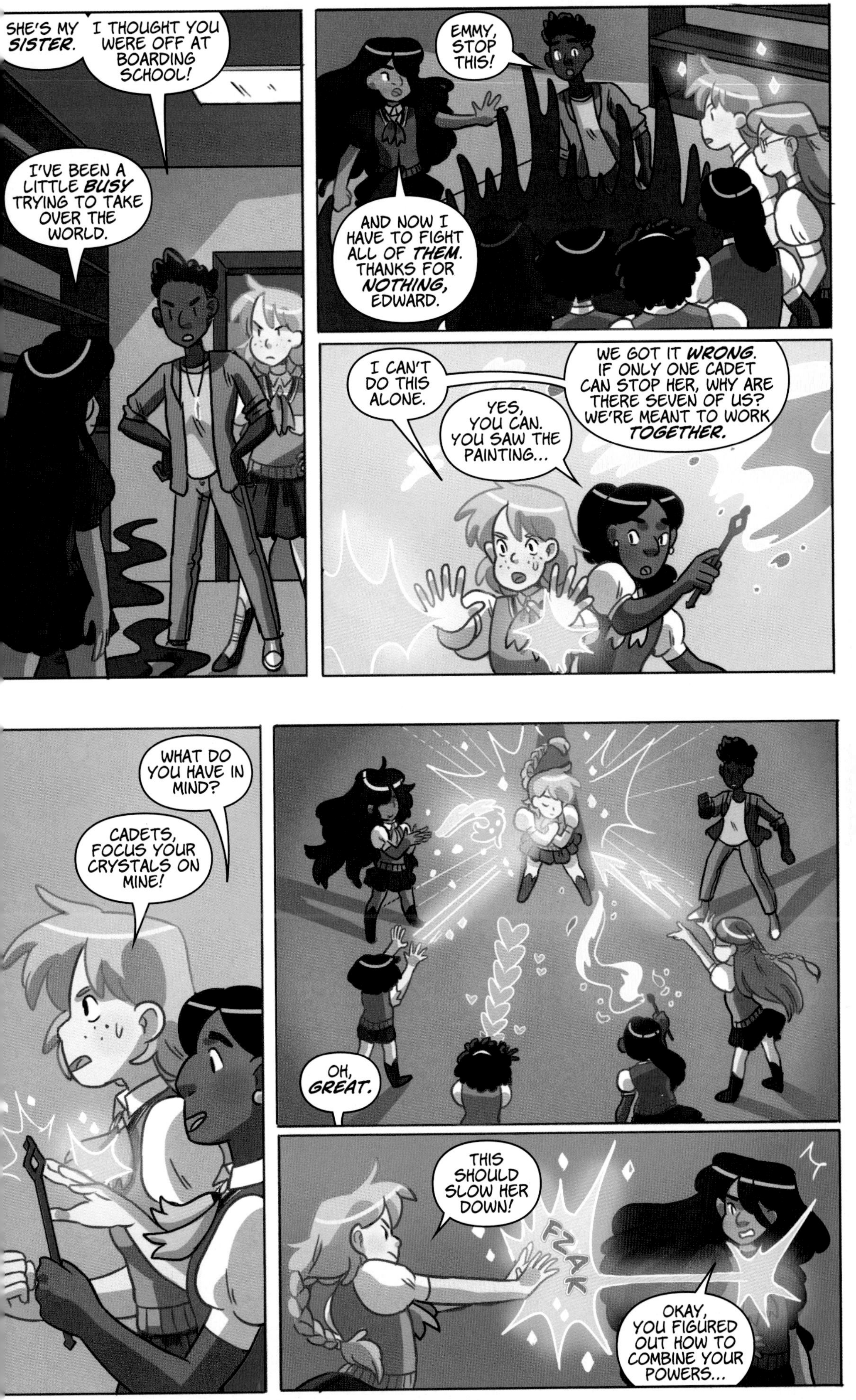
SHE'S MY *SISTER*.
I THOUGHT YOU WERE OFF AT BOARDING SCHOOL!
I'VE BEEN A LITTLE *BUSY* TRYING TO TAKE OVER THE WORLD.
EMMY, STOP THIS!
AND NOW I HAVE TO FIGHT ALL OF *THEM*. THANKS FOR *NOTHING*, EDWARD.
I CAN'T DO THIS ALONE.
YES, YOU CAN. YOU SAW THE PAINTING...
WE GOT IT *WRONG*. IF ONLY ONE CADET CAN STOP HER, WHY ARE THERE SEVEN OF US? WE'RE MEANT TO WORK *TOGETHER*.
WHAT DO YOU HAVE IN MIND?
CADETS, FOCUS YOUR CRYSTALS ON MINE!
OH, *GREAT*.
THIS SHOULD SLOW HER DOWN!
FZAK
OKAY, YOU FIGURED OUT HOW TO COMBINE YOUR POWERS...

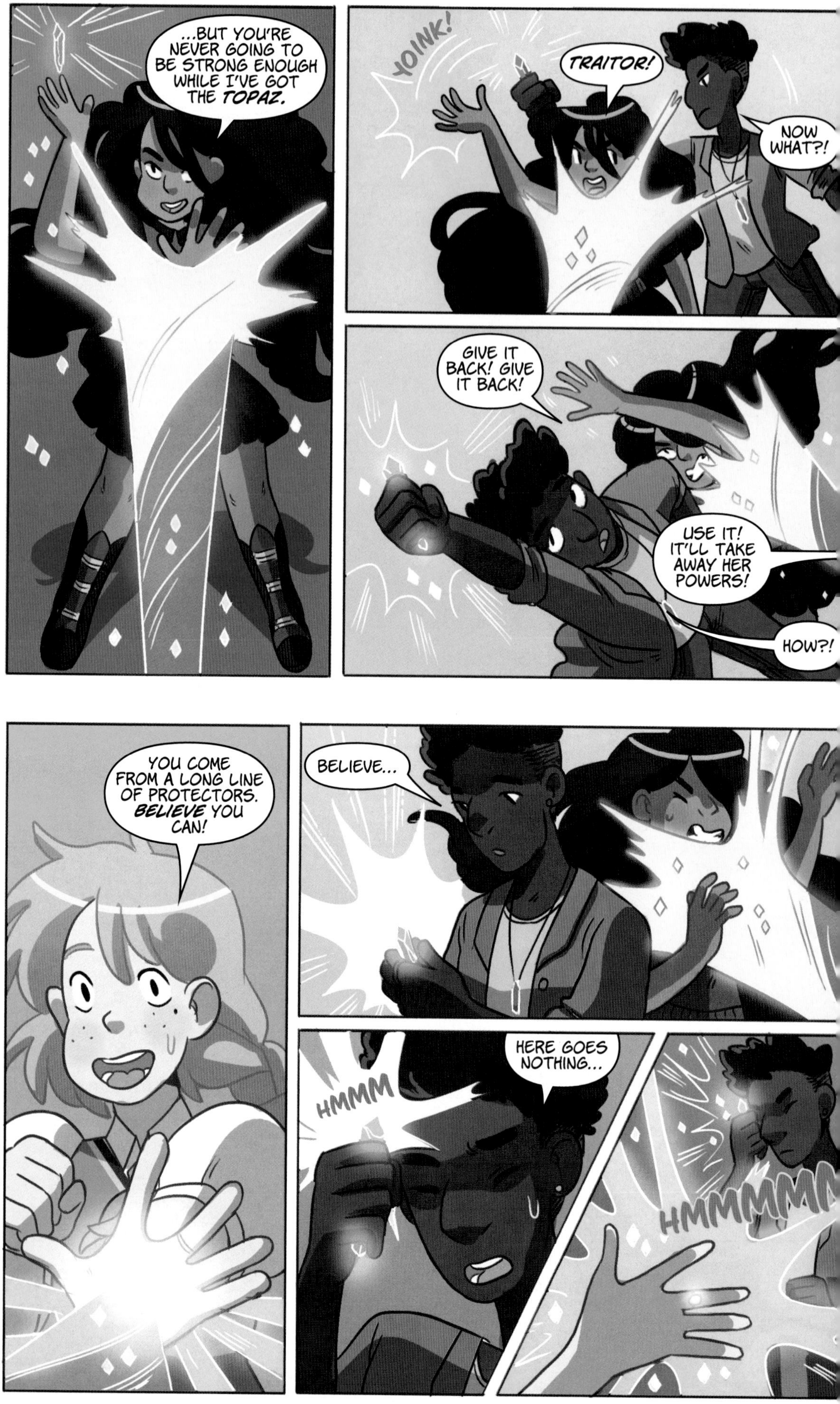
...BUT YOU'RE NEVER GOING TO BE STRONG ENOUGH WHILE I'VE GOT THE *TOPAZ.*
YOINK!
TRAITOR!
NOW WHAT?!
GIVE IT BACK! GIVE IT BACK!
USE IT! IT'LL TAKE AWAY HER POWERS!
HOW?!
YOU COME FROM A LONG LINE OF PROTECTORS. *BELIEVE* YOU CAN!
BELIEVE...
HERE GOES NOTHING...
HMMM
HMMMMM

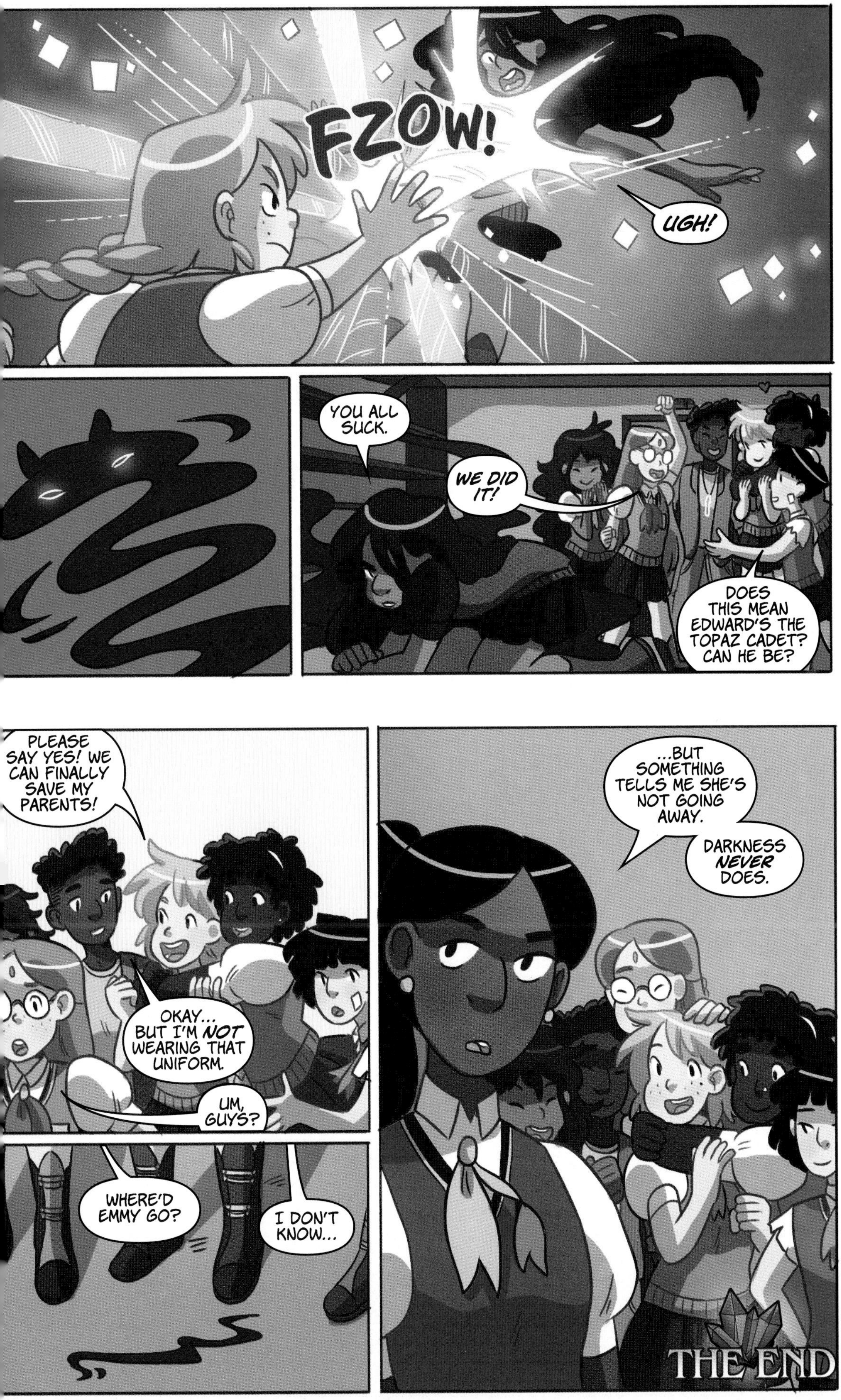
FZOW!
UGH!
YOU ALL SUCK.
WE DID IT!
DOES THIS MEAN EDWARD'S THE TOPAZ CADET? CAN HE BE?
PLEASE SAY YES! WE CAN FINALLY SAVE MY PARENTS!
OKAY... BUT I'M *NOT* WEARING THAT UNIFORM.
UM, GUYS?
WHERE'D EMMY GO?
I DON'T KNOW...
...BUT SOMETHING TELLS ME SHE'S NOT GOING AWAY.
DARKNESS *NEVER* DOES.
THE END

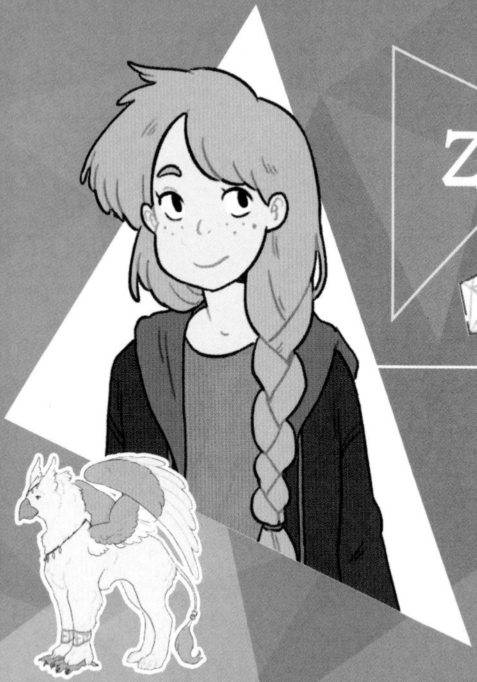

Zoe

DIAMOND CADET

Summon: Gryphon
Special Abilities: Diamond Dust, Lightning Bolt

Zoe is a fast thinker with natural leadership skills, but she's sometimes afraid that she doesn't belong in the group. With her friends helping to build her confidence in herself and her powers, she's starting to realize her full potential!

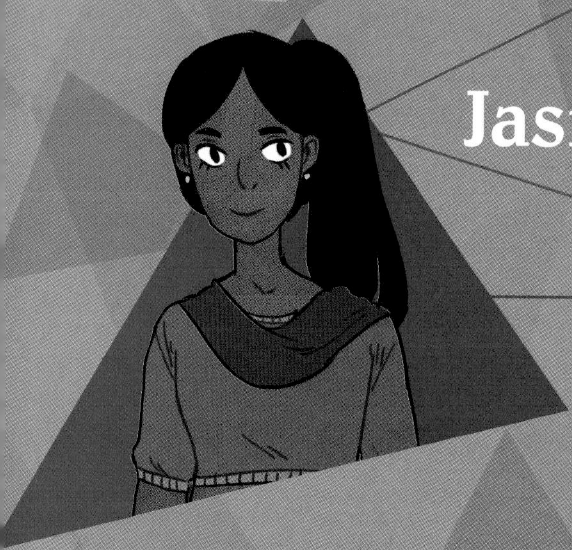

Jasmine

RUBY CADET

Summon: Flaming Phoenix
Special Abilities: Fire Blast

Jasmine is in charge, and likes to take care of her Cadets. She is much more forceful and inspiring than her sister Nahla. Her fire attacks are the most powerful of the group, but she also has the greatest weakness—because she loses her powers when she gets wet.

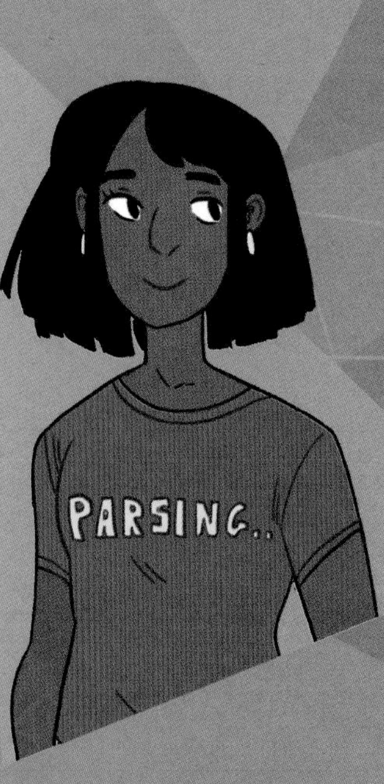
PARSING..

Nahla

Jasmine's older sister Nahla is innovative with computers and the internet, and has figured out ways to combine tech with Crystal magic. Although she could use the Ruby Crystal, she let Jasmine take it and become the Cadet, preferring to work behind the scenes.

Olivia

GARNET CADET
Summon: Giant Butterfly
Special Abilities: Love Chain

Olivia is incredibly nice, loving, and supportive. As one of the veteran members of the Cadets, she tries to welcome and train the newer members. She was once a prototypical "mean girl," but after rejecting The Darkness and becoming a much nicer person, Jasmine found Olivia and brought her into the group.

Gwen

EMERALD CADET
Summon: Pegasus
Special Abilities: Energy Bow & Arrow

Gwen is a bright and energetic talker, though she's not always plugged into what people around her are feeling. She moved around a lot as a kid, so to make new friends, she always tries to befriend the queen bee and to be as lively and entertaining as possible.

Liz

PEARL CADET
Summon: Unicorn
Special Abilities: Moon Disc, Moon Beam Attack

Liz is a kindhearted but tough skater who's not afraid to say the unpopular thing. She's outspoken and may seem like a rebel, but she actually likes to play fair. She's used to hanging with a diverse group of friends, but sometimes acts out to assert her individuality.

Milena

SAPPHIRE CADET
Summon: Leviathan
Special Abilities: Typhoon, Storm Waters Attack

Milena may seem shy, but she likes to make mischief, though sometimes it's by accident. She learned to use her powers "wrong," and she actually prefers to use them backwards, creating unexpected payoffs. Although she is very powerful near large bodies of water outside, she is weak indoors and away from water.

Edward

TOPAZ CADET
Summon: Unknown
Special Abilities: Unknown

Edward is cocky, goofy, and likes to tease the other Cadets. Still, when things get tough, he'll run into harm's way to save his friends from danger—even when the danger is his sister, Emmy! He often goes on sailing trips with his wealthy father, who is the owner of Violet Lab.

Emmy

DARKNESS CADET
Summon: Darkness Dragon
Special Abilities: Darkness Mist, Mind Control, Call Darkness Creatures

Emmy is the most powerful of all the Cadets. She is intelligent, funny, and selfish. When she combines the Topaz Crystal she was destined to have with her talent for commanding the Darkness, she seems unstoppable!

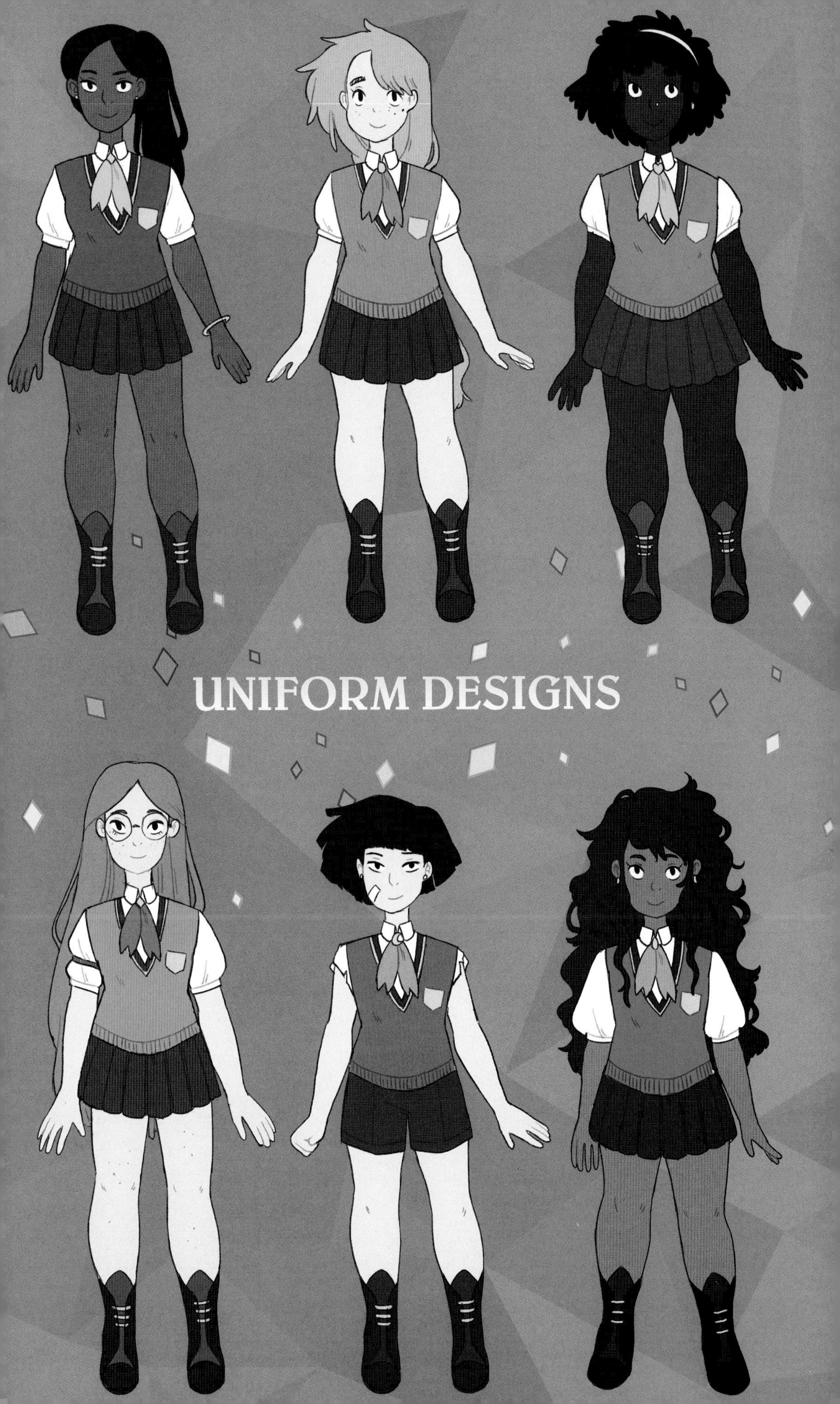
UNIFORM DESIGNS

ANNE TOOLE

is a WGA-nominated writer for video games, one-hour television, webseries, comics, and short fiction. Her credits include the Emmy-winning webseries THE LIZZIE BENNET DIARIES and the dark fantasy game THE WITCHER.

KATIE O'NEILL

is a New Zealand-based cartoonist and illustrator. She has made several comics that were serialized online, including PRINCESS PRINCESS.

PAULINA GANUCHEAU

is a Maryland-based illustrator and sequential artist. She is the artist of ZODIAC STARFORCE from Dark Horse Comics and ANOTHER CASTLE from Oni Press. You can find her drawing at her desk blasting K-pop most hours of the day.

ERIKA TERRIQUEZ

has been working in the publishing industry since 2006. She's done lettering, design, and pre-press during this time. Erika spends most of her time lettering manga and in the last few years has dabbled in lettering American comics.

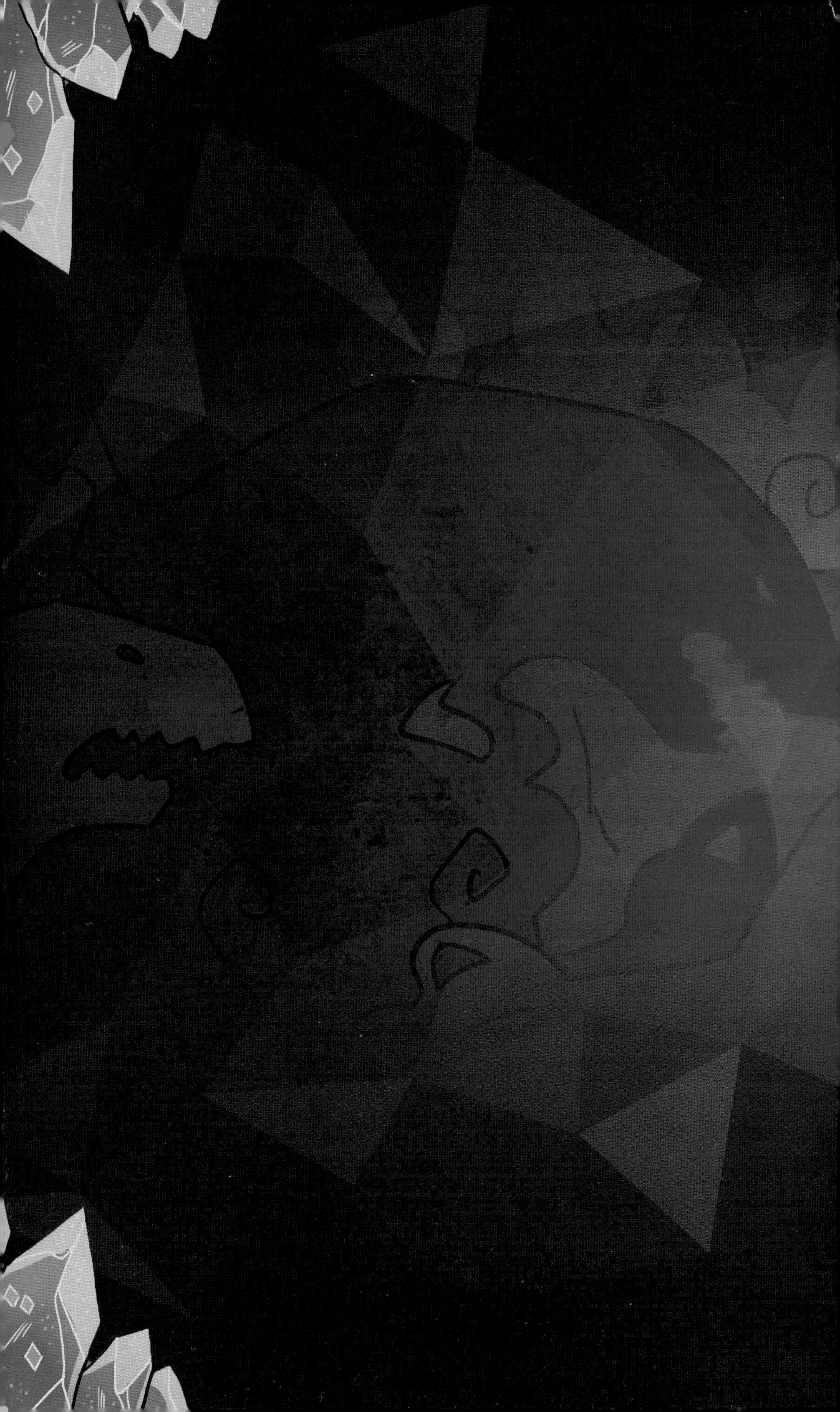